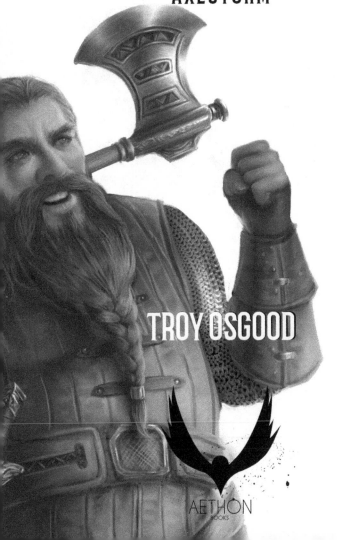

LITR

SKY REALMS

— ONLINE —

AXESTORM

TROY OSGOOD

AETHON
BOOKS

Prologue

HE TOOK THE BOOK OFF THE SHELF. IT WAS LARGE, A FOOT tall and a couple inches wider, a couple inches thick. Bound in thick leather with brass bindings. Gold etched lettering flowed across the front as he examined it.

The History of Hankarth, Volume 3
Jorat of Alberstan

It was covered in a fine layer of dust that he had to blow away, fighting back a cough. Holding the book against the ladder, one arm curled around the upright to hold himself in place, he opened the cover and flipped through the pages. Skimming the text, he nodded and closed the book.

Holding it against his body, he started climbing down the ladder. It was attached to runners set along a rail far above, leaning out at a steep angle. He descended, not looking below, carefully placing his feet and one free hand. His robe kept getting in the way, the ends swishing and getting caught on the rungs. The ladder, made of ironwood uprights and rungs, still flexed under his weight, even with the extra support railing halfway down.

Cursing, he finally felt his feet hit the hardwood plank flooring. He looked up the ladder at the fifty shelves before him. He could see the one empty space on the forty-fifth shelf, so high above. Hundreds, thousands, of books filled the shelves of the spherical room, the iron runners circling along the top and halfway point with two ladders attached. Only the single opening marred the surface of books.

"No wonder I haven't read this one in a while," Bastian the Sage said to himself, looking up at the lone spot so high above. "Of course, Jorat was never that good a writer."

He had only read Jorat's Histories twenty times. Which was nothing compared to the number of times he had read all the others. The most was in the hundreds now.

Turning away from the stacks, he walked out the opening and into the next room. This one was large, with light wood flooring and dark wood paneling. A large window opened out onto the sky of Hankarth. Clouds drifted by, the sun high, with dark specks of other islands visible. Tapestries hung on either side of the window, another opening leading to the rest of the tower. A large stone hearth was on the far wall. Assorted couches and chairs filled the room, some alone and others in clusters. Different styles and colors. A small bar was set up next to the hearth. Wine bottles, their corks visible, filled a shelf behind it, more bottles and glasses on top.

He walked across the room, choosing a spot at random. All the seats looked worn, well used. Bastian paused as he was about to sit down. He looked down the room at the hearth and a seat.

The seat was occupied.

A man was sitting there, glass of wine in hand, staring into the flames of the hearth.

With a sigh, setting the book down on the chair, Bastian walked down to the hearth. He paused next to the chair, thinking to get his own glass of wine but decided not to. The guest would not be staying long. He took another step and turned to look down at the man.

Dressed in elegant clothes. Well-tailored, the latest style in the lands of the Highborn Confederacy. Clean lines, simple but ostentatious at the same time. Bright colors that seemed to stand out alongside the man's light gray skin. His head was shaved, the only hair was a braided beard hanging from his chin. Black eyes stared into the flames, not bothering to look up at the Sage.

"Feardagh. I would say that it has been too long, but that is not true," Bastian said in greeting.

"That is not my name," the man in the chair said. Fingers tightened around the wineglass. He turned and glared at Bastian, who returned it.

The black eyes smoldered, the man radiating anger even if he did not appear it.

Bastian shrugged.

"It is your name," he said.

"No," the gray-skinned man said slowly, powerfully. His voice was deep, the echo of years within it. The words carried a threat. "It is not."

Bastian just sighed, shaking his head.

"It is since I saved us all by creating this," Bastian told the man, his arms rising to indicate everything around them.

"We created this," the man said, still staring. He forced himself to relax and took a sip of wine.

Bastian turned his head and glanced out the door toward the map room across the hall. In that room was the map of the fractured islands of Hankarth, the only complete one in existence, with the black iron nail stuck in the middle piercing map and thick wood table. He returned his gaze back to the Feardagh.

"It was your power that caused it," Bastian said, his own voice containing threats. "It was my power that used yours to save us."

The sky outside darkened, and Bastian felt as if the walls, floor, and ceiling were closing in. He could feel the gathering power, the storm that was starting. A great weight started to press in on him, fears nipping at him.

With a wave of his hand, the feelings vanished, the sun returning outside the window. He glared down at the seated man, more annoyed than angry.

"Do not play games with me," Bastian said. "Why are you here?"

The Feardagh stared hard at Bastian, eyes boring into the man, before his expression changed in an instant. One second, hard and anger, the next, happy and calm.

"Things are progressing," he said with a smile.

"I know," Bastian replied and walked toward the bar.

He saw the open bottle sitting on top. A rare vintage, one of only a dozen bottles still in existence, and the Feardagh had just opened it. Picking up the bottle, taking a sniff, Bastian poured himself a glass. He swirled it, seeing the red liquid move and change colors. A deep maroon to a light pink and back. Taking a sip, he enjoyed the flavor. Quite possibly the finest bottle of wine ever produced on the islands.

"Is that why you are here?" Bastian asked. "To tell me something I already know?"

"I just wanted to remind you of the deal," the Feardagh said, taking the final sip of his wine.

He stood up and crossed over to the bar, coming within a foot of Bastian, staring at the man. They were of equal height, the Feardagh a little more muscular. He reached for the bottle, but Bastian grabbed it and moved it away. The Feardagh chuckled.

He placed the wineglass on the bar, hard, and the glass cracked.

"It has been a long time," he said and walked away, feeling Bastian's eyes upon him.

The Sage knew the Feardagh, the demon of deals, was trying to make up for his earlier mistake. Always a showman, the Feardagh had let pride get in the way of his performance. He was working to get that standing back. *Why bother?* Bastian thought. It wasn't going to work. He wasn't one of the common people, swayed by pretty words and cheap theatrics.

He glanced out the doorway again, toward the map and the black iron nail.

No, he hadn't let words and tricks sway him. He had made his deal knowing the consequences of his actions. But it had been the only way, the only choice.

"How many hundreds of years?" the Feardagh asked, turning back to Bastian. He had stopped walking at the book, looking down at the cover, running his fingers over the text. Bastian did not respond. "So long with no action, but now things are moving quickly." He turned and looked back at Bastian. "Almost too quickly. The time is coming."

"Yes," was all Bastian said, and he cracked a smile seeing annoyance flash across the Feardagh's face. A small victory, but still a victory, showing that he had the upper hand.

"A final reckoning," the Feardagh said, sweeping his hands out in a flourish.

Bastian made a quick 'get on with it' gesture while taking a drink of wine.

The Feardagh smiled, tilting his head as he studied Bastian.

"Have you been out in the world?" he asked, knowing the answer. "It has changed in the centuries. Adapted to survive. No longer the world we once knew."

"Of course," Bastian said. "That was the plan. It was the only way."

"Things have changed," the Feardagh continued. "People, cultures, animals, names." He finished with an emphasis on the last word. "Things are no longer what they were," he spat, angry now, his mood changing quickly again.

Bastian remained calm, taking another sip of wine. It was very good.

"We survived," he said with a hard edge to his voice. "That is all that matters."

Taking a deep breath, the Feardagh visibly calmed. He smoothed out the folds in his jacket, showing long and sharp-looking black fingernails that were neatly manicured.

"Are you nervous?" he finally asked with a sneer.

"Not at all."

The Feardagh laughed. The sound echoed around the room, bouncing off the hard walls. There was nothing joyful about it. Sharp and harsh, the laugh hurt to hear. Bastian managed to ignore it.

"You should be," the Feardagh barked, the word sharp. "If you lose, all that you have worked for will be lost."

There was a minute or two of silence, the two staring at each other. Sage and demon. The Feardagh smiled, arrogant. Bastian was calm, knowing.

"That was the deal," Bastian said, breaking the silence.

"I have seen your Champions," the Feardagh said. "You should be very worried."

"And yours?" Bastian asked. "When will they arrive?"

"Soon enough," the Feardagh answered. He glanced up at Bastian. "Will they still be your Champions when they learn what you have done? What you did to them?"

Bastian stared at the gray skinned demon, studying him, ignoring the question. The Feardagh was looking at his long, sharp fingernails. He picked at them, acting as if bored. Bastian sighed.

"It saved you as well," Bastian said slowly, sadly. "You would have been destroyed. We all would have been. Why force the deal?"

He watched the Feardagh's expression. The demon glared at him sharply, hatefully, but there was a hint of fear. Desperation. Despair and sadness. Regret. Guilt. So much guilt. It flashed across the Feardagh's face quickly, gone in a blink. But it had been there.

"I am what I am," the demon answered with a wicked smirk.

The Feardagh picked up the book from the chair, flipping through the pages. He pretended to read a couple. The emotions still fought within the demon. Bastian could see the inner conflict before the demon's normal nature dominated and its arrogance resurfaced.

"Trash," he said and threw it on the floor where it landed with a thud, sliding a couple inches across the smooth planks. The Feardagh looked back down at it. "What the histories do not say, none of them ever do, is that in all the deals I have ever made, I always come out on top."

He laughed again, staring at Bastian in amusement. And then he was gone. No smoke, no clap of thunder, no gesture of spell. The Feardagh just disappeared.

"Not this time," Bastian said quietly, setting down the glass of wine. "Not this time," he said again, a note of desperation creeping in.

He walked past the clusters of chairs to where the book lay on the floor. Crouching down, he picked it up, running his fingers across the cover. The Feardagh's sharp nails had cut the leather, leaving a scar. Bastian sighed and placed it carefully on the chair.

He no longer felt like reading.

PART I

PART ONE

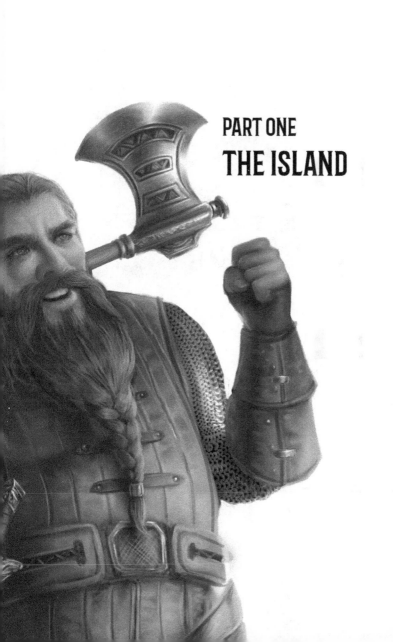

PART ONE
THE ISLAND

CHAPTER ONE

THE AX SWUNG DOWN AT AN ANGLE, SLAMMING INTO THE THICK trunk of the tree. Splinters of wood pulp flew in all directions as the ax head was pulled back. Another swing and more chunks were removed, a growing pile on the ground. The notch grew bigger and bigger with each swing.

Pulling the ax up, laying it across his shoulders, Hall took a step back. He wiped the sweat off his brow, pushing a few strands of his loose shoulder-length hair away from his face, staring at his handiwork. He had never swung an ax in real life, but this was the third tree he was chopping down in the Green-height Vale. The large forest was just south of Breakridge Meadow, where his village of Skara Brae was located. Surrounded by the Thunder Growl mountains on all sides but the north, the Vale was at a higher elevation above the meadow.

Old growth, the Vale had stood undisturbed for a long time.

Until Hall and his friends had arrived and started rebuilding the ruined town.

He wasn't a fan of chopping down the trees, but they needed the wood and they were being selective about what they took. Under the guidance of the Valedale Gnomes and the forest's Leshy guardian, Smol, Hall only took what they said he could. It was an effective pruning method. Cleaning out dying wood, or trees that were choking the growth of others, but it was a slow process getting the wood they needed.

Duncant, the Bodin carpenter they had gotten from Silverpeak Keep, was outpacing the production of the wood. His need was greater than the supply. But Hall was okay with that. Slow and steady. He had no desire to destroy the forest just to build his village.

Leaning the ax against the tree, he walked a couple steps back and picked up his waterskin. Taking a drink, he dumped some over his head to wash the sweat away. He shook his head, drops spraying everywhere, more dripping down his beard. It wasn't hot in the Vale, but the sun did beat down and the work was strenuous. The mountains protected the forest from the ever present wind that blew across the meadow. Dropping the skin, he stretched his arms to work out a knot that had started to form in his shoulders from the repeated swinging action.

He wore no shirt, the linen tunic bunched on the ground near the waterskin and his pile of weapons. Green tattoos ran across his chest, skin the color of bark, some bisected by long healed scars. Swirls, runes, and other symbols ran up his arms, across his chest and back, then down his other arm.

Hall glanced up into the sky, seeing the black speck that would be Pike circling above. The dragonhawk spent most of the day hunting in the woods and the mountains. Distant but never truly far away.

Picking up the ax, he set his feet and went to take another swing.

"Halls," a squeaking but rough bark-like voice said.

He turned and saw Smol, the Leshy of Greenheight Vale. The creature was only about three feet tall with brown skin covered in light fur except for the lower half which was all fur. It had four-toed paws for feet and four long fingers that ended in claws. Green moss-like hair spilled down its head, onto its back, and covered its shoulders. The face was like a bear with a small nose and two small eyes. Small pointed ears poked out from the green hair as well as two small horns from the forehead.

Leshies were forest guardians. Solitary, they protected the woods also serving as gardeners. Not all forests had one. A Leshy's presence showed how magical a forest was. Hall had yet to find out exactly what it meant that Greenheight Vale had one.

He had first met Smol a couple of days after defeating Vertoyi, the original Custodian of the Grove. The Leshy was being attacked by two corrupted bears, the corruption of the grove starting to seep into Greenheight Vale. They discovered that the corruption had attracted a tribe of Spriggens that had taken over the small village of Gnomes that lived in Greenheight. Hall and his friends had defeated the Spriggens, saving Smol and the Valedale Gnomes. Also making the first allies of Skara Brae.

As thanks, the Gnomes were serving as laborers in the rebuilding of Skara Brae. For which, Hall was eternally thankful. There were thirteen people living, somewhat, in the village now and not all of them would make productive carpenters. The thought of Timmin swinging a hammer brought a smile to Hall's face.

"Good morning, Smol," Hall said, bowing to the small Leshy.

"Good morns, yes," Smol replied and bowed. "The Duncants wants ta talks."

Hall sighed. Of course. The carpenter always wanted to talk. It was annoying, but Hall was quickly learning to listen to Duncant's ideas. It just meant more time away from what he needed to be doing himself.

Picking up his shirt, waterskin, and weapons, Hall nodded toward Smol.

"Thank you, do you know where he is?"

"Docks."

————

Hall stepped out from the line of trees and onto the slope that led down to the meadow. He could already feel the constant wind coming up the hill, funneled between the mountains on either side. The peaks towered above him as he looked out over what was becoming his home.

To his right, the east, the mountain turned into the high ridge that gave the area its name. Breakridge, with its grass and stone-covered steep sides, cut the meadow off from the rest of the island of Edin. Standing tall, stone arch on top, it was a wall spanning from the Thunder Growls to the Frost Tips to the north. Those mountains stood far away, most of the tops lost in the clouds and those he could see covered in the snow that gave them their names. He could just make out the flat plateau that was where the Branch of the World Tree was located, the Meadowsheight Grove.

The wind that blew in off the open edge of the meadow, the broken edge of the island of Edin, pushed against the tall grass. It always blew strong. He could just make out the grass-covered mounds that were the roofs of the village, the rest sunken into the ground.

Smol trotted along behind him. The Leshy had taken an interest in the various construction projects that Duncant had underway. The only construction Smol had ever seen was what little the Valedale Gnomes did in their village. What Duncant was doing was vastly different. With Leigh taking over as Custodian of the Grove, cleansing the corruption, it was leaving Greenheight which left Smol with little to do.

"Docks nice," the small Leshy said, and Hall chuckled.

It wasn't, not yet, not even close. But maybe someday it would be.

They got to the bottom of the hill and turned west around the bottom of the peaks that wrapped around Valedale protectively.

Both mountain ranges formed the edge of the island until they got to the gap that was the Breakridge Meadow. But on the south, the Thunder Growl turned inland to shelter the forest. It was along this part of the mountains that Duncant had decided to build the docks. With guidance from Hroth-grav, the captain of the *Frozen Blade*, the ship that had brought them from Silverpeak Keep back to Skara Brae over a month ago.

A couple hundred feet away, protected from the wind by a spur of the Thunder Growls, was the start of the docks. A large platform that would have slips for two medium-sized airships, a crane between them, raised about twenty feet off the ground. The whole thing would be supported by a series of beams and columns with bracing set into the ground around it, accessed by a switchbacking ramp that was wide enough for a single wagon.

That's what it was going to be, but currently it was just a series of poles set into the hard ground and some cross-bracing. It didn't look like much to Hall, but he hoped Duncant knew what he was doing.

The Bodin was up in the structure, banging away at one of the cross braces. The whole thing shook with each impact of the small hammer. Gnomes moved about the bottom of the columns, some tying off other braces, others cutting lengths of wood. About a half-dozen of the small creatures were working around the future dock.

As he walked across the meadow toward the docks, Hall brought up the Settlement Interface to check on the Bodin's progress. It had been a couple days since he had last looked and figured he should be up to date.

Skara Brae Town Stats:
Lord: Hall
Status: Ruins 25%
Morale: Productive
Government: N/A
Appointed Officials: Timmin, Administrator Brient, Sheriff
Population: 13
Production: Carpentry Rank One – 25%
Farming Rank One – 15%
Faction: None
Allies: Gnomes of Valedale
Brownpaw of Fallen Green
Trade Partners: N/A
Enemies: N/A

The main page of the interface was the overview of the town. Each listing had more options once that specific page was accessed. The more the village was repaired and upgraded, Hall noticed that more information was revealed on the main page.

Since he had first touched the Settlement Stone and activated the village, it had always been listed as just *Ruins*, but now there was progress shown for how far it had to go to get out of that state. *Morale* had always been blank but now there was a setting. One of these days, he promised himself, he'd take the time to look into what all that meant.

Mentally, he clicked on *Carpentry Rank One* and a new

translucent menu opened up, replacing the previous. Along the top was written *Maximum Daily Output* over a progress bar. A measure of efficiency that Hall assumed took into account Duncant's knowledge and the Valedale Gnome's labors. It currently read at seventy-five out of one hundred percent.

Along the bottom was another progress bar that read twenty-five out of one hundred percent. Hall had not spent much time researching what was required to get to Carpentry Rank Two and what exactly being that rank would mean. He assumed it would open up more plans and ways to upgrade the existing buildings.

In the main part of the menu, Duncant was listed as a Level Six Carpenter with a series of buildings under his name and more progress bars. It wasn't all the buildings in Skara Brae—for that listing Hall would need to go to another page of the Settlement Interface. This listing just showed the projects the Carpenter was currently working on and their progress.

Airship Docks Level One 25%
House Level One 25%
House Level One 25%
House Level One 25%
House Level One 25%
Inn Level One 40%
Town Hall Level One 30%

Closing out the menus, Hall stopped at the base of the Dock supports and watched the small Bodin at work. He held on with one arm wrapped around a beam, the other beating on a wooden spike with the hammer. A length of rope was hung loosely off the beam, dangling and not connected to the Bodin's tool belt.

"Duncant," Hall called up, waiting until the Bodin had

finished his hammering. "You wanted something?" he asked when the carpenter looked down.

Nodding his head rapidly, Duncant slipped the hammer into his tool belt and scrambled down the beams, columns, and braces. Hall winced a couple times as Duncant moved without care, not paying attention that he had no safety harness. Wrapping his legs around the corner post, Duncant shimmied down, hopping the last couple feet. He turned to Hall, smiling broadly.

"What do you think?" he asked in his slightly high-pitched voice.

"Of," Hall prompted.

Duncant huffed, sighed, and waved at the dock.

"Oh," Hall said, trying to hide his own annoyance. "It's coming along. Is that why you called me down from Greenheight?"

He watched the Leshy start to climb the bracing, looking over the top of Duncant's head. Smol's claws were digging grooves into the wood as he climbed toward the top.

"No," Duncant muttered. "I wanted to know where the next batch of logs was."

Hall rolled his eyes. He should have known.

"They'll be here when they get here."

"But I need them," Duncant said, his voice starting to whine.

Hall held up his hand and the Bodin stopped. Looking down at his feet, kicking the dirt, the carpenter muttered something. Hall thought he heard it but decided not to press the point. Where the Bodin was concerned, they both needed each other, but it was best not to press. Duncant was talented but unguilded, which made him cheap. He hadn't been able to find work in Silverpeak Keep, at least not work equal to his talents, so had leaped at the chance to rebuild Skara Brae. If pushed, he could just up and leave.

Which Hall did not want.

"I made some modifications to the plans," Duncant said, looking back up and smiling.

Hall didn't know why Duncant had been removed from the guild in Silverpeak Keep, but he wondered if the constant modifications was part of it. Duncant was never satisfied with a design. He kept messing with it, even while construction was underway.

Duncant headed toward a large table set closer to the mountain, in the shade. Crates of supplies were stacked around it, and across the top were papers held down by rocks. Rolls of other papers and a stack of folded plans were to the side. Duncant pointed to the one plan unrolled. Hall couldn't understand most of it and doubted anyone but Duncant could. He looked at the carpenter, who shrugged and started speaking, fingers pointing at parts of the plans as he talked.

"I added a third dock," he explained. "See it here? For a smaller ship, of course as you can tell by the size compared to the others. Shouldn't take that much more lumber, only a half dozen columns and two cross-braces, another one hundred square foot of planking, another week of work."

Hall sighed.

"Why?"

Duncant reached for the folded stack of plans, holding them up.

"I used this to size the new dock," he said as if Hall had not spoken.

Hall looked at the plans the Bodin held and reached for them. He recognized them as the airship plans he had taken from the Cudgel in Silverpeak Keep. It was some new Dwarven design that had been stored in the chest in the building currently serving as the village's Bank. In a chest that Duncant shouldn't have taken them from.

Duncant pulled them out of Hall's reach, pretending not to notice the angry scowl he received.

"Two medium freighters and a small one should be all that we need to handle here for a number of years," he continued, ignoring Hall. "The crane can easily be modified to unload from any of the three and... wait... why what?"

"Huh," Hall stated, caught off guard. He had only been half-listening.

Duncant had been rambling and Hall had been stewing over the borrowing of the plans. He had no idea what he was going to do with them but figured they would be valuable to someone. When the Cudgel, who had been revealed as Councilor Cronet, had been caught trying to take over Silverpeak Keep, he had run. Hall and the others had found him, confronted him, and killed him. In the single chest that Cronet had tried to take were the plans. One of the few items Cronet had run with, Hall assumed it was because they were valuable.

And here was Duncant with them out in the middle of the meadow in the weather where it could rain or the wind could take them or any number of other accidents.

With Duncant going on and on, Hall had drifted until the carpenter brought him back.

"Why what?" Duncant asked again.

Hall thought back through the conversation and remembered when, and more importantly why, he had asked the question.

"Why did you decide to make three berths?"

"Oh, well," Duncant started a little shyly. Hall had discovered early on that Duncant was not a fan of talking about his own ideas, where they came from. He had no problem putting them down on paper and then talking about the specifics, but the origins was when he was hesitant. Again, Hall wondered if it had anything to do with why the Bodin was unguilded. "We needed the two for deliveries and outgoing, and I figured since you had these plans, it meant you wanted to make your own ship and that meant it would need its own berth."

"Why would we need our own airship?" Hall asked. The idea had never occurred to him. He had made an arrangement with Hrothgrav and the *Frozen Blade* to come back every couple of months.

Duncant looked away and then back down at the ground as if afraid to speak.

"Well, we're isolated here," he said, still looking down. "And can't be reliant on other ships coming randomly. And that takes time. Give them an order and wait a couple months for supplies to arrive. What if need something in an emergency?"

Hall took a step back, cursing himself. He glanced at the plans for the Dwarven airship laying on the table. Duncant was right. Breakridge was weeks of hard overland travel from any civilization. The closest were Silverpeak Keep along the coast of the island and the Firbolg village of Green Ember more south into the heart of Edin. If they needed anything, it would be at least a month to make a trip to either place and back again. By airship, they were only a couple days to Silverpeak Keep. He thought back to when he had first seen an airship not on a restricted flight path. It had been flying along the southern edge of Edin as they had walked from Fallen Green to Silverpeak Keep. He had thought about getting their own airship then, but the plan had been pushed from his mind with everything that happened after. It just took Duncant to remind him.

"Duncant, you're a genius," Hall said and picked up the plans. The Bodin looked up and smiled.

A notification appeared in front of Hall's vision.

Your Settlement's Airship Docks have been upgraded to Level Two.
Progress has been changed to fifteen percent.

That surprised Hall. It was interesting that Duncant had somehow managed to adjust the Docks to Level Two by changing the plans. He wondered if the Carpenter had gotten any kind of experience or skill gain.

Hall tapped a finger against the plans. "How much do you think a ship like this would cost to build?"

CHAPTER TWO

Hall woke up, turning over onto his back.

He was alone in their bed. Leigh had again gotten up early and left for Meadowheight Grove. He was surprised she had been in the village last night. Glad of it, but surprised. They didn't see much of each other, both so busy and she spent more nights in the Grove than she did in the bed they now shared, in the room they shared in what would be the village's Inn.

Much had progressed in the village during the month plus they had been back. While Hall had been in Silverpeak Keep, the Valedale Gnomes had worked hard on the village. They had made a couple of the buildings livable. Walls and doors that would keep out the weather was the extent, but they were livable. No one was sleeping in a tent anymore.

After the first few buildings, they had started on the Inn, getting the few rooms on the second level up to living standards. It was there that Hall and Leigh had settled in the larger room. Roxhard and Jackoby had each taken a room. Caryn and Sabine had claimed one of the houses, the two growing close in recent weeks. The other citizens in the small village had spread out into the buildings as well, with Timmin, the new administrator, claiming a spot in what was planned to become the Town Hall.

Most of the village was still considered ruins, but it was a start.

It had not taken long after their first kiss for Hall and Leigh's relationship to go further. He was comfortable with her. In fact, he was falling in love with her and she with him. Even when they spent time apart, which was happening a lot lately, he missed her but was still comfortable in their relationship. It was an odd place to be in, he thought as he sat up.

He had missed the notification when they had accepted their feelings for each other and became a true couple. His Alliance Reputation with her had jumped. They had been at *Trusted* but now were maxxed out and even beyond. The maximum level had been *Respected* with a total of 5000. His connection with Leigh had jumped the value beyond from 5000 straight to 6000 and *Respected* to *Dedicated*. It had never wavered even when they went a day or two without seeing each other. Both were busy.

Standing up, naked, he searched through the small room for his clothes. They had been thrown all over the place last night. He was surprised that he had not heard Leigh get up, get dressed, and leave. How tired had he been? Between the day's labor and last night's fun, he had been very tired apparently.

Pulling his shirt on to finish dressing, Hall opened the door and walked out into the hallway. His was the last room on the left, an equal size one across. Three other rooms, each much smaller, lined the wall next to him, mirrored on the other side. The hall ended at a balcony overlooking what would be the Inn's common room someday. He was on the second of three stories, another set of rooms above.

Walking down the stairs, he was still thinking about what

Duncant had said. He had been thinking about it all day and into the night when the few people in the village had gathered for the communal meal. All except the latest two citizens. Braniff and Garick were up north in the Frost Tips, exploring.

Duncant had a good point about them needing their own ship. But did that mean having their own crew? Hall knew nothing of airships and had not shown the plans to Hrothgrav when he had the chance the last time the captain was around, but from what Duncant said looking them over, this new design allowed for a smaller crew and had a ship that was easier to handle.

Would it be worth the expense?

He walked outside and could feel the sun on him, some of the light making it through the roofs and down into the sunken pit that was the village. Skara Brae was unique. He had never seen or heard of a design like it. All the buildings were sunk a story or so into the ground, all opened onto the main street, the only street. A ring with buildings on either side. All the roofs were above ground, covered in grass and moss. A path ran across the homes on the inside of the ring, creating two tunnels with stone arches that were needed to pass through. A ramp led down into the road, stairs between the homes leading up to the meadow.

Outside the three-story Inn was the village's Settlement Stone, a square gray obelisk about five feet tall. The first time they had come to the village, on Leigh's quest to investigate the Grove, Hall had touched the stone out of curiosity. That touch had reactivated the village and he had become the Lord of Skara Brae.

He was only just now coming to realize what that meant, now that there were people living in the village that were making it their home. Their lives were in his hands. They were here based on faith in him.

Not exactly true, he knew. All of them had nowhere else to go, but they were still counting on him to provide them a place to live. That was the promise, spoken or not, that he had made. One he intended to keep.

Turning his attention away from the stone, Hall listened to the sounds of Skara Brae. It was morning, the sun just rising and it was still dark on the street. Breakridge, as well as the roofs of the buildings, blocked a lot of the morning sun, casting it all in cool shadows. Mostly it was silent, just the creaking of wood as the wind brushed along the grass covered roofs. With just over a dozen people, it was easy to consider even the small village as empty.

There was still so much he didn't know about the village. Why had it even been built here? The meadow was so isolated. The wind coming in from the edge of the island was constant and fierce, hitting the Breakridge and coming back into the meadow. There was a lack of resources. The land wasn't that great for farming.

Adequate was how Dinah and Hitchly had described it.

Was it because of the Grove? He had never seen villages near other Druid Groves.

When the demons Surtr and Ymir had fractured the world, causing Hankarth to explode into the fragmented islands it now was, it was the World Tree that had kept those pieces floating in the air. Yggradisil had spread Branches out across each of the islands, no matter how small, and around those had grown the Groves where the Druids protected those Branches.

They were in out of the way places. Not near civilization.

So why here?

The previous Custodian, Vertoyi, had killed himself to end the corruption he had caused. No way to ask him. The village had been long abandoned, fallen to ruin, possibly even before Vertoyi's time as Custodian. Someone had to have the answers.

A story for another time, Hall knew, which seemed to be a running pattern. There was always something pushed off for other more important things. Learning about the history of Skara Brae would have to wait, as it wasn't as important as preparing the village and his people for the future.

Being self-sufficient was a start. The isolation worked against them. They would be able to grow their own food, hunt in Greenheight and beyond the Ridge, but there was a lot that they would still need to get from Silverpeak Keep or Green Ember. There might even be something closer to the north, which meant time to explore.

But no matter what, they needed an airship to get to any of the places. Overland travel would just be too dangerous. They couldn't count on regular trips from Hrothgrav or any other ship captain. The cost in gold would be incredibly high.

The more he thought about it, the more it made sense.

Hall turned toward the right, crossing through the arch where the meadow above passed over. The short tunnel wasn't that much darker as it wasn't deep enough to keep the light from either side from illuminating the interior. Square stones, tightly joined together, formed the arch, and Hall had been amazed they were still standing. They should have fallen from erosion and the weight of the meadow they supported. But they were still standing with no sign of weakness.

Just on the other side of the arch was a two-story building, slightly taller than the others. The only difference between it and the homes was the remains of a balcony off the second story. The road had been widened into the meadow, an open space where a home would have been, to give an area for the villagers to gather as they were addressed from the balcony.

Double doors led into the building, and Hall pulled one open. Inside was a wide-open space, a staircase in the back along with a single office. The floor had been stone blocks, most of which still remained. A few had been cracked, a couple pushed up. Stone formed the walls of both stories, with the wood plank flooring above resting on thick and heavy beams. It all looked solid. The Gnomes had done good work, under Duncant's supervision, at reinforcing or replacing the existing structure. The stair was still a little rough-looking, no railing and a couple of loose steps, but it worked. Hall had been up to the second floor himself. Just a series of offices, with a large meeting room connected to currently missing doors that would lead to the balcony.

Timmin wasn't as sure about the stairs and so had set up in the large area on the first floor, claiming the room in the back as his quarters. The tall and thin administrator was not at the desk that had hastily been constructed and set up for his use. Papers covered the surface, all in Timmin's small and neat hand. Most of it was in shorthand, a form of which only the administrator could read.

Hall wasn't sure how far he could trust the man. Timmin was indebted to him. Together with the others, they had rescued Timmin from the Cudgel. The leader of the Silver Blades, a thieves' guild in Silverpeak Keep, had intended to use Timmin to forge the official ledgers kept by the Councilor of Coins. The plan was to undermine the citizens' faith in the records, make it look like the Councilor was stealing from the city treasury. With the Cudgel dead, the city's original thieves' guild, the Door Knockers, had taken an interest in Timmin's talents.

Coming with Hall had kept him out of their hands and put his talents to better use. Besides being an expert forger, Timmin was an excellent administrator. He thought of things Hall had no idea even existed. He was thankful to have Timmin but wasn't sure how far to extend trust.

"Timmin," he called out. "You here?"

The door to the office opened and Timmin stepped out. Long gray hair tied back in a ponytail, tall, thin and older.

Somehow always clean shaven, he had black eyes and a long-beaked nose. Besides being clean shaven at all times, somehow Timmin kept his rich-looking clothes clean.

The only person in Skara Brae to manage such a feat.

Even in the dark room empty of furnishing and barely repaired, Timmin looked every bit how a government official should look. He carried himself with the same air. Stuffy and formal, as if annoyed at every interruption.

"Good morning, Milord," he said with a slight bow of his head.

"Hall."

"Apologies," Timmin said without a hint of apologetic tone in his voice. "Milord Hall."

"Just Hall."

"Hmm?" Timmin asked with a raised eyebrow.

Hall sighed and just shook his head. It was the same in almost every conversation between the two. Hall hated the use of the title, and Timmin refused to stop using it.

"I have a question for you," Hall said as Timmin sat in his uncomfortable-looking chair behind the desk. "Maybe a couple." He remained standing a couple feet from the desk as Timmin picked up some of the papers and started scanning through them.

"Yes?"

"What do you know about airships?"

Timmin looked up at Hall curiously. He tilted his head, tapping on his long nose. It was a motion Timmin used absently as he was thinking.

"That we would benefit greatly from having one of our own," the administrator finally said, returning his gaze to the papers. He started shuffling some of them around, searching. "I assume this has to do with those plans you found in Councilor Cronet's chest?"

"Yeah," Hall replied. "Duncant already revised the Dock plans to include a berth."

"Two or three airships would be best. Three preferably," Timmin said, continuing to look through the papers. "It would be the most beneficial to have one ship outbound, one inbound and one docked for emergencies. But I suppose we can make one ship work."

Hall stared at the man to see if he had been joking. He wasn't.

"I had a quick look at those plans the other day," Timmin added, still not looking up from the papers. "It is a new Dwarven design, and there are parts that are missing."

Feeling himself deflate a little bit, Hall sighed. Of course it wouldn't be that easy.

"Why did Cronet have them then? What good did they do him?"

Timmin did look up, his left hand again tapping on his nose.

"I assume he thought any shipbuilders would be able to make use of the plans and use their knowledge to fill in the missing parts," the administrator said and returned his attention to the papers. He started making some notes with the ink quill kept at the side. "He would have been wrong. No shipbuilder in Essec, Arash, or Storvgarde could finish those plans. Not even any Highborn."

"Only the Dwarves?" Hall asked, knowing the answer.

"Indeed. I recognized the crossed ax rune of Axestorm Hall, which is on the realm of Huntley."

You have discovered that the airship plans recovered from the Cudgel can only be used by a Dwarven engineer. Without that input, the plans are worthless.

Once completed by a Dwarven engineer, the plans will allow a new design of an airship to be built. Find an engineer that can complete the plans. Timmin recognized a rune for Axestorm Hall on the realm of

Huntley, indicating that is a good place to start.

AIRSHIP MODEL X I
Travel to Huntley and discover who drafted the plans 0/1
Rewards: +100 Experience

ACCEPT QUEST?

Conversations with the Skara Brae Village Administrator, Timmin, have shown a need for the village to have its own airship. Get a ship constructed for Skara Brae.

A SHIP OF OUR OWN I
Commission the construction of an airship 0/1
Rewards: +100 Experience

ACCEPT QUEST?

"Interesting," Hall said aloud, surprised when the notifications flashed across his vision.

"Hmm?" Timmin prompted without looking up.

"Apparently, I'm supposed to get an airship for the village," Hall said. "Got a couple quest prompts."

"Of course," Timmin said. "Was that not the whole point of this conversation?"

Hall sighed. Learning to trust Timmin might not end up being the real struggle. Learning to put up with him would be.

He read the quest notifications again as he accepted them.

The experience reward was higher than previous quests. Hall wondered if it was adjusting for the increased experience required to level. He was still not used to how slow leveling was in this new version of the game.

"Any ideas on where to find a Dwarven engineer?" he asked.

"Axestone is known to have the best," Timmin replied, making more notations.

"In the Hard Edge Mountains on Huntley?" Hall asked.

The administrator made a motion of his head that Hall took to mean yes.

Huntley was an island that belonged to the kingdom of Storvgarde, one of the three human kingdoms in Hankarth. The islands were mostly ice-covered mountains and frozen tundra as they floated further down, below all the others, further away from the light of the sun where it was colder and the shadows from islands higher above fell.

Hall had been there many times during his Pre-Glitch gaming days. It was a harsh realm. The Dwarves that made their home in the Hard Edge Mountains were an unfriendly lot. He thought that the clan that Roxhard's gaming backstory gave him, the Stonefire clan, was from Hard Edge, but he couldn't remember. The clan had been just a name, no other information. Biography filler.

The question now was how would he get there to even try to commission an engineer to build him a ship?

"And how much will it cost," he muttered quietly.

"That is a good question," Timmin replied, hearing the comment.

"Any idea?"

"No. It is not my concern," Timmin said and started moving the papers loudly, shuffling and stacking them, banging them together on the table.

Hall shook his head and turned to leave the Town Hall, taking the hint that he was keeping the administrator from his work. Timmin was right. It was not his concern how Hall got the gold. As the Lord of Skara Brae, it was Hall's issue to find the necessary gold and he had an idea where to start.

CHAPTER THREE

"Seriously?" Sabine asked, surprised. "An airship?"

The Witch leaned back against the outside wall of the Inn, her short blonde hair blowing in the breeze. She angrily pushed pieces out of her eyes as she stared at Hall in annoyance.

They were gathered in the tight space of the road outside the building. Sabine, with Caryn next to her, Roxhard standing in the street, and Jackoby leaning against the unfinished house across from the Inn. Leigh was still off at the Grove, and Hall would visit her with the same question later. It had been asked of only Sabine and Roxhard since they had been there when he had gained the item, so it was partly theirs.

In his left hand, Hall held a pouch of gems of various sizes. It was all the jewels they had collected since he had first left Grayhold. A sizable amount. There hadn't been a chance to convert them to gold yet. He had no idea how much they were worth but assumed a decent amount.

Holding his right hand out, palm up, he showed off the last gem. The one he had asked them about. Could we use this to purchase an airship?

Laying on his hand was a rough stone about an inch long and high. Green but with a strange inner light, a tint that was part of the interior of the stone. It sparkled as it caught the light.

A Sun Emerald.

They had found it back on the island of Cumberland in a cave deep in the Far Edge Peaks. A treasure map had led them to the cave, which had apparently been a Redcap's trove. It had been a worthwhile trek, Hall's first deciphered treasure map. Each had gotten magical items they were still using along with some gold and the gems. The Sun Emerald had been the biggest find. A gem of the size he held was worth hundreds of gold.

But enough to commission an airship?

Even if it wasn't enough to get the ship detailed in the plans, it had to be enough to get a small and older airship.

If the others would let him use it.

He looked at Roxhard.

"Sure," the Dwarf said as Hall knew he would.

The brother-like bond they had started to develop had only grown in the last few weeks while in Skara Brae. A fourteen-year-old kid trapped in the body of a couple-hundred-year-old Dwarf, Roxhard needed that bond to hold himself together.

"Of course Leigh said yes," Sabine muttered.

"Haven't asked her yet," Hall replied.

"Of course Leigh will say yes," Sabine amended with annoyance.

It was no guarantee, but considering Hall and Leigh's relationship, which was now common knowledge, everyone knew the way Leigh would vote.

Hall had to wonder if Sabine was upset because she was being outvoted or because Leigh would even get a vote. Hall, Roxhard, Sabine, and Caryn were all Players. People from the real world that had gotten trapped in Sky Realms Online by the Glitch, the weird event that had occurred which forced their consciousnesses to somehow transfer into the game. None of them could log out, and they had been told by the game's developers, Electronic Storm, that this was their new life and the only way they would exist. Everyone else in Skara Brae were NPCs, computer-generated characters. That included Jackoby. And Leigh.

They were unlike any NPCs Hall had ever encountered in any game he had ever played. The AI was light years beyond what had been in Sky Realms Online Pre-Glitch. They were real people as far as Hall was concerned. Sabine had initially had some issues with NPCs like Leigh, but Hall thought she had gotten over that.

Apparently not.

Or was she just jealous?

Hall had thought Sabine was interested in him at one point, but she had never really shown much interest. Caryn's light touch on Sabine's arm, seeming to calm the Witch, told Hall that maybe Sabine had no need to be jealous.

"Fine," she said finally with a sigh. "Let's go buy an airship."

———

Pike soared above, flying in a wide circle over the meadow. Using the magical connection between them, Hall was able to see through the dragonhawk's eyes. The level of detail he could see, especially from so far up, was breathtaking. The power in the bat-like wings as they moved, gliding along the wind currents, was amazing. He could see other birds flying around the mountains. Cliff Shrikes possibly or Hawks. They didn't bother coming closer.

Somehow, they knew that the meadow belonged to Pike.

The circle widened, and Pike glided toward the Grove. The

most southern peak of the Frost Tips was a large mountain, the base the entire northern edge of Breakridge Meadow, with the eastern edge turning sharply north where the Ridge itself turned west to meet it, creating a shadowed and somewhat hidden side to the mountain. Steeply sloping, there were two long areas of flat ground along the lower slope. A path had been carved into the slope, giving somewhat easier access to the two plateaus.

The higher one, also the smallest, overlooked the meadow and the edge of the island, giving a good view of the surrounding sky and the entire land. Hall had gotten up there once. A long and difficult trek up the steep trail, the view had been amazing. The angle of the plateau allowed clear views of the meadow, most of the southern edge of the Ridge, the sky to the south and west and partly to the north. He had decided it would be a good place for a Watchtower.

Except for the cold. The wind was brutal that high up and with nothing to block it.

Meadowsheight Grove was most of the lower plateau, the larger part of it curling back out of view from the meadow along the eastern edge of the mountain. Standing stones separated the exposed rock of the mountain from where the green grass of the Grove started. Trees, flowers, and bushes dotted the landscape leading to the large pool. Beyond was a thick forest and a clearing with the Custodian's Cave at the end. Reflecting silver in the sunlight was the Branch itself, a large tree growing on an island in the middle of the pond.

What Hall saw was so different from when they had first come to the Grove. Then it had been corrupted, poisoned by the power of Vertoyi. The former Custodian had made a deal with a demon, granted power but it had quickly corrupted him which had, in turn, corrupted the Grove. If they had not arrived when they did, the Branch might have died.

In the short time they had been in Skara Brae, Leigh had

made great strides in repairing the corruption. The Grove and the Branch were doing some with their own power, but they still needed the Custodian. Reluctant at first, as she was during her entire training as a Druid, Leigh had come to fully embrace her new role.

With Pike's vision, he could see her now. She glanced up at the circling dragonhawk as she walked across the stepping stones set just below the surface of the pond. Waving, she stepped onto the land and headed toward the standing stones.

Hall closed his eyes, opening them to see the broad meadow laid out before him. He stood at the top of a set of stairs leading up from Skara Brae. Tall grass shifted in the wind, a sea of it before him and the distant mountain. He started walking, enjoying the feel of the breeze and sun against his face and bare arms.

It was a couple of miles between the village and the mountains, a pleasant and easy walk through the grass. He crossed a couple of small streams, easily hopping over. Trees were grouped in tight clusters, using each other for support against the wind. Lone trees were gnarled and bent, devoid of leaves. Silent specters.

He saw small animals dart through the tall grass, birds taking flight as he walked past.

An hour later, he arrived at the base of the mountain. *It needs a name*, he thought as he looked up at the sheer cliffs of gray stone, the flat higher plateau visible as a sharp edge. The high peak was obscured by clouds, and a higher and distant island could be seen just past the edge. A black spot against the blue sky.

A couple of worn totems stood on both sides of the steep path carved into the side of the mountain. They had once been stone trees, but time and weather had cracked and broken them. Running his ungloved hand across the surface, he started walking up the path. It switchbacked a couple of times, a hard climb due to the steepness. Like the totems, the path had been worn by weather and time. Loose rocks that had fallen from the walls, grooves that running water had eroded, all made the walk harder.

Finally, he got to the top, his head clearing the elevation of the plateau, and he smiled.

Leigh sat on the ground between the standing stones that led to the Grove. She sat cross-legged, hands resting on her knees, her staff leaning against the stones. Still in the same leathers she had worn when they met but with more wear and tear, she smiled at him. She was beautiful. Gael, like his human half, she had pale skin. Light blue tattoos ran up her exposed arms, stopping at her shoulders. Long, very curly, bright red hair with streaks of green framed a pretty face with blue eyes and freckles. Two braids hung down over her shoulders, exposing her ears and the two earrings she had in each ear. Small green gems hung on dangling chains and rings high up in the lobe.

She stood up as he came closer and they hugged, arms wrapping tight. She was shorter than Hall, head just below his chin. Leigh leaned back, and he bent down for a kiss.

"What brings you up here?" she asked, breaking off the kiss and stepping away. "Not that I mind the visit."

"I had a thought I wanted to discuss," he started, and she held up a hand.

Taking his hand in hers, she pulled him through the standing stones, taking her staff in hand.

"Talk as we walk," she said, and he laughed.

The first time they had been to the Grove, reddish-purple moss had grown everywhere and the plants and trees had been wilted and dying. Everything had been corrupted. Now, there was green and life. Some were still wilted and the wrong color, the corruption still trying to fight, but they were being overpowered by the strength of life that now flowed through the grove.

Hall could feel it. The air was cleaner, fresher. He could feel the magic. Small animals, squirrels, and rabbits and more, ran through the grass, climbing the trees and jumping through bushes. Birds sang everywhere.

Protected from the worst of the wind, the Grove was warmer as well. It was pleasant, tranquil. Nothing like it had been.

Releasing his hand, Leigh walked over to one of the small purple plants. Her free hand started to glow a soft blue that spread up the tattoos along her arm. Crouching down, she cupped the flower in the glowing hand, not quite touching it. The glow spread from her hand to the plant, and Hall watched as the green of life spread through the leaves. When she stood up, there was still some purple in the plant, but it was mostly green and standing stronger.

It was an ability she called *Revitalize* and she had been granted it when given the title of Custodian of the Grove. Title Abilities was new, something else added Post-Glitch.

"Where's Angus?" he asked, noticing the shaggy cow was missing.

Leigh's Druid Companion, Angus was rarely ever far from her side.

"Playing with the Shamblers," she replied, cupping her still glowing hand around another small plant.

Hall stared at her in confusion. Shamblers were large creatures, basically walking piles of mud and vines, that served as guardians of the Grove. They had been corrupted, and it had been a corrupted Shambler heart that had finally shown Vertoyi what he had done. The corrupted Custodian had been blinded by power, thinking he was making the Grove a better place. He had been moments from killing them all when the sight of a corrupted Shambler heart had broken through his madness.

Leigh laughed when she saw his face.

"He's fine," she said. "The new Shamblers are safe. All the corrupted ones fell apart, and I had to start growing new ones. They're the same size as Angus right now."

He shook his head at the thought of the small cow running around with smaller Shamblers.

"What did you want to talk about?" Leigh asked.

"Remember that Sun Emerald?"

———

"I can't," Hrothgrav said.

The large Storvgardian sat on the grass sloped roof next to Hall, taking a long pull from his mug. The two men sat facing the open edge of the meadow and the moon that shone down on them. They could hear the nocturnal animals coming awake, the distant hoot of owls coming from Greenheight Vale and a long howl of a wolf out beyond the ridge. Hrothgrav's ship, the *Frozen Blade*, sat tethered a ways out in the meadow, moving with the wind. It had arrived earlier in the day, a scheduled delivery. Unloading without a dock was difficult, which meant the cargo had to be smaller. When the dock was finished—*soon*, Duncant kept saying over and over—it would be much easier and Hrothgrav could bring larger shipments.

Since the first time the *Frozen Blade* had brought Hall and his companions back to Skara Brae from Silverpeak Keep, the ship had made two return deliveries. It was costing Hall a lot of gold, which he was rapidly running out of, but it was needed for them to get the supplies they required. In the couple of days since he had come up with the idea, Hall was second-guessing it. Was putting all that money into an airship really a wise investment at this time?

"Don't get me wrong," Hrothgrav said, taking another long pull from the mug. He pulled it away, looking at it sadly. Holding it upside down, he watched a last drop fall to the grass. With a sigh, he set it down next to him. "I would love to fly back down to Huntley. Been a long time since the crew has been in home skies. But just can't do it now. Contracts," he finished with a shrug.

Sitting next to him, Hall saw the motion and understood. He had been lucky enough to get the two shipments he had gotten from the *Frozen Blade*. Hrothgrav had told him it would be many months before he could return again.

Which was an incentive to get their own ship.

"I can get you to Auld and should have good luck finding a ship there," Hrothgrav said, pushing himself up. He stood a bit unsteadily. Picking up the mug, he slowly made his way down the steep roof, almost slipping a couple times. "But we need to leave tomorrow," he added over his shoulder as he walked down the stone steps toward the Inn and more ale.

CHAPTER FOUR

THEY SAILED OVERLAND, THE *FROZEN BLADE* A COUPLE hundred feet above the surface of Edin. What had taken Hall and the others a couple weeks of walking was only taking the airship a couple of days. Standing against the railing, wind whipping in the wind, Hall looked down at the world below. He could see the Fallen Green Forest, home of Jackoby's Firbolg tribe the Brownpaw. The clearing that contained the huge tree laying on its side, the Fallen Green itself, was visible, and he thought he could see where the village of Green Ember was.

Jackoby had taken one look at the forest from this height and retreated to the shared cabin below deck. The men had one, the women another. Hall wondered what it must have been like, seeing your home that had always seemed so large, now looking so small. In the real world, Hall had flown all the time and gotten used to the sensation. This was only the second time Jackoby had ever been on an airship. The first, he had spent most of the time in the cabin.

He had come out a little bit more each day. When they had passed over Fallen Green, Roxhard had coaxed the Firbolg out.

One look at the huge forest looking so tiny had been enough for the large Warden. Hall didn't expect to see him again all day.

Which was fine with him. Jackoby was not the most entertaining or pleasant traveling companion. The Firbolg was only there because he felt he owed Hall a life debt. Hall had saved his life and hadn't expected a reward. The last thing he had wanted was to force the Firbolg to follow him around. Now, he had a reluctant bodyguard. Jackoby was an excellent Warden. A strong fighter. He had proven himself many times over. But he still did not get along with the others.

Not all of them had come, and Hall was missing her already. Leigh had stayed behind in Skara Brae. Her responsibilities in the Grove required her to be there. She couldn't leave for the length of time this trip would take. A month, at least. Hall was just glad that Braniff and Garick had returned before they had left and agreed to stay around the village.

The two higher level adventurers, a Skirmisher and Warden, had answered Hall's letter by showing up in Skara Brae, quicker than he had expected. They had already been in Auld, Braniff had explained. Hall's letter had been simple. Could he turn Skara Brae into an adventuring hub, a kind of Guild Hall? A place where mid to high-level adventurers, like his companions and himself, could explore out from. He had been told all the Great Dungeons had been cleared out, but they had found something in the mountains that had never existed. Skara Brae and the Sage's cave. If there were two new places, could there be more?

Come to Skara Brae and help us explore, the letter had said. The two adventurers had been bored and were eager for new places to adventure. The day after arriving in Skara Brae, they had already set out to explore the Frost Tips, after Braniff had given Hall training in *Leap* Rank Two. They had only just returned the morning Hall had left. Not enough time to learn what, if anything, they had found. Just long enough to get them to agree to stay close to the village while he was away, to provide extra security.

The way they had acted, Hall had a feeling they had found something.

Two things that made him want to go back to Skara Brae: Leigh, and what new mysteries Braniff had found. Three things, really. He was feeling guilty for leaving the village.

Before, there had been no citizens. Now, there was, and while Timmin was an able administrator and would do a better job than Hall could, he was still not Hall. He was the reason all those people had come to Skara Brae. And he was abandoning them.

And why Hard Edge? He could get a ship from the yards at Spirehold, the capital of the Kingdom of Essec. The island of Essec had plenty of shipbuilders where he could find a cheap enough vessel, and it was much closer than Huntley.

He had the quests and his adventuring self wanted to complete the quests, see where they led. But was that the best move for his people? Was he making decisions based on what he wanted and not what was best for his people?

That was not what a good leader did.

Sighing, Hall stepped back from the railing.

It was the flight with nothing to do; it let his mind wander. He had never had much responsibility in the real world, his old life, and now, he was taking a lot on. He'd read or heard that leaders were always troubled by self-doubt and second-guessing but that the good leader put it in the back of their mind and did what they had to for their people. They didn't always do the popular choice or the easy choice, but always the choice that was for the long-term benefit of their people.

That was what he would try to do.

Instead of flying a straight southeasterly course from Skara
Brae to Auld, the city on the southern edge of Edin, the *Frozen
Blade* turned sharply south halfway through the journey. They
spent a day or more flying over the land of Edin before the
island ended. The sharp and jagged edge of land disappeared
beneath them, and the airship was flying over nothing.

Hall, again at the railing, looked down and saw nothing. As
far as he could see. Just blue sky, clouds, and the shadows of
other floating islands. But directly under the ship was straight
emptiness. A drop of miles and miles with nothing to stop the
fall. He was not afraid of heights, did not suffer from vertigo,
but he still felt a little uneasy looking at all that nothing
below him.

Further east, he could make out a large island almost
directly below Edin and a strange shimmering in the air. A thin
strip of air shone, catching the light from the sun and reflecting
it across the sky. He realized it was the waterfall that fell from
Edin and landed on the edge of Cumberland, the large island
down and to the east, that formed the Green Flow. He had
never seen it from this angle.

The *Frozen Blade* flew away from the island's edge a couple
of miles before it turned to the east once more. He shifted to
the other side of the ship where land was visible. They stayed
relatively even with their prior elevation, and Hall could see
mountains forming in the distance, the hills and forests of the
island's edge. Trees were leaning out over the sky, roots digging
deep into the side of the island, holding on as tight as they
could. Rough dirt sides of hills were exposed, revealing where
the grassy mounds had once continued and completed their
shapes. Like all edges of the islands, he could see and follow
the jagged and uneven line. Small streams spilled off the edge,
disappearing as they evaporated or just faded.

As many times as he had flown or walked along the edge of
the various islands, it never ceased to amaze him. The amount

of processing power to create all the islands was immense and that the developers had spent so much time and energy creating each of the many unique island edges had always baffled him.

Why?

No player would have cared if they had copied the same elements over and over or smoothed the edges. If they had treated the edges like beaches or cliffs, it would have been fine. All other games he had ever played ended that way. Beaches and cliffs. But not Sky Realms Online. Here, the developers had let their imaginations run wild. No effort had been spared, and they had created something that was truly amazing.

It was another day of travel before the docks of Auld came into view. Thick wooden posts and crossbeams attached to the stone of the island supported the large planks that formed the docks. Cranes were set at various points, allowing for loading and unloading of cargo from the airships. The flag of Essec flew over the easternmost set of docks. A pair of long docks hanging over the sky, the wooden planking u-shaped, with berths for two airships to a side for a total of eight. All ships that flew out of Essec, or were registered as Essecian, had to dock there. There was another set, similar shaped, but more to the west. The unassigned docks and it was there that the *Frozen Blade* headed. Four ships, including the passenger liner that made the regular trip from Land's Edge Port to Auld, were parked at Essec's docks. Hall counted another four ships at the other docks. There were none with Storvgardian flags. One was Arashi from the islands further above, two were unmarked and one was Highborn.

He started to worry. The plan had been to book passage on a ship headed down, most likely a Storvgardian ship. With none in port, how would they find a ship heading that way? Would they have to hop from one ship to another?

From his position next to the helm, Hrothgrav barked

orders to his crew. Hall looked to the bow of the ship where a signalman was waving different colored flags. He couldn't see the man but knew there was a worker on the dock with flags. The two communicated on where and when to dock. Hall felt the airship lurch as the engines shifted and rotated, allowing the ship to hover in place.

A half-hour later, Hall watched the crew work as they guided the ship into a berth near the island's edge and in front of another ship. They brought the *Frozen Blade* high, fifty or more feet above the other ship, their shadow covering it and the crew as well as the docks. Bringing the ship about, lining it up with the docks, Hall again felt the lurch as the engines rotated. The loud noise, ever-present that he had gotten used to hearing even at night, lowered. At low power, the engines were a small roar instead of the constant thumping they had been at full power. Slowly, the *Frozen Blade* lowered itself down until it was hovering above the dock. The crew made small adjustments as it lowered, and four sailors brought stout-looking long poles to the railing. They reached out and down, the poles hitting the docks of Auld. One of the sailors yelled and together they all pushed, sending the *Frozen Blade* a foot or so further away from the wooden planks, giving it more clearance. Another couple feet and the engines settled into standby, just enough power to keep the ship afloat.

Lines were thrown out, and the ship was tied off.

As the *Frozen Blade* settled with sailors rushing to open the large cargo hatches in the middle of the ship's deck, Hrothgrav walked down toward Hall.

"Here is where we part, my friend," the big Storvgardian said, clapping Hall on the shoulder.

"You'll return to Skara Brae?" Hall asked.

"Aye," Hrothgrav replied. "We'll sail from here to Silverpeak Keep and then back up the edge to your little village. Hopefully that Bodin carpenter has the dock done by then. The boys hate unloading without a crane."

Hall laughed. The Skara Brae docks should be done by that time, he figured, as long as Duncant didn't keep making changes.

Sailors set the gangplank out, and it landed on the docks with a thud followed by a screech as Pike flew out of the stairs that led to the cabins below. He spiraled into the sky, each rotation widening his circle until he disappeared over the island. Flexing his wings, free to fly for the first time in days, Pike was off to hunt. With the winds while sailing, the dragonhawk had to spend his time below decks where there wasn't any room to spread his wings.

Hrothgrav followed the flight of the dragonhawk and turned back toward Hall.

"You picked up after him, right?" he asked and laughed at Hall's nod. "Safe travels my friend," he said and extended his arm.

Hall clasped it, warrior to warrior.

"Safe travels."

He moved toward the gangplank as the others all came up from below, Roxhard with Hall's gear. Seeing them made him miss Leigh even more. She should have been there, with Angus by her side. He was even missing the constant mooing complaints of the shaggy cow.

"Come up with a name yet?" he asked Roxhard as the Dwarf handed him his traveling pack. Most of his inventory was contained in the magical pouch at his side, but each of them still had traveling packs filled with items to sell or gear for the trip.

The Dwarf chuckled and shook his head. Roxhard had been trying to come up with a guild name for the group of adventurers since they had first met. A couple months and while he had come up with ideas, none of them seemed to fit.

"Let's go find an inn and see about booking passage down," Hall said and led the group down the gangplank.

He stopped right before his foot was about to touch down on the dock. A woman walked by, stumbling, supported by a man on her side, heading toward the ship further back.

"Beg pardon," the man muttered as he helped the woman to walk.

A very pregnant woman.

Hall watched her for a moment, caught off guard. He had seen pregnant women before, but he couldn't remember if he had seen any in-game, now or before. With NPCs being static, not aging, there was no need for pregnancy. Children NPCs stayed as children; adults never aged. He shook his head, refocusing his thoughts on what he needed to do.

Pregnant women had to exist in the game, he just must not have noticed.

———

"It has been a long time," Captain Hart said with a smile and exaggerated bow.

He nodded to Hall and Roxhard, eyebrows raised at the sight of Jackoby, leaned out to kiss Sabine's hand and stopped speechless when he saw Caryn.

"How did you travel to the spirit world?" Hart asked as he bent down and kissed Caryn's hand. "For that is the only place you could have found such beauty."

Hall saw Sabine's face stiffen and her eyes cloud in anger. *Which was strange*, he thought, as the first time they had flown with Captain Hart and his ship, the *Twisted Gale*, Sabine had completely ignored Hart's flirtations. And now she appeared jealous as he gave his attention to Caryn.

The small Duelist's dark skin blushed and she laughed.

Hart stood up and turned back toward Hall.

"It is good that you found me," he said.

Which was true, Hall thought, but it had been a surprise.

They had left the docks, stepping from the wood planking to the hard-packed dirt street when Roxhard had noticed Captain Hart exiting a tavern fronting the docks. The sharp-dressed man had stumbled a little but recovered when he saw Hall and the others.

Long black hair tied back, neatly trimmed beard, dark eyes and the pale skin of the Gael, Hart cut a dashing figure. He wore black boots polished to a shine, black pants, sleeve-less leather vest over a white shirt that kept his dark blue tattoos visible. A red sash belt gave him a bit of color as did the green gem set into the pommel of his scimitar that hung off the belt.

Hall had not expected to see Hart, the only other ship's captain that he knew. The timing was simply too good for it to be pure luck.

"Why is it good?" he asked, hoping for a good answer.

Hart stepped back, giving them an exaggerated once-over.

"You have the look of people in need of a ship," he said with a laugh. "And I happen to be in the need for cargo or passengers," he finished, walking over to Hall and putting his arm over Hall's shoulder. He steered Hall toward the Essec dock. "Paying passengers," he added.

"What about Dyson?" Hall asked. "Don't you still work for him?"

"Of course," the ship's Captain said. "But his business has..." he paused while searching for the right word. "Let's just say, the heat has risen and he has had to cut back a bit. Which leaves me with some holes in my schedule."

They neared the docks, and Hall could see the *Twisted Gale* bobbing up and down where it was tied off. He was surprised he hadn't recognized the ship when they had first approached.

"I was wondering what the ship and I would do when you

appeared," Hart continued. "What a fated meeting. An old friend in need of a ship and me with a ship in need of a task."

They stopped at the gangplank, and Hart released Hall. He turned to face the Skirmisher.

"And where shall the *Gale* and I be taking you?"

"Huntley," Hall answered.

Hart's eyes widened in surprise. It was not the answer he had been expecting. Hall could see Hart's mind thinking, working through the numbers. He looked confused at first, but it changed quickly and Captain Hart smiled.

"It's been a long time since we've been that far down," he said and gestured to the gangplank. "Please, come aboard."

———

Hall found himself standing at the railing of an airship.

Again.

Only a couple hours after leaving the *Frozen Blade*, the *Twisted Gale* had taken off. The first hour had been spent with Hart's first mate, an Arashi half-elf named Milinar, tracking down the rest of the crew. The *Gale* was smaller than the *Blade* and had less crew, but they had scattered throughout Auld and it took time to round them up. None had been happy about setting sail so soon after spending only a couple days in port, nowhere near as many as they were used to.

The *Gale* had been in port for three days prior to Hall's arrival, Hart had explained. They'd restocked, thinking the quartermaster could find a new cargo quickly. That hadn't happened and with nothing coming from Dyson, legitimate or not, Hart had been eager to leave Auld. With dock fees adding up, the *Gale* needed a job. Hall provided that.

Sailors pushed the *Gale* away from the dock, where the arms of the sails would clear, and Hart signaled his helmsman. Hall felt the deck drop beneath him as the ship quickly fell down. Hart kept it falling, a controlled descent with the engines provided some uplift. Hall could see the underside of Edin, jagged faces of brown and gray rock that sloped in toward the island. Over a hundred feet deep. The *Gale* only went half that distance, enough to be below the ships above, before the engines engaged. They rotated and pushed the ship away from the island, spinning it around so the bow faced east.

Rotating again, Hall felt the lurch as the airship started traveling at a southeasterly direction away from Edin. The bow was pitched, a slight downward angle. He could see the reflected light that was the great waterfall. The ship was coming closer, the falling water becoming visible. Blue water on blue sky, it was a unique effect that had Hall captivated. He saw the rest of his companions on deck, all of them likewise entranced.

The water didn't fall in a sheet; it fell in undulating waves. Front and back, splashes falling off. There was no noise, nothing for the water to hit against as it fell. Hall could see rainbows everywhere, small ones as the sun hit the water drops misting into the air. The ship passed a hundred feet away, and Hall could feel the mist cool against his skin.

He turned and watched as the falling water disappeared behind them.

CHAPTER FIVE

HALL STARED AT THE CHARTS LAID OUT IN FRONT OF HIM, trying to understand what he was looking at. Many of the islands were represented in the ship's charts. Each to a single sheet, laid out with wind patterns out to five miles from the island's edge. But there was nothing to show how they all linked together, which ones floated over others. There were numerous notations, taken from Hart or some other ship, detailing how islands close together affected the winds between. Notes about which islands had sudden outcroppings from the rocks beneath. Other notes about distances between islands, what upward or downward pitch to set the ship.

He had tried to do an accurate map of the travel from Edin to Huntley, but five days out and halfway there, the attempt was failing. He had managed to get five skill gains in *Cartography* but no useful maps. Even his mental map wasn't a help. When they were between islands, it just showed the blinking cursor that was him floating in the middle of nothing.

Hart had explained that navigation was done by placement off a fixed point; a star, the sun, another island. That point changed depending on where the airship was coming from and heading to, as well as if it was traveling up or down. There was a skill, *Navigation* in the Environment tree, that was used, and those high in the skill were sought after and paid accordingly. Briefly, Hall thought about training in it but didn't want to use up one of his three skill slots in that tree for *Navigation*.

Characters were able to learn up to one hundred and fifty skill points in both the Activity and Environment skill trees. They could learn two hundred in Combat and Magic and another one hundred and fifty in Professions or tradeskills. He just wouldn't use it enough to justify points in *Navigation*.

He still tried to make maps.

There wasn't anything else to do on the voyage.

Hart had said it would take ten days to get from Edin to Huntley, and that was because they were flying down. It would be fifteen or more going the other direction. It was always faster to go down instead of up. The air would get colder the deeper down they went as those islands were further from the sun and fell under the shadows of the higher islands.

Hall was also finding that there were a lot of unclaimed islands floating around Hankarth. Small pieces of rock, some only a mile across, filled the sky. They were so small that normally they wouldn't be visible from any of the bigger and populated islands. He didn't remember these existing in the pre-Glitch game, but then air travel had mostly been automatic. Get on the ship, hang out on the deck, and a couple minutes later the ship would arrive.

The idea of spending days on board had seemed crazy.

Now, he missed the old way. The sailors had plenty to keep them busy. The passengers had nothing.

Trying one last time to map the route from Stark to Riven, two mid-sized islands that were unclaimed by any of the kingdoms and they had passed yesterday, Hall just gave up. It wasn't working. He knew that Stark was above Riven by five hundred feet and north by two hundred. His *Cartography* Skill had managed to map that as long as the edge of Stark was visible, but as soon as the lost site of the island, even though they were hovering over Riven, the Skill failed to connect the two points. He had tried sketching, forcing the map to connect them, but had just failed for the third time.

With a sigh, he left the room, an office used by the Navigator and Quartermaster, closing the door behind him. The ship was swaying slightly, and Hall adjusted his gait. It had taken a couple of days to get used to the motion of an airship traveling along the winds, but he had been on enough of them since awakening in Grayhold that it was becoming easier to adjust each time. He turned down the small hallway and headed aft toward the lower balcony. It was there that he had first met Dyson, the merchant that also ran a smuggling operation between Edin and Cumberland that involved a couple of the Essec Guards on that island.

The door had a pane of glass set in it, looking out over the balcony. Looking out the glass to see if the space was empty, Hall was about to open the door when he noticed some odd specks in the distance.

SKILL GAIN!

Increased Perception Rank Two +.1

They appeared to be moving, coming from a small island they had just passed. A half dozen of them, very small but getting larger as they appeared to be moving. And yes, they were moving. He had no idea what they were, still too far for details, but they were coming closer.

Cursing, he ran back down the hallway and up the stairs to the deck. He emerged just under the command deck, having to turn and run up another set of stairs. Hart was standing in his customary position next to the helmsman.

The Captain looked at Hall, confused at the Skirmisher's sudden appearance.

"I think something's chasing us," Hall said and ran toward the railing at the back of the deck.

Hart followed, his eyes roaming the sky to where Hall pointed.

The half dozen objects were much closer now, and Hall could start to see shapes. They were all black, shadowed by the sun, but he could see long wings flapping and something atop the wings. He had an idea of what he was looking at.

"Glass," Hart yelled, and a sailor standing on the deck ran to the Captain.

Taking the spyglass, Hart looked through the smaller end. He tracked the glass across the sky, looking for the objects. His movements stopped as he focused on them.

Hart cursed and let the spyglass down.

"Roc Riders."

Large birds, the size of small dragons, Rocs were the only other creature capable of flying from island to island. More common than dragons, the great birds had sometimes been tamed by smarter and more civilized humanoid inhabitants of Hankarth. Or the wild people that lived on random islands, apparently.

Even though airship travel was only minutes long in the pre-Glitch game, it had sometimes been longer as the voyage would stop for a kind of mini-event. Rocs with Riders were the most common, and those were still rare, one out of every seven to ten voyages. The ship would be attacked by a number of Rocs and riders, depending on the number and levels of the passengers. These attacks usually yielded excellent loot, and some players even camped the ships in hopes of hitting the attacks multiple times.

The fights were hard with the birds hovering above the

airship and the riders jumping down to attack. Players died, but the airships were never destroyed.

"Just our luck," Hart muttered. "I knew we should have stayed further away from those debris realms," he added, using the term for the many small and unclaimed islands.

The term referred to the idea that there was no reason to land, no one had ever settled, and the floating islands were just obstructions to avoid. Some, most, were only dozens of feet in size. Very few were miles long but still not large enough or too far away from civilization to settle. Islands that were nothing more than debris in the sky.

Lifting the spyglass to his eye again, Hart started muttering to himself. Hall knew he was calculating the distance between the ship and the Rocs, figuring out how long it would take before the Riders were upon them.

"Can we outrun them?" Hall asked, wondering why Hart wasn't ordering the engine room to pour on the power.

"Not a chance," the Captain replied, which gave Hall his answer. Hart wouldn't waste the fuel or put the wear on the engines if it would not matter.

"Get your weapons and your friends," Hart said, stepping away from the rail. He handed the spyglass to the other sailor. "We're about to be boarded."

He started shouting some commands to the other sailors and to a man, the crew of the *Twisted Gale* responded quickly and efficiently. Some ran for the sails, to bring them down before the sharp talons could rip them to shreds. Others ran to get out the weapons while still more headed for the large ballista mounted to the bow and aft of the ship.

Hall had never seen Rocs flying from so far away, and their speed was surprising. Airships were relatively slow and ponderous. They were not built for speed. But Rocs were. The ship did not seem to be moving at all.

The giant birds were fast approaching.

Hall ran for the stairs down.

———

He heard the screeching as he stepped back on deck, spear in hand and sword strapped to his waist. He had left his javelin below. Without the magical ability to return, he would lose the weapon with any attack, a miss or a hit. The others all armed and rushing up behind him except for Pike and Salem, who had stayed below. Rocs surrounded the ship, three to a side, sailors trying to get off shots with the crossbows. The great birds opened their razor-sharp beaks, screeching as they used their wings to hover and hold themselves steady, claws raked out as the Riders fired back with their bows.

Fights in the air were chaotic, more missing then hits, as both sides had to try to stay aloft. The Rocs were agile, able to move around the *Twisted Gale* which had to force its way forward. Sailors ran across the deck, avoiding the attacking arrows, trying to find openings. There were only half a dozen crossbows, most of the crew armed with swords and spears which they jabbed out when a bird got too close.

Skill gain!
Identify Rank One +.2

Redclaw Roc (blue)
Serenti Roc Rider (white)

The Roc's wingspan was easily fifteen feet across, the body close to ten feet long. Foot-long talons ended in razor-sharp points and the beak was at least the same size. The colors ranged from deep red to orange and every shade between. No two looked exactly alike.

Unlike the Riders. The six men were all dusky-skinned,

covered in white tattoos, wearing no armor and bare-chested. They sported bone-white masks in the shape of demons. Thick vines encircled the Roc's lean bodies, running over the men like harnesses that held them in place. Each had a small bow, firing arrows rapidly.

The last sail was finally pulled down but had been damaged by one of the birds. Hall watched as part of the deck's railing was pulled off, ripped and broken by a Roc's grasping talons.

They all stood in the middle of the deck wondering what to do.

Hall had been on airship's during Roc attacks before but this was not like that. There, the Roc had landed on the deck, allowing the melee fighters to fight. These birds and Riders flew just out of reach, flying over and under the airship, firing as they went.

"Watch for an opening," he yelled to Jackoby, Roxhard, and Caryn. He signaled to Sabine, and the Witch nodded.

Their only true ranged attacker, she watched the birds and waited until three of them were lined up. Waving her fingers and chanting, Sabine launched a *Hexbolt*, the crackling purple energy split and slammed into the three birds and riders. Bolts surrounded them, streaking across their bodies as the Riders tried to fire their arrows.

Unable to move, the three Rocs were large targets for the *Gale's* sailors. The sound of crossbows firing filled the air, bolts streaking toward their targets. Hall launched one of his small throwing knives, the blade striking a Roc just below the eye. The knife's special ability didn't activate, only doing minimal damage.

Hall saw Health drop from the three birds' health bars. The Riders were relatively unharmed, no bolts striking them, but in this fight, they weren't the targets. Kill the Roc and you'd kill the Rider.

The Rocs continued to screech, and now Hall could hear war cries from the Riders in a language he did not know. Behind the cries, he heard something else. A singular voice rising in volume above all the other noises. The words, in that same language, were spoken with a cadence and pattern.

A chant.

"Spellcaster," Hall yelled, turning around rapidly looking for the Rider.

It was too late.

Out of the clear blue sky, a bolt of blue-white lightning shot down, slamming into the deck of the *Gale*. The force caused the ship to shake, listing to one side. Sailors fell to the ground as the deck shifted under them. Smoke rose up from where the bolt had struck. No flames, just the smoke coming from the large scorched deck.

Hall scanned the sky.

Skill Gain!
Increased Perception Rank Two +.1
Skill Gain!
Identify Rank One +.1

Serenti Bonespeaker (blue)

He saw the spellcaster, a Shaman. Dressed the same as the other riders, carrying a bow, the man and his dusky red Roc hung back from the fight. *Clever*, Hall thought, having the man dressed the same. Spellcasters were usually easy to spot as they wore no armor and just looked different. This group, the Serenti, were smart. The only reason Hall knew the Rider was the Shaman was because he hung back and didn't have hold the bow in hand. It was a detail that would be easy to miss in the chaotic fight.

"Sabine," Hall shouted and pointed. "That one."

The Witch held herself steady against one of the masts. Her eyes tried to follow Hall's extended arm. She shook her head, unable to tell which one he meant.

Hall cursed. It wasn't her fault. The birds and Riders moved in no evident pattern. It was chaotic, meant to distract, to make it hard to follow any one Rider. And it was working.

He felt the rush of air as a ballista bolt, a three-inch round and six-foot-long missile, shot past. The bow crew had managed to rotate the weapon, pointing it almost over the ship. The large bolt slammed into one of the Rocs, piercing the bird's side. Wings fluttered as the creature was pushed backward. The Rider lost his bow, the weapon dropping down into the nothingness to fall forever. He managed to stay attached, leaning forward and laying across the spinning Roc.

It tried to get control of its flight, but the bolt was lodged in the chest, knocking the balance off and the added weight dragging the bird down. It gave one final squawk, and the wings just stopped moving as all strength left it. Down the Roc fell, disappearing out of sight below the ship, the screams of the Rider following.

Hall felt useless. There wasn't much he could do. He ran to the railing where the three Rocs hovered, the talons trying to grab at the ship. He joined the sailors with spears, jabbing at the creatures if they got too close.

His ironwood spear slid across a Roc's talon, leaving a scratch and causing the bird to pull back. He pulled the weapon back and slid it out rapidly to the side, catching another Roc in the leg. The tip penetrated the feathers and muscle, hitting the thin bones. The creature squawked in pain as the spear activated its special ability.

Exceptional Breakridge Ironwood Spear
Attack Power +2
Damage 1d6 +2

Agility +1
Durability 12/12
Weight 3 lbs.

On successful hit, has a 50% chance of causing Splinter. A shard of wood lodges within the wound causing 1 DMG every 3 Seconds for 15 Seconds.

Blood leaked out from the wound where Hall could see the magical splinter lodged in the Roc's leg. The spear was almost knocked from his grasp as the Roc kicked out. He slid back out of the way as talons grabbed the decking and pulled.

Wood cracked, snapping as railing and decking were ripped away.

Hall slid further back, away from the section of the ship now exposed to the sky.

He felt the *Twisted Gale* turning and lurching as the ship tilted at a steep angle. The roar of the engines increased in pitch as they ramped up to full power. The Rocs fluttered and screeched as the ship momentarily pulled away.

Both ballistae fired as the birds hung back. One more Roc fell from the sky as a bolt pierced its chest. The second bolt missed, becoming a speck in the blue as it disappeared from sight.

The remaining Rocs pulled in their wings, diving as they chased the ship. Hall looked toward the bow and could see a good-sized island floating ahead. They were far above it, angling down. He wondered what Captain Hart meant to do. Lose the birds around the island? The ship got closer, and Hall could feel the wind ripping at them, pushing against them, and he realized what Hart's plan was. The wind currents around the islands could be wild and chaotic. Rocs could manage to fly in the winds, but the Riders would need to decide what they wanted to do. Chase after the ship, where they would lose speed against the wind, or try to fly through the winds and slow down and potentially lose the ship.

There was a third choice. They had all forgotten the spellcaster.

A bolt of lightning streaked down from the sky and slammed into the starboard engine. Sparks erupted as the metal engine was torn, smoke billowed out of the wound. The port kept going, the aft sputtering. The *Gale* started to turn, pushed by the full power of the port engine.

"Shut them down," Hart shouted over the wind and the noise, Hall somehow hearing the Captain's words.

It was too late. The *Gale* turned so the port side was facing the island and the wind. The ship shuddered as the engines both stopped, smoke drifting up from the starboard side. Wind slammed against the ship as its speed and momentum carried it toward the island. Another bolt slammed into the ship, wood cracking and splintering.

"Brace for impact," Hart shouted as the shore of the island came closer and closer.

The command was passed from sailor to sailor, all hands grabbing for anything to hold on to. Those that could ducked under cover. Hall's friends all ran for the stairs to below. He tried to follow but knew there was no time. He grabbed the railing that led to the upper deck, bracing himself against the side of the stairs and looked toward the island that now filled his vision.

Almost perfectly round in shape, the edges of the island were rough and jagged. A lone mountain, the top bald, stood to one side, a large lake in the middle. Trees and hills covered the entire island save for a small strip of clearing along the edge.

Which was where the *Gale* was heading.

Hall closed his eyes.

He could feel the wind, hear the creaking of the ship and

the distant screeching of the Rocs. There was a whistling as the wind cut through the ship. Men yelled and screamed.

Bracing himself the best he could, Hall waited for the impact. He had no idea when it would happen. Wood cracked as pieces were pushed off, splintering with the force of the wind.

And then the boom, more wood cracking as the ship slammed into the island.

The force of the impact broke the railing, and Hall lost his group. He forced his eyes closed as he fell. He felt the impact as he slammed into wood, once and then twice and again, his body thrown around.

Hall landed hard, feeling soft grass beneath him.

CHAPTER SIX

SOMEHOW, HE WAS ALIVE.

By some miracle, he lived.

But he hurt. Hall could barely move. He could barely breathe. Every movement was pain, every breath was searing, causing him to cough, which hurt even more. Cursing with each small movement, Hall forced himself to turn over. Coughing, breathing heavy, he pulled up his Status, looking at his Health.

Health 20/59
Energy 81/81
Vitality 8/22

He tried to sit up but couldn't. He didn't think his back was broken; it was just too painful to move. His lung was punctured, that much he knew. He was bleeding from multiple wounds but didn't have any kind of icon indicating the bleeding was damage over time. That was a relief. A minor one, but still a relief.

Groaning surrounded him along with the creaking of the ship. Wood banged against wood, men muttered and cried out in pain. He couldn't see anyone else. Just wood above and to the side, unable to identify what part of the ship he was seeing. Deck or wall? To the other side was the blue sky beyond the edge of the island, soft grass of the clearing visible. It looked peaceful, inviting.

Hall knew he had to move, to find the others.

Reaching down toward his belt, he fumbled for the potion pouch he had looted a long time ago. Somehow, painfully, with the awkward angle, he managed to open the pouch. By feel alone, he found the potion he wanted and pulled it up. The vial was small, filled with a golden liquid. *A Minor Health Potion.*

Grunting in pain, having to stop for a time, he managed to pry the cork off without spilling any of the contents. Bringing it to his lips, he drank it all. Hall felt the thick liquid flow down his throat, feeling warmth spreading through his body. It started in his chest, radiating out from there to every part of his body. He cried out as bones realigned and fused together, flesh knitted itself together, and the wall of his lung was repaired.

Minor Health Potion has healed you for +15 Health

Letting the empty vial drop, he reached back toward the pouch but stopped. He heard a new sound. The thud of something hitting the ground. Turning, he saw two Rocs in the clearing, the birds crouching down and the Riders sliding off their backs.

Hall cursed.

Forcing himself to move quick, still in tremendous pain, Hall pulled a vial filled with a light green liquid out of the pouch. This time he was able to remove the cork quicker and dump the liquid down his throat. Immediately, he felt like he had drunk a gallon of coffee. His nerves were on fire, full of energy.

Minor Vitality Potion has recharged you for +10 Vitality

He pushed himself up, eyes scanning the ground for his spear. He saw the weapon in the clearing, ten feet away— between him and the approaching Riders.

They didn't see him, lost in the shadows of the crashed ship. He saw the two gesturing, talking, moving cautiously with weapons drawn and ready. Each held an ax, the handle wooden with a rough chiseled stone head fastened to it. Their language was full of quick and short sounds, not quite grunts but nothing recognizable as words. They understood each other easily enough.

Skill Gain!
Identify Rank One +.2

Serenti Roc Rider (white)
Serenti Roc Rider (white)

Hall sighed. Of course neither was the spellcaster. He was still in the air, circling above the wreckage and ready to rain spells down. Not ideal.

Slowly, carefully, Hall pulled his legs in under him so he was crouching, leaning deeper into the shadows of the ship. The two Serenti Riders spread out, causing Hall to curse. He couldn't lose sight of them, but he wanted them closer to the ship before he attacked. If he could keep more of the *Gale's* bulk around them, it should limit the interference from the spellcaster. He tried to listen, straining to hear, but there were no more noises coming from the rest of the ship. The groans of pain had faded, most likely falling silent as they caught sight of the Rocs overhead.

Realizing he had to act, Hall drew his short sword and activated *Leap*.

He soared through the air, a quick and low jump, landing between the startled Serenti. Without the spear, he didn't have the reach for *Leaping Stab*, but he did get his Attack of Opportunity. Hall swung to his right, the short sword slicing across the Serenti's back. The warrior fell forward, blood flying through the air. Stopping his swing, Hall pivoted and turned his blade. He stabbed straight out and caught the second Serenti in the gut as the warrior reacted by turning. The Serenti folded in half, dropping his weapon as his hands reached for the wound. Hall kicked out, pushing the warrior back and off his sword. He turned and blocked the weak swing of the stone ax. Metal hit wood, and surprisingly, the ax shaft did not break. It didn't appear to be ironwood, the color too light, but was just as strong.

Though wounded, the Serenti was still quick. He pulled the ax back and swung, adjusting the arc and pulling the ax back again. Hall avoided both attacks, stabbing out with his sword but missing. He glanced at the Serenti's Health bar, seeing that it was only down to seventy-five percent. Which was where his own Health was. He hurt, his muscles stiff and not moving as fast. Hall knew he was barely blocking the much faster warrior's attacks. Metal against wood, whoosh of air as weapons barely missed. Hall shifted, trying to adjust so he could see behind him at the second warrior, making sure the Serenti was down and out.

A screech filled the air. Not as loud or ear-splitting as the Rocs. It was strong, powerful, and familiar. Hall smiled.

Pike flew out of the *Gale's* wreckage from above. The dragonhawk swooped down, and Hall jumped back. A bolt of lightning shot out from Pike's open mouth, slamming into the

Serenti. The warrior spasmed, shaking, smoke rising from where the blue-white lightning hit. Before the warrior could recover, Hall stabbed out with his sword and the warrior dropped.

He glanced behind him and saw that there was no threat from the second warrior. The Serenti lay unmoving.

SLAIN: *Serenti Roc Rider*
+10 Experience
SLAIN: *Serenti Roc Rider +25 Experience*

Skill Gain!
Small Blades Rank Two +.1

Hall looked up into the sky, searching for the other two Rocs. He couldn't see the great birds but heard the sounds of fighting from the other side of the ship. He looked across the clearing, seeing the two riderless birds eyeing him warily. Well-trained, they did not react to the deaths of their riders.

Taking a couple steps toward them, eyes watching, Hall reached his spear. The birds hadn't reacted, and Pike was now perched on his shoulder. Bending down, he picked up the weapon and gave it a quick look.

Durability 10/12

It had taken some damage but nothing obvious.

With eyes still on the riderless birds, Hall stepped back toward the ship. He turned around and looked at the *Gale*.

It wasn't as damaged as he had thought. The ship lay on its side, the deck facing to his right. Hall had been thrown from the ship, landing past the bow and under some of the deck boards. One of the masts lay shattered, broken. Most of the deck itself was missing, more pieces of the rail gone. Moving to look at the deck he could see sailors now, some visible in the gaps of the decking. Others crawling along the rail. Two were helping an unmoving comrade down the side to the ground where others were gathering. He couldn't see Captain Hart.

And behind the ship, he saw flashes of light and the sounds of battle. Rocs squawked and cried.

Hall ran with the deck to his side, sliding under the broken mast where it lay against the ground. He passed the sailors, turning around the aft of the ship and saw the battle.

A Roc lay motionless, a pile of feathers with purple crackling lightning still shooting around its body. The Rider fought against Jackoby. The spellcaster was still in the air, hovering above the ground, and throwing fireballs toward the back of the ship. Where the others must be, Hall thought, wondering if they were okay. He couldn't see them, hoping they were all still alive. The bar of black light that shot out and struck the Roc told him that at least Sabine was in the fight.

Hall wished he had his javelin. The spellcaster was too far and too high for him to use *Leap*, the ranged attack with the javelin would have been welcome.

Instead, he pulled out one of the throwing knives from his bracer and let it fly. The small weapon struck the spellcaster, and its special ability activated. Lightning erupted at the impact, small bolts flickering around the Serenti Bonespeaker. The spellcaster yelled in pain, almost slipping from the Roc. He turned toward Hall, raising his hands, and was struck by blue-white blobs of energy. Sabine's *Arcane Missiles* slammed into the Bonespeaker. He raised his hands in defense, trying to stop the barrage. The Roc screeched, great wings beating the air as it tried to raise into the air. Dust and dirt, leaves and small rocks, were kicked up as the great wings buffeted the ground. The great bird formed a shield, protecting its rider as the Bonespeaker tried to recover.

Hall ran across the ground, ignoring the fight between

Jackoby and the Serenti. He closed the distance, angling to come in to the side of the Roc. When he was close enough, he used *Leap*. Jumping high, he covered the distance and landed on the back of the Roc, using *Leaping Stab*. The spear slammed into the back of the Bonespeaker. Pulling it back as he landed, Hall stabbed forward again. The tip burst through the chest of the spellcaster, blood flying out. The Bonespeaker sagged, the weight pulling Hall forward.

The Roc reacted madly, bucking and tilting. Hall lost his balance and fell, holding his spear tightly. The weapon pulled out of the Bonespeaker with a loud smacking noise, the lifeless body sagging in the harness that held it tight to the Roc. The great bird flew into the air, twisting and trying to dislodge the body.

Hall yelled out in pain as he crashed to the ground, rebreaking bones that had previously been healed. He hurt all over, glancing at his Health to see it had dropped drastically. Laying on the ground, he watched the Roc fly higher and higher into the sky. With squawks and screeches, the other two flew into the air and followed the first. They disappeared into the blue sky, large bodies disappearing into small specks before vanishing completely.

SLAIN: Serenti Bonespeaker
+10 Experience

Skill Gain!
Polearms Rank Two +.1
Skill Gain!
Thrown Rank Two +.1

Breathing hard, Hall just lay on the ground, too hurt to move.

———

"It's repairable," Henrik, the *Gale's* engineer, said. His arm was in a sling and a bandage lay over a gash across his forehead. "We'll limp along to the next port, but she'll fly."

Hall was standing in front of the ship's deck, which lay facing them. With Captain Hart and the engineer, they were inspecting the damage. By some miracle, everyone had survived the crash and the Serenti's attack. They were all hurt; no one had escaped unscathed. Injuries ranged from broken bones to a shattered spine. One of the ship's gunners had snapped his back during the crash and no amount of magic potion would heal the wound. He needed a high-level Druid.

There were very few Health potions, and they used them all up in getting most of the crew mobile. A good amount still lay in the makeshift camp they had constructed under the shade of the trees. Hall had set a guard rotation using some of the crew and his companions. They had no idea if the island was inhabited and what kind of creatures made their home on it.

Hall himself was still hurting. He had used two more Minor Health potions and another Minor Vitality. His Health was full, but his Vitality was still five points below the maximum. Evidence of the wear and tear his body had gone through. Because they were out of potions, he had gotten to use his *Triage* skill and raised it a couple of points.

"How long?" Captain Hart asked.

"Hard to say," Henrik replied. "Depends on what we can salvage and what we can make from that," he said, pointing at the forest. "Also depends how quick we move and well, we won't be moving quick," he finished and gestured at the wounded sailors.

Hart nodded, looking back at his men. The Captain, like them all, was hurt. His arm was in a sling, a bandage covering a wound on his other arm that had finally stopped bleeding. His fine clothing was ruined, ripped and torn. He walked with a limp, grimacing with each step.

"Get started," Hart said, reaching out and clasping Henrik's shoulder. "Get what men you can to start work."

The engineer nodded and walked toward the men. He called out for a couple, motioning them to tasks. Hart gestured to Hall, and they walked away from the ship and the crew.

"We got lucky," Hart said.

Hall nodded. Everyone knew the crash could have been much worse.

"But we're still in it pretty deep," Hart continued. "Food is scarce, as is drinkable water. We're days away from any kind of civilization. It could be weeks before the ship can fly again, and when those Roc return home with no Riders, the Serenti could come looking for us."

"And none of us are at full Health," Hall said.

The two fell silent, both knowing how bad off they were.

"Any of yours an Alchemist?" Hart asked.

"Sabine is," Hall replied, but he wasn't sure what level. She had mentioned it in passing once that she had taken *Alchemy* as her a Profession along with *Enchanting*. *Herbology* was the third Skill she had chosen. With all that they had been through since Grayhold, he doubted she had had a chance to level the Skill at all. "But we need materials."

They both turned to the forest around them. It wasn't a jungle, but it wasn't a forest like they had on Edin. Somewhere in the middle. The trees were tall, thick with branches. Vines hung down, coiling on the ground where exposed roots criss-crossed. Small birds and animals could be heard running through the trees.

"We need as many able-bodied as we can get to work on the ship," Hart pointed out. "Could use the Firbolg and the Dwarf."

With the two Wardens working on the ship, using their size and greater strength, Sabine staying in the camp to make potions and all the sailors working on repairs or turned into guards it left only Hall and Caryn for foraging.

"Might as well get started," Hall said, and the two walked back toward the camp.

CHAPTER SEVEN

NONE OF THEM WERE HAPPY ABOUT STAYING BEHIND, BUT THEY all understood why. Except Jackoby. The Firbolg grumbled loudly. He was only with them because he felt a debt to Hall for saving his life and he could not repay that debt by staying behind while Hall went into the depths of the unknown island.

"I am going with you," Jackoby growled, staring down at Hall.

The two stood face-to-face, the Firbolg a head taller and much bulkier. He glared at the Half-Elf, his tone and eyes proof that he did not want to go because he had any liking for Hall. Hall didn't back down, craning his neck to stare right back.

"You are staying," he said again, filling his voice with authority.

Hall could feel all the eyes on them. Sabine, Salem in his customary position over her shoulders, was behind Jackoby, rolling her eyes. Caryn looked nervous. Roxhard was kicking at the sand, trying to ignore it all. Captain Hart and the sailors of the *Gale* weren't sure what to make of the exchange. Hall could see some of the sailors looking like they were laying bets, thinking it was going to come to blows.

"Captain Hart needs you here," Hall explained, or tried to. He could tell Jackoby wasn't listening, but he still tried. "Your strength is needed here."

"Then you will stay as well," Jackoby said, jabbing a thick finger into Hall's chest.

The force made Hall stumble back a step. Jackoby sneered. Now Hall was starting to get angry. This was ridiculous. He felt his hand tightening against the shaft of his spear. Taking a deep breath, he forced himself to calm down. This was useless and getting into a fight would accomplish nothing. There had to be a better way.

"I get it," Hall said, taking a step back and relaxing. "The debt and all that, but look at it this way: if the ship doesn't get repaired, none of us are getting off this island and the debt won't get repaid. In a way, helping to repair the ship is saving my life."

He watched the Firbolg's brown fur-covered face with the darker markings. Hall knew the plea hadn't worked. If anything, it looked like Jackoby was madder. *Did I somehow offend his honor?* Hall thought, watching the Firbolg's fiery eyes. Jackoby looked like he was going to step forward, his shoulders tense, arms slightly raised.

"I will not be dishonored if you die from stupidity," Jackoby barked and turned, stalking away.

There were some mutterings from the sailors, disappointed there was no fight and no betting. They dispersed, going back to their tasks. Sabine rolled her eyes, and Hall thought he heard a quiet and annoyed "NPCs" as she walked away. Roxhard looked up at Hall, shrugged, and smiled and followed Jackoby and Captain Hart.

Hall shook his head and sighed. He had to do something to make life with Jackoby easier. If the Firbolg was going to be part of their group, they had to learn to trust and listen to each other. The Firbolg did neither.

"Where do you want to start?" Caryn asked.

Hall looked up into the sky where he saw Pike circling the clearing. The dragonhawk screeched and flew south across the clearing and over the trees. Hall pointed in the direction Pike had gone.

"Might as well start that way and circle the island unless Pike sees something interesting from above."

"Sounds good," Caryn agree and fell into step beside Hall.

————

Skill Gain!
Herbology Rank Two +.1

Success!
You have harvested a stalk of Green Root

Hall stood up and stretched his back. He was getting tired from having to bend down so much. They were having great success at finding herbs, flowers, and roots for Sabine to use in potion making. Getting good Skill gains as well. Seven skill ups in *Herbology* and that had gotten him to 15.5, enough to gain an Attribute Point in *Intelligence* and the bonus one hundred experience.

The island was teeming in *Green Root*, a small root found at the base of trees that provided healing and many others. Caryn apparently had a higher Skill as she was finding and harvesting more. She had mentioned she had a Skill called *Foraging*, which seemed to help as she managed to find edible nuts and berries. Hall wondered how that differed from his *Survival* Skill. He had almost forgotten he had it, as there had been no gains in a long time, until he received a couple while hunting for the roots and flowers.

He chewed on his third piece of *Green Root,* which worked to restore some of his Health. The root was bitter tasting but it helped, so he kept eating. The gains were greater when used in a Potion, but he needed to get his Health up and it was working.

The forest around them was thick and old. They had found and started following an animal's trail, figuring it would lead them toward a source of water and where there was water, there were herbs, roots, and flowers. Possibly an animal to kill for meat. It had been over an hour, thirty minutes of walking the trail, and they had seen nothing living.

That the trail existed was evidence that animals did live on the island. It looked well used, the leaves and sticks broken, the grass trampled and the small branches bent back on either side. It also looked recently used.

He heard sounds to the left, underbrush crunching and snapping. Caryn stepped out onto the trail a couple feet ahead of him. She had a handful of *Ginseng Root* in her hand, she tossed him one and started to put the rest in the pouch on her belt. Like Hall's, it was small, only a couple inches long and deep, but it opened to a magical pocket dimension that was much larger. Catching the root, he watched as she started putting the bundle of six-inch-long roots into the bag. He turned away as they started to distort at the bag's mouth, folding and twisting, shrinking as they somehow managed to fit into the much smaller space.

Taking his water flask out of his own pouch, he poured some over the root to wash away the dirt. Satisfied it was as clean as he could get it, Hall started to chew on the hard and spongy root. He could feel little bits of energy pushing through his veins as he ate. Where *Green Root* worked on Health, *Ginseng* worked on Vitality.

He noticed Caryn looking at him, head tilted and unsure of herself. She was never the most confident of people, had a naivete about her. He knew she wanted to ask him a question but wasn't sure if she should. A small Gael woman with dark skin, she kept her hair in thin tight dreadlocks, no tattooing and dark eyes. She wore a reddish leather kilt and calf-high boots, bracers on her bare arms, leather armor and shoulder pauldrons. Her long thin-bladed swords were sheathed at her hips. Those two blades bore the same maker's mark as Hall's own short sword but had been found in different places. His had come from a Red Cap's treasure cache in the Far Edge Peaks on the northern edge of Cumberland. Hers had been used by Cronet, the former Councilor of Silverpeak Keep on Edin, also known as the Cudgel, leader of the Silver Blades thief's guild and a man that had led a failed coup to take over Silverpeak Keep.

Hall didn't know what the mark meant or who the weapons were made by. It was a mystery for another day, just one of many that were being added almost daily it seemed.

"You have a question," he prompted.

Caryn nodded, a shy and small nod, trying to smile but failing.

"It's kind of personnel," she started, glancing at him but moving on quickly. "You don't have to answer but..." she trailed off.

"What's the question?" he asked with a chuckle, making a motion with his hand to get her moving. They could walk and talk.

"Well... uhm... What's it like with an NPC?" she asked, almost blurting it out. "The... you know..." she waved her hand absently.

It took Hall a minute to get what she meant, and he started to get mad. She meant his relationship with Leigh. He was a Player and Leigh was an NPC. He knew that, for a time,

Sabine had harbored resentment toward Leigh and the equal status Hall gave her, but he thought she had moved on. He hadn't expected the same prejudice from Caryn.

She must have sensed something from his silence because she looked at him, holding out her hands.

"It's not like that," she said, trying to calm him. "I love Leigh. She's great. It's not a Players are better than NPCs thing. We're not. We're all equal."

The way she said it, not quickly and with conviction, told Hall that she truly meant it. He calmed down, sighing and forcing a smile to show he wasn't offended. He carefully thought about her question before answering.

"We're all just bits of data now," he said with a shrug. "So I suppose it's no different from a Player and a Player," he finished with a glance at Caryn. He could see her blushing a little. "Why do you ask?"

This time it was obvious that Caryn was blushing.

"I guess you know about Sabine and me," she started with a glance at Hall. He nodded. The two women didn't exactly advertise their relationship, just like Hall and Leigh, but Skara Brae was small and with only about a dozen inhabitants. It was hard to hide anything. The relationship had somewhat surprised him at first because he had known Sabine had been interested in him at the beginning, before realizing how much he was attracted to Leigh. "Was just curious if there was any difference."

Hall realized that Sabine must have said something about NPCs being different, probably something negative, and that was what prompted Caryn's question. Silence fell as they continued walking, eyes roaming the foliage to the sides of the trails for more roots.

"She's loud," Caryn said with a chuckle before stepping off the trail and disappearing into the trees.

Hall stood there looking after her, embarrassed.

Shortly after, Hall was connected to Pike, watching what the dragonhawk was seeing. From the dragonhawk's eyes, he saw a large clearing ahead of them, trees tight all around. Broken trees at one end, snapped and dead with new growth coming in around them. Deep furrows in the ground, where the dirt had been kicked up but new grass had grown over them. The clearing wasn't flat, twice the size of the one where the *Gale* had crashed, and filled with dozens of grass-covered mounds. Some big, some small.

The trail led right to it.

They slowed as they got closer, Caryn drawing her twin blades. Through Pike's eyes, Hall saw nothing alive in the clearing, but they felt better with weapons in hand. Ahead, they could see the brightness that was the clearing, a light at the end of the somewhat darker tunnel of the forest. Pausing at the edge, they looked out in confusion.

The clearing sloped down to the south. They had entered at the high side, from the east, and had a clear view down to the southern line of trees, where the deep grooves had been pushed into the ground and the trees beyond were smashed and broken. It was like something had been thrown into the clearing, coming in low over the trees before slamming into them and ending up into the side of the hill.

Grass-covered mounds filled the space, and Hall could see some bits and pieces of what they originally were poking through. Thick timbers, some wrapped in rusting metal. The largest mound was in the middle, and even more of the wood and metal showed through the grass.

A crashed airship.

It had to have been here for decades, Hall thought as they stepped into the clearing, working their way down to what had to be the main deck and hold of the ship, the largest mound in the clearing. It looked to be half-buried in the side of the hill. The grass had grown thick over the structure, moss and small trees growing out of the wood.

"Wow," Caryn said.

Hall agreed with her assessment.

Ever since the *Gale's* crash, he had been wondering if this island was one he had visited in his past life, expecting something familiar to appear as they had explored. He had been all over Hankarth, every place that a Player could get to, multiple times as he had spent some time leveling alternate characters. There had been plenty of quests that took Players to different debris islands, but he had never seen anything that looked like this.

They came around to what Hall thought was the deck of the ship, which appeared to be a little larger than the *Gale*. It appeared to have crashed into the hill keel first, laying on the port side. There had been nothing to see on those sides, the dirt and grass covering everything. The deck was different.

Vines grew up the twenty feet of the deck, moving in and out of the many holes in the heavy timbers. Small holes with only one large opening into the hold. The ship had been mostly intact when it had crashed, somehow not splintering on impact. An impact that was harder than the *Twisted Gale's*, from all the evidence. The unknown ship had come in hard and fast, the snapped trees stopping its momentum enough to keep it from exploding into splinters on impact.

Hall stepped toward the large opening, a gash in the boards. He doubted there would be anything salvageable, time seemed to have worn the ship down, but there was nothing lost in looking. His foot stepped over the broken boards, setting down on the inside of the dark ship when he heard a noise behind him. It sounded like something digging through the ground.

Turning, spear held ready, Caryn turning as well, they saw

a small explosion of dirt and grass. It was like something was pushing up from below, the hole erupting in the ground. A long and bony arm, covered in exposed muscle and sinew, shot out. It reached for the sky, fingers clacking as they opened and closed. Another arm shot out, more bone than anything else. The fingers dug at the size of the hole, making it larger and larger.

They watched as a skull appeared, strips of flesh laying loose as the dirt fell from the bone. More and more of the creature was revealed as it pulled itself from the ground. Hall could see two more behind it.

Skill Gain!
Identify Rank One +.2

Rotting SkyBreeze Sailor (white)
Rotting SkyBreeze Sailor (white)
Rotting SkyBreeze Captain (blue)

Hall stepped back out into the clearing, quickly looking for any other explosions of dirt and grass that would indicate more Undead. He saw nothing, just the three. Caryn was walking slowly toward the first Rotting Sailor. Hall activated *Leap* and jumped high into the air. A short arc he soared over Caryn and the first two Undead, aiming for the Captain in the rear that was just fully emerged from the ground.

The Undead held a rusty cutlass in its right hand, the left hand had long bony fingers ending in sharp points. It stumbled as Hall stabbed down with the spear, using *Leaping Stab* to score the first hit. Looking at its Health bar, Hall saw the bar drop a little. He landed behind it, pivoted, and stabbed out with the spear. The sharp weapon pierced the Captain's rotting chest, bursting out the other side.

Dumbly, the Undead tried to turn, the spear and Hall

holding it in position. It reached behind itself, trying to swing the sword or swipe at Hall with the claws, but it could not reach. The thing was strong, and Hall had to work to hold it still. With a screech, Pike swooped down out of the sky. A crack echoed through the clearing as a stuttering blue-white bolt of lightning shot out from the dragonhawk and slammed into the head of the Undead.

It exploded, pieces of gore and bone flying everywhere. Hall turned his head, avoiding any to the face. He felt small pieces hit his armor and bare arm. The body attached to the spear kept moving for a couple more seconds before it fell still, arms hanging limp and sword dropping from bony fingers. Hall kicked out, pushing the rotting corpse off his weapon.

He turned to see how Caryn was doing. The duelist was holding her own against the two Undead Sailors. Her twin blades moved in a blur, blocking attacks and delivering them. Each slice took off pieces of the Sailors. Bit by bit, she was whittling them down.

That was a Duelist strength. They moved so fast, able to evade attacks against them and deliver multiple ones quickly. Each attack was not that strong, but it was the frequency that caused the overall damage. A little bit at a time. Like a Skirmisher, they couldn't wear heavier armor, just the light leather armor, so their defense came from their speed.

Wiping the pieces of Undead off his body and his spear, Hall watched as Caryn finished off the two Rotting Sailors. Pieces fell to the ground until there wasn't enough to sustain the creatures and they just collapsed in a heap.

SLAIN: *Rotting SkyBreeze Captain*
+30 Experience

Skill Gain!
Polearms Rank Two +.1

"Yuck," Caryn muttered as she flicked her blades, throwing small pieces of Undead to the ground.

Hall pushed at the corpse of the Captain. A few threads of clothes remained, the rest just rotting meat that was starting to gather flies now that it wasn't magically animated. The cutlass was rusty, not worth salvaging, and he saw nothing else. Looking up, he saw Caryn shake her head. Her two piles of corpse yielded no loot either.

"At least we know the name of the ship," Hall said, pointing toward the vine and grass-covered wreck. "Let's check it out and head back to the *Gale*."

Standing at the opening, he glanced back at Caryn. She wasn't watching him, but her eyes scanned the trees and the hill, waiting for any other Undead to appear. Slowly, carefully, Hall stepped into the darkness of the ship. Nothing happened this time as his foot came down on the curved planking of the hull.

It was dark within the hold, but enough light leaked in that his *Limited Night Vision* was activated. He saw everything as shadows. Light gray on darker black and gray. Not enough for details, but instead it was definition that he saw. He could make out the shapes and depth. Enough to walk without tripping.

It was awkward as he was walking on the ship's side. Rotted crates lay in pieces on the hull, the contents long rotted away. Stepping carefully over them, he finished his examination of the hold and found nothing. Moving back a couple feet, he crouched and stepped into the upper hold, moving in what would have been up but was now sideways. It was awkward to move as the hallway was only a couple feet high. He had to almost lay down and crawl. Rooms lined the hallway on both sides, and he had to step carefully over door openings. Crouching down, he looked in each of the rooms and saw nothing, everything rotted or removed.

Sighing, he looked at the rooms on the upper side of the

hallway and maneuvered to where he could pull himself into the space. Sitting on the wall to the side of the door, he gave the room a quick review. Nothing. The next one was the same. But the last held a chest.

Sitting on the wall next to the door, he saw it in the corner across from him. Small, about a foot long, a couple inches deep and a foot high. It was wooden, banded in metal, and Hall was surprised that it had not rotted like all the others.

Tentatively, he reached out and pulled it close, expecting a trap to be triggered. He looked around the room, listening hard, waiting for something to happen. But nothing did. Sliding the chest closer to the edge, he dropped out of the doorway and reached up to grab it. The small chest wasn't heavy, and he managed to get it down to his level, hearing the jingling of coins and jewels within. Along with something else. It had thumped as he moved the small chest, sliding around and hitting the walls. Not hard, softly, but heavy enough to make an impact noise.

The lock looked simple, but he knew better than to play with it.

Not when he had someone with lock picking skills.

"Present for you," Hall said as he stepped back out into the sun, blinking as his vision returned to normal. Hearing a squawk above him, Hall looked up to see Pike perched on top of the ship. He handed the chest to Caryn.

She set it down on a rock and crouched down, running her fingers lightly along the surface. Leaning close, she looked at the lock, reaching into her pouch and pulling out a set of lock picks. Caryn set to work. Hall stepped back, putting some space between him and the chest just in case something went wrong. He trusted Caryn's skill but didn't need to be right on top of her and the chest either.

She moved the picks slowly but deftly, and he heard a faint click as she stood up, letting out a breath. Caryn quickly hopped back as she lifted the lid. They both waited a bit with nothing happening.

"Was it trapped?" Hall asked, stepping forward.

"Yeah," Caryn replied. "Minor explosion wards," she added and pointed to markings along the bottom edge of the cover and the top edge of the sidewall. The two scratchings, too small for Hall to really decipher, would have lain over each other when the lid was closed, touching. Lifting the lid without disarming them would have activated the ward and caused an explosion.

Stepping closer, Hall looked down into the small chest. The walls were exposed wood, dented and scratched. Laying on the bottom of the chest were loose piles of coins. He saw a couple gold and copper but mostly silver. A good-sized handful. A couple small jewels poked up from between and around the coins. He saw red and green, rubies and emeralds.

But what really had Hall's attention was the small scroll case on top of the coins. About an inch in diameter and six inches long, made of leather with intricate rune work along the edges at the top and bottom. He hadn't seen many in his new life on Hankarth, but Hall recognized a Treasure Map.

Maps were a new feature post-Glitch. Just like the name implied, they led to a treasure of some kind. He had deciphered and used one which led them into the Far Edge Peaks on Cumberland and a Red Cap's treasure hoard. Another had been found in a random tower in the Green Flow Forest, also on Cumberland, but he could not use that one yet. It was a Masterwork Map, and he was not high enough Level in his class and in the *Cartography* skill to read it yet. And wouldn't be for a very long time.

The *Cartography* skill was new as well and from what he had learned, it was rare. There was a Cartographers Guild, and they controlled and heavily restricted the use of the Skill, having a monopoly on it. As Leigh had explained, Treasure

Maps were more like keys that not just lead to the treasure's location but allowed for the unlocking of it. Without the Map, and someone to decode it, the treasure could not be found or claimed.

Hall had yet to meet anyone else with the Skill or anyone from the Cartographers Guild. He wasn't sure what he would do when it happened. It could be trouble.

Pushing those thoughts to the back of his mind, he pulled out the scroll case.

"Is that what I think it is?" Caryn asked, and Hall nodded.

She had yet to see one with them, but they had explained them to her.

"We should head back," Hall said, putting the case in his pouch. "I'll take a look back at camp." He reached down and pulled out some of the coins, about to put them in his pouch when he paused. He stared at the pile in his hand and the rest in the chest. With a sigh, he let them fall back into the chest, coin clinking against coin. "We should give these to Captain Hart," he said, looking to Caryn for confirmation. "It'll cost a lot to fully repair the *Gale*."

Caryn looked down at the coins for a moment before looking back at Hall and smiling. She nodded in agreement.

Closing the lid, Hall picked up the chest and started for the trail that would lead back to the crash site.

CHAPTER EIGHT

HALL SAT WITH HIS BACK AGAINST A TREE, WATCHING THE LATE-night activity around the wreck of the *Gale*. Hart had organized the sailors, Jackoby and Roxhard into two shifts. He had them keep working well into the night, to the point where it got too dark to work with even torchlight. They would get to sleep for a couple of hours before starting again, the ones not working right away getting to sleep even longer.

If they could sleep through the noise.

Sabine had set to work immediately after they returned with the supplies. She was making as many potions as she could, as quickly as she could. Especially Vitality. With the hard work in repairing the ship, they would all need the Vitality potions. No one was getting a full night's rest, and they would all take Vitality hits. The potions would help.

A fire burned between the tree line and the ship, casting odd shadows everywhere. The last workers had just descended from the *Gale*, coming to get a late supper. Hall knew that tomorrow they would need to start hunting for fresh meat and forage for fruit and other food items. Their supply would not last long, and they would need it for the much slower trip to Huntley once the *Gale* was repaired.

No one said the word *if*. They were all operating off *when* the ship would get repaired. It was too soon to start worrying about the *if*.

He could hear light snoring, the sound of people rolling as they slept, from all around him. No one had set up camp in the treeline, they all wanted to be around the fire and the protection from predators it would give them. Guards were posted just outside the range of the firelight, watching the forest and the skies.

Hart was the last off the ship. He had been examining the afternoon's work. The Captain had been grateful when Hall had given him the chest of coins and jewels. It wouldn't come close to paying for all the repairs the ship would need, but it was the gesture that counted. It had also earned Hall some Alliance Reputation with Captain Hart.

Captain Hart is appreciative of the coins and jewels. He does not blame you for the crash of his ship and would not have charged you anything for repairs, but the gift is most welcome and he takes it as it was meant. A gift. This, along with his general friendly feelings toward you from before, has earned you +1000 Alliance with Captain Hart.

You are now Known and Friendly to Captain Hart.

Hall had been surprised at the amount of Alliance Reputation he had gained. He wondered why any gain had not happened the first time he had met Hart, or even before the current voyage had started. Why did it all accumulate now? He still wasn't sure how the Reputation system in Post-Glitch Sky Realms Online worked.

The moon was out but covered, most of the stars also blocked by the other islands floating above them. This part of the world seemed to have a lot of small debris islands floating around. It was going to be a dark night. The watch would have to keep the fire going throughout and into the morning. They hadn't heard any noises in the forest, not yet, but there would be predators out there. And they would be curious about these newcomers to the islands.

Hall fully expected one, or more, of the predators to brave the fires tonight. He planned to sleep lightly.

But he was still too worked up to sleep. He had been going nonstop since earlier that morning. The crash, the battle with the Serenti Roc Riders, and fight with the Rotting SkyBreeze Captain. It had all left him wired. He could feel himself jittery. He had never been a coffee fan in real life, but he knew the effects of too much caffeine and he was feeling something similar now.

Needing something to do, he pulled up his Character Sheet and looked it over.

Character Name: Hall
Race: Half-Elf
Class: Skirmisher

Level: 5
Experience
Total: 305
Next Level: 2,400

Unassigned Stat Points: 0

Health
Base: 59
Adjusted: 0
Total: 59

Energy
Base: 81
Adjusted: 0
Total: 81

Vitality
Base: 22
Adjusted: 0
Total: 22

Attributes
Strength
Base: 11
Adjusted: 0
Total: 11
Agility
Base: 17
Adjusted: 4
Total: 21
Wellness
Base: 13
Adjusted: 0
Total: 13
Intelligence
Base: 12
Adjusted: 0
Total: 12
Willpower
Base: 10
Adjusted: 0
Total: 10
Charisma
Base: 12
Adjusted: 0

Total: 12

Attack Power
Base: 1
Adjusted: 2
Total: 3
Attack Speed
Base: -4 seconds
Adjusted: -1 second
Total: -5 seconds
Spell Power
Base: 1
Adjusted: 0
Total: 1
Spell Resistance
Base: 0
Adjusted: 0
Total: 0
Protection
Base: 3
Adjusted: 9
Total: 12
Carrying Capacity
Base: 30
Adjusted: 0
Total: 30

Elemental Resistances
Air: 0%
Earth: 0%
Fire: 25%
Water: 0%

Racial Ability

Limited Night Vision

Class Abilities
Evade (Rank One)
Leap (Rank Two)
Leaping Stab (Rank One)
Shared Vision

Skills
Combat
Light Armor (Rank Two): 12.9
Polearms (Rank Two): 16.3
Small Blades (Rank Two): 14.4
Thrown (Rank Two): 11.9

Activity
Identify (Rank One): 9.1
Strategy (Rank Two): 10.3
Triage (Rank Two): 10.5

Environment
Camouflage (Rank One): 0.8
Increased Perception (Rank Two): 10.4
Stealth (Rank One): 1.9
Survival (Rank Two): 13.6
Tracking (Rank One): 2.6

Professions
Cartography (Rank Two): 16.9
Herbology (Rank Two): 15.5
Skinning (Rank Two): 12.5

Reputation (Faction)
Druids of the Grove: 1500, Known and Friendly

Kingdom of Essec: 1600, Known and Friendly
Valedale Gnomes: 1000, Known and Friendly
Brownpaw of Fallen Green: 1000, Known and Friendly
Peakguard: 750, Known
Door Knockers: 625, Known

Reputation (Alliance)
Guard Captain Henry: 1300, Friendly
Watchman Kelly: 800, Known
Merchant Dyson: 700, Known
Druid Leigh: 6000, Loved
Smol, Gardener of Greenheight Vale: 1200, Friendly
Jackoby of the Brownpaw: 350, Known
Sergeant Brient of the Peakguard: 1200, Friendly
Captain Hart: 1000, Friendly

Not much had changed. Leveling was slow, both Class Level and Skill Level. That meant the gains in everything came slow. He could remember when maintenance of his Character Sheet had been an almost daily thing. Once he had hit endgame and no longer advanced, rarely changing gear, it had been infrequent. Now he barely remembered to even look at it. Some days he barely remembered even having a Character Sheet.

Scanning down the list of Skills, he knew he still had decisions to make about some of them. Seeing Cartography, he remembered the scroll case he had found. The one thing he had kept from the chest. He reached into his inventory pouch, looking too small for his hand to fit into. He mentally thought about the scroll case and pulled it out.

Looking it over, he figured out which end to open. He hoped it wasn't trapped, not sure how to even tell if it was. Nothing happened as he pulled off the top and looked inside. He had to shift to catch the light from the fire better but could see a rolled-up parchment inside. Upending the case, he tapped it against his palm a couple times until the parchment slid out.

Setting aside the case, Hall unrolled the paper.

Smaller than the others he had, this map was well preserved. The paper was thick, the edges fairly crisp without rips or tears. There were numerous notations along the edges surrounding a roughly oval-shaped island, or at least part of one. Only a portion of the island was revealed. The island's edges were rough and jagged, with barely any identifying features. There was a large pond or lake in the middle with a small 'x" marked on an island in the lake. Another mark, some kind of symbol, was drawn in the middle of a clearing, almost directly south of the lake

CONGRATULATIONS!
You have uncovered a Treasure Map Level I.

X MARKS THE ISLAND
Rewards: +50 Experience

ACCEPT QUEST?

Success!
You have deciphered: Treasure Map Level I
Cartography Rank Two +.3

Hall turned the map around, on its side and even looked at it diagonally. He had no idea what island it was showing. He read the notations, and they seemed to tell a story.

We crashed twelve days ago, and most of the crew has died. Fallen prey to the predators of the island, died from their wounds received from the crash of the SkyBreeze or from hunger. There is just the six

of us left. No matter what, while there is still one of us alive, we will fulfill our charge. The treasures have been hidden, and I have had Urisif our Navigator create this Treasure Map as a key to prevent just anyone from finding and uncovering them. I hope and pray that it is our brothers in the Confederacy that are reading this now and that you find what we have hidden and complete our task.

Yumagar of Clan Soris, Captain of the SkyBreeze

Hall read the story a couple of times, trying to understand what he was reading. He understood now that the map depicted the island they were on. Only part of it had been explored and uncovered by the Cartographer, this Urisif that was mentioned. The *SkyBreeze* had to be the second symbol, which was possibly Captain Yumagar's personnel mark.

He thought about the Undead he had destroyed. That had been Captain Yumagar, what was left of him. Bowing his head and offering a quick prayer to the Spirits, Hall hoped Yumagar had at last found his rest. There were no Gods on Hankarth, just Spirits. Hall supposed they were essentially Gods, just not as all-powerful. And he wondered which ones the Highborn Confederacy said prayers to for the dead.

The *SkyBreeze* was a Highborn ship. The names and the reference to the Confederacy confirmed it. He wondered what these treasures Yumagar mentioned were. More gold and coins? Magical items?

Holding the map up to the light, Hall mentally opened his personal map. Barely any of the island was revealed. He and Caryn had only explored the southern part, a couple of miles in a straight line from the *Gale*. But he was able to scale his map to match the treasure map and align the symbol that was the *SkyBreeze* wreckage with the clearing on his map. He mentally marked that spot and used the scale he had developed to estimate the distance from the *SkyBreeze's* clearing to the lake on the map.

Skill Gain!

Cartography Rank Two +.1

Only a couple of hours walk.

Would it be worth the trek?

———

"Are you sure it is worth the risk and time?" Captain Hart asked the next morning.

Already, the sailors assigned to this shift were hard at work. Hall could hear the sound of construction all around the ship, metal on metal and metal on wood, saws cutting through wood. From the forest, they could hear the chop of axes and cutting of branches. One tree had been cut down, and a couple sailors were working at removing the limbs and bark. A long process.

Hall shrugged in response.

There was no way to know unless they tried.

"The treasures, whatever they are, will still be hidden," Hall said. "No one has decoded the map until now. As for what it is? Only one way to find out."

"You'll be gone for at least a full day and night," Sabine pointed out.

She stood in the small group with Hall, Hart, Caryn, and Hart's First Mate a Storvgardian named Ragtar. The big man said nothing, just listened. Hall knew he would support whatever his Captain chose.

Hall had presented the map and his desire to seek out the treasure as a choice that Hart would make. If Captain Hart said no, Hall would honor that decision. The *Twisted Gale* was Hart's ship, he the Captain, and he was in charge while sailing. As far as Hall was concerned, this salvage and repair operation still fell under Hart's command. Hall knew that Hart wanted to get safely and quickly off the island, and taking them away from their foraging duties would be a distraction and loss of workers. And that was if only Hall and Caryn went.

Hart pulled at his short beard, absently scratching the healing cut on his cheek. He stared at the *Gale*, the sailors moving all over it. They had cleared away the broken pieces, making a large pile of salvage off to the side. Deck boards that were cracked or fallen off, hull planks in similar condition, pieces of furniture and even doors from inside. Saws cut into the wood, removing the broken and useless pieces.

"Okay," Hart said finally, turning back to Hall. "We can't spare you for more than a day," he added. "And just you two."

Hall nodded as the group dispersed. He could tell that Sabine was disappointed and jealous. The Witch wanted to go with them but knew she was needed here at the wreckage. She had potions to make. Caryn walked off with her, the two talking quietly. He looked toward the camp and the sleeping, or trying to sleep, forms of the second shift of workers. Roxhard was among them, the Dwarf's stocky but smaller form standing out from the mass of Humans. Jackoby was in the forest, serving as a lumberjack.

Should he tell either of them that he was leaving? Probably not Jackoby. The Firbolg was upset that Hall had left on the foraging mission, leaving his unwanted protector behind. He would be even more upset about this excursion. Better to just leave and let Jackoby think it was another foraging trip.

But Roxhard? The Dwarf would be hurt if Hall just up and left. Would be disappointed that he didn't get to go, but would possibly understand. Or wouldn't he? It had been a long time since Hall had been fourteen, and he thought back to how he would have reacted. He would have been angry, hurt, resentful. He would have felt excluded. Even if he understood the reasons, and the logic, he still would have felt that way. But it would be worse if he just left.

Hall sighed.

———

Roxhard took it well. The Dwarf was disappointed that he could not go but understood. Or at least said he understood. But there was nothing to be done for it.

Hall and Caryn set off as soon as they could. They grabbed a couple of potions from the supply Sabine was back to making. The Witch had almost used up all the supplies they had brought back with them yesterday. Promising to search for more as they journeyed, Hall stepped away to allow Sabine and Caryn to say goodbye in private.

He opened the potion belt he had looted from a smuggler back on Cumberland, outside of River's Side. Small, the leather thick to protect the contents, it could hold six vials of Minor potions. He had used up some after the crash and now filled it up, putting the extras in his magical inventory pouch. Two *Minor Health Potion*, two *Minor Vitality Potion,* and two *Minor Energy Potion*.

Caryn joined him, and they walked out of the clearing and into the forest. They passed freshly cut stumps where the sailors had cut down trees to use as masts and make into planks for new decking. Hart planned to only repair the decking needed to keep the ship airborne. That was all he wanted to do for now. Get the *Twisted Gale* airborne. Hall had decided to not return to the wreckage of the *SkyBreeze*. He had the treasure map and the location marked on his personnel map. With that and his *Cartography* Skill, Hall thought he could lead them to the lake from this direction and it would save time.

They heard the sounds of animals as they walked, much as they had yesterday. Small creatures scurrying through the trees, rustling through bushes. Nothing large. Not yet. There had been no predator attacks last night, and no one reported seeing any signs of anything.

Pulling up his map every couple of minutes, Hall kept them on course. The scenery didn't change. A forest of green trees, thick canopy above, grass and bushes along the ground. More of the same for the couple miles they walked. The sun rose high above them and started to set, marking the progress of time.

Past noon, they stopped to rest and eat. A small brook meandered around the trees and some boulders, which Caryn hopped on top. Hall crouched down next to the water, watching a small fish swim. He glanced up at where Pike circled above. He couldn't see the dragonhawk through the tree canopy but knew the bird was there. Should he call out to let Pike know about the fish?

The little creature swam further downriver, Hall watching it go. With a shrug, he stood up.

"I haven't seen any tracks," Caryn said as she lay back on the stone. "Have you?"

"No," Hall replied. "But I haven't really been looking."

"Me either, but we should still see some right?"

Hall shrugged. He would have thought they would have come across some. Either yesterday or today.

"We should keep moving," he said.

With a sigh, Caryn jumped off the boulder. "Lead the way."

———

"How is that possible?" Caryn asked.

Hall had no answer because he had no idea.

As they had gotten closer to the lake, when they were able to see that the trees were starting to thin and they could see more light and sky ahead, Hall had led them around to where the trail from the *SkyBreeze* would have come. He reasoned that any search for the hidden treasure would be easier from that direction as it was how the map had been made.

Once on that trail, they had left the trees and stepped out into the clearing that surrounded the lake. The land sloped gently down, covered in tall grass and loose boulders. Clumps of flowers grew around the clearing, standing tall above the grass. The lake itself was calm, crystal blue waters. It was a good-sized body of water, and Hall could see a river flowing into it on the far bank. They found the island, the only island in the lake, easy enough.

But that island was a surprise.

It floated above the surface of the water.

They could see the jagged underside of the rocky island, the top an almost mirror. Not large, the island was a single large hill that came to a flat top of exposed rock. The underside was jagged, sloping to a point that floated only a couple feet above the water. Vines ran from trees on the lake's edge to the island only twenty feet offshore.

Hall had never heard of a floating island within a larger floating island. The fractured realms of Hankarth ranged in size, but they were singular floating islands of rock. How could this smaller one be floating above the larger? Legend had it that each island had a Branch of the World Trees on it, some-where. Did this debris island somehow have two?

Only one way to find out, Hall thought.

They walked down to the shore, the grass ending at the water but a foot or two higher. Hall led them along the shore, watching for a way to cross. The floating island cast shadows along the shore as did the vines as they walked under. Hall looked up at the vines, wondering how they could have grown. The small floating island would have risen out of the water, which meant the vines would have been there from before that event happened.

It didn't make any sense. They looked old, covered in moss that hung down. The more he looked, the more Hall realized there was something odd about them.

Skill gain!
Increased Perception Rank Two +.1

"They're ropes," Caryn said at the same time the thought came to Hall.

Thick lines that resembled those used on the *Gale*. *They must have come from the SkyBreeze*, Hall thought. They hung tight from island to shore, tied to trees on the shore side. He couldn't see what they were tied to out on the island. Hanging twenty feet above water and the shore, they seemed to dive into the island halfway up.

"I guess that's how we get across," Caryn said, walking toward the treeline where one of the moss-covered ropes came out of the thick canopy.

"Hold on," Hall said and looked up into the sky, trying to find Pike. "Let's make sure it's worth risking those first."

Pike streaked across the sky, circling the lake and flying over the floating island. The dragonhawk swooped lower, flying low over the island, scaring a flock of small birds that took off into the air with protesting chirps and rapidly flapping wings.

Through their *Shared Vision*, Hall looked down on the floating island. The grass and bush-covered slopes were steep, exposed rock in many places. They tapered to a flat top of stone. Boulders covered it with what looked to be a raised portion set back from the edge which was why it wasn't visible from the shore. It appeared that just the birds had been living on the island and they were now gone, nothing else was visible to Pike's sharp eyes. The raised rock was covered in sticks, twigs, and leaves as if the birds had been nesting there.

Pike studied the raised portion as it seemed the perfect

place to put a chest, but there was nothing beyond the birds' nests. The top of the island showed no indication of the potential treasure. There was a chance it had been claimed already, Hall knew, but the map hadn't been taken so the treasure most likely remained. It wouldn't have been left on top of the stone, exposed to anyone passing overhead.

The sides were too steep to have dug into. Any loose dirt that had been used to cover the hole would have been washed away in the rain. Hall had Pike fly lower, even with the island. The dragonhawk scanned the steep sides, looking at the slopes for any possible caves. Nothing was visible on the sides of the island that they could see, but around the backside there appeared to be a shadowed niche halfway up the steep side, a ridge of rock curling around to the front.

"Got it," Hall said. "I think," he added as Pike's view faded from his vision.

He quickly described what he had seen to Caryn.

"Looks like we're using the ropes," she said brightly and started climbing up the tree.

Hall watched her crawl out along a thick branch, one hand running along the moss-covered rope. She pulled at it, testing the strength and how well it was tied off. Putting both hands on the thick rope, she pulled herself up, legs stretched out, and hung. The rope seemed to sag a bit but held. Looking up, Caryn started bouncing, watching where the rope disappeared into the tree's canopy. There was more sag to the rope as it bounced up and down under Caryn's weight, but it still held.

Satisfied, the small Duelist shifted her grip on the rope and swung her legs up. Hooked around the rope, she started moving across it, feet sliding along the slick rope and hand over hand. It was slow, painstaking and Caryn had to stop a couple of times. She paused when she hit the end of the branch, looking down at the distance to the ground, before fixing her eyes resolutely on the island out in the lake.

Hall watched her progress. She looked graceful and seemed to move quickly to his eyes. He knew she was being purposely slow and careful, but he was impatient, wanting her to get across so he could make his attempt. The rope bounced up and down with each of her movements, the distance it moved grew larger as she got toward the middle where it had been sagging to begin with. Hall listened, watching the end of the rope where it disappeared into the tree. He waited for the sound of it snapping or the end flying out. However, it had been since the rope had been tied to the tree, it managed to hold against Caryn's weight and movements.

It took another fifteen minutes for Caryn to make it all the way across. At the end, where she was only a couple feet over the sloping surface of the island, she released her legs and dangled over the ground. Looking down, she took a deep breath and let go. She landed on the steep slope, leaning forward into the slope, but still almost fell back before catching her balance.

She took a couple steps higher and examined where the end of the rope was hidden in the thick grass and bushes covering the island's surface. Grabbing it, she tugged hard. Letting go, still looking at it, Caryn finally shrugged. She turned back and gave Hall the thumbs up.

He wasn't that comforted by Caryn making it across the rope line. Hall probably weighed twice as much as the small woman. But standing around didn't get him onto the island.

Climbing the tree was easy enough. Fighting through the thick branches with spear and javelin wasn't as easy, but he made it, after getting both caught a couple of times. It took some grunting and cursing, but he got onto the branch just below the rope.

Reaching up, Hall grabbed the rope and pulled. He felt it give a little but not much. Holding onto it with one hand, he slid out along the branch, which started to sag under his weight. Sighing, knowing he might as well get it over with, Hall grabbed the rope with both hands. He swung his legs up, wrapping them around loosely. His gloves seemed to slip on the slimy moss. Caryn had pushed most of it off, but removing the moss had left a layer of slime. Hand over hand, Hall started to slide his way across the rope.

The branch disappeared from beneath him, and he could see the hard grass-covered ground below. He tried not to think about how much it would hurt if he slammed into it, especially with no true healing magic. Inch by inch, he moved down the rope. The shore passed beneath him, and he was out over the dark blue waters of the lake. The waters were murky, and he could not see the bottom; no way to estimate how deep it was.

The distance felt longer than it looked. The rope was tight, but it bounced under his weight, each movement threatening to dislodge him. His shoulders ached, his legs tired. Above him, he could see Pike circling in lazy circles, gliding on the wind currents. Looking ahead, he saw Caryn a couple feet off to the side, not watching him but looking worriedly past him. He wanted to resist the urge to look but couldn't.

Stopping moving, Hall tilted his head to look at the trees and cursed.

Stepping out of the branches, pushing the green canopy aside, were two creatures. They stood about three feet high. Thin, with long legs and arms, hands that ended in sharp claws. Each was covered in thin scales, different shades of green. They had the heads of lizards, flat yellow eyes, and mouths filled with sharp teeth. Raising above their heads were long and thin tails. A cross between lizards and monkeys.

"What are those," Hall exclaimed aloud.

Skill gain!
Identify Rank One +.2

Howling Jungle Monmodo (white)
Howling Jungle Monmodo (white)

They watched him, pointing with their long fingers, barking and hooting at each other. One jumped up and down, batting at the other which was slightly smaller. He wasn't sure if the creatures were aggressive. He hoped not.

Hall looked down at the waters, across at Caryn and back at the lizard monkeys. He felt exposed hanging onto the rope over the lake. It was sagging down under his weight as he lay there, and he knew he couldn't wait any longer. With his weight just hanging, the rope would come loose and he'd fall. No telling what was in the waters or the depth, and it would be hard to swim with his armor and weapons dragging at him.

Eyes ahead, Hall started moving again.

The rope started bouncing, hard and fast. He stopped and looked back at the trees. One of the Monmodos had grabbed the rope and was shaking it.

"Stop that," he yelled.

Starting to move again, Hall tried to slide faster. Looking up he sent a mental message to Pike. With a screech, the dragonhawk stopped circling and dove down toward the trees. Pike wanted to unleash a lightning bolt breath attack, but Hall stopped him. Too dangerous. It would be too easy to hit the rope and send Hall flying. Instead, Pike flew close, leading with his talons, trying to distract the Monmodos.

The two creatures hooted and hollered, crying as Pike screeched. Hall didn't look back, just continued on. Inch by inch, foot by foot, he made his way across the rope. Glancing down, he saw the blue water turned to green and brown land with some gray stone. He was over the island.

Speeding up, he got near the end and released his tired and cramping legs. They hung about a foot or two over the steep slope. Taking a deep breath, Hall let himself drop. He tried to lean forward but failed. His feet hit the slope on an angle and he started to fall backward, arms flailing as he tried to fight gravity.

He felt a hand grab his arm, pulling at him, and it was just enough for him to regain his balance.

"Thanks," he said to Caryn as he leaned forward against the sloped island.

It was steeper than he had thought it would be. A hard climb to the top, but there was plenty of handholds with all the exposed rock, the bushes, and the scraggly trees.

He looked back toward the trees on the shore, watching as Pike squawked and flew into the air. The Monmodo's still barked and hooted, but now they weren't alone. Four more of the creatures had come out of the trees, drawn by the noise. The first two were grabbing onto the rope, hooking their long legs over it, the newcomers climbing the tree.

"Incoming," Hall muttered with a curse. "Up to the top."

Quickly, the two worked their way up the steep slope toward the flat top.

CHAPTER NINE

THE CLIMB WAS TOUGH. THE DIRT THAT COVERED THE ROCK OF the island was loose and slid underfoot. Hall had pulled out a couple of scrub bushes before he gave up trying to use them to help pull himself up. He glanced back at the shore a couple of times and saw the Monmodos moving across the rope quickly.

All four of them.

Caryn was having an easier time with the climb. She was already well past him, nearing the top. Giving up, Hall activated *Leap* and jumped into the air. He landed right at the edge but was able to lean forward. Off-balance, he took a couple steps before able to catch himself from falling. Caryn climbed over the edge a couple seconds behind.

Hooting and barking told him the first Monmodo had made it to the island.

Large boulders dotted the flat top, the raised portion a couple dozen feet away. No birds had returned, leaving the nests empty. The top was littered with loose leaves, grass, and sticks. Together they stepped away from the edge and turned, drawing weapons.

The first Monmodo crested the top, its lizard head visible

and catching a throwing knife. Lightning sparked on the impact, and the creature yelped in pain, falling back. It disappeared from view.

They waited and two of the Monmodos jumped up high, landing on the edge. They quickly ran, catching Hall and Caryn by surprise. He hadn't expected them to move that quickly, especially after jumping. Long arms swung in the air, sharp talons extended. The creatures hissed and growled, hooting and barking. Hall braced himself and stabbed out with his spear.

And missed.

The Monmodo jumped up out of the way. Hall didn't react in time, feeling the weight of the creature as it landed on his shoulders. He fell backward, the creature's momentum pushing him down. He landed hard, the breath forced out of his lungs. He looked up into the manic eyes of the Monmodo. Bright yellow, thin black iris, saliva dripping from the creature's snout. Hall could see the many small and sharp teeth that filled the mouth.

It snapped at him, trying to bite, but Hall managed to get his left arm up to block. He got it under the thing's chin, strong enough to keep the wildly snapping head back. But not the arms. The Monmodo pounded at him. Hands and feet. The blows weren't strong, but they were adding up. Hall watched his Health dropping.

He reached with his right, trying to find the spear he had dropped. Searching fingers found it, and he grabbed the shaft. It was an awkward swing, but he managed to hit the Monmodo in the head. The creature yelped and jumped off. Hall managed to sit up before it attacked again.

The lizard-monkey darted in from the side, arms swinging. Hall got the tip of the spear up and stabbed, catching the Monmodo in the shoulder. It spun the light creature, knocking it down.

Pushing himself up, Hall took the couple steps needed and stabbed down with his spear. The Monmodo jerked, yelping, as the spear slammed into its chest. It spasmed and then lay still.

SLAIN: *Howling Jungle Monmodo +25 Experience*

Skill Gain!
Light Armor Rank Two +.1
Skill Gain!
Polearms Rank Two +.1
Skill Gain!
Thrown Rank Two +.1

Hall turned to Caryn in time to see her Monmodo fall, the creature covered in dozens of cuts.

"Look out," she called just as Hall felt something small but hard slam into his shoulder.

He turned to the island's edge and saw the other two Monmodos. They were picking up small rocks and throwing them, most missing and just becoming noise as they clattered along the top of the island. But some hit, and Hall grunted with each impact.

Like the punches of the dead Monmodo, each attack wasn't doing much damage, but they were adding up. Ducking, throwing his arm up to stop a rock from hitting his face, Hall tried to estimate the distance to the edge. Could he land the *Leap* and not fall? Another rock hit his chest, a larger one, and he grunted in pain.

Activating *Leap*, he jumped into the air. His arc was high, the distance short. Just before he landed, he used *Leaping Stab* and scored a quick hit on the left Monmodo. The creature shrieked and dropped its rock. Landing next to it, he thrust the spear into its side. It staggered and slipped, hitting the other one. Pulling out the spear, Hall quickly attacked again. The sharp ironwood tip hit the Monmodo in the neck, ending its life.

Shrieking, the last tried to escape, but Caryn's swords sliced through its back. It fell forward and off the island, bumping and rolling to the bottom where it splashed into the lake and disappeared.

SLAIN: *Howling Jungle Monmodo +25 Experience*

Skill Gain!
Light Armor Rank Two +.1
Skill Gain!
Polearms Rank Two +.1

"That was fun," Caryn muttered, flicking her swords to get the Monmodos' blood and guts off the blades. "Yuck."

"Let's get that treasure," Hall said.

———

He could see the ridge that Pike had spotted. From the top of the island, it was about twenty feet down the steep side. Only a couple feet wide and running close to ten feet in length. Hall thought he could see a deep shadow where the niche would be. If the shelf had been deeper, he would have used *Leap* to jump down, but it was too thin. Not enough space to risk it.

"Any rope?" Caryn asked.

Hall nodded and reached into the magical pouch on his belt. Before they had set out exploring yesterday, he had switched around some of his inventory. The main goal had been to clear up space in the pouch for any herbs and other items they found, but it had also been to add the items he thought they might need. He hadn't wanted to bring the travel pack he had managed to recover from the *Gale's* crash, wanting to travel light. The long coil of rope had been almost an afterthought. He was glad he had thought to take it.

Holding the coil in his arms, taking the end, he looked around the top of the island. There wasn't much that he could see to tie it off to. No trees grew, or at least none thick enough to support their weight. The boulders were all too big and round.

"You think you can hold it as I climb down?" Caryn asked, looking from Hall to the ridge.

In answer, Hall walked to the edge and let the rope down. He kept feeding it until the end coiled loosely on the ridge. Stepping back, he wrapped it around his waist, making sure to throw the excess out of the way so it wouldn't tangle in his legs.

Caryn took hold of the rope and stepped off the edge. She held it in both hands, slowly walking backward. Hall leaned back, holding it tight in his gloved hands, adjusting his stance to take the weight with his legs. Step by step, Caryn walked down the slope.

Hall felt her weight pulling at him, wanting to drag him forward, but he fought against it. She slipped at one point, almost dragging him forward, feet slipping an inch or two, but he caught himself.

Then the weight was released off the rope. His shoulders and legs felt relief, but he didn't let go.

"I'm down," Caryn shouted up.

He stepped to the edge and looked down, rope still running through his hands. The Duelist was walking carefully along the ridge, the rope coiled around her waist and held in one hand. She got to the darker spot, where the slope seemed to just stop as it went down. Crouching, Caryn drew one of her swords and poked it toward the island. Hall watched the tip and a couple inches disappear from view. Caryn waved it around, and he heard a faint tapping sound as she checked for traps.

Withdrawing the sword, replacing it in the sheath at her

waist, Caryn reached forward. Her arms, head, and part of her body disappeared. It was weird seeing her lower body and not the rest. It took a minute but Caryn's full body returned to view as she dragged a long wooden chest out of the small cave in the side of the island.

Looking up at him, she flashed a thumbs up.

Still crouched in front of the chest, she reached for the clasp, trying to open it, but it wouldn't budge. From what Hall could see, there was no lock, just the clasp that wouldn't open.

"It won't open," she growled.

"Treasure maps are like keys," Hall said, yelling down. "I should be able to open it. Bring it up."

Shifting her body, Caryn tried to lift the chest. She managed to get it off the ground, holding it awkwardly as she tried to maneuver it toward the small pouch on her belt. If she could get it close enough, the magic would catch the chest and shrink it enough to fit. She couldn't manage it. The chest was too long, too heavy, for her to get it to where she needed it. Caryn set it back down

"It's heavy," she called up. "I don't think I can hold it and climb."

"Tie the rope around it, and I'll try to pull it up," Hall called down.

Caryn did so. She managed to lift the chest enough to thread the rope under it a couple of times, crisscrossing it like straps. Pulling on the knots to make sure they were tight, Caryn flashed Hall a thumbs up. She stepped back, as much as she could on the thin ridge, moving out of the way.

Hall set his feet, adjusted his grip on the rope and started to pull. Hand over hand, he hauled the rope up, standing near the edge to watch it. The chest was as heavy as she had said. Caryn took another step back to avoid the wildly swinging object. Try as hard as he could, Hall could not stop the awkward chest from swinging as it banged and bumped its way up the steep slope. It caught a couple of times, but he was able to shake it loose, and finally, he hauled it up onto the flat top of the island.

Dragging it back a couple of feet, he untied the knots and lowered the rope down to Caryn. She tied it around her waist and gave a tug. Bracing himself, he started pulling on the rope as she climbed her way back up.

She crested the top and lay on the ground, not bothering to untie the rope yet. Hall released it and stood panting, bent over with his hands on his knees, wishing he had invested more Attribute Points in Strength.

Standing up, he moved over to the chest. It was close to three feet long, a foot wide, and only six inches or so tall. Made completely of wood, there didn't appear to be any seams to the sides and bottom. It had been carved from one giant log. The top was a separate piece, fit tightly onto the sides with no hinges and just four clasps. One to each side. The clasps were the only pieces of metal on the entire chest. They looked to be made of thin iron, delicately carved. There were designs etched into the wood, leaves with long stems that swirled around the edges. The top was clear of design save for one small one in the lower right corner.

"Caryn," Hall said and pointed. She was now standing, untying the rope.

"Holy..." she started to say and stopped, staring down at the small symbol.

Only an inch long and half an inch high, it was one they both recognized. Hall drew his short sword, while Caryn pulled out one of her long blades. On the metal of each of the blades, just above the hilts, was the same symbol.

"That's a little weird," she said, running her fingers over the mark etched into her sword.

All of their blades, his one and her two, were magical. He

wasn't sure about the stats and powers of her swords, but he knew his very well.

Exceptional Short Sword Of Fighting
Damage 2d4 (+3)
Agility: +2
Strength: +1
Durability 16/20
Weight: 5 lbs.

"Some kind of maker's mark," Hall said.

A triangle with the point up, halfway up the sides of the triangle was a straight line connected to an arc. Hall thought of it as a triangle with a half moon behind it, the point penetrating the moon. The mark was simple, not much to look at.

"Very odd that we're seeing it everywhere," Hall continued.

He had thought it odd enough when it had just been his short sword and Caryn's twin blades. Now that there was the chest, he started to wonder what the mark really meant. There were so many crafters in the fractured realms of Hankarth that seeing the same mark multiple times was a little disconcerting. He had already decided that he needed to learn more about the mark, seeing it here and now just cemented that decision.

Crouching down, he undid all four of the clasps. Taking a deep breath, assuming there would be no traps as he had the key map, Hall lifted the wooden cover off and set it aside. Together they both looked inside, Caryn whistling in surprise. *No wonder it was so heavy*, Hall thought as he looked at the contents. The note had called the contents treasures, and Hall agreed. The chest wasn't that big, and Hall couldn't imagine how so much had been crammed into it.

Four coin purses lay on top and Hall removed them. He handed two to Caryn and undid the ties on the two he held. Looking inside, he saw silver and copper coins. Highborn

Confederacy size and style. The value of all coins across the varied kingdoms and races of Hankarth remained relatively the same to make for easier transactions. A gold coin was a gold coin regardless of where it had been minted. A quick count showed there to be over a hundred silver and twice as much copper.

"Gold," Caryn said, bouncing a pouch in her hand. Hall could hear the metal on metal jingling of the coins. "And jewels," she said, indicating the other pouch.

Neither of hers was as big as the two Hall had, which meant a lower amount of gold coins and not that many jewels. But it was still a good haul in just coins. And there was still more. The purses had been laying on top of a rolled cloak, which was wrapped around something. Hall could just make out the shape. It looked like a sword.

Carefully, not wanting to rip the cloak, he pulled it out. Made of a thick cloth, not quite wool but similar. Dark brown, the inside a light green. He lay the bundle down on the ground and slowly unwrapped the cloak to reveal a sword. The blade was between the length of his short sword and Caryn's long swords. Thin at the hilt, the top curved back without widening but thinning to a sharp point. Even with the amount of time the blade had been in the chest, there was no sign of rust or wear and the edge caught the sun showing how sharp it still was. The hilt was small, but thick where the blade met. The shining metal of the hilt was wider there, two emeralds on either side cut into a diamond shape. Leather-wrapped, the handgrip with no pommel but the metal turning slightly and ending in a point facing toward the front. And there, just above the emeralds, was the familiar mark.

Hall lifted the sword up, surprised at how light it felt in his hands. Standing up, he gave it a few practice swings. It sliced through the air, making a whistling sound.

"Magic?" Caryn asked.

"Probably," Hall answered, still swinging the sword. "The craftsmanship is amazing."

Caryn bent down and picked up the cloak, giving it a shake to knock off the leaves and twigs it had picked up from being on the ground. She let it fall, revealing a deep hood and a total length that would fit her. It would have been short on a High Elf, the Highborn usually having a height between the average Human and average Firbolg.

Giving the strange sword another swing, Hall looked back down into the chest. Leather shoulder pauldrons were the next thing he pulled out. Two pieces that would fit over the shoulders with straps that would cross over the body to hold them in place. A dark leather, Hall didn't recognize the hide. He tried to remember what animals roamed the Highborn's islands that didn't exist elsewhere and couldn't think of any. But he knew the leather wasn't that of a cow or wolf or any of the other common animals. Two leather belts and a baldric with a loop at the bottom, most likely to hold the sword. Each of those was made of the same dark leather. Also inside the chest was a pair of green cloth gloves, fingerless with golden runes stitched along the end. Underneath it all was what looked to be a rolled-up painting. He picked it up and examined the canvas. Thick, tightly woven, and old. He didn't bother to unroll it, not out there. That was something to be done in a cleaner and safer environment. There wasn't much he could make out of the outside of the canvas, but he did see a small mark in a corner. Faded, but enough to see the lines and swirls. Two wavy lines, one over the other, with an arched line above them. A moon hanging over a river.

He had a feeling that the painting was the true treasure of this chest.

QUEST COMPLETE!

X MARKS THE ISLAND
Rewards: +50 Experience

You have found a painting within the treasure of the SkyBreeze. It appears to be of great age and possibly valuable, the true treasure of the map. There is a maker's mark on the canvas. Discover more about the painting and who painted it.

THE PAINTED SKYBREEZE I
Learn more about the painting 0/1
Rewards: +100 experience

ACCEPT QUEST?

"This is a nice haul," Caryn said, folding the cloak.

"Yeah. Too bad we won't know the stats of anything until we can get somewhere with a Witch that can Scry."

"Giving the coins to Captain Hart?"

Hall looked down at the two purses he had set near his feet. There was a lot of money in the four purses. It would go a long way to helping fund an airship for Skara Brae. But Hart could use it to help repair the *Twisted Gale*. Hall sighed.

"We'll keep a small handful, but the majority goes to Hart."

Caryn nodded in agreement.

Crouching back down, taking the cloak from Caryn, Hall repacked the chest. Not as good as the first time, but he managed to put the cover on and lock the clasps. Struggling with the awkward sized chest, he managed to get it hovered over his pouch. Pushing it down, he turned his head to avoid watching the distortion effect as the magic of the pouch shrunk the chest. It disappeared and he pulled up his inventory menu, surprised to see that the individual items in the chest didn't show as taking up space. Just the chest itself using up one slot.

Together they walked to the edge, staring out at the trees across the lake and the rope leading from island to those trees. Hall paused as he looked down at the body of the Monmodo. He studied the scaly hide, wondering if it could be skinned. Bending down, he withdrew the small skinning knife and made a quick cut along the belly of the small creature. He worked quickly, pulling at the hide which surprisingly didn't seem to be leaking much blood. It took a couple of minutes but he cut off a decent-sized piece of the Monmodo's hide.

Success!
You have gained Rough Monmodo Leather

Skill Gain!
Skinning Rank Two +.2

Rolling the hide up, he stuffed it into his pouch. The first he had skinned anything in a long time. He still wasn't sure if he was going to keep *Skinning* as one of his Profession Skills, but he could utilize it when the opportunity arose.

"Think there's any of those in the trees?" Caryn asked, pointing at the corpse.

Hall looked up at the sky where Pike circled above. With a screech, the dragonhawk swooped and dove toward the trees just offshore. He flew into the trees, his squawking and calls audible as he scouted under the canopy.

"Guess not," Caryn said with a chuckle.

"Ladies first," Hall said smiling, waving to the rope midway down the slope.

Smiling, Caryn practically slid down the steep slope, hopping and skidding. She came to a stop where the rope was tied to a rock outcropping. Testing the rope, pulling on it to make sure it remained tied, she grabbed it in both hands. Holding onto it, walking down until her arms were extended, she swung her legs up and wrapped around the rope. She started working her way along the rope, hand over hand, legs sliding.

Caryn made it look easy.

She was across the lake and shore quicker this time than the first. Caryn disappeared into the thick canopy of the trees. Hall could see the leaves shaking as the Duelist moved through them. She dropped to the ground, brushing off loose leaves and twigs. Taking a couple steps away from the tree, she waved to Hall.

He made his uneasy way down the slope. He was agile, just not anywhere near as agile as Caryn. The loose stones slid under his feet as he leaned back for more balance. Slowly he made his way down to the rope and copied Caryn's maneuver. Arms extended, he swung his legs up and felt the rope bouncing under his weight. Going back was easier, he found. He knew how the rope moved, where it would dip and bounce the most. Hall knew he wasn't as graceful as Caryn had been, but he made it across.

The bright sun dimmed as he pushed his way into the thick canopy of leaves, the larger branch appearing underneath. When he felt he was close enough to the trunk, Hall unwrapped his legs and set them down on the branch. Holding his balance, he let go of the rope and made his way to the trunk where he climbed down to the ground.

Landing on the ground, he also brushed off some extra leaves and twigs as he stepped out from under the canopy. Caryn was standing down by the shore, and Hall joined her. She looked wistfully across the lake at the floating island. Hall glanced down at her, confused by her expression.

"You okay?"

Caryn didn't reply for a minute, just watched the island. The birds started to return, circling and flying back down to their nests. Birdsong started to fill the air around them. With a squawk, almost indignant, Pike landed on Hall's shoulder. The talons dug in and Hall winced.

"I miss home," she said.

It was an odd comment at that time. Hall didn't know much about Caryn, even after the last month or so he had known her. There wasn't much time to sit down and chat while they had been rebuilding Skara Brae, and he had yet to learn Caryn's history from before she was trapped in Sky Realms Online.

"I'm not sure why this," Caryn paused and waved her hand at the floating island, "triggered my homesickness. It's not like my old life was all that exciting. I had my girlfriend, but that relationship wasn't..." She paused again and chuckled. "She was a hardcore gamer and I wasn't. Remember I told you that I had just started playing?"

Hall nodded.

"I really only did it to be closer with her," Caryn admitted. "To spend more time with her doing something she loved. I wasn't even sure that I was enjoying it. It had only been three hours or so and then..." Again, she waved her hand absently, moving her fingers in an odd motion that Hall took to represent static and the Glitch.

"And now you're stuck here in something you weren't sure you wanted," Hall finished and Caryn nodded.

Hall had always been a gamer, the same with Roxhard and Sabine. Living in Sky Realms Online was, in many ways, a dream come true. While playing a VRMMORPG, the Player was lost in the immersion, some games better than others, but there was always the call of Real Life to bring them out of it. They knew it was just a game. That was no longer true.

But if you hadn't wanted to play the game and were now stuck in it? What would that be like?

Caryn was always so upbeat, energetic but a little naïve.

Hall had to wonder how much of it was a defensive and coping mechanism.

He looked up at the sun, measuring its distance across the sky.

"Let's get back to the ship," he said.

———

They walked in silence, following the same trail they had used to get to the clearing and the lake. Hall left Caryn to her thoughts, her mood not improving. Pike soared lazily above, disappearing for a time as the dragonhawk went off to hunt. In no real hurry, they stopped and gathered more roots and flowers, Hall gaining another three points in *Herbology*.

It took almost four hours of walking to get close to where the *Gale* had crashed. Hall had to keep checking his map, adjusting their course. As they neared the crash site, Hall started to sense something was wrong. He couldn't place why he thought that, but he knew it. A glance at Caryn showed she felt the same, her eyes darting around the woods surrounding them, her hands tight on the hilts of her swords. The forest had fallen silent, no small animals running over branches, nothing but the wind blowing through the leaves.

Hall stopped, listening.

"What's that noise?" Caryn whispered from just behind him.

He couldn't hear it at first, but as soon as she mentioned it, he caught the sound. Growls. The clang of metal. Shouts and curses.

"Come on," he said and took off at a run.

Hall mentally called for Pike, getting an image of the dragonhawk sitting in a tree, something in his talons. Pike squawked, annoyed, but pushed off the branch. The meal fell to the forest floor, forgotten, as Pike flew into the air.

Running hard, Hall passed the new stumps of the felled trees. He stepped out of the forest and into the clearing where the *Gale* lay. The sounds of fighting were louder, the crack and boom of magic. Men shouted, calling out curses and screams. Hall took it all in quickly as Caryn burst out beside him.

The sailors and his companions were backed up against the hull of the *Twisted Gale*, using it to protect their rear. Hall could see a couple of bodies, human and monster, scattered around, packs and tools forgotten. Just beyond the ship were large and thick logs laid in a pile, smaller ones stacked around them, piles of rough planking alongside. Other smaller piles of broken timber were loosely stacked near the front of the ship. All signs of a worksite that had hastily been interrupted. Jackoby and Roxhard held the flanks of the group, weapons swinging. Sabine stood in the back, higher than the others as she had climbed up part of the ship's hull to get a vantage point to cast spells.

Giant lizards crawled everywhere. A couple dozen of the creatures. They were long, six to eight feet, with thick tails of the same length. A foot or so off the ground. Scaly skin in shades of green with brown stripes. Four short legs ending in long claws. Flat heads, with long forked tongues and mouths full of razor-sharp teeth.

The creatures hissed and growled as they stalked toward the sailors.

CHAPTER TEN

"What are those?" Caryn said, trying to keep quiet and not alert the creatures.

The monsters were moving like a swarm, pushing and prodding at each other to be the ones closest to the sailors and potential food.

Skill Gain!
Identify Rank One +.1

Deep Forest Ghiler (white)

Hall saw a couple of the creatures' heads lift up, forked tongues out as they tasted the air. The heads turned and caught sight of them. Four of the Ghilers hissed, their long bodies turning quickly. The creatures growled and charged, their small legs carrying them quickly across the open space.

Caryn took a couple steps away from Hall, finding a large tree and putting it to her back. She drew her swords, watching as two of the Ghilers angled to face her. They slowed down, tongues flicking out quickly, shaking as they did. The other two faced off with Hall, one further ahead of the other.

Activating *Leap*, Hall jumped over the first creature. His spear stabbed down into its body as he soared past, the weapon scoring a deep hit. He landed just beyond the second creature, turning quickly and stabbing out and down with the spear. The tip struck the creature along its spine. The scaly hide absorbed most of the blow, but it still hurt, drawing a line of blood and the Ghiler hissing in pain. Raising the spear to attack again, Hall felt a strong impact against his legs. The Ghiler whipped its thick tail, knocking Hall off balance. A small amount of Health was lost as he stumbled back, trying to avoid another quick attack from the tail. The first Ghiler had turned, stalking toward him. He couldn't set his feet, having to avoid the swift tail attacks. Fast as a whip, thick as a club, the tail slammed into his shins. The pain was intense. He didn't think the bone was broken. Not yet. Another hit and it would break.

Hall jumped forward, feet landing on the back of the Ghiler. He ran, taking a couple steps and using the creature as a springboard. He jumped and landed almost where he had begun. Turning, he stabbed down with the spear, catching the surprised Ghiler in the head. The sharp ironwood tip penetrated the weaker hide between the creature's eyes. With a final shake, the Ghiler stopped moving.

The second creature turned, growling in frustration. Hall set his feet, watching as it slowly approached. It moved warily at an angle where it could use the tail to attack. Hall waited and then *Leapt* into the air when it got within tail-attack range. He stabbed down as he jumped up, scoring a quick hit. The creature's head bent up awkwardly, watching the Skirmisher as he came down, spear tip leading. Hall slammed into the Ghiler's back, the extra force and momentum pushing the spear through the Ghiler's body. With a shudder, the creature died.

SLAIN: Deep Forest Ghiler +10 Experience
SLAIN: Deep Forest Ghiler +10 Experience

Skill Gain!
Polearms Rank Two +.2

Pulling his spear out of the Ghilers body, Hall saw Caryn running toward the larger group of Ghilers attacking the sailors. She had already killed her two. Jumping off the dead body, Hall ran after her. A screech from above told him Pike had arrived. He saw the dive-bombing blur that was the dragonhawk as Pike cut across the backs of the Ghilers, talons out. Turning back, Pike hovered in air and let loose a blue-white crackling bolt of lightning.

Caryn's twin blades slashed across the backs of unprepared Ghilers, as she used her speed and agility. She pretty much ran along the tail of one, onto its back, attacked, and jumped onto the back of another. Her weapons were a blur, turning and stabbing as she moved, blood spraying into the air with each hit.

Hall used *Leap*, knowing his best tactic was to land on a Ghiler's back. There were so many of the creatures, he couldn't land on the ground in the middle; he would be overwhelmed. He slammed down onto the back of one of the creatures in the rear, spear slamming through its back. He activated the ability again, landing on a Ghiler ten feet to the side. He stabbed down just behind the Ghiler's eyes, the creature not even giving one last move as it dropped dead.

Keeping an eye on his Energy, Hall *Leapt* from Ghiler to Ghiler. Not all attacks were kills, but most were. He crisscrossed the back ranks of the creatures with Caryn, sometimes next to each other and sometimes further apart. Not all her attacks were kills either, but between the two, they managed to grab the attention of the mob.

Risking a glance to the ship, Hall saw Roxhard and Jackoby pushing back. Without the constant pressure of the horde, they were able to thin out the Ghiler rushing against them. With the sailors' help, they started to move away from the ship, stepping over the dead and dying creatures. The attack from the rear proved to be the difference. Within minutes, all the Ghilers were dead. Hall stood with one leg on a dead Ghiler, the other on the ground, bodies of the creatures all around him. He leaned on his spear, breathing heavy. His Energy was drained and he had taken some hits near the end.

SLAIN: Deep Forest Ghiler +10 Experience
SLAIN: Deep Forest Ghiler +10 Experience
SLAIN: Deep Forest Ghiler +10 Experience
SLAIN: Deep Forest Ghiler +10 Experience
SLAIN: Deep Forest Ghiler +10 Experience
SLAIN: Deep Forest Ghiler +10 Experience
SLAIN: Deep Forest Ghiler +10 Experience
SLAIN: Deep Forest Ghiler +10 Experience

Skill Gain!
Light Armor Rank Two +.2
Skill Gain!
Polearms Rank Two +.5

"Welcome back," a deep voice said, drawing Hall's attention.

He looked up to see Roxhard picking his way over the corpses.

"Good timing," the Dwarf said with a chuckle. He stepped on one body, and it shifted under him. Roxhard jumped, ax raised to attack. He laughed, realizing the body had just slipped and wasn't still alive.

"Where did these things come from?" Hall asked, his eyes roaming the dead Ghiler.

Roxhard shrugged and waved his hand to the west.

"Somewhere over there," he said. "One of the sailors was foraging that way and came running back screaming. These followed him."

Hall shook his head. The poor man must have accidentally stepped into a nesting ground. He looked around, doing a quick count of heads.

"Didn't make it," Roxhard said sadly.

"Lost another three," Captain Hart said as he made his way over the bodies. He stepped carefully, trying to avoid the growing pools of blood. "I'm glad you arrived when you did."

"I'm sorry we weren't here," Hall said angrily, upset with himself.

"It wouldn't have mattered," Hart told him, clapping Hall on the shoulder. "You would have been trapped against the ship with the rest of us. The surprise attack from the rear is what turned the tide."

Hall nodded. He knew it was true, but it didn't make him feel any better.

"We need to clean up this mess," he said, standing up straighter. "We'll have to drag the bodies as far away as we can. They'll attract scavengers."

Captain Hart grumbled and Hall shrugged.

"I'll order up a detail," Hart said and walked away, calling out to some of the sailors.

Sliding the spear into his harness, Hall bent down and grabbed a Ghiler tail. He pulled and cursed. The creature was heavy. With a sigh, he started to drag the body away.

———

Congratulations!

You have received Rough Ghiler Hide.

Skill Gain!
Skinning Rank Two +.1

Hall stood up, throwing the large piece of hide onto the pile off to the side. It was a big pile and growing. He had already gotten almost ten gains in *Skinning* with at least twelve more corpses to go. Raising his hands above his head, holding the bloody skinning knife off to the side, Hall stretched out his sore muscles. He had not received any slashing hits from the fight with the lizard-like creatures, just bashing from the tails and bodies, so he had not bothered using one of the healing potions. As a result, his body was bruised and battered. Crouching for almost an hour to skin the bodies hadn't helped.

With a group of six sailors, Roxhard, and Jackoby, Hall had dragged the bodies of the Ghiler a couple hundred feet into the woods. They had gone west, the way the creatures had come. The low-to-the-ground Ghiler had left a trail of smashed logs and sticks, flattened grasses and ripped up bushes. In their haste to chase the sailor, they had just stampeded over anything in their way. Hall had been tempted to follow the trail all the way back to the nesting ground and leave the bodies there but the creatures were just too heavy. They dragged them as far as they could into the forest.

The sailors had gone back to help with the ship, leaving the two Wardens and Hall with the dead Ghilers. Hall figured he was safe enough to skin without anything else attacking, but he felt better having them there, even though they were bored as he skinned the Ghiler. It did provide a nice distraction from the back-breaking work they had been doing to repair the *Gale*. Being two of the strongest, it had fallen on them to lug the large timbers out of the forest. Both wanted a break. Hauling dead lizards wasn't much different but it got them away from the ship.

"Did you find the treasure?" Roxhard asked as Hall stuffed the last leather into his pouch.

Congratulations!
You have received Rough Ghiler Hide.

Skill Gain!
Skinning Rank Two +.1

Out of the last dozen Ghilers, Hall had only gotten four skill gains. It seemed to be a system put in place to prevent Players from leveling the Skill off repeated kills of the same monster, forcing them to find different things to hunt. Another reason why NPCs didn't seem to get as high in Skill as Players or Adventurers. Most NPCs never went far from their homes so what they had to kill would not change often.

He looked down at the long claws on the creatures, wondering if it would be worth breaking them off. Looking up at the sun, how high it was in the sky and how little daylight was left, he decided not to.

The three started walking back to the ship and the work. Hall knew he'd be roped into helping with repairs. He was tired, just wanting to rest after the hike and the Monmodos along with the Ghilers, but that was still hours away.

"Yeah," he answered Roxhard. "Found a floating island too."

The Dwarf gave him a funny look, not sure if Hall was joking or not.

"Uhm... we're on a floating island."

Hall laughed.

"True, but this was a floating island on a floating island," Hall said and explained the odd island he and Caryn had found. He glanced at Jackoby. "Ever hear about something like that?"

"No," Jackoby grunted. "But then I have never been off Edin before."

Hall nodded. The Firbolg was not an Adventurer, at least he didn't use to be. There would have been no reason for him to travel far past Fallen Green Forest. Hall had to remember that most NPCs were villagers with no reason to travel and wouldn't know much beyond their local area.

"I didn't think that was possible," Roxhard said as they walked through the forest.

It was silent, all animals having fled while they had labored to haul the Ghiler corpses far enough away from the crash site.

"Me either," Hall replied.

———

"Are you sure?" Captain Hart asked, hefting the bags of coins that Hall handed him. They were heavy and clinked loudly as metal hit metal.

"It's going to cost a lot to fix the *Gale*," Hall said, repeating what the statement he had made earlier when giving Hart the bags from the *SkyBreeze's* chest.

Hart nodded, pocketing the bags into the small pouch at his waist.

Everyone, including NPCs, had the magical inventory pouches. Each was different in style and shape, but they all had the same basic properties. Hall had known that Leigh and Jackoby had the pouches, but he hadn't noticed that all NPCs had one too. Or did they? Hall pushed it from his mind as it wasn't important.

The important thing was getting off the island.

"Where do we stand?" he asked Hart.

"Most of the materials we'll need are ready," Hart replied

as he led Hall toward the ship. "We've gotten the damaged parts ready for the new material." He paused and glanced back at the piles of wood. "They're more patches," he admitted. "They should hold until we get to Huntley."

"Should?"

Hart shrugged, not answering him, which Hall did not find reassuring.

"Anyway," Hart continued. "It'll be a couple days to get the patches on, and then we'll work to set the ship upright and repairs can start on the engines and new masts."

"And," Hall prompted.

"At least two to three days after that we should be able to fly," Hart replied. "We'll be much slower but we'll get there."

Captain Hart led Hall to the aft of the ship. The *Twisted Gale* was a flat-bottomed vessel, like most airships, but its aft still tapered to a point. It lay on an angle, one engine high in the air and the other against the ground. It was that engine that kept the *Gale* on the angle and probably had prevented the ship from rolling over. Which would have most likely killed everyone. If not, the ship would have been damaged beyond all repair.

But would they have died? Would he and the other Players have respawned? And if they did, where? There were no more bind points. Not anymore. At least not that he knew of.

Hall walked over to the engine, running his hand over the metal.

"We got lucky," Hart said, joining Hall. He rapped his knuckles against the engine and pointed at the strut that connected it to the hull of the ship. "The *Gale*, she's tough. If that had broken, we would have lost the engine. Without both engines, we'd be stuck level and couldn't rise or descend."

He led Hall around to the other side of the engine where they were in the shadow of the ship's leaning hull. Hart crouched down and looked where the engine had pushed up the ground, burying part of the rounded iron casing.

"What can I do?" Hall asked.

"Vines," Hart replied standing up. "We need lots and lots of vines."

CHAPTER ELEVEN

Hart had them wait until the next day. He sent everyone to bed, even the late shift of workers. The only ones up were the guards. Hall took his turn at watch, midway through the night, sharing it with Roxhard and four of the sailors. He took the side that faced where they had dragged the dead Ghilers, figuring any wandering predators would come from that direction.

Midway through his watch, he heard loud growling from deep in the forest. Yapping, cries of pain and howls, as the island's predators fought over the carcasses. It went on for minutes until a single loud roar silenced everything. It echoed through the night, the trees shaking. Hall stared out into the dark, wanting to see what had made that sound and at the same time not wanting to see it. He hoped that whatever it was would be content with the Ghilers.

Branches cracked and snapped, something uttering a low growl. For Hall to hear it as far away as he was, the creature had to be massive. The sounds that came out of the deep forest, heightened by the dark of night, were horrific. Rending and tearing, more cries of pain ending in strangled shouts. Fighting and eating.

Gripping his spear tighter, Hall listened and waited, tense. The sounds went on for minutes, seemingly forever, then just stopped. The forest was quiet, none of the normal nocturnal sounds. Hall glanced behind him where the fire still roared. He saw faces all looking his way, shadowed by the flames behind them, some standing up and clutching weapons. Turning back to the dark forest, Hall heard new sounds. Branches breaking and a tree being knocked over. The roots ripped out of the ground, the sharp cracking of branches being broken and then a ground-shaking thud. Followed by nothing. Whatever had made all the noise, whatever massive creature it had been, was gone.

Hall didn't release his tight hold on the spear. He expected something to come bursting out of the trees.

It was a tense rest of the night and when he was relieved, he could not get to sleep. He doubted anyone would.

———

"Heave," Captain Hart yelled.

Hall, standing in line with six sailors, pulled on the thick vine he held in his hand. Hand over hand, he pulled, standing still and not moving. The others in front and behind doing the same. Next to him, on both sides, were lines of men all doing the same. Pulling.

He was the second to last man in his line, second in from the bow of the ship, with Captain Hart just behind as the last man in the first line. The six lines of men were all on the keel side of the angled ship. Thirty feet out, the long vines had snaked across the ground, up the side of the ship and over the hull to the other railing where they had been attached to cleats, the remainders of the masts and anything else Hart and the ship's engineer were sure would not break off. They had spent hours digging out under the keel of the ship to help encourage it to move.

At Hart's first command, the men on the vines had lifted and pulled them tight. At his second command, the first 'heave,' they had pulled and continued to pull with each shout from Hart. Four sailors, with broken bones or shoulders or some other unhealed injury that prevented them from standing on the lines, stood guard. They held weapons, if they could, and stared out into the thick forests. Their jobs weren't to defend but to warn. Hall had Pike up in the air, circling. The dragonhawk flew wide arcs over the island, watching for anything coming toward the *Gale*.

Hall couldn't spare a thought for Pike. None of them could spare a thought for anything besides pulling. They had to get the ship as horizontal as they could. Hart had said it didn't need to be perfect. The port side had to be off the ground so they could get at the engine.

The only way to do that was to pull the great ship over through brute force.

Caryn and Sabine were at the bow and aft, watching the timbers of the ship. Their job was to call out if anything started to buckle or break. Roxhard and Jackoby were on the hull side with long poles. Their job was simple but hard. Instead of pushing, they were going to use their greater strength and lever the ship over. The only other person not pulling was the *Gale's* engineer, who ran back and forth around the engine, watching every piece of it as the rest strained to lift the heavy ship.

"Heave."

Hall pulled. Sweat rolled down his forehead and into his eyes. It stung, but there was no way to wipe it away. His hands burned; he could feel the blisters forming as the vine rope moved through his tight grip. There was no way to loosen his hold. To do so would allow the vines to slip and the *Gale* to slide back. Once they had started to pull, there was no stopping until the ship was righted. The engine had somehow survived one crash into the ground. It would not survive another.

"Heave."

Holding tight with his left hand, Hall released his right hand and grabbed the vines ahead of the left. Both hands tight, he pulled back. At the next yell from Hart, he released the left and grabbed the vines ahead of the right hand. Holding tight, he and all the others pulled.

The *Gale* groaned, moving an inch at a time.

Already his muscles hurt with the strain. If he was hurting, the sailors had to be worse. None of them were at peak Health or Vitality. And this exertion would sap even them even more. He fought the urge to look at Sabine and Caryn, to see what they were doing or how they were reacting. Was the ship holding? Hart had warned that the strain could be too much for the damaged ship. It, or 'she' as Captain Hart referred to the *Twisted Gale*, wanted to remain as she was. Not be pulled over. He wanted to shout out encouragement to Roxhard and Jackoby, wanted to help them push while everyone else pulled.

But he couldn't. It took all his concentration to just pull on the thick vines, hoping they wouldn't snap.

Hall knew he was a reluctant leader. He hadn't wanted to be, it had just happened. But as he was the leader of his companions, he now hated being put in a position where he wasn't in charge or at least not involved. Here and now, he was just one of many pulling on the vines. He knew this was where he needed to be and was the most useful, but it still bothered him.

"Heave."

Hall pulled on the vines. In the next line over, he saw one of the sailors stumble. The man recovered quickly and got back into rhythm with the others. A quick glance at Captain

Hart showed the man worried. Once a man had stumbled and slipped, it would be a domino effect and more would follow. The *Gale* wasn't anywhere near where the ship needed to be for her own weight to finish the job.

"Heave."

Arms shook, muscles spasmed, but Hall kept pulling. The ship groaned, creaking. Something snapped, but Hall kept pulling. They all did. Hand over hand.

Shouts of alarm came from two lines down, and Hall saw that vine go slack, dangling and useless. The *Gale* shuddered, seeming to fall back an inch or two. Hall could feel additional weight through his arms, the shudder of the ship. Gritting his teeth, hearing grunts of effort around him, they adjusted and pulled. The other line remained slack.

"Out, out," Hart shouted. "Move back, don't trip them."

The voice was frantic, desperate, worried.

There were cries of pain, curses, and another line went slack. The *Gale* groaned, loudly, followed by more creaking. Hall's line was pulled forward. They couldn't adjust for the additional weight, the pulling lopsided. Hall thought he saw the *Gale* starting to twist.

"Don't stop," Captain Hart shouted. "Get back on the vines. Quick. Hurry."

The *Gale* twisted, the bow sliding toward them and the aft away from them, leaning back down. The ship's wooden structure groaned, and Hall saw the railing along the deck cracking. He heard snapping from the deck side, Jackoby's deep voice crying out in pain and shock.

"Get the pressure off," came a shout from that side. The engineer. "Don't let it fall."

Cursing, not thinking, Hall activated *Leap*. He jumped sideways, over the heads of the other sailors. He landed near the aft, two loose vines at his feet. Behind him, sailors were scrambling to pull others out of the way. There were cries of pain, some holding their legs and arms. Hall imagined there were broken bones. Some tried to stand but could not, arms and legs tired beyond use. Bending down, Hall grabbed both of the loose vines, one in each hand. Setting his feet, he pulled, taking steps backward. He growled, muscles protesting.

He knew he couldn't pull it on his own, but maybe he could keep it from twisting.

Hall strained. His arms felt like they would be pulled out of the sockets. But he held on. He felt the slack behind him tighten as sailors grabbed the vines and started to pull. There was a stronger tug on the vine in his left hand. Hall stopped moving, glancing behind him just enough to see two men on the vine in his right hand. On the other side was just one person. The Firbolg. Jackoby. The Warden growled as he pulled, and Hall could see the pain in his face.

Releasing that vine, Hall concentrated on the one he now held.

"Heave," Hart yelled.

The captain's shouts became faster. He knew they had to get the ship righted quickly. The men were tired. It was only a matter of time before they all collapsed and the ship would fall back, the engine would be destroyed, and they would be stuck.

"Heave."

They did.

Hall felt more pressure against his arms, weight trying to pull the vines out of his grasp, to let the ship fall back down. He fought against it. Jackoby roared. The sailors picked up on it, copying it. The sound was loud. Hall joined in. He felt the guttural sound, felt the power in the cry from all those around him. As one, they pulled.

The *Twisted Gale* seemed to hover just on the edge. The keel slipped a little, down into where they had dug, leaning. Just waiting for the final decision on which way to go.

"HEAVE!" Hart yelled above the roar.

One last effort, one last great pull, and the ship decided.

Hall watched the railing of the ship. It was moving. Not away but toward them. With a crash that shook the island, the *Gale* fell down and lay almost flat. The vines went slack, all the pressure off them and the sailors all fell backward. There were grunts of pain, curses as they all collapsed to the ground. It was followed by cheers and sighs of relief.

Hall sat on the ground, arms held out in front. They didn't want to move, seeming stuck like that. His knuckles were white, finger cramped and unable to unfold. He bit back a cry as sharp needles of pain spread through his legs. Shifting, barely able to move, he turned his body to look at Jackoby.

The Firbolg was also on the ground. One arm was moving, the other he held tight to his body. His teeth were ground in pain, his breathing heavy.

"Are you okay?" Hall asked, knowing it was a dumb question. Of course Jackoby wasn't.

The Firbolg shot him a sharp look that softened quickly.

"Broken," he growled, indicating the arm curled tight to his body. "The pole snapped and so did the arm."

"How did—" Hall started to say looking at the vine that Jackoby had single-handedly held. He just shook his head.

"I want off this island," Jackoby muttered, each word labored.

Arms stiff, not wanting to move, Hall reached down into the potion pouch on his belt. Fumbling with the tie, he pulled out a *Minor Health Potion*. Shifting again, pushing his body closer, Hall uncorked the vial with his teeth. Spitting the cork on the ground, he handed the small vial to the Firbolg. Nodding his thanks, Jackoby swallowed it all in one gulp. He grimaced at the taste.

Hall watched as the pain left the Firbolg's eyes and features. The broken arm moved a little, causing Jackoby to gasp in pain, but at least it was moving.

Hall pulled a *Minor Vitality Potion* out of the pouch. Closing his eyes, he put it to his lips and tipped the vial. He felt the thick liquid wash down his throat, a tingling spreading out from where it touched. He felt energy coursing through his veins. Not much but enough that he could move again. Forcing himself to stand, he saw Sabine and Caryn walking through the crowd of exhausted sailors, handing out potions and herbs.

Captain Hart stood looking up at his ship, relief all over his face.

"We still have a lot to do," he said, not directed at anyone. "But I think that can wait for tomorrow."

———

The great beast was back that night.

Hall could hear it moving through the forest, branches snapping and the thud of the feet on the ground. It was silent except for the movements, no growl or call. All was silent as the unknown creature stalked through the woods. The fire was high, a bright and flickering flame sending heat and light out into the night. He didn't think the beast would come that close to the camp.

He hoped it wouldn't. They were in no shape to deal with anything that night. Everyone was exhausted. Passed out. Even with a couple of *Minor Vitality Potions*, Hall still felt worn out. Legs were hurt, aching, as were his arms. He moved them now, stretching, feeling muscles protest.

Hall glanced behind him at the fire and the camp. No one moved. Turning back to the woods, he took a step in that direction and then another. The light from the fire disappeared as he stepped into the canopy of the trees.

Looking back, he could just make out the flames, flickering and casting odd shadows between the tree trunks. He wasn't sure what he was doing. There was no need but he was curious.

Hall pushed through the trees, his *Limited Night Vision* activating. Everything was in shadows, shades of gray and black. No detail but enough to walk by.

He made his way through the thick forest, following the trail they had made yesterday with the Ghiler corpses. He moved slowly, quietly, still not sure what he was doing.

But something nagged at him, pushed at him. It wanted him to see.

It took thirty minutes to get to where they had left the corpses. He had smelled it long before that. The carrion smell of death and blood. The area was a mess. Broken trees, some snapped completely off. Others lay on their sides. Ghiler corpses were torn to shreds, ripped apart. And there were others there. Newer ones, fresher ones. Flies buzzed through the air, but there were no scavengers. Everything left the bloody mess alone.

Hall skirted the edge, holding his nose and trying not to breathe. The trail of the creature was easy to find. Broken trees, snapped branches, and footprints the size of his body.

Congratulations!
You have discovered Unknown Print.

Skill Gain!
Tracking Rank One +.1

He shook his head, somewhat amused. He didn't need any Skill to follow this trail. He hesitated before following, looking back the way he had come. It wasn't too late to turn around. Did he really want to find out what was out there? He took one step back but stopped.

There was a low growl from further ahead. Loud, pushing through the trees. *They were going to be on this island for another week at least*, Hall thought. They needed to know what this thing was. Now determined, he started down the large creature's trail.

The tracks were not placed on the ground so much as they were forced. Deep, a couple inches, they showed a foot with three toes and claws on the front and one large on the back. Each was spaced at least four to five feet apart. Whatever the monster was, it was huge.

He couldn't move quickly, keeping an eye on the tracks but mostly on the debris the creature left behind it. Broken branches, rocks pushed aside, stumps and roots. Things that didn't bother a creature of its size, but did anything smaller. It left behind a mess. Surprisingly, there wasn't that much destruction the deeper into the forest Hall went. He had expected more trees to be uprooted or pushed aside, picturing scenes from movies he had seen. Which really didn't make much sense, he realized. If the creature destroyed everything as it walked, there would be nothing left. The creature was selective in the path it took, avoiding the tighter clusters of trees and moving where there was more space.

The land sloped down ahead, and Hall could see the decline through the trees. The night also seemed to brighten, more moonlight showing through the gaps. A clearing of some kind. Hall stopped at the edge of the trees, the grass sloping down to a small pond and river below. About fifty feet down, no trees on the slopes or along the banks. The small dell was bright, the moonlight shining down unblocked by trees or higher islands.

Crouching by the pool was the creature. Somehow with the moonlight and stars, Hall was able to see it clearly. A Monmodo, but huge.

It was drinking from the pond, the large hand cupping water that it brought to its mouth, the many teeth catching the light. The head lifted as something caught its attention.

Hall crouched low, ducking behind a tree, watching the giant Monmodo.

Skill Gain!
Identify Rank One +.1

Konglo, Monmodo King (Purple)

It stood up, head still lifted and sniffing at the air. The giant Monmodo stood at least twenty feet tall, the tail around ten feet long as it whipped through the air showing the creature's agitation. It uttered a low growl as the eyes darted around the clearing and treeline. Hall crouched lower, hoping to be lost in the shadow, glad he was downwind.

Skill Gain!
Camouflage Rank One +.5

He had no hope of really remaining hidden. Even with the gain, his *Camouflage* Skill was still too low. If he moved, he knew he was dead. This creature, Konglo, was a Boss level monster. No way to know what the actual Level was, but it would be high. There had always been World Bosses, high-level creatures that roamed the world. Lore had been developed to explain their existence. There had never been a creature with the name of Konglo. Like Skara Brae and all of Breakridge, this was a new creature in the game.

Holding his breath, Hall watched the giant creature settle down. With a quiet hoot, the Monmodo hopped halfway up the other side of the dell. Its feet dug into the ground and it leapt again, catching gracefully at a thick tree along the edge. Hall expected it to crush the trunk, but for all its size, the Monmodo was like a monkey, barely touching as it moved. It grabbed the trunk just enough to support itself on the edge before it disappeared into the trees.

Hall didn't move for a long time, watching where the giant Monmodo had disappeared. He listened to the sounds of the night returning. Slowly, but coming back.

The best indication he would get that Konglo had left.

Hall stood up, turning but stopped. Something was rustling in the leaves near. He waited. A crunch of leaf, then another, but a little further away. He watched as a shadow jumped into a patch of moonlight, something glinting. The shadow made a noise, a croak. Stepping forward, Hall made out what looked to be a large frog. Six inches or so, maybe more and glinting in the moonlight, sitting on the creature's head, was a small golden crown that seemed to glow in the moonlight.

What is that? he thought, watching as the creature hopped away and disappeared into the bushes. He shook his head, wondering if the frog with a crown had even been real. A loud crash from behind him refocused his thoughts. Konglo was moving, but away luckily.

Quickly, worried, Hall made his way back to the *Gale*.

Another week on this island with Konglo roaming around was not something Hall was looking forward to.

PART TWO
AXESTORM HALL

CHAPTER TWELVE

HALL STOOD JUST OUTSIDE THE TREE LINE, THE OTHERS aligned around him. They all watched as Captain Hart, the engineer and the helmsmen stood awkwardly on the deck of the *Twisted Gale*. The ship was relatively flat, only a slight angle which made standing difficult, but it was possible. They conferred together quietly, the engineer gesturing wildly. Hart made a placating gesture with his hands. While Hall couldn't see it from where he stood, he knew the engineer had rolled his eyes.

They had done all they could for repairs. It was time to test the ship.

It had gone quicker than Hart had estimated. The threat of Konglo seemed to be a motivating factor. All had heard the noises in the night, and once Hall had reported what he had seen, that was enough to light a fire under the sailors. The repairs had been completed in record time.

The engineer moved across the sloped deck, moving awkwardly. He disappeared down the stairs to the engine room below. Hart stepped back from the helmsmen who gripped the wheel. Hall could see and sense the man's nervousness. A lot could go wrong and if it did, they were all in serious trouble. Hart gripped the railing and gave the quiet command. The helmsman relayed it to the engineer and all standing by the trees held their breath in anticipation.

The Twisted *Gale* shook. Small at first but growing larger and stronger. The ship groaned and creaked. A loud noise grew from beneath its decks. A rumbling and rattle. Hart looked down at the deck beneath his feet in fear.

Hall watched as the two engines started to shake, separate from the ship itself, in counterpoint, working opposite. The barrel-shaped metal engines started to hum, that was the only way Hall could describe it. The humming turned to a dull roar as they flared to life. Hart turned, still clutching the rail, and watched as the port engine started to rotate. Creaking, groaning, protesting, the engine faced down. Both of them did and the *Gale* started to rise from the ground.

Slowly, lumbering, without any of its usual grace, the ship lifted. A foot at a time, groaning and creaking the whole time. It shuddered again, a spasm that started at the engines and moved to the bow. The ship had once been beautiful, but the crash had damaged it in many ways. They had patched the holes, the new construction standing out against the old. It wasn't just the newness; it was the ugliness. The patches were obvious, thrown together and barely holding.

Higher and higher it rose.

The shaking stopped, the noises quieting. It hovered in the air, the sails tied to the new masts.

Without the prior groaning, the engines rotated again and the ship slowly lowered back down to the ground. It stopped about ten feet off, hovering, and sailors quickly ran forward from the sides. They threw ropes up to the deck, Captain Hart running around and tying them to cleats, the other ends tied to stout trees. The wind blew through the clearing, gently rocking the ship.

"All aboard," Captain Hart yelled from where he now stood against the railing.

Hall looked down the line, both directions. No one seemed that eager to board the damaged ship. With a sigh, he took a step forward, grabbing his pack off the ground.

Hall sat alone in the cabin, the others helping out with the damaged ship or relaxing on deck. They were five days out from the island, which Hall had decided to call Bow after the town he had grown up in. No one had charted or claimed the debris island, so he felt justified in doing so. His physical map was spread out on the bunk, showing the half of the island he had explored. A couple locations were marked and that was it. So much more to see. Maybe someday he'd get a chance to fully explore the island, but not now.

They still had to get to Huntley.

Captain Hart had debated the course with himself and the ship's officers. The navigator and the engineer had suggested altering the course and flying to one of the closer inhabited islands for full repairs. The *Twisted Gale* was holding together but not close to peak. It was the helmsman that said it would take less time to fly straight to Huntley. Hall had heard the discussion, though not invited to take part. It had involved velocity, wind currents, that a ship falling was faster than going level and put less stress on the structure and other statements that Hall knew nothing about. He had zoned out for most of the technical aspects, only paying attention when Hart had finally agreed.

Skill Gain!

Cartography Rank Two +.1

The name of the island appeared on the map, text scrolling along the bottom edge. The font matched the rest of the maps, flowing and embellished lettering.

You have laid claim to a previously uncharted island. The claim must be secured and notarized with The Guild of Exploration.

CLAIMING YOUR LAND
Register the uncharted island with the Guild of Exploration 0/1
Reward: +100 Experience; a new island

Hall stared at the quest prompt hovering before his eyes. He reread it a couple of times, still confused. Somehow, by naming the island and possibly mapping it, he had laid claim to it? What was this Guild of Exploration?

Mentally dismissing the quest after accepting it, not even sure he wanted to lay claim to an island with a Boss level monster living on it, Hall sighed. Just one more thing added to the long list of questions and mysteries he had to deal with. On top of the current problems.

He was starting to feel overwhelmed. There had never been this much to deal with before. It was too much. He thought about opening up his quest list and canceling it, but something flashed up from his memory.

Opening the Settlement Menu, Hall searched for the bit of text he was vaguely remembering. He was having a hard time finding it. Something about the Settlement Ranking of Skara Brae and how he could still have a lower rank Settlement. A lower rank like an outpost.

That had some possibilities, he thought.

Menu after menu passed by his vision as he searched for what he wanted, unable to find it. The thought tickled at his memory.

The door opened and Roxhard strode into the room.

"What are you doing?" the Dwarf asked, and Hall lost his place in the menus.

"Nothing," he replied, dismissing the menus, the nagging thought pushed to the back of his mind with so many others. "You?"

"Just got tired of seeing nothing but the blue," Roxhard said.

The last day, the *Twisted Gale* had been flying through an area of the sky with no visible islands, just the vast expanse of blue with clouds visible all around. Above and below. With nothing to shade the light of the sun, it was bright on the eyes and all suffered headaches when on deck for too long. The sailors had hats, some of which had survived the crash, but the passengers did not. It helped but not much. Most sailors that sailed beyond the main islands had spent weeks of time in the expanse of blue, and they had gotten used to it. For Hall and the others, days of blue was somewhat scary. It made them feel alone. They all knew there were islands not that far away. A couple miles shift in any direction and the black dots would start to appear and grow larger, becoming the floating islands of fractured Hankarth.

But knowing was not the same as seeing.

"Have you had any more ideas?" Hall asked.

Roxhard sat down in the only chair in the room, nailed to the floor and unable to move. It was behind a desk set against the wall, also nailed. Made for a human, the chair was a little tall for Roxhard and his feet did not touch the floor as he hopped up onto the seat.

"Huh?"

"Guild name," Hall prompted. "Any ideas?"

Roxhard stared at the wall, looking at a picture hanging over the desk. A painting depicting one of the many floating islands with clouds beyond and the sun shining down. Hall wasn't sure what island it was or who painted it, but thought the quality was decent enough. Roxhard seemed to be lost in the colors.

"Rox?"

The Dwarf stirred, looking over at Hall. It was not the first time in the trip that Hall had noticed Roxhard spacing out. Something was bothering the Dwarf, the others starting to notice it. He was quiet and withdrawn, not typical Roxhard. Hall would have dismissed it, but with Roxhard being fourteen, he paid more attention. It was odd seeing the Dwarf, looking like he was carved from rock, seemingly lost in a mood.

"What's up?" he asked. "You okay?"

The Dwarf's attention returned to the painting, his eyes tracing the lines.

"Nothing," he started to say and stopped. "I… uhm… Well… Did you ever play a Dwarf?"

Hall thought back to his playing days. He had tried every class and race in every combination possible. His first character had been Hall, the Half-Elf Skirmisher, and had always returned to play the same even with brief play times as other characters. It had really always been Hall. Bu there had been a couple Dwarves for a brief time.

"Yeah," he replied. "A little."

Roxhard gestured at himself, pointing at his face.

"I played nothing but," he said, and Hall was remarked at how adult his mannerisms were at that moment. Nothing like the teenager he really was. "I'm a Dwarf, but I'm not."

Hall nodded, not saying anything but letting Roxhard talk.

"All Player Dwarves are part of a handful of Clans. We get to pick at creation," Roxhard continued.

Again, Hall nodded, vaguely remembering. Humans were the only races that were distinct enough to be different at creation. The other races each had Clans that only added to their background, each Clan story adding immersion and depth. There were no physical differences.

"My Clan is the Stonefire," Roxhard said, and Hall started to understand.I don't fully remember the lore, but the Stonefire Clan of Dwarves lived in Axestorm Hall," he said and trailed off.

"Which is in the Hard Edge Mountains," Hall finished.

Roxhard nodded. Hall realized that the Dwarf was worried about being around other Dwarves, these ones being true Dwarves. Roxhard might know the lore, but he hadn't lived it. He might look over a hundred years old, maybe two hundred, but he was not.

Hall thought about how he would react if he encountered a village of Wood Elves. Would he have the same issues? It hadn't been something that had come up yet. He had been lucky to get by so far as they had yet to leave Gael lands, but he could see how Roxhard would be so worried. He didn't know what to say to help his friend.

Not knowing the culture you were supposed to belong to would be embarrassing for anyone, Hall knew, let alone a four-teen-year-old kid. Being a Dwarf made it even worse. As a race, the Dwarves were big on their clan histories. In any game he had ever played, a hallmark of the race was their adherence to tradition and ancestors. None of which had been important for Players in the old game. But it would be now.

Wouldn't it?

Hall wasn't sure. Would that be one of the areas that the game's mechanics would gloss over?

"You weren't raised in Axestorm," Hall said, deciding that it wasn't something he wanted to risk Roxhard's mental well-being over. He remembered what it was like to be that age, and this visit to the Hard Edge Mountains was going to be rough enough for the Dwarf. "No one there will recognize you, so we make up a story about you being an orphan or something."

Roxhard looked at Hall, hope and relief in the deep-set

eyes. It was odd seeing that expression on the rough face of the Dwarf.

"Will that work?"

Hall nodded, hoping it would.

———

The voyage was another ten days. The *Gale* was hurting, each day the engines laboring harder and harder, the ship slower. It shook more. Small shudders, but Hall could feel each one through the decking. Islands started to appear, closer and closer. Small ones like they had crashed on and even a couple bigger.

It made the shaking of the ship easier to bear. Any of the islands were close enough to get to without crashing, and there would be enough traffic in the area that rescue would happen. They had passed three other airships in the last two days. Each encounter was tense, the ships passing and hoping the other wasn't a pirate.

Hall would be glad when the trip was over.

It was midmorning, the sun rising over his shoulder. Most of it was blocked by higher islands as they had been descending for the last couple weeks. There was a chill to the air, not just from the wind. Less sunlight and more shadows. Standing in the bow, Hall saw a large dark line along the horizon. The engines had rotated to be parallel with the ship. They were no longer descending but now flying straight toward the dark line.

The ship flew on, the line gaining in detail. An island, one of the many realms. A large one, stretching along the horizon. Hall could see the dark underside of jagged rocks. Mountains ringed the island, the parts that they could see. High and snow-capped, the clouds hovering just above.

"That's Huntley," Captain Hart said, coming to stand next to Hall. "Those are the Hard Edge Mountains."

Hall had never seen them from this angle. He had been to Huntley, just a couple of times when quests brought him there. The island had been a Level Twenty realm for Storvgardes and some Dwarves with very little reason for anyone else to visit. Access to the island had been by airships on prescribed routes. They had never come from this direction. As the *Gale* got closer, Hall finally understood why they were called the Hard Edge Mountains.

Like all the islands, the edge of Huntley was jagged and rough, like it had been pulled straight out of the ground. Both Cumberland and Edin had mountains along the edge, ending in cliffs and broken rock. Huntly was the same, but also vastly different. The Hard Edge Mountains were split down the middle of the peaks. Sheer sides facing the sky. It wasn't rough but almost smooth like the mountain had been cut in half. It had none of the ripping aspect the other ranges had.

"Wow," Hall said.

The *Gale* turned, coming alongside the mountains.

"You haven't seen anything yet," Hart chuckled.

Over the next hour, the others all came on deck. They stood along the railing. There were a couple of new sailors among the crew, those who like Hall's companions had never seen the Hard Edge Mountains before. Word had passed that there was something they would want to see.

They watched the smooth-sided mountains pass, running south along the island. There were no birds of any kind flying among the cliffs, either above or below the grade line of the island. The sides of the peaks were so sheer and sharp that there was nowhere to nest. Ahead Hall could see the island start to turn to the east as they approached the southern end. It wasn't a gradual turn or a curve, but an almost perfect square corner. The mountain's edge was sharp.

But it wasn't just that corner that caught the eye; it was everything that dotted the mountain.

Parts of Axestorm Hall were visible. The mountain had been sheared off and so had the Dwarven fortress.

Hall could see the mouths of tunnels carved out of the mountain, arches laid with square blocks, that just ended with nothing but the drop. Rooms, large and small, cut right in half and open to the sky. Lines along the faces that were part of tunnels that had run parallel with the mountain, now just grooves cut into the side.

The *Gale's* Helmsman brought the ship as close to the side of the mountain as he dared. The wind around the mountains wasn't as strong as Hall thought it would be. The constant wind across Breakridge Meadow had more force.

He heard Sabine gasp in surprise. They could see Dwarves in the exposed rooms and tunnels. Some sat at furniture, others walked the halls. Even those that were sheared along their length, only having a depth of five feet or so. In some places, railings had been installed, metal and stone, ornate and plain. Nothing projected beyond the edge of the mountain. No balconies, statues, or docks. The straight and smooth cut edge of the mountain was maintained. They were a good distance away from the sheer face, but Hall could see that time and weather had dulled the once beautiful carvings and rune work in the rooms and tunnels.

It was jarring, Hall realized, seeing worked rooms with columns and etched rune work just open to the sky. He expected there to be more, to see the rooms hidden behind tons of rock. But seeing them exposed with Dwarves treating it as nothing, it was scary. Here at the Hard Edge Mountains, the truth of what the fracturing had caused was revealed. Hall had seen the ruins of cities, the remains still on the islands with the other half gone into the nothingness below. There were even the two islands, Orliss and Crawlit, where a city on Orliss had fallen onto Crawlit. The resultant earthquake had ruined the lower island with the great mounds of stone from Orliss remaining. But what he was seeing now was different. A stark realization of what had been done to the world of Hankarth.

An entire mountain, filled with thousands of years' worth of Dwarf halls, just ripped apart. Gone as if it never existed but the evidence was there. A constant reminder of what had been lost.

But there was also evidence of life going on. The Dwarves went on. Known for their stubbornness born of granite, they went on.

The *Gale* turned the sharp corner around the mountain and Hall saw more of the exposed tunnels and rooms of Axestorm Hall. Up and down the length of the mountain, even below the main elevation of the island.

"Oh my god," Caryn exclaimed pointing.

Hall saw it too. On the southern side of the mountain was a huge chamber, at least half of it. Rectangular with the ceiling curved, the top fifty or seventy-five feet above the floor, the sides covered in carvings and busts between black stone buttresses. Statues stood in front of each buttress that ran the length of the room. A long and high tunnel led to the large chamber, half of it remaining. Against the far wall, opposite the tunnel, was a raised dais. Steps upon steps, a dozen or so. At the top was a chair, carved from gold and obsidian. Both were sheared in half. Half the steps, half the throne. Everything in the room looked old and worn. Time had worked its hand on the throne, statues, busts, and carvings. Even with half of it missing, worn down by wind and weather, the majesty had not left the ancient throne room. It was not used anymore, that was obvious, but Hall could imagine how the room had been before the fracture. It would have awed any visitor, made them feel small with the weight of the stone pressing down on them.

It was the largest room they could see but just one of

dozens. Rooms upon rooms, tunnels running parallel and many others just dead ending.

How big would Axestorm Hall have been when whole? How much was lost?

It took Hall's breath away. He had seen some beautiful sights while playing Sky Realms Online but never anything like this. Had it existed before the Glitch? It couldn't have. Even if Players only saw it from the inside, they would have discovered the tunnels and rooms open to the sky. It would have been talked about, screenshots taken, and Hall would have visited Axestorm Hall to see it for himself.

And he had visited the Hall. There had never been anything like this.

He looked to the east, watching the mountain fall away, the last in the range. It gave way to foothills, the Greystones, and then to a stark plain. The tundra stretched for miles, further than his eyes could see. Once past the mountain, the *Gale* turned back to the north, passing over the edge of Huntley. This edge was jagged and rough. What Hall was used to seeing. And as the *Gale* traveled over the Greystone Foothills, Hall saw the Axestorm Hall that he thought he knew.

The mountain towered over the foothills, a long ramp built from stone block on stone block, leading up to the great doors that were carved into the side of the mountain. Twenty feet wide, forty feet high, made out of bronze and etched with scenes of battles. Carved out of the mountain's face were two huge crossed axes hanging over the doors. The stone heads were not plain, runes and other carvings filled the surfaces. More runes and carvings down the thick stone shafts. Time had not affected the axes or the doors. Round buildings stood out from the mountain's slopes, above and below the doors. More built into the foothills. Domed roofs, open-top floors, and thin windows on the lower. Dozens of them, some built from the gray stones of the mountains and others in different colors, made from stones taken from deep underground and brought up to the surface.

A loud roar filled the air as the *Gale* flew across the face of the mountain. Above and to the side of the great doors, a thick sheet of water fell from the mountain. It shot out from the face, falling hundreds of feet to slam into the ground, forming into a wide pond before a raging river flowed its way through the foothills pushed by the force of the waterfall. Rounded stone buildings jutted out over the pond, built into the wall of stone.

This is what Hall remembered, but at the same time, it wasn't.

Like everything else in this new version of Sky Realms Online, it was bigger. More defined. More developed. But just as amazing.

Jackoby's eyes were wide in amazement, the Firbolg never having been out of his forest before. Something like Axestorm Hall was beyond anything he had imagined. Hall glanced at Roxhard, seeing the Dwarf almost as amazed as the Firbolg. Roxhard would have been to the original Axestorm, but like Hall's own reaction, this was completely different.

None of Hart's crew seemed to notice that Roxhard was so shocked and amazed. This was something that the Dwarf should have seen multiple times, the amazement long since faded. It appeared that they were buying the story Hall had come up with. Because of that story, it was understandable that Roxhard was surprised and amazed.

The ship continued past the entrance to Axestorm Hall, and they saw that the pond was larger than they first thought. The width continued around the curve of the mountain and into the valley framed by the Hard Edge Mountains and the foothills, becoming a large lake nestled at the bottom. Trees lined the shores on the side of the foothills, more Dwarven buildings along the mountains. A large one stood out above the lake, almost hanging out over it. Like the others it was rounded, half-in and half-out of the mountain, the sides sloping up with a flat roof. A parapet ran along the edge, and Hall could see two large ballistae and a catapult on the roof. The small figures of Dwarves moved about on the roof and on the stone docks below jutting out into the lake. Small ships could be seen sailing and rowing across the surface.

Along the edge of the mountains, almost a hundred feet above the surface of the lake, a broad road had been cut. Wagons moved in both directions, a short stone wall along the edge. The road followed the curve of the mountains, staying high until it hit the far end of the lake where it sloped down toward the surface.

Hall felt the shift in the *Gale* as it started to slowly descend. They crossed over the surface of the lake, the ship's shadow rolling across the blue surface. Heads turned to watch them. There wasn't much airship traffic, only two other ships, which Hall found odd for a place renowned for their shipyards.

Which he saw just past the edge of the lake. A wide-open area, cleared of trees and quarried rock to create a bowl of steep-sided cliffs surrounding the flattened land. Thick, square, huge blocks of stone-lined the ground, raising the floor of the shipyard a couple feet above the roiling surface of the water. Buildings were carved into the side of the bowl, openings dotting the ground level and higher stories, large enough to push ships in and out. Hall could see the metal rails that led into each one, extending out into the docking area. Long docks of stone hung out over the lake, the majority of the arched buttresses supporting them hidden under the water. Two airships hovered in the air, tethered to the docks, cranes loading or unloading cargo from the holds. Hall placed them to be of Storvgardian design. He could see half-finished ships and others that were just the structure filling out the open space of the shipyards. A busy place, the front half near the lake devoted to merchant and passenger ships with the back half under the shadow of the cliffs being used for the ship building.

There was a slight turn to the *Gale*, the descending angle changing, as the Helmsman adjusted to get the ship lined up with an open berth at the end of the stone docks, no other ships near. Hall noticed that the crane there was larger. All cranes had leather tarps held together by thick ropes hanging from the wooden arm. A simple design. The crane at the dock the *Gale* was heading for had a larger crane and tarp with two smaller cranes at the ends. Hall realized it wasn't used for unloading cargo but lifting ships. A ramp, not noticeable until at the angle the *Gale* was flying, came out of the water with metal rails which led into the shipyards. A way to get a ship in need of repairs into the yards.

As they got closer, Hall could see the network of rails spread across the yard. It was hard to trace, so many rails moving back and forth, crossing and overlapping. It seemed impossible for a large ship to move across those rails, but Hall knew it happened. He saw Dwarven workers running across the shipyards, heading for the dock and the ramp, waiting for the *Gale* to land.

It was obvious to all those below that the *Twisted Gale* was limping along through the sky.

———

"Thank you," Hall said to Captain Hart, extending his hand.

He took it, holding one of the bags of coins Hall had given him in the other.

"I don't know how long repairs will take, but I will check with you before we leave," Hart said.

Hall nodded and Hart turned away, hurrying to deal with an impatient Dwarf a couple feet away. The Dwarf was the Dockmaster, in charge of all ships coming and going as well as coordinating repairs and launching of new ships. Even though the Axestorm Shipyards, called Axeport, were not that busy, the Dockmaster was still wanting to get Hart and the *Gale's* repairs into the schedule. Hall walked toward the others, Pike on his shoulder. They were gathered at the end of the dock, watching the activity in the shipyards, waiting on him.

"The Inn is that way," Hall said, pointing across the length of the shipyards to the last collection of windows and door built into the stone cliff.

Sabine looked over her shoulder and across the lake at the twin axes carved into the mountainside.

"There are better inns probably within the city itself," she suggested.

"We can't enter the city yet," Hall replied. "Something about getting our papers first. The Dockmaster. Hall said, pointing at the Dwarf down the docks that was now angrily arguing with Captain Hart "He said thatIt's too late in the day. We'll have to go to the Port Office in the morning."

"Of course," Sabine muttered.

The group walked across the wide shipyards, stepping over iron rails. The stone blocks under their feet were large, at least ten feet square, and set tightly together with barely a joint. There were no settlement issues, each corner and side level with the next. Hall had never seen such level pavers anywhere, not even real life. There was always one that was higher, a corner chipped away, or a loose block. But not at the Axestorm Shipyards.

No signs hung over any of the openings into the cliff wall, which varied greatly in size. Some were large enough for a ship to pass through, others just big enough for a person. Other openings were meant to be windows, only a couple filled with glass, heading up the stone wall to indicate upper stories. Nothing extended past the wall, everything flat.

Opening the last door on the wall, a stout wooden one

made of planks held by metal bolts, Hall could hear the noises coming from within confirming he had picked the right door. Pike stretched his wings, flapping and lifting off. Hall watched as the dragonhawk spiraled into the air, disappearing into the mountains to hunt. Stepping through the door, Hall saw a tavern, a room that was recognizable as such no matter where in the world it was. The room was large, the only light coming from the two windows to the right of the door, these filled with glass. A large hearth stood at the far end, two more on the side walls. No fires were lit as there was enough light from the windows and it was not that cold yet. Huntley was a lower realm, the island far from the sun's rays. It was never hot but it was not the cold season yet. The walls were worked stone, patterns carved into the walls depicting scenes of battle and ships flying over mountains. Paint had been applied to the lines, making them stand out and giving the gray stone some color. Next to the hearth on the far wall was an arched opening that led to a dark hallway. Two bars stood in the corners of the room with tables scattered throughout.

Surprisingly, the ceiling was wood, light-colored planks supported by dark and heavy looking timber beams.

Storvgardes, Gaels, a couple of Arash, and even a crew of Highborn sat at the tables and the two bars. They talked loud, laughing and drinking. The few Dwarves in the tavern were even louder. Hall had expected more Dwarves. It was their shipyards, after all. There must have been another tavern elsewhere nearby for the use of the shipyard workers. This was where the visitors came.

Hall led his companions through the tavern, weaving around tables and the short and stout Dwarven servers. He stopped at the bar in the left corner, noticing that the floor behind it was raised to get the shorter Dwarf to be head height with customers sitting at the human height bar counter.

"What can I do ye for?" the black-bearded Dwarf behind the bar asked, towel in hand as he cleaned a pewter mug.

"Rooms," Hall replied. "Food and drink."

The Dwarf glanced beyond Hall, eyes taking in the group. They focused on Roxhard, who was looking around the room before returning to Hall.

"Can do ye two rooms," he said, giving a price that Hall agreed to. "Ye'll be wanting to go up to the Hall, will ye not?" he asked, again focusing on Roxhard who didn't appear to hear the Innkeep.

Hall nudged his friend.

"Huh?" Roxhard asked, focusing on the Innkeep. "I'm sorry, what did you say?"

"I asked if ye would be wanting to go up to the Hall," the Innkeep growled, a little annoyed. "To yer clan rooms."

Panic came over Roxhard's face. Hall was about to speak up, but Roxhard took a deep breath, got control of his face, and answered the Innkeep.

"No," Roxhard said, not confidently. "Not tonight. I'll be staying with my companions."

The Innkeep studied Roxhard. There was curiosity in the Dwarf's face, questions he wanted to ask. *Was this going to be the first test of Roxhard's story?* Hall wondered. He had hoped it would be longer before they had to attempt it. He was worried that Roxhard wouldn't be able to pull it off effectively. Already Hall was seeing big differences between Roxhard and the Dwarves of Axestorm Hall. The speech patterns were different. The accent was basically the same, created and assigned by the game based on starting race, but Roxhard still talked like an American fourteen-year-old kid.

"Suit yerself," the Innkeep said with a shrug. "Take a table and I'll have one of the lasses bring ye the food and drink."

Hall looked out into the tavern, noticing that his strange group was drawing stares, and indicated a table off in the corner. The others, including Roxhard who looked relieved to move away from the Innkeep, started that way.

"I wonder if you could identify something for me?" Hall asked the Innkeep, who grunted an affirmative.

Reaching into his pouch, Hall felt the strange emptiness around his hand. It was an odd feeling, one he wasn't sure he liked. The pouch was much larger on the inside, feeling like a giant void. With a thought about what he was looking for, Hall felt it appear in his hands. He pulled out the set of folded airship plans he had looted from Cronet. The bundle was fairly large, wider than the mouth of the pouch, Hall looking away as the plans distorted and enlarged as they were pulled out.

Before he had left Skara Brae, Timmin had suggested he keep the plans secret. There were a half dozen shipbuilders in Axestorm Hall. The Administrator cautioned about showing the new style of airship to the designer's potential rivals. Better to go straight to the designer him or herself.

Carefully, only revealing the part with the rune that Timmin had identified as Axestorm Hall, he held it out to the Innkeep. Other runes and markings surrounded the crossed ax symbol that he knew. Hall was hoping the others would spell out who the designer was.

"Ship plans?" the Innkeep asked, recognizing what they were from just the few lines he could see.

"Do you know where I can find who these plans belong to?" Hall asked.

The Innkeep studied the runes, motioning Hall to reposition so he could get a better look. He ran a beefy finger along some of the text before turning a sharp-eyed glare on Hall.

"Where did ye get these?" he asked, a faint note of threat in his voice.

Hall wondered how to respond. The Innkeep was suspicious. He had recognized something in the writing. *Does he think I stole them?* Hall wondered. Did he tell the Innkeep the truth, which might result in the Dwarf requiring Hall to turn them over? Did he lie, which might not end up getting him any closer to the designer? Would the Innkeep demand Hall return them, right then and there, no matter how he answered?

"We found them as loot," Hall finally replied.

He didn't think lying to the Dwarf would be the right move, but he also wasn't going to reveal too much.

The Innkeep's gaze hardened. He seemed about to say something but stopped, the eyes softening.

"Bah," he barked, sounding like a kind of chuckle. "They shouldn't have lost them in the first place, eh?"

Hall smiled as the Innkeep slammed his fist on the counter, his laugh loud and long.

"Those plans there belong to the Battleforges," the Dwarf said once he stopped laughing. Why he was laughing, Hall wasn't sure. "That's their mark," he added, pointing at a small symbol next to the crossed axes. "One of the smaller shipbuilders. They spend more time tinkering with ships than actually building them."

QUEST COMPLETE!

The Innkeeper of the Axeport Lodgings has told you that the airship plans belong to a small shipbuilding clan named the Battleforges.

AIRSHIP MODEL X I

Travel to Huntley and discover who drafted the plans 1/1
Rewards: +100 Experience

You now know who drafted the plans in your possession. Return the airship plans to the Battleforge Shipbuilders.

AIRSHIP MODEL X II

Return the plans to the Battleforges 0/1
Rewards: +50 Experience, Unknown Reward x1

ACCEPT QUEST?

He wondered at the *Unknown Reward*. The last time he had that listed for a quest, he had received two new and previously unknown Skills. What would this one give him? Those had been from an Elite quest. This was not. He didn't think he'd get Skills this time.

Hall refolded the plans and placed them back in his pouch.

"Where is their shop?" he asked.

"Directly across," the Innkeep said, already stepping away from Hall. A Storvgarde down the bar had her hand raised, shaking an empty mug. "Last one on that side before the lake."

Turning away from the bar, Hall silently cursed. Of course, the shipbuilders he would be looking for would have been the closest to where they started. If he had known that, he could have gone directly there but now would have to wait for the morning. With a sigh, he threaded his way to the table in the corner. There were already plates of food and mugs of ale waiting.

CHAPTER THIRTEEN

CROSSING THE YARDS TOOK A LONG TIME AS THEY WERE VERY active in the morning. Ships were being loaded, wagons and carts on rails moving haphazardly across the space. They had to pause and wait as a large ship was pulled out of one of the openings, the entrance to one of the larger shipbuilders. A very large ship, three-masted and standing tall, was resting in a wooden frame attached to a wide and long flatbed. Ropes led from brackets to large animals that grunted and pulled. A dozen of them, arrayed in two long lines. Shaggy creatures, five or more times the size of Angus, Leigh's Highland cow. Hair hung down to the ground, dragging across it and covering tree trunk-like legs. Short and powerful, the creatures had huge heads with long horns curling off to the sides. Yaks from high up in the mountains.

Dwarves used large mountain rams as mounts, but the Yaks were their pack animals.

The ship was heavy, the Yaks struggling as they slowly moved the great ship out into the yards. Everyone stopped to watch, sailors marveling at the craftsmanship of the ship. Dwarves walked proudly in front of it, the designers and builders. Hall didn't know much about airships, but this one was obviously special. Three levels under the main deck, elevated forecastle, and sterncastle, a keel that wasn't as flat as normal. Two huge engines were mounted to the side, the sails furled and wrapped around the masts. He couldn't make out the name painted along the side.

Once it was past, Hall led Roxhard and Jackoby across the yard, stepping over rails and the piles of smelling offal the Yaks had left behind. Caryn and Sabine had remained behind in the Inn, sleeping in. Or so they had said. Hall assumed they just wanted some privacy after being stuck in the crowded *Twisted Gale* and the debris island for so long.

The outside of the Battleforges' shop was similar to all the others. Nothing fancy, no ornamentation. Hall had missed them before, but he now noticed that all the shops along the curved wall of the cliff had a small rune carved above the doors. The only signage. This one was a double-headed ax carved vertically with a flame behind. Both doors, the small and large, were closed.

Pushing open the door, Hall walked inside with Roxhard. Jackoby leaned back against the stone wall, eyes roaming the shipyards. He wasn't looking for trouble, the Firbolg was still amazed at the sights.

The inside of the shop was not what Hall had expected.

It was a large space, one giant room. Easily thirty feet high, a hundred feet deep and forty wide. Two iron rails led in, the large wooden doors notched around them. Stone buttresses were spaced down the walls, arches holding up the rough stone ceiling. Hall had expected to see a large ship being worked on, but there was nothing. Just a small, single-masted ship down at the far end, hidden in the dark. There were no piles of wood, nails, or any other parts that would indicate a ship being worked on.

Gaslamps lined the walls, every ten feet and about twenty

off the floor. There was plenty of light to illuminate any work, but it was obvious no work was being done or had been done in a long time. The small ship at the far end was in the dark, obviously pushed out of the way. Workbenches and desks, set at Dwarf height, lined one wall. Cabinets and shelves lined the other. Another small door was barely visible at the far end.

Hall heard a strange noise, something smacking against wood. Not a hammer, but more of an ax slicing into wood. It wasn't a regular pattern. They heard the thwack once, as they stood just inside, and then another a minute later. The third was twice as long. Hall led Roxhard toward the sound, which was coming from the dark far corner on the right.

There was light down there, not as much as the rest of the shop. As they got closer, Hall could see three Dwarves, two off to the side and one standing facing the wall. That one held a throwing ax and was moving his arm up and down, getting ready to throw. About twenty feet away, mounted to the wall was a large piece of wood planking. There were two other axes lodged into it, set in the dripping painted red lines set in a circular pattern. A bullseye.

The Dwarf cocked his arm back and threw it forward, releasing the ax. It spun, end over end, in a low arc. The ax head spun and slammed into the wood planking, closest to the center of the bullseye.

One of the Dwarves against the wall said something in their language, mocking words of short syllables and hard consonants. Hall didn't know the language and a glance at Roxhard showed that he did not either. The thrower responded, angry, barking a long response. The third joined in, yelling at both of the others.

Hall and Roxhard stopped a dozen feet away, watching the growing argument.

The three Dwarves formed a circle, shouting at each other. Hall was no judge of Dwarf age, but he thought them to all be about the same, a hundred or two hundred years old. One was blond, the other brown, and the last black-haired. Thick beards and long hair. Each was the spitting image of the other besides the hair. They barked and cursed at each other, pushing and shoving.

Hall coughed, trying to get their attention. It didn't work, their shouting just getting louder.

"Excuse me," Hall said, loudly.

The Dwarves still fought, now closer and in each other's faces. More shoving and pushing.

"Hey!" Hall yelled.

Still ignored. He glanced down at Roxhard, who shrugged.

"Don't be minding them," a voice said from across the room. It was female but still deep.

Hall tried to see the speaker but couldn't; the small airship, that was as dusty as he had assumed, was between them.

Small was a relative term, Hall realized as he looked at the bulk of the ship between him and the speaker. It was close to fifty feet in length, a one-story high stern castle that took up most of the back half with the single mast in front. It appeared to be able to hold a decent amount of cargo for its size. Hall could see the engine mount attached to the side.

"When they get like this, me brothers are useless."

A female Dwarf walked around the airship. She was shorter than the other three, four inches or so shorter than Roxhard. Her hair was blond, done in two thick braids that hung over her shoulders. Stout as were all Dwarves, she was softer in appearance with a cute and cheerful face. She rolled her large green eyes as she glanced at the three fighting Dwarves who were now rolling around on the ground wrestling, punching and kicking while still shouting curses.

"What can I do ye for?" she asked, her eyes lingering on Roxhard.

Barely visible through his thick beard, Roxhard's cheeks

grew red and he glanced away. The female Dwarf's smile widened.

"We're looking for the Battleforge Shipbuilders," Hall told her, glancing at the fighting brothers as they slammed into the airship making it rock.

"That be us," she replied. "I'm Gerdi. Those there are my brothers: Borden, Norden, and Korden."

The three brothers still fought, kicking and cursing, the pile now rolling away from the airship.

Gerdi said something to Roxhard in the Dwarven language. His attention was on the fighting brothers and didn't realize she was talking to him. She said it again and he turned, eyes widening in shock and fear. Roxhard took a step back, panicked, shaking his head.

She said something else in Dwarven, quieter, questioning.

"I... I... don't understand," Roxhard managed to get out.

Gerdi looked up at Hall, confused, her eyes returning to Roxhard who seemed to shrink away.

Hall sighed. He knew this moment was bound to happen and had just been hoping it would have been later. He had thought about leaving Roxhard in the Inn and wished he had.

"Ye donae understand yer own language?" Gerdi asked, surprised but also a little intrigued.

Roxhard didn't say anything, and Hall nudged the Dwarf with his boot, hoping the motion went unnoticed. Roxhard swallowed and took a deep breath. He started reciting, acting like he was drawing from memory and not naturally speaking. His dictation became smoother the more he talked, sounding more natural and not as mechanical.

"I wasn't born in a Dwarf settlement," he said, not meeting Gerdi's gaze. "My parents were killed by Trow raiders, and I was taken in as a child by Gael farmers. We lived outside of Grayhold on the island of Cumberland. When I was old enough, I joined the Essec Guards. Spent time with them before deciding I wanted to be on my own."

It was a good story, Hall knew. Simple enough and they had worked out more details if needed, but it explained the major points of why Roxhard wouldn't know Dwarf culture. Or their language.

"That ax is of Dwarven make," Gerdi mentioned, pointing at the battle ax hanging off Roxhard's shoulder.

It wasn't an accusation, more a question.

"My father's," Roxhard replied. "Dwarf father, I mean. My Gael father saved it for when I came of age."

Gerdi nodded, apparently buying the story. Or at least her curiosity was satisfied.

For now.

"What clan are ye?" Gerdi asked. "Sorry, I mean what clan were yer Dwarf Da and Ma."

"Stonefire," Roxhard answered without thinking.

Hall grimaced at seeing Gerdi's reaction. They really should have done more research into the name, but both had assumed it was a made-up clan chosen by the game with no connection to an existing NPC clan. It appeared they were wrong. Very wrong.

Gerdi's eyes were wide. The young Dwarf was shocked and surprised. It had not been an answer she had expected, and her reaction told Hall that apparently the Stonefires were of some importance or fame.

She was about to say more when another voice boomed out of the back corner, coming from what Hall thought was the office. Deep, craggy and old.

"What is going on out here?" it bellowed in common.

The voice was followed by an old Dwarf. His long beard and hair had gone to gray, a deep color that resembled that of stone. All of the Dwarf looked like he had been carved from stone. Wrinkles, like cracks, in the visible parts of his skin. A thick brow over small deep-set eyes. He moved like a younger Dwarf, no hitch or limp, no hesitation. There was strength still in the old shipbuilder.

He paused as he rounded the small airship, surprised at the two guests. Then his eyes quickly turned to the mass of fighting Dwarves.

"Lads," he said.

A single word, not spoken loudly, but somehow the three brothers heard it.

Instantly, they stopped fighting. Still pushing at each other in their haste to get up, they managed to separate and get to their feet. Each brushed himself off, still staring daggers at the others. They turned to face the old Dwarf, who Hall assumed to be the father, but stopped when they saw him and Roxhard.

"We have guests," the old Dwarf said with a sigh, rolling his eyes.

Gerdi just smiled and held back a laugh.

Skill Gain!
Identify Rank One +.1

Corben Battleforge
Master Shipbuilder

The old Dwarf was dressed in workman's clothes. Thick trousers, cotton shirt with a leather apron and tool belt. The apron was practically useless as Corben's thick beard covered most of it. The beard was braided, but there was so much to it that the braid was almost as wide as his chest.

Looking at the other four Dwarves, Hall could see the family resemblance in all of them.

Skill Gain!
Identify Rank One +.4

Gerdi Battleforge
Journeyman Shipbuilder

Borden Battleforge
Journeyman Shipbuilder

Norden Battleforge
Journeyman Shipbuilder

Korden Battleforge
Journeyman Shipbuilder

Congratulations!
You have gained Identify Rank Two.

With a last look at his sons, Corben turned to Hall.

"What can we do for ye?" he asked. "As ye can see, we're not currently commissioned to build a ship, but I must warn ye: us Battleforges can build ye a grand airship, but we donae have the capacity of some of the others," he finished and motioned at the shop. There was a note of sadness to his voice as he spoke.

Hall wondered if the Battleforges had fallen on rough times or if it was something else. It was odd to see the shop empty, not even the small ship was being worked on.

Reaching into his pouch, Hall removed the plans. He unfolded them so that Corben could see. Gerdi and the three brothers had crowded in close. The brothers glanced at Roxhard but didn't say anything. Each of them studied the blueprints, Corben leaning in closer. At the same time, all five pairs of Dwarven eyes widened in shock.

"Hey," Borden, the blond-haired brother barked.

"That's," Norden, the brown-haired one followed.

"Ours," finished Korden, who belonged to the black hair.

The three of them glared at each other, about to start pushing and arguing when a glare from their father stopped them.

"Where did ye get this, lad?" Corben asked softly. His old eyes roamed the plans, taking them all in. There was recognition in those eyes, as if seeing an old friend. His mouth moved silently as he read the various notes, all probably written by him.

Hall held the plans out to him. Corben looked up in surprise, hesitantly reaching out and taking them. There was joy to the old Dwarf, the family around him practically beaming. It was like Hall had returned a long-lost family heirloom.

Maybe he had.

"A man named Cronet had them in a chest," Hall started to explain but stopped.

Anger filled Corben's gaze as the Dwarf stepped back. He was almost spitting, growling. "Cronet?" he roared. Corben looked old, but Hall could see the fight in the Dwarf. He would have been a terror in combat when younger. Most likely still would be. "That thieving dung. Where is he?"

The reaction took Hall by surprise. He hadn't expected a direct line between Cronet and the Battleforges. He had assumed that Cronet had gotten the plans from someone else that had gotten them from another person and so on down the chain to the Dwarves.

"Cronet is dead," Hall stated.

Corben stopped his tirade, glancing at Hall.

"Truly?"

Hall nodded.

"You killed him?"

"Yes," Hall said, giving a brief recap of the events in Silverpeak. Corben and the others listened intently.

"Good," Corben said, folding the plans. "Bastard got what he deserved."

He went to hand the plans back to Hall, who held up his hands.

"Those are yours," he said.

"Nay, lad," Corben told him, pushing the plans back toward Hall. "Ye won 'em fair and square."

"Take them," Hall insisted.

Corben nodded and Hall could see that the old Dwarf was truly thankful. It was as if something long lost was returned.

QUEST COMPLETE!

You have returned the ship plans to the original designer, Corben Battleforge. You can tell the old Master Shipbuilder is thankful.

AIRSHIP MODEL X II

Return the plans to the Battleforges 1/1
Rewards: +50 Experience, Unknown Reward x1

"What can I do to thank ye?" Corben asked, still staring at the plans held almost reverently in his hands. "I donae have much gold, but…"

Hall held up his hands, stopping Corben. He hadn't immediately gotten the *Unknown Reward* from the quest but thought he would soon. It seemed there was more to the quest, the reward possibly coming after the conversation. He didn't think it would be just gold and the *Unknown Reward* hinted that he might get the airship after all. Hall had started to have doubts when he saw the emptiness of the Battleforges' workshop.

"I don't want gold," Hall said.

"Ye must want something," Corben said, almost pleading.

Hall pointed at the plans in the Dwarf's hand.

"That," he said.

———

"Do ye know anything about these?" Corben asked, looking down at the plans thoughtfully.

His children had stepped back, watching. Gerdi was still staring at Roxhard, her eyes had barely left him. For his part, Roxhard was trying hard to not stare back.

"Nothing," Hall replied. "We just found them in the bottom of a chest, and the Administrator at my town recognized the Axestorm Hall mark."

"Yer town?" Corben asked and looked at Hall in a new light. His eyes went blank for a second, Hall recognizing the signs of someone using the *Identify* Skill. "Ah, I see now. Sorry, Lord," he said and gave a slight bow with his head. "These plans are useless now," he began and glanced out the large doors and into the yard. "Did ye see that large ship that was hauled out this morning? Those buggers looking all proud? Bah," he said and spit on the ground. "Honorless dung beetles."

"What kind," Borden interjected angrily.

"Of Dwarf," Norden added, a little angrier.

"Steals plans," Korden finished, angrier than his brothers.

"The cursed Oakenstones built our ship," Gerdi growled. "Parading it around like it was theirs. They were already the largest shipbuilder clan in Axeport. No need to steal from us. But they up and did it anyway."

Corben raised his hands, moving them in a gesture to calm his children.

"That bastard Cronet came down here looking for an airship," Corben explained, calmer than his children. "Came to us, heard we had a new and revolutionary design. I worked out a deal with him and next thing I know, the bastard stole the plans and sold them to the Oakenstones." Corben sighed, shaking his head. "I went to the King but without these," he continued and held up the plans. "I had no evidence and was laughed out of the Assembly."

"Business fell apart after that," Gerdi explained.

Hall felt sorry for them. It was a common story, someone higher up the chain stealing and profiting from those lower down, taking their hard work and benefiting from it by thievery.

"I assume that ship was commissioned for Cronet?" Hall asked.

He pictured the ship and imagined a fleet of them, armed to the teeth, sailing over the lands of Edin. Cronet had wanted to take over Silverpeak Keep, set himself up as ruler, and Hall's fear had been that he would then expand to take over all of Edin. Including Skara Brae. The airship only reinforced that idea. Hall was doubly glad he had removed Cronet and stopped his plans.

"Aye," Corben muttered, a sad sound at first but then the Dwarf brightened and chuckled, realizing what Hall was leading to. "But he's dead now, isn't he? Won't be paying the rest of his bill."

The three brothers looked at each other, not sure they understood, but Gerdi did. She started laughing with her father.

"When they fly the ship all the way up there, won't be anyone to take it," Gerdi said around her laughter. "They have this huge expensive ship and no customer."

Now the brothers got it and started laughing. Hall looked at Roxhard, who shrugged. The Battleforges were an odd bunch. The laughter finally died down, and Corben looked at Hall seriously.

"Ship like that is expensive," he said. "We can't build it ourselves. I'd need to hire extra hands and as you can see, we're short on materials."

"How expensive?" Hall asked, afraid to know the answer and wishing he had kept more of the gold they had given Captain Hart.

Corben looked up at the rough stone ceiling, thick fingers playing with his braided beard. His mouth moved as he mumbled to himself, adding and subtracting figures. The fingers on the hand not playing with his beard tapped against his leg. Behind him, Borden whispered something to Korden that Norden didn't hear. This caused Norden to push Borden, who pushed back. Korden tried to get between them and got shoved, so he naturally shoved back. The three of them fell to the ground. Gerdi took her eyes off Roxhard and sighed, watching her brothers brawl. She lazily kicked at them, causing one of the three to yelp. That made Gerdi chuckle.

It just made Hall wonder who he was getting involved with.

Finally, Corben arrived at a number. It was higher than Hall had expected. Way higher. The gold he had didn't come close, but did the Sun Emerald and other jewels? He stopped before even offering them to Corben. Why was he so set on that particular ship? Now that he had seen what it really looked like, it was far more than he needed or should be spending gold on. He thought about the mega-rich back in the real world that bought these huge yachts for one person that were the same size as cruise ships that carried a hundred people. It was insane and he was falling into that trap. That ship was too much. The gold and jewels could be better spent on materials needed for Skara Brae.

And he still hadn't gotten the *Unknown Reward* from the quest.

"Just a bit out of my price range," Hall admitted.

Corben nodded, as it was the answer he had expected. The old Dwarf looked at Hall shrewdly.

"What do you be needing an airship for, lad?" Corben asked.

"My village of Skara Brae is isolated," Hall explained. "Couple weeks of hard travel overland to the nearest city so getting supplies is difficult. We'll have a dock for airships, but we can't be forced to rely on others. At some point, we'll need our own."

Corben was nodding.

"Aye, that you will," the shipbuilder said, his voice drifting off as he became lost in thought. "Ye donae need a large ship. Nae like this," he said and waved the plans in his hands. "Ye need something smaller and fast. But it needs to be able to take on some cargo. Large orders ye would still want a bigger ship but for emergencies and getting ye adventurers around. Something like a cog would do ye."

He turned and looked at the dark ship to the side. Walking over, Corben ran his hands along the curved hull. Turning back to Hall, he was smiling.

"Ye need this," he said proudly and thumped the hull with his open hand. The noise echoed through the large room. "She'll do ye for what ye be wanting. And not bleed ye dry."

Walking back to Hall, Corben clapped him on the shoulder and chuckled. The hit almost caused Hall to stagger.

"Here's a secret, lad," Corben said with a grin. "The big ships cost ye two arms and three legs to just maintain. Not even repairs, but just in regular maintenance." He paused, cocking his head in thought. "Well, maybe that be not accurate. It's really five arms and seven legs." Corben laughed at his own joke.

Hall walked toward the small ship. A cog, Corben had called it. He left Roxhard standing alone and Gerdi took a couple steps closer to the Dwarf Warden. Roxhard tried, and failed, to pretend not to notice. Running his hand down the wood hull, Hall walked the length of the ship. It wasn't a big ship, but would it be big enough? Corben was right. They didn't need a freight ship, just something capable of hauling a small amount of cargo and most often just passengers. He turned back to look at the old Dwarf.

"Crew of six, the cabin can sleep more. Can also modify

the cargo hold to add more sleeping space," Corben said, reciting some of the specs. "This girl here, she has some of the elements I put into this design," he continued and waved the ship plans again. "Just on a smaller scale. She's fast, light, and can carry more than a normal ship of her size. Also has some attachment points for weapons."

The way Corben was talking, Hall was starting to get an idea of what the quest's *Unknown Reward* was going to be.

"And the cost?" he asked.

Corben smiled, walking over to him.

"She's maybe half done," the old Dwarf started. He paused in front of Hall, looking up. "Tell ye what, since I owe ye, if ye pay for the materials then she'll be yers."

He held out his hand, which Hall took. The two shook.

QUEST COMPLETE!

Master shipbuilder Corben Battleforge has agreed to complete work on the cog in his shop for your use. You just have to pay for materials.

A SHIP OF OUR OWN I

Commission the construction of an airship 1/1
Rewards: +100 Experience

Once complete, take possession of your new airship.

A SHIP OF OUR OWN II

Claim ownership of an airship 0/1
Rewards: Airship, +100 Experience

ACCEPT QUEST?

"Deal," Corben said, and Hall echoed. "We can get started right away, will just need to get the materials…" he trailed off, waiting on Hall.

Reaching into his inventory pouch, Hall brought out a bag of jewels. He had consolidated them all into one bag and it was a heavy one. Corben's eyes lit up as he saw the bulges in the bag, hearing the rock hitting rock sounds as Hall untied it and reached into the bag. He searched around inside and found the one he wanted.

Hall held the Sun Emerald between his thumb and forefinger, watching it reflected in Corven's eyes.

"Will this do?"

CHAPTER FOURTEEN

Now that the business was out of the way, Corben finally seemed to notice Roxhard. Or more accurately, he noticed that his daughter kept staring at the other Dwarf.

"And who are ye?" he asked. Not unkindly but there was a bit of steel to his tone. Hall figured the old Dwarf had used *Identify* on Roxhard but wasn't sure what the result had been. The question, though, was one that fathers of daughters had asked no matter the world, digital or real, and no matter the race.

"He's a Stonefire, Da," Gerdi blurted out.

The three brothers behind Corben stopped their fighting. They all stood up, crowding in close again.

Corben studied Roxhard intently, the younger Dwarf wilting under that gaze.

"Ye aren't from Axestorm," Corben said finally. "So how are ye a Stonefire?"

"He was raised by Gael," Gerdi said before anyone else could say anything. "His Da and Ma were killed when he was a babe."

Corben and the three brothers all shared similar expressions. Ones of shock, surprise, and pity. The old Dwarf recovered quickly, leaning in close, the fingers of his left hand playing with his braided beard while his right hand tapped against his leg.

"Now, isn't that interesting?" he said as he stared at Roxhard. "What do ye know of yer clan and heritage, lad?"

"Raised by humans," Borden exclaimed.

"How shameful," Norden continued.

"That's horrible," Korden finished.

It was Gerdi's turn to flash them a glare. Surprisingly, the three brothers backed down from their sister's angry stare. For his part, Roxhard tried to stand tall and proud. He did mostly, but anyone would have a hard time under Corben's intent gaze.

"Next to nothing," Roxhard admitted, wincing somewhat as Corben's eyes widened even more.

"That can be fixed, can't it, Da?" Gerdi asked, drawing a nod from Corben.

"Aye," he replied with a grin. "That it can."

He motioned Hall and Roxhard to follow him as he headed toward the front of the shop. The three brothers started to follow, but a single glance over his shoulder stopped them. Gerdi continued walking and smiled smugly at them. It didn't take long before the three were pushing and shoving each other again, and Hall could hear a crash as they fell to the ground wrestling. Corben stopped in front of the large doors. Thirty feet high, twenty feet wide, thick wooden planks held together by iron bands. Hall was amazed that each plank was a single long piece. The doors were two leaves, meeting in the middle, with a single crossbar set at Dwarf height. Without struggling, Corben lifted the heavy looking beam and set it aside. He pushed the doors open, the large leaves moving silently and easy on hidden hinges. Only opening them a couple feet, he stepped out into the hall, followed by the others.

Hall looked to the side and saw Jackoby notice them. The Firbolg pushed himself off the wall and walked over to join them. Corben looked the large Firbolg up and down, a quick glance at Hall, who nodded, confirming that Jackoby was with them. Corben promptly ignored the Firbolg. The shipbuilder's gaze lingered on the docks where the large airship from earlier, the one built by the Oakenstones, was in the water and still on the rails. It appeared the Dwarves were having some trouble getting the engines to ignite, the ship held in place by the cranes. Corben shook his head ruefully, lost in thinking about what could have been. It was a minute or so later when he smiled, big and wide.

"Ha," he barked, drawing Gerdi's attention and pointing. "They can't even get the engines going. That's the problem with just looking at plans," he said sagely, looking up at Hall to make sure the Skirmisher understood. "Ye get just the details but not the soul. There's more that goes into making a ship than the plans say."

He stared at the massive ship for another minute before shaking his head and muttering something in Dwarvish. Hall glanced at Gerdi to see her looking at her father with sad eyes. Not pitying, but understanding, acceptance, and grief. Hall didn't know much about the Dwarves beyond that they were a proud race and if his visit to the Assembly, whatever that was, had gone the way Corben described, the Master Shipbuilder would have been embarrassed and somewhat disgraced. No matter how badly the Oakenstone's failed with the ship, nothing would replace Corben's lost honor.

"Ye saw those buildings along the shoreline between the doors and the falls?" Corben asked, pointing at the lake and the collection of structures just below the main gate to Axestorm Hall. "That there are the halls of the Stonefire. Old Matron Lydi runs the clan nowadays, has for a hundred years."

Hall remembered seeing the structures as they had flown

over the lake in the *Twisted Gale*. Round buildings built off the face of the mountain, domed roofs. There had been stone docks out into the lake, the buildings built into and out of the mountainside.

"Ye should go and see her, lad," Corben said turning to Roxhard. "Learn of ye heritage."

Roxhard looked nervous, extremely so. This was pushing what he and Hall had talked about. How would the story they had created for Roxhard hold up to the actual Stonefire clan itself?

"Might as well," Gerdi said. "Yer going to be here awhile waiting on the ship."

Your companion Roxhard has been offered a quest that you are eligible to participate in.

Roxhard was raised by humans and knows nothing of his heritage. Accompany him as he meets the clan of his ancestors, the Stonefires.

A DWARF IS A DWARF NO MATTER WHAT I
Accompany Roxhard to meet Matron Lydi of the Stonefires 0/1
Reward: +50 Stonefire Clan reputation; +25 Experience

Waiting on Roxhard to Accept or Refuse Quest.

Hall read the quest prompt and then reread it. It appeared that the quest was Roxhard's, and he was just along for the ride. Was this similar to what Roxhard, Sabine, and the others got when they followed the quests he received? The rewards were lower as well. Less reputation and experience.

He glanced at Roxhard and saw his friend staring out across the lake, nervous and scared. The Dwarf was hesitant. Hall laid a hand on Roxhard's shoulder, not able to touch through the leather shoulder pauldron, but the pressure was still reassuring and comforting.

"You got this," Hall said and Roxhard nodded.

*Roxhard has Accepted **A DWARF IS A DWARF NO MATTER WHAT I***

ACCEPT QUEST?

Hall quickly accepted the quest. He glanced at Jackoby, who nodded. He had gotten it as well.

"Yer going to need to prove yerself, lad," Corben said gently. "The Matron might not be believing yer word."

Under his hand, Hall felt Roxhard tense. He pushed down, trying to let Roxhard know it was okay. They could handle whatever was to come.

Roxhard nodded.

"Ye'll need to enter Axestorm and go down to the Stonefire halls. There is no outside entrance that strangers can use. Ye got plenty of day left, but I'd hurry if ye were thinking of going today."

"No reason to put it off," Hall said, knowing that Roxhard would push to wait. But Hall didn't want the fourteen-year-old doing nothing but thinking about the meeting. Over and over. It would do more harm, just making the already nervous teen even more anxious.

"True," Roxhard stammered, forcing the words out.

"They'll be needing an introduction," Gerdi pointed out and Corben nodded. "I can do it. Ye won't be needing me here today."

Already nervous, on the point of panic, at Gerdi's suggestion, Roxhard paled and looked like he was ready to run away.

Hall and his companions, along with Gerdi, made their way up the long road. To their right was the steep slope of the mountain towering high above them. It was hot, the sun to the east shining directly onto the road with no shade. The heat soaked into the stone of the mountain, reflecting off. It would be dark once the sun went beyond the mountains, casting the road in shade, but Hall imagined it would stay warm enough for hours after as the ambient heat leached out of the mountain.

They hugged the wall, carts and mounted travelers passing in both directions. The road was wider than Hall had thought, able to take three wagons side by side. That width allowed for the two-way traffic and some space to get around the walkers. Of which, there were more than the wagons and mounted. Which Hall had found odd at first. The road from Axeport to Axestorm Hall was long, a couple of miles, and it would take an hour, if not more, to cross by walking. Taking a wagon or mount of some kind, Hall had only seen Rams and Yaks so far, would cut the travel time down a lot. Gerdi had laughed at him. She'd muttered something about weak humans and walking. Hall had caught enough of it that he didn't bring the subject up again.

Sabine did. A couple of times. Especially when she'd brush dust away from another passing wagon. The road was smoothed stone, but there was still dust and dirt kicked up by the rolling wheels and pounding hooves. Gerdi had started to ignore the Witch, had almost instantly, not liking Sabine from the start. The young Dwarf chatted with Caryn, the two clicking right away. Which was also causing Sabine's annoyance to rise.

Both women had been eager to see more of Axestorm Hall.

The first part of the hike had been the hardest. The road was a couple hundred feet above the lake, which put it the same above the shipyards. The Dwarves had kept the road's pitch as shallow as possible, but it was still a long climb by foot. Hall was tempted to walk to the other side of the road, along the low stone wall and look down into the lake far below, but the traffic prevented it. The wagons heading to Axeport kept tight to the wall, leaving no room to walk.

Once it leveled out, the walking became easier if still boring. Nothing to see but the mountain and the road. All the travelers were Dwarves, Hall and friends getting a lot of attention and curious stares.

For her part, Gerdi seemed to bask in that attention. Hall wondered if her father, Corben, would have approved. If the Battleforges had suffered a loss in honor due to what had happened at the Assembly, they should have been keeping a low profile. Gerdi seemed to want the other Dwarves to know the Battleforges were bringing non-Dwarves into Axestorm. Hall sighed. Dwarven politics was not something he wanted to get involved in. He just wanted his airship and to return home to Skara Brae.

And to Leigh.

He was missing her. It was an ache, growing stronger every day. Not having a way to communicate with her was the worst. He had come from a world with cellphones and instant messaging. No one was unreachable no matter where they were. Sky Realms Online had a postal service, a letter sent from one office somehow making its way to another office many unconnected islands away. He had seen evidence that the system still worked Post-Glitch. He had sent a message to Sabine on that first day, writing it in Grayhold and she had received it in River's Side. But both were on the same island. Maybe the service no longer worked from island to island? Hall knew he would need to start running some tests. And to figure out how to get a Postmaster in Skara Brae. Was that something the village could even have? How would he even go about finding out if it was possible?

They walked in silence, most of them. Caryn and Gerdi kept chatting away. Hall heard Roxhard's name mentioned many times. Each time the Dwarf seemed to jump. Hall was starting to worry. It was becoming obvious that Gerdi had some interest in Roxhard. Why, he wasn't sure. He hoped it wasn't because she was seeing him as an oddity, a curiosity. If that was true, Roxhard could be hurt. Hall remembered being fourteen and how rough a time it could be. Especially when starting to navigate interactions with girls or boys or relationships. If the interest was genuine, Roxhard could still be hurt in the long run. Gerdi had to be at least a hundred years old, mentally and physically. Roxhard looked older but was still a teenager. Any relationship between the two would be awkward.

Taking a deep breath, Hall tried to focus on something else. Thinking about relationships was giving him a headache. His and Leigh's, Sabine and Caryn, whatever was going to happen with Gerdi and Roxhard.

Looking over his shoulder to make sure no wagon or rider was approaching, he stepped out into the middle of the road. From there, he could see down the length of the road, which was relatively straight, only curving out when it got near the waterfall. There, at the far end, he could just make out a dark opening. A cave. The entrance to Axestorm Hall.

The noise of the waterfall was deafening. Cold spray hit the side of the mountain, mist filling the air. The ground was covered in a thin layer of moisture, puddles in the lower areas of the road. Wagons and hooves splashed the water, throwing more into the air and adding mud. Hall couldn't hear any talking over the roar of the falls.

Looking up, he couldn't see the top, the sheet of water lost in the shadows of the mountains. *It had to be a couple hundred feet up*, he thought. Fed from somewhere deeper in the mountains, the falls were cold, never warming up.

The cave entrance was almost flush with the edge of the falls, a couple feet in. A dark hole leading into the depths of the mountain. Hall could feel the mist as they got closer, clinging to his face and leather armor. He pulled up the hood of his cloak, shielding himself from the splashing. He could still feel the cold water as it struck his bare arms, causing a shiver.

Traffic had slowed the closer they got and came to a stop just outside the cave entrance. Hall could see glowing globes of gas lamps attached to the smooth walls, a line of them illuminating the entrance to Axestorm Hall.

Square gray blocks, an angled capstone at the top, framed the opening. There had once been runes and carvings in the blocks, but constant exposure to the falls had worn them away. The tunnel beyond was carved square. Floor, walls, and ceiling all smooth. The floor showed grooves, a result of centuries of use. Once past the opening, the tunnel widened, gaining an extra five feet or so on either side.

"Donae," Gerdi said, Hall able to hear her now that the tons of stone around them deadened the sound of the falls. Caryn had taken a step toward the new width, meaning to get out of the way of the wagons. "That's fer the guards."

Sure enough, as Hall looked down that space between the wagons and wall, he saw armored Dwarves standing at attention. They were wearing the first plate armor Hall had seen in the game for a long time. Players, and most NPCs, could wear only Light Armor and Medium Armor. Light was defined as leather or hide armor, no iron or other metal. Chain mail was the extent of Medium Armor, at least for the chest. Shoulder Pauldrons could be metal, iron or something else. Iron plates were worn on the upper legs, attached to leather pants. Iron boots and gloves and sometimes helms. In the case of Firbolgs, like Jackoby, a form of pliable and

204 • TROY OSGOOD

strong wood was substituted for the metal. Ironwood or
similar.

The theory was that full plate armor was too bulky and
heavy to wear out in the wilds. It took too long to get into in
the mornings, made too much noise, and wore a Player's
Vitality down just by wearing it.

These Dwarves wore full plate chests. They still wore
leather leggings with the iron plates and bolts, but their upper
bodies were fully encased in iron. Thick pauldrons, solid-
looking helms, gloves with overlapping wrist protection and a
full iron chestpiece. Shields were held in front of them,
diamond-shaped that would cover the Dwarf's whole body. In
their dominant hands, each Dwarf held a halberd with a
double-headed battleax over their shoulders. The helms were
open-faced, showing the Dwarf's carved from stone faces,
which stood impassively as if truly stone. From the top of each
helm were curling rams horns, detailed to look like bone.

Formidable looking guards.

Skill Gain!
Identify Rank Two +.1

Axestorm Hall Guardian (white)

Even though Hall knew all their gear was of excellent
quality and they would all be well-trained fighters, there was
still something overtly ceremonial about them. Why were they
needed? Who, or what, could attack this entrance to
Axestorm? Any invaders would have to first fight their way
through the shipyards and run down the road, exposed the
whole way. He hadn't seen any defenses along the road, but
Hall knew there would be traps of some kind.

The chances of any attacking force making it to this tunnel
were slim.

So why the guards?

And why so many?

They lined both sides of the tunnel, one standing under each of the gas lamps, which were mounted every twenty feet.

Hall finally decided that the guards were just part of the game's design. It was one of those things that leaned toward form over function. Looking cool rather than making real sense. There were a lot of those elements in Sky Realms Online. No matter how immersive the developers, Electronic Storm, had tried to make it, there had always been some elements done more for the mechanics of the game or the aesthetics. This was one of those elements.

Because the armored guards standing at silent and motionless attention did look formidable.

And cool.

Hall tried not to stare at the first as they walked past. The Dwarf's eyes were constantly in motion, small movements of the head as he scrutinized every person walking into the tunnel. The face didn't change expression, the Dwarf focused. NPC guards, at least in the old game, had served no purpose. They were there, always there. No life outside of being a guard. Hall assumed these did have a life, fully fleshed-out NPCs like others he had encountered. How did they manage to stay alert all day when they just stood there, staring at lines of people?

Slow-moving lines.

Hall glanced ahead, down the long tunnel where the line disappeared into an open set of doors. Smaller doors, more crowded. More guards. It was a checkpoint of some kind, Hall realized, watching people shuffle forward and stop. They talked to an official-looking Dwarf, maybe argued a bit, and then moved on. Unlike the Guards, that Dwarf wore robes of a dark blue with gray trim.

"Is it always like this?" Caryn asked Gerdi.

"Aye," the young shipbuilder replied. "There's been talk of widening the entrance, adding more inspectors, but it never happens." She shrugged, shifting her feet in impatience.

The line moved quicker than Hall had thought it would. Not as quick as he wanted, but quick enough. A wagon just ahead moved through the opening, the inspector glaring at it. There had been a very loud and vocal argument between the wagon's owner and the inspector, all spoken in Dwarvish. Gerdi had winced a couple of times, and Hall had wondered if it was going to come to blows. The guards never shifted, used to this sort of occurrence. Finally, with one last word, the wagon driver lifted his reins and spurred his Yak team on and into the deeper corridors of Axestorm.

Skill Gain!

Identify Rank Two +.1

Axestorm Customs Inspector (white)

The Inspector, an older Dwarf with long gray hair and beard done up in multiple braids, turned to look at the next in line, Hall and his companions. The Dwarf's eyes widened in surprise at the mixed group, focusing on Roxhard and then recognizing Gerdi.

"What do ye bring to us today, lass?" he asked, his voice rough but not unkind. The eyes roamed the group, lingering on Jackoby. He looked the Firbolg up and down, seeming to sneer at the wooden weapons and armor. A thick medallion hung on a gold chain around the Dwarf's neck, positioned over his thick beard. Some kind of badge of office, Hall assumed. As the Dwarf moved, Hall could hear the clink of metal under the robe. Hall reassessed his assumption of the Dwarf. He figured the Inspector to be a clerk, but this one was every bit the warrior the guards were.

"Friends of me Pa," Gerdi replied. "And a long lost Stone-fire," she added with a mischievous smile.

Eyes widened quickly before narrowing as the Inspector studied Roxhard. The eyes were measuring and Roxhard did good not to shrink under the intense stare. Instead, Roxhard stood straighter, eyeing the Inspector with a look that dared him to say something. Nodding, the Inspector turned back to Gerdi.

"Pass on through," he said and waved them on as if Gerdi's revelation was no big deal, his attention already turning to the next in line.

Hall saw through the act. He knew the Inspector was intrigued, and as soon as the shift was over and he could go to one of the many taverns in Axestorm, he would start talking about the lost Stonefire Dwarf. The story would spread across the Dwarf city.

Which is what Hall now realized Gerdi wanted. Or, more accurately, her father wanted. Hall wasn't sure if the Battle-forges believed the story of Roxhard's parents being Stonefires, but soon, it wouldn't matter. Corben wanted the story to spread. And it would, like wildfire. Matron Lydi would be hard-pressed to deny Roxhard after the story spread through the city. A side benefit would be the increased attention the Battleforges would get for being the ones to find the lost Stone-fire. By having Gerdi start the rumor, Corben was ensuring that his clan would reap some benefit.

Once through the doors, they entered a large and open room. Numerous openings led off the domed space. Buttresses stood out from the walls, one between each open-ing, curving up the dome and meeting at the top. Where all the supporting buttresses met, a large lamp hung giving off a soft glow that illuminated the room. A curved dish, the lamp was made of a clear stone that let the light through and reflected it, making it greater. Chains supported the dish, hanging from the stone ceiling, which contained numerous small glowing crystals.

It wasn't bright or harsh, the glow easy on the eyes but still providing enough light to see the details of the room. Each opening was arched, carvings along the edges with single large runes at the top. The floor was made of large stone slabs, a brownish color giving some contrast to the gray walls.

The travelers coming in from Axeport moved quickly, not bothering to glance at the directional runes above the openings, each already knowing where they were going.

"This way," Gerdi said and led them straight through the room.

Hall didn't know what the rune above the opening said as it was in the rune language of the Dwarves. He didn't have time to ask as Gerdi led them on quickly. The tunnel was only wide enough for a single wagon, but Hall saw no evidence that one ever came down this way. No ruts were worn into the stone slabs of the floor. The walls were exposed stone, worked smooth, with small gas lamps every ten feet or so. An arched ceiling hung ten feet or so over their heads, stone blocks fit tightly together. Every twenty feet down the hundred-foot length were support beams of thick stones along the wall and ceilings. A bright light down at the end led them on. They passed a couple of Dwarves walking, dressed in the clothes of workmen, each stopping to stare at the odd group.

Almost near the end, but far enough back that they could not see out the opening, Gerdi stopped them. She turned to face them, that mischievous smile on her face.

"How many of ye have been to Axestorm before?" she asked.

Hall glanced at the other Players, who had undoubtedly been here before pre-Glitch. Except for Caryn, who had only been playing a total of three hours before the incident. Sabine and Roxhard shook their heads, acknowledging that their previous knowledge was wrong. Hall also shook his head no.

Gerdi's smile widened.

"It's always fun seeing a newcomer's first view," she said and led them on the last two dozen feet.

CHAPTER FIFTEEN

HALL HAD PREPPED HIMSELF. HE THOUGHT ABOUT WHAT HE had seen of Axestorm Hall before, imagining how it could have changed. Every other city had gotten bigger, turning into real cities instead of the game version. He imagined how that would be applied to Axestorm.

He could never have imagined what he saw as he stepped out of the opening.

The mountain had been carved out, sloping down from a high top lost in shadows far above. The bottom was immense, over a hundred feet across and they weren't even on the lowest floor. *How wide a diameter must it be at the very top*, Hall thought. Buildings lined each level going up the slope. Multiple openings, exterior stairs leading to higher levels. Some of the structures were flush with the mountains, others built-out. And through it all the open center. Low stone walls lined the center, some areas jutting out.

Hall stared up and up, seeing birds flying from ring to ring, so high up that details were lost. *How high up?* Hall wondered, trying to count rings and stopping at twenty-five with more still to go. The way the rings widened as they rose made it difficult to follow.

Wide and ornamental stone stairs stood at the four directions, right at the edge of the opening. This main central level ran to the stairs, but as they rose higher and higher with the rings moving further and further away from the center, there were long bridges connecting the stairs to the rings. He saw that the stair towers from this level stopped five or so levels above, with a new set just barely visible rising up another ten levels but built somewhat closer to the rings of that level. It continued like that until the stairs were lost in the shadows above.

Statues were everywhere, some set on the walls around the perimeter of the center opening, others against the walls of the mountain. No signs hung from any of the buildings, just runes carved above wooden doors. What had to be windows lined the buildings facing the center, torch and gas lamps visible through the openings. Large metal poles were set into the railing, holding gas lamps aloft, with more set against the walls.

Hall walked to the railing, which stood only three feet high, Dwarf height. Carefully he leaned out, looking down another ten or more stories, each ring shrinking beneath him. Down at the very bottom, he could see a bright red glow and feel the heat rising up even at this distance. The Great Forge of Axestorm.

"Holy," he started and just stopped. No words were adequate to describe his awe.

Axestorm Hall was the largest of the Dwarven settlements, the capital of their widespread kingdom. And it showed. This was their crowning achievement.

He heard the noise before he saw it, drawing his attention. A splashing and crashing sound, like the waterfall outside but not as loud. Turning he saw the source of the noise to the left of the opening where his awestruck friends still stood. Water falling through an opening above and down to the next level through another wide opening. Somehow the Dwarves had diverted part of the immense waterfall outside into their city. It crashed down from somewhere above, through all the rings and most likely down to the forge below.

And the number of Dwarves was staggering. They were everywhere. Dark-skinned, light-skinned, every shade of hair and all of the males bearded. He could see almost a hundred on this level alone. There would be thousands living in Axestorm Hall. The noise was loud, deep and gravelly voices echoing across the stone. Hundreds of voices talking and barking, rising and falling. It was hard to tell where each voice came from, this level or those above.

"Something, isn't it?" Gerdi asked with a chuckle as she walked over to stand next to Hall, the others followed.

He just nodded.

"How long does it take to walk all the way up?" Roxhard asked, staring at the stairs, thinking the same thing they all were.

They had already been walking a couple miles from the shipyards, and none were looking forward to walking up thousands of stairs.

Gerdi laughed.

"No one uses the stairs," she said, motioning them to follow her. "Not anymore."

She led them to the back of the hall, directly in line with the stair towers. Two large openings faced them, square, framed in small brown stones against the gray of the mountain. Beyond was nothing but darkness, the shape of smoothed and worked stone visible. Open shafts heading up and down. Hall stepped closer and saw what looked to be iron rails mounted on the sides of the shafts.

"I'd step back if I were ye," Gerdi said, grabbing Hall's leather jerkin and pulling back.

She reached past him and touched a rune-covered stone next to the opening. It flashed red, staying lit with a dull glow. Taking a couple steps back, gently pushing Hall further back, she waited patiently.

Hall glanced at her, confused, but turned sharply back to the openings as he heard a thunderous noise. Flickers of light could be seen from above, bright and orange, sparking. Then there came a screeching and more sparks. A dark box came to a slow stop in the opening, sparks flying on both sides as something gripped the metal rails. Made of iron, the box filled the space and contained a handful of Dwarves. One of them took a step out, looking at the buildings and ring they were on. He stepped back in.

"Down or up?" he asked Gerdi, eyes studying the others but only in mild curiosity.

"Down," she replied.

The Dwarf nodded and stepped back, the other four in the strange box doing the same. Gerdi stepped on, turning back to the others and motioning them to hurry up. They glanced at each other, a little fearful, but slowly and tentatively stepped into the box. Hall looked down into the gap between the stone and the metal floor of the box, a couple inches wide. There was nothing but black, the stone walls disappearing in shadow.

"Welcome to Axestorm," the Dwarf that had been in the front said to Hall.

"Thank you," he replied as he looked around the box.

Welded dark iron plates formed the walls, floor, and ceiling. Featureless with no light except that from the floor beyond. Hall could see a series of levers mounted to the wall, just right of the opening. It was an elevator, he realized, marveling that such a thing existed in Sky Realms Online.

It shouldn't have surprised him though. The Dwarves were

engineers. It was they that had invented the first airships, creating the mechanical vehicles. Eventually, humans and the other races had co-opted the designs, making their own, but the Dwarves were the first and still the best airships. Hall had always wondered why the Dwarves hadn't built other mechanical wonders, like the airships. It seemed that in this post-Glitch world, they had.

He felt the box lurch as Gerdi moved the levers. Managing to hold steady, he saw the stone floor rise, or more accurately, the metal box was descending.

It moved slowly, whatever controlled the speed and descent screeching against the rails to the sides. Hall could just see the flickering of sparks at the edges of the open front of the elevator cab. He had to stop thinking of it as a box. It was an elevator. He just found it odd that it existed. It felt a little out of place, but he didn't have long to dwell on it.

They passed two more levels, the elevator cab going dark between them, only lighting as they passed. He saw an odd glow just above each of the openings, a bright red rune. Some kind of floor marker. Hall didn't get a chance to see what was on the levels. The cab wasn't moving fast, but it didn't pause at each level. It appeared to be more of the same. Dwarves going about their business and lives.

With a slight bump, the cab slowed down even more, the screeching louder, as Gerdi flipped a couple more levers. Once it came to a complete stop, Gerdi led them off and the other Dwarf stepped forward, moving some of the levers. Hall glanced back as the box disappeared, heading down.

The level she led them out onto was different from the one above. They stepped out into a wide tunnel, quartz stone lamps mounted to the wall in regular intervals provided light. There were two other openings to each side twenty feet away from the elevator. At the far end, they could see light, the open space of the spire. The walls were carved, elegant runic script about five feet off the ground lined both sides. Equally spaced along the arched ceiling were circular openings. Hall assumed them to be vent holes, connecting to the outside to allow clean air to flow into the caverns and tunnels.

Instead of straight ahead to the spire, Gerdi turned right at the first intersection. They followed her into another set of tunnels much like the first, passing more intersections that led toward the spire and deeper into the mountain. Hall slowed his pace, coming alongside Roxhard. He indicated for the Dwarf to slow and let the others get ahead.

"You ready for this?" he asked quietly.

Roxhard didn't answer, turning his head to look at the carvings along the walls. He reached up, running his hand along the etched stone as they walked, feeling the smooth edges.

"I think I am," he replied, sounding confident. "I wasn't at first. That walk from the shipyards to here was hard. I kept wanting to run and hide, but now…" he paused and shrugged.

"What changed?" Hall prompted.

"I don't know," Roxhard admitted. "As soon as we walked into the spire… I… I wasn't nervous anymore." Roxhard fell silent and Hall let him think, work through what he was feeling. "It felt like coming home," the Dwarf finally said, quietly. The silence lingered as they passed another intersection, Roxhard looking toward the light of the open spire. "That's weird, I know. This isn't home. The story we came up with is more accurate, but just being in here…" he paused again and shook his head. "It doesn't make any sense."

Hall agreed. It didn't. He could believe a Dwarf raised somewhere else might have some connection to the ancestral home. But the story of Roxhard being raised in Gael lands was just that, a story. Roxhard wasn't native to Hankarth. He was from Earth. An American teen wearing the body of a Dwarf.

But that wasn't accurate, not anymore. Roxhard, like Hall

himself, was just bits of data. Maybe the developers of Sky Realms Online had coded in some form of racial memory, an added layer to the immersion since this was now their new life. That was beginning to make sense. A way for the Players to fully immerse themselves in Hankarth by fully becoming their characters.

For Roxhard, that meant embracing what it was to be Dwarven. Including a connection to Axestorm Hall.

But what would that mean for me? Hall thought. He was a Half-Elf, Gael and Wood Elf mixed. Unlike Dwarf characters, who had a clan, Human and Wood Elf characters had nothing similar added to their backstory. There was no village they were born in, no noble family missing an heir. Or had that changed too?

Out of curiosity, Hall was about to open his Character Sheet and delve deeper into the menus when he heard a noise from above him. Looking up, he saw a small form jump out of the vent hole. It slammed into him, heavier than it looked, the weight and momentum forcing Hall down. He hit the stone ground hard, head knocking back.

You have hit your head and received Light Concussion. -5 Health, -2 Vitality, +2 Seconds to Attack Speed. -2 to Protection for one minute.

Groaning, reaching up and feeling the bump on his head, wondering why he didn't start wearing a helmet, Hall pushed himself up. What had hit him? He looked down the tunnel to see almost a dozen small forms running around his companions. Four-legged, they stood only about a foot off the ground, two or three feet long. Stocky-looking creatures with short and compact legs. Long thin heads and snouts, wide tails and three long claws on each foot. They were covered in a kind of armor, overlapping plates of thick hides. Two sharp and strong-looking horns grew out of the sides of their thin heads. Fast, the creatures were swarming over his companions, who had a hard time hitting them as they were so low to the ground.

Skill Gain!
Identify Rank Two +.1

Enraged Deep Pango (white)

Hall barely recognized the creatures. He had rarely encountered them as they were only found in deep mines within Hankarth. The creatures used their strong claws and horns, along with an ability to eat rock, to dig through the mountains. For the Dwarves and their mines, Pangos were like rats in a city.

Jackoby was having the best luck against the Pangos. His hammer slammed down on the back of one, crushing the creature within its armored plating. There were three crushed shells around him. Roxhard kicked and swung, keeping the biting and clawing creatures away from him. His ax slammed into one, the blade screeching along the plating. Sabine was casting *Hexbolt*, purple streaks of lightning striking a handful of the creatures. They shuddered, crackling energy surrounding their small bodies. Caryn had the hardest time. Her twin swords were not strong enough to pierce the hard shells and not strong enough to push them away.

One of the Pangos noticed Hall stirring. With a sharp chittering sound, it rushed him, claws glinting in the light. The creature jumped into the air.

Hall felt slow, sluggish, due to the debuff, but he was still fast enough to grab his spear from the ground. He held it awkwardly, not able to brace it, but the point was out and the leaping Pango impaled itself on the spear, the Ironwood tip piercing the creature's soft underbelly.

Cursing, Hall dropped the spear and the still shaking body

of the Pango. He drew his short sword and stalked toward the group of creatures harassing his companions. Most were already down, dead or dying. The size and quickness of the nimble creatures made them hard to hit, but it only took a blow or two to end the Pango's life.

Swinging his sword, Hall sliced across the armored back of the Pango. The blade cut, but not as deep as he would have liked. The creature yelped and turned to attack, exposing its soft underbelly. Another strike and the creature was dead. Another struck at him with its long front claws, Hall parrying the attack. The claws sparked as they slid along the blade. He kept the creature's attention and Roxhard's ax ended its life.

Glancing around, Hall saw that all the Pango were dead. They had spread out from the defensive circle, finishing off the wounded Pango. Even Gerdi got in on the fighting. She had a small hammer in hand, the blunt end dripping black blood and flesh.

SLAIN: *Enraged Deep Pango +10 Experience*
SLAIN: *Enraged Deep Pango +10 Experience*
SLAIN: *Enraged Deep Pango +5 Experience*

Skill Gain!
Polearm Rank Two +.1
Skill Gain!
Small Blades Rank Two +.1

"What was that?" Hall asked, eyes searching the tunnel above him. He turned, looking at all the vent openings he could see.

"Pesky buggers are always running around the vents," Gerdi replied, not a hint of fear in her voice. She kicked at one of the corpses with her booted foot. "They usually stay further down. I've never seen any this far up the mountain."

Hall bent down, examining the corpse. The plates were flexible but tough.

"Any use for the plates?" he asked.

Gerdi shrugged.

"Someone, somewhere has a use for everything," she said, uttering a phrase that Hall had heard many times over his gaming career. It was the reason given for why almost any creature dropped some loot, or had a part of its body, that was useful for something. Crafting materials, alchemical reagents. Someone could find a use for anything. "No one in Axestorm uses Pango parts," she finished.

Standing up, Hall decided it wasn't worth the time to try and harvest the plates. He had never heard of an armor recipe that used Pango plates. Was he able to sell them to a General Goods vendor? He thought so, but only for a couple of coppers. Not worth the time. Not anymore.

They all turned at a noise coming down the tunnel. Weapons raised, they waited. Four Dwarves ran out of the shadows. They were dressed in leather armor with iron plates on the legs and gloves, iron pauldrons and overlapping thin iron scale mail. Each wore a close-fitting helm with no major ornamentation and a bar between the eyes. They held large iron shields before them with a mixture of hand ax and hammers for weapons. Etched into the center of their shields was an anvil with flames behind it. The symbol of the Stonefire Clan.

The Dwarves came to a stop about ten feet away, eyeing Hall and the others warily.

"What happened here?" one of them said in the common language since most of the group were not Dwarves. He was a couple steps in front of the others. The leader of this squad. Dwarves never led from the back.

Skill Gain!

Identify Rank Two +.1

Stonefire Hall Patroller Officer (white)

"The Pango attacked us," Gerdi answered, stepping forward, making sure not to avoid touching the bodies of the creatures.

The lead Patroller growled a curse in Dwarvish. He motioned to his men and spread out, avoiding the bodies, but looking up into the vent holes.

"They've been getting more aggressive lately," the Officer growled, motioning to his men to spread out. "Where are ye heading?"

"To yer halls," Gerdi answered.

The Officer examined the group, gaze lingering on Jackoby and even longer on Roxhard who hovered near the back.

"Yer a strange lot," he grunted. "Off with ye. We'll clean up yer mess."

"Thank ye," Gerdi replied with a brief nod of her head.

Hall picked up his spear, the Pango still impaled. Pointing the spear down, he lifted a leg and pushed on the dead creature as he pulled the spear up. The Pango fell to the ground, popping off the spear. He gave it a shake, getting rid of the loose blood. The Patroller Officer was glaring at him. Hall shrugged and carefully stepped around the dead bodies.

———

Gerdi led them down a couple more tunnels. Left turn, right turn, and straight before they came to a large and open area. The room was a dome, the walls, and floor lined with square blocks. A light brown color, contrasted with smaller blocks framing the archways of the three tunnels that led into it. On the fourth wall was a set of large double doors, wooden with metal plates attached. Scenes of battles and crafting were carved into the plates.

Before the doors stood five guards, four dressed the same as the Patrollers from the tunnels. The fifth was different. Her armor was more formal. Instead of chain, she wore plate, carried no shield, but bore a two-handed mace.

A loud noise filled the room, echoing across the rounded chamber. Water rushed out of two round openings above and to the sides of the doors. It fell into a moat carved into the room's floor. A half-circle in front of the doors, a stone bridge across the twenty-foot width.

The plate armored dwarf stood in the middle of the bridge, mace over her shoulder. The bridge itself was a marvel. Four posts at the end rising above the low walls, statues carved along the top depicting four Dwarves. Each was different, but they were so well detailed that the family resemblance was immediately apparent.

Hall glanced at Roxhard, trying not to gasp in surprise. Looking at his friend, he could see the resemblance to the statues. But how was that possible? Roxhard's avatar was like Hall's and the others. His features from real life, just fantasized and altered to fit the race. But it was still their real features.

Nothing about Roxhard had changed. He was still the same as the day they had met months ago. But the resemblance to the ancient Stonefires was there.

Hall shook his head, not sure how to process it. What did it mean? Did the game create the clan to fit Roxhard's backstory? That made no sense. The amount of processing power that would be required would make it prohibitive. Especially since there could be dozens of Dwarf Players trapped in the game like they were.

They had no idea how many Players were trapped in Sky Realms Online. Hall remembered seeing a handful in Grayhold on that first day. If there was an equal number at each of the potential starting areas, that could still be close to one hundred. Hall had a hard time believing the developers would make one hundred new Dwarf clans just to fit back-stories.

But he had no other explanation.

"Good evening travelers," the armored Dwarf on the bridge spoke in the common language, drawing Hall's attention and forcing him to focus.

Skill Gain!

Identify Rank Two +.1

Stonefire Hall Gatekeeper (blue)

"Good evening to ye," Gerdi said with a bow of her head. "We seek an audience with Matron Lydi."

The Gatekeeper nodded, shifting to look past Gerdi. Her eyes moved over each member of the party, measuring and studying, before stopping on Roxhard. She stared hard, her eyes widening a fraction.

"Why do ye speak for our brother Stonefire?" she asked, staring directly at Roxhard who seemed to wilt under that penetrating glare.

Part of Hall had thought Roxhard's resemblance to the Stonefire statues was only in his imagination. It was comforting to have confirmation from someone else, but scary at the same time.

Gerdi turned to look back at Roxhard. He took a step forward, back straightening, his eyes looking up to match the stare of the Gatekeeper.

"My parents were Stonefires but died when I was young," Roxhard said, voice strong and confident. Hall was proud. There was where he would have thought Roxhard would fall, let the story fall apart, but instead the opposite was happening.

Somehow from somewhere, Roxhard was drawing strength. "I was raised by human parents."

Behind the Gatekeeper, the other guards shifted, murmuring to each other. The Gatekeeper looked back at them sharply, the guards coming back to attention and stopping any chatter. She returned to look at Roxhard. Finally, after what felt like minutes but was only seconds, she motioned to the great doors behind her.

"Follow me."

CHAPTER SIXTEEN

THE GREAT DOORS WERE OPENED, AND THE WHITE ARMORED Gatekeeper led them into the halls of the Stonefires. The entry chamber was three stories high and perfectly square. Width, length, and height all the same. Pillars lined the walls, spaced evenly, heavily detailed. Stone blocks filled the space between, along the floor and the ceiling. Light brown, the pillars a darker tan. The clear crystal gas lamps lined the room, attached to the pillars, providing plenty of light throughout. Across from the entrance was a smaller set of double doors. Balconies lined the two floors above with Dwarven guards, each armed with a crossbow. Hall could only see two on each balcony but had no doubt more could be called upon in a moment's notice.

He studied the balconies, thinking he could use *Leap* and get up there before the other guards could arrive. It seemed such an obvious weak link in the defenses. But appearances could be deceiving. There would be traps up there, only one way on or off, possibly even secret doors to get defenders behind attackers. He looked around at the walls, wondering if there were secret doors there as well.

Hall hadn't known what to expect. Were all Dwarf clan halls like this? Fortresses within the greater fortress of Axestorm? Because that is what this room was. The entry to a fortress.

The crossbow dwarves watched as Hall and the others followed the Gatekeeper across the room, their footsteps echoing along the stones, the only sounds. When they were halfway across, the great doors leading out to Axestorm closed with a clash causing them to jump

Hall felt twitchy, feeling the eyes of the Dwarves watching him, crossbows resting easily on the stone walls. He glanced at Jackoby, the large Firbolg visibly tense, a low growl coming from deep in his throat. Hall agreed with the Warden. It felt unnatural to be walking so calmly through a room where death could come from above any second.

The Gatekeeper had given them no reason to feel that way. He just did. The long walk was tense. Only Gerdi didn't seem to feel it.

Hall felt better when the doors before them opened out. Two more guards stood at attention, each holding a door open, armed with shields and halberds. They stared straight ahead as Hall passed.

The corridor beyond was bright. Walls, ceiling, and floors were all a light tan square block. Pillars lined the wall, stone beams across the ceiling at each set of pillars, more decoration than structural. Gas lamps on each pillar, pedestals with a variety of statues and busts between. Fifty feet long, no doors at the far end. Two more guards stood on either side. Again, their footsteps were the only sound.

Passing the two motionless guards, they came into the middle of a long corridor. Turning left, the Gatekeeper silently led them down the new corridor. Designed like the first, pillars with gas lamps and statues between, double doors at the far end.

They opened out into the corridor, two guards with hammers and shields held them. Hall could see a larger room beyond, flooded with daylight. His eyes blinked as they stepped into the larger chamber, having gotten used to the diffuse glow of the gas and crystal lamps. The daylight was much brighter and harsher.

The room they entered was an audience chamber. Across from them was a curved stone wall, larger blocks with wide openings that led to a balcony. Hall could see blue skies and clouds beyond, realizing they were in the chamber that hung out over the large lake below. Behind them was a straight wall, the sides straight until the curve. No longer were their footsteps the only sound, there was a quiet roar that filled the background. Not loud but constant.

The waterfall.

Tapestries lined the walls, more statues, and even some weapons and banners. Trophies, animal heads, and full mounts filled some of the space. There was not a clear bit of wall. Dwarf guards stood at attention, a variety of weapons, spaced evenly around the room. Ones armed with crossbows were across the room, standing between the openings to the balconies. Against the right-side wall was a long stone table, a mixture of stone and wood chairs down the sides. Enough seating for over a dozen.

To the left at the far end stood a raised stone dais, a simple stone chair on top. Two white armored guards stood on either side of a sitting elderly female Dwarf. At the base of the dais was another elderly Dwarf, male, sitting at a table with a large book open in front of him. His eyes never left the writing, ink quill moving quickly. Three others dressed in chain and leather, with weapons sheathed, stood off to the side, eyeing the group warily. Two males and a female.

The older Dwarf on the throne wore simple tan robes lined in brown trim, a large double-headed war hammer leaning against the stone chair. Her eyes followed them as the Gate-keeper led them toward the dais.

Skill Gain!

Identify Rank Two +.1

Matron Lydi Stonefire (orange)

Her arms rested calmly on the arms of the throne. Her expression showed nothing. The gray eyes watched them approach, focused on Roxhard. Who didn't notice. His eyes roamed the hall, studying the tapestries and banners, noting the weapons and trophies. He didn't feel the elderly clan mother's eyes on him. Or if he did, Roxhard was doing a good job ignoring it.

"Who have ye brought me, sister?" Matron Lydi asked, leaning forward in her chair, eyes never leaving Roxhard, who finally noticed her stare.

He looked up at her and quickly shifted his gaze. He looked anywhere but at the elderly Dwarf.

The Gatekeeper stopped a couple of feet from the base of the dais, looking up at the Matron. She shifted and motioned back to Roxhard. Hall watched as his friend took a deep breath, steeling himself and stepped forward.

"This one claims to be one of us," the Gatekeeper said, her voice loud in the room, each word spoken clearly. "A Stonefire."

Matron Lydi leaned forward even more, staring down at Roxhard. Hall could see the cracks, wrinkles in her aged face, but wisdom still shone in her eyes. All eyes were now on Roxhard. The elderly male sitting at the table was looking up in surprise. The first time his eyes had left the book, almost dropping the ink quill. Hall noticed the other three, all middle-aged Dwarves, were staring at Roxhard with a mixture of curiosity and trepidation. He assumed those to be Matron Lydi's children. The heirs to the clan leadership.

"Greetings. I am Matron Lydi, the matriarch of the Stonefire clan," she said formally "Welcome to our halls." Her gaze was soft, kindly. "What is your name, child?"

QUEST COMPLETE!

Together, with Roxhard, you have traveled to the halls of the Stonefires and been introduced to Matron Lydi, matriarch of the clan.

A DWARF IS A DWARF NO MATTER WHAT I
Accompany Roxhard to meet Matron Lydi of the Stonefires 1/1
Reward: +50 Stonefire Clan reputation; +25 Experience

You are now Known to the Stonefire Clan.

Roxhard glanced nervously back at Hall who nodded, motioning at Roxhard to talk to the Matron. Hall glanced at the others. He wasn't offended that they were being ignored, but he could see a flaring of Sabine's eyes. She was offended.

"Roxhard," he said with a bow.

"And ye claim to be one of us?" Matron Lydi asked.

Roxhard took a deep breath. He looked at the tapestries and statues that surrounded the Matron's dais. The history of the Stonefires. Their deeds and battles. The victories and their greatest craftings. This was what Roxhard was claiming to be part of.

Hall could imagine the thoughts running through the fourteen-year-old's head. It was overwhelming. Up until this moment, the full weight of what it would mean to claim lineage with the Stonefires had not sunk in. Here in this room with all the history, Roxhard was understanding what it truly meant. He looked back at the Matron.

"I do, Matron."

Eyes locked with Roxhard, she seemed to look into his soul. She smiled.

"Tell us yer story," Matron Lydi said.

Roxhard did. The same story he had told Gerdi's father, almost word for word. Matron Lydi, everyone in the room, listened intently. Roxhard told it slowly, clearly and with conviction. When he was done, silence fell over the room. The three heirs looked up at the Matron. The male clerk looked down at his book, quill pen resting and waiting to write. No one said anything, no one moved. Silence stretched. Matron Lydi leaned back, fingers tapping on the stone arm of her throne. Her eyes roamed the hall, stopping at each statue, studying the tapestries.

"Step closer, young one," she said finally, leaning forward again, beckoning to Roxhard.

He took a couple steps closer to the dais.

"We have heard of yer coming," the Matron said with a quick glance to Gerdi, who looked chagrined. "And ye do look like one of us," she added, fingers still tapping on the stone arm. "Who are yer parents?"

Hall cursed quietly, working hard to not speak aloud. This was what he was afraid of. They had carried the story too far. It was all going to fall apart now. He wished they had never come here. It was going to crush Roxhard and who knew how angry the Stonefires would be. And the Battleforges? They would be embarrassed. What would this do their already fragile standing within Axestorm? He looked to Roxhard, expecting to see the Dwarf Warden panicking.

Instead, Roxhard looked calm, his eyes unfocused like he was looking at his Character Sheet. Focus returned to his dark eyes, a small smile on his face.

"My father was named Dern and my mother was Carli of the Amberbars."

Hall somehow managed to keep the surprise from his face. A glance showed that Sabine wasn't so successful. Where had those names come from? Roxhard had said them with confidence. They were not names he had made up on the spot. The information had to have come from his Character's Backstory. But they had not been there before. Backstories had never had that much detail.

Matron Lydi's eye's flashed recognition. She knew the names. But instead of saying anything, she looked down at the clerk. The man flipped back through the pages of the book, eyes scanning, thick fingers running over lines of text.

Time slowed, all eyes focused on the clerk. He flipped through more pages, read more lines. Keeping his finger on a specific line, he looked up at Matron Lydi.

"Dern of the Stonefire was joined to Carli of the Amberbars near one hundred and twenty years ago," the clerk said, his voice deep and old but still strong. "The two were lost on a trade mission to the Gael islands soon after. All on that mission were lost, and it was not known if any had ever arrived on the islands. Carli was pregnant when they left Axestorm Hall."

He fell silent, the full weight of his words filling the chamber.

Hall was shocked. It made no sense. How did the names appear in both Roxhard's Backstory and the Stonefire clan history? He and Roxhard had made up the story about the dead parents on the voyage from the debris island to Axestorm. How had it made it into the histories? Roxhard's Backstory didn't have that information before they came up with it. They had created it. And there had been no names. Roxhard just made those up after questioned by Matron Lydi.

There had been no patch since the Glitch. How had the game files been updated with that story? And so quickly?

Matron Lydi looked out the openings and onto the blue sky beyond. Clouds drifted by along with the black masses that were other islands. Her finger of one hand tapped on the stone arm of the chair, the others curled around the handle of the hammer. No one moved or said anything, all eyes on Matron Lydi.

Finally, she turned and faced Roxhard. Her gaze was stern.

"It appears that yer story is true," she said. "At least, as ye know it. Yer resemblance to our clan is undeniable." Two of the three offspring looked up at her sharply, the older of the males and the female. Most likely worried about their status as heirs. Lydi paused, eyes roaming the chamber, settling on Hall for a moment before moving on. Her fingers continued to tap but she no longer held the hammer. "But we cannot accept ye into the clan until ye have proven yerself a true Stonefire."

The words had weight to them. Almost a challenge.

Hall watched Roxhard's reaction. The Dwarf locked eyes with Matron Lydi and simply nodded.

Matron Lydi, matriarch of the Stonefire clan, has accepted the evidence that Roxhard is indeed a long lost Stonefire but she still requires him to prove himself.

A DWARF IS A DWARF NO MATTER WHAT II
Assist Roxhard in proving himself to Matron Lydi and the Stonefires
0/1
Reward: +200 Stonefire Clan reputation; +25 Experience

Waiting on Roxhard to Accept or Refuse Quest

Hall barely had time to read the quest fully before a new message flashed across his vision.

*Roxhard has Accepted **A DWARF IS A DWARF NO MATTER WHAT II***

ACCEPT QUEST?

"What must I do?" Roxhard asked.

———

Matron Lydi smiled, satisfied.

She pointed to the largest tapestry hanging in the chamber. It depicted a Dwarf standing on a cliff edge, a wide opening behind him. He was dressed in full plate, functional armor and not ceremonial, holding a double-bladed, two-handed ax. The sun shone down on the Dwarf, bathing him in light. Fiery red beard, deep-set eyes. Hall hadn't noticed before, only giving the various items in the room a cursory glance, but the Dwarf was almost a dead ringer for Roxhard.

Hall studied the opening behind him. Not overly large, carved stone blocks framing it, a symbol carved at the top. An anvil with flames behind it. The Stonefire clan emblem. Two statues stood to either side of the opening. He assumed it to be a dungeon of some kind and whatever Roxhard had to do would involve it.

He was right.

"That is the founder of our clan, Brignar Stonefire," Matron Lydi explained, pointing at the tapestry. "He stands in front of the entrance to our crypts. What ye must do is twofold." Her gaze returned to Roxhard, who pulled his away from the tapestry.

Hall saw the surprise in Roxhard's face when he saw his own features depicted in the tapestry. Focus returned as he listened to the Matron speak.

"First, ye must lay the spirit of yer father to rest in his ancestral crypt," Matron Lydi said.

Roxhard must travel to the ancient Stonefire Crypt to lay the spirit of his father to rest with the spirits of his ancestors, then he must enter the Amberbar Crypt to lay the spirit of his mother to rest with the spirits of his ancestors.

THE FINAL REST

Accompany Roxhard to the Stonefire Crypt and lay the spirit of his father to rest 0/1

Accompany Roxhard to the Amberbar Crypt and lay the spirit of his mother to rest 0/1

Rewards: +200 Stonefire Clan Reputation; +25 Experience

Waiting on Roxhard to Accept or Refuse Quest.

*Roxhard has Accepted **THE FINAL REST**.*

ACCEPT QUEST?

Hall reread the quest text. There wasn't much to go on. It was Roxhard's quest. Had he received more information? Or would more be revealed when they got to the Crypt?

"When a young Stonefire comes of age," Matron Lydi continued once she was sure Roxhard had accepted the quest, "they make the journey to the Crypt and the tomb of Brignar. There they spend the night in communion with our ancestors and learn our history. Through that learning, they become Stonefires. That is what ye must do."

Roxhard must find the tomb of Brignar Stonefire and spend the night in communion with the Stonefire ancestors. If he does so, Roxhard will be accepted into the clan.

A CLAN'S HISTORY I

Assist Roxhard in communing with the Stonefire ancestors 0/1

Reward: +200 Stonefire Clan Reputation; +25 Experience

Waiting on Roxhard to Accept or Refuse quest.

*Roxhard has Accepted **A CLAN'S HISTORY**.*

ACCEPT QUEST?

"Beware, young Roxhard," Matron Lydi said, leaning forward, her voice grave. "If ye are not a true Stonefire, the ancestors will destroy ye."

CHAPTER SEVENTEEN

"WHY ARE WE DOING THIS?" SABINE ASKED, HER VOICE LOW.

She was walking with Caryn at the rear of the group as they exited the side entrance to Axestorm Hall, heading down the road toward the shipyards. Gerdi Battleforge was in the lead again, along with one of the sons of Matron Lydi. Urit Stonefire had agreed to accompany them, to be their guide to the Crypts. He had been the only one of the three Stonefire heirs that hadn't appeared angry and jealous at Roxhard's appearance.

The sun was rising to the east, a red glow along the far horizon. The morning was chilly, a cold wind blowing across the mountains. They had risen early after spending the night in the guest chambers of Stonefire Hall.

It had been at Matron Lydi's suggestion. It took almost over a day to reach the Crypt, and it was not wise to venture there at night. Dinner had been served in the chambers where they had been left alone until the morning when Urit had come to get them.

Hall wanted to turn back and snap at Sabine, but he somewhat agreed with her. Why were they doing this? The rewards, for them at least, were low. Roxhard had told them his part of the quest came with much better experience and reputation rewards. Which had prompted Hall to review his quests with his friends, finding out that the others had gotten similar rewards as his was with Roxhard's.

That had come as a surprise.

This current chain didn't really advance any of his personal goals or those of the others. And was becoming a true Stonefire something that Roxhard needed? It was hard to tell what effect it would have but if the Dwarf was going to stay in Skara Brae, it was not that important.

So why were they doing it?

Hall wasn't able to talk with Roxhard much because Gerdi had been there. The young Battleforge had taken a liking to Roxhard and hadn't left his side for most of the night. From his reactions in the audience chamber, Roxhard seemed to want to be legitimized.

Really, Hall thought, turning his thoughts away from Sabine, that was all that was important. If it was something Roxhard wanted to do, then it was something they would do.

"Donae mind me siblings," Urit was saying to Roxhard, who followed behind the Stonefire. "They're just jealous and worried."

"About what?" Roxhard asked.

"Ye," Urit answered with a chuckle. "Me mother didnae tell ye, but yer Da was her brother. Me uncle. Yer Da was in line for the throne of the clan."

That brought the group to a complete halt, including Gerdi. Urit had gone a couple paces more before he realized they weren't following. Turning back, he looked at them confused but then chuckled, understanding.

"Donae worry," he said, motioning for them to continue. "They won't try to kill ye." They still hadn't moved, and he shrugged. "Not like ye would get the throne. Not now."

There was almost a sigh of relief from Roxhard.

"Why not?" Sabine asked, suddenly interested.

"Long and complicated," Urit replied. "Dwarf politics," he added, his tone saying they wouldn't understand.

They probably wouldn't.

Urit was a young Dwarf, about the same age as Gerdi and what Roxhard looked like. Dark red beard that hung down to his waist. He had shaved the sides of his head, keeping the hair long in the middle, the sides tattooed. Dressed in chainmail, the clan tabard over it, and leather pants. He carried a small metal buckler on his back and a one-handed hammer in his iron gloved hand. He hadn't given a reason why he had chosen to guide them.

They continued in silence for the hour it took to walk to the shipyards. Already the yards were bustling with activity. Ship captains wanted to be off, to get a full day's sail in the air. Shouts overlapped as they pushed to get the ships loaded and be the first one off.

Weaving their way around the activity, Gerdi stopped them at the entrance to the Battleforge shop. Noises could be heard coming from within, through the large doors. They were open a foot or so and Hall walked toward them, wanting to get a look at the progress on his airship. Gerdi stopped him, waving her hand in a no gesture.

"No peeking," she said with a laugh. The smile dropped as she looked at Roxhard. "This is where I leave ye." She stepped away, reaching for the door. "Not much for roaming the mountains, ye understand." She turned away with a small shrug and stopped just before stepping through the door. "See ye soon," she added, looking straight at Roxhard.

She closed the doors behind her, blocking off the noise. Roxhard just stared at where she had been.

"I think the lass likes ye," Urit said, clapping Roxhard on the shoulder.

Roxhard was still stunned as Urit directed them to the end of the shipyard. The cliff came to a stop just short of the water, a wide trail leading along the edge of the lake. Single file, they started down the trail, which began as smooth blocks but changed to hard-packed dirt and exposed rock.

The path paralleled the lake running east for half a mile before the shore turned to the south. The cliff rose to their left, high above, the risen sun glinting off the surface of the water. Foothills continued to the south along the shore of the lake, the path straight through the hills with an offshoot turning north into the mountains.

Urit turned them north, the trail running through the higher Greystone Foothills for a mile before it turned back into the mountains. Wide and smooth, well-traveled, it cut across the side of the sloping mountains with the foothills spreading out before them. Scrub oaks and bushes, random collections of boulders, lined the rocky slope of the mountains. The peaks towered above them, high tree-covered ridges.

The higher they went, the more of the land Hall could see. Tundra spread out for miles, another mountain range barely visible in the far distance. He could see the edge of Huntley to the south and southeast, a large forest along the jagged line. The foothills became the plains, dotted with small forests and ponds. Thin drifts of smoke could be seen curling into the sky, a half dozen visible throughout the plains. A large concentration coming closer in the foothills, hidden down in a valley.

Hall lifted his head, looking out across the plains. They all stopped, following his gaze, seeing a black dot coming closer. It flew toward them rapidly, growing in size and detail. Pike screeched as he circled above them, spiraling lower and lower. Dust was kicked up as his powerful wings flapped, hovering in the air. He settled on Hall's shoulder, causing the Skirmisher to wince as the talons dug in.

"I've missed you too," Hall said, reaching up and scratching the dragonhawk's chin.

Behind him, Hall heard a hiss and Sabine whispering soothing words to Salem. He wondered what had gotten into the minx cat, who normally didn't mind Pike. The cat was probably picking up on Sabine's mood. It had not gotten any better. The Witch had gotten more annoyed as the hike had gotten harder, the bottom of her long dress dragging in the dirt.

———

It was well past midday when the group climbed onto a small plateau. The trail had gotten steeper as it cut across the mountains, making for hard travel. Most of the flat area was taken up by a large and round building, made of gray stone, with a domed roof. A watchpost. Half the structure was on the plateau, the other built onto the mountainside and into it. Hall could see that at least a story, maybe two, extended below the elevation of the plateau. He tried to find a joint between the walls and the rock, but there was none. It was as if the structure had been carved from the mountain, not built onto it.

The walls were open beneath the dome, columns spaced every couple feet. Dwarf crossbowmen could be seen patrolling, looking out over the foothills. Urit led them around to the back side where a low wall formed a marshaling yard. Ramps led down to the watchpost's entrance, a wide wooden door. The trail continued into the mountains past the watchpost.

Hall heard noises, the braying of Rams and mooing of Yaks, coming from the mountain. Where the cliff face turned, Hall could just make out a cave opening, wooden fence across. Some kind of stable.

"Welcome to Greystone Watch," Urit said as he led them down the ramp. "We can stay here fer the night."

Hall glanced up at the sun. It was starting to set, but there was still a couple hours of daylight left. He looked up the trail, seeing the shadows already falling across it as the peaks and ridges hid the light from the sun. They could probably get another couple miles in, maybe three if they were lucky, but at what risk?

The Hard Edge Mountains were Urit's home. He knew them best. If he didn't think it wise to keep walking, Hall would listen. He glanced at Pike who spread his wings. Pushing off against Hall's shoulder, the dragonhawk flapped his wings. He gained altitude and spiraled higher, circling over the plateau.

At the door, Urit pounded on it, repeatedly. No specific pattern, just pounding.

It was a minute later that the door was pushed open, forcibly, making Urit step back. The Dwarf was smiling though as he stepped out of the way. Another Dwarf stood in the doorway, looking annoyed. His brown eyes were furrowed, barely noticeable though the bushy black hair and beard. He wore leathers, chest and leggings, a hand ax through his belt. A steel-gray tabard hung across his chest, trimmed in blue. The dual crossed ax sigil of Axestorm Hall was stitched on the tabard. Another symbol, smaller, was above. A stone boulder with a crescent moon behind it.

Skill Gain!

Identify Rank Two +.1

Greystone Watchman (white)

The Dwarf glared at Urit, eyes widening as he took in the strange group standing behind the Stonefire Dwarf. He had been about to speak, most likely shout, something in the Dwarf language but stopped and changed to the common tongue.

"What do ye want?" he grumbled, the glare softening as he spoke to Urit.

"Lodging," Urit replied, smiling, his tone suggesting the answer should have been obvious.

"Did ye bring ale with ye Urit Stonefire?"

"Sadly no," Urit replied. "Not this time."

The Watchman grunted, eyes returning to Hall and the others.

"Who did ye bring with ye then?"

Urit made the introductions, not bothering with more than names. The Watchman's eyes rose in surprise as Urit introduced Roxhard with the Stonefire name. He looked questioningly at Urit who just nodded in a reply that said questions would be answered later.

"I be Dreden Blueboulder," the Watchman said. "Commander of this here Watchpost. If the Stonefires be vouching for ye, ye be welcome."

He stepped back and gestured them inside.

———

The first level was one large round room. Stairs curving along both sides, with no railings, were the only feature. One set leading up, the other down. Most of the space was taken up by crates of various sizes. Racks of weapons and armor lined the wall and stacked on shelves. Hall saw small ballista mounted on wagons, two of the weapons. The large bolts stacked between.

Dreden led them to the left set of stairs, leading up to the next level.

Bunks filled one half of the level, a wooden railing around the stairs, a long wooden table with bench seating and a larger central stair leading to the top level. The other half of the level was divided into smaller rooms. Wooden doors were closed, but Hall guessed them to be a kitchen of some kind and possibly the commander's office. He counted a dozen bunks, sleeping for twenty-four, ladders leading to the top.

"A Watchpost serves two purposes," Dreden said, pointing out the bunks. "We keep watch over the surrounding lands but also provide a place fer travelers to rest."

Hall nodded. He could see evidence of six bunks being used, the bottoms only. Wooden chests sat at the ends of these and the bedding was rumpled. It seemed that only six Dwarves manned the Watchpost.

"Any changes at Crackleberry?" Urit asked.

Dreden shook his head.

"Crackleberry?" Hall asked, curious. He didn't remember a town by that name in the region. It didn't sound Dwarven.

"A Bodin community in the Greystone Foothills," Urit answered.

"Used to be Bodin," Dreden muttered angrily.

The Watchman caught Hall's confused look and motioned them to follow him upstairs.

They walked out onto the top level, the sides open to the elements, a wooden trap door with hinges attached to the stone floor next to the stairs. Two Dwarven crossbowmen stood on the east side, looking out onto the plains.

"Any change?" Dreden asked, leading the group to that side.

"Same as before," one of the crossbowmen answered.

Hall looked out and saw the same plains he had seen before, but further out and greater detail due to the higher elevation. He looked for the large collection of smoke, assuming that must be Crackleberry.

Eyes scanned the hills, looking for smoke or other signs of civilization. He found it, barely visible as the homes were part of the hills. He could see doors, cobblestone paths, windows.

Bodin homes were buried in the hillside, most of the rooms underground. Chimneys poked out of the mounds. What he couldn't see were the Bodin themselves.

He looked over at Dreden.

"About a month ago, maybe a little less, the town was raided by Storvgarde tribesmen from the plains," Dreden explained.

"That's not normal?" Hall stated more than asked. If it had happened before, the Dwarves wouldn't have found it odd enough to watch. And Hall had to wonder why anyone would attack the peaceful Bodin. It's not like they had resources worth taking.

"Nay," Dreden replied. "The Storvgarde left the Bodin alone."

"What happened to change that?" Sabine asked.

"Some new chieftain from what we hear," Dreden answered. "Has the tribesmen whipped into a frenzy. Crackle-berry isn't the only place they've raided." He leaned against the stone railing, watching Pike circling above. "Funny thing is, the new chieftain isn't a tribesman. Came out of Colds Ridge, settlement more east."

Hall knew of Colds Ridge. It was a Storvgarde port town, just past the forest along the islands edge and where another range of mountains started. The place most players landed at when venturing to the island of Huntley. The Storvgarde people were spread out over four large islands and many smaller ones. They were a kingdom in the loosest sense of the world. There was a high king, called the Jarl, and the Storv-garde that lived in the towns and cities followed him, the ones that lived on the island of Katten where the Jarl kept court. The more wild Storvgarde, the ones living in the tundra and mountains, paid lip service but largely ignored his rule. They still followed the old ways, clashed with their neighbors, and wanted nothing to do with the larger world. There was constant tension between the Jarl's civilized Storvgarde and the barbaric Storvgarde.

"Did you aid them?" Caryn asked.

"Nah lass," Dreden answered, a bit sheepish. "Not our place."

She started to say something else but stopped, letting it go.

Leaning forward, feeling the wind biting his face, Hall found Pike high above. He connected with the dragonhawk and sent Pike soaring out over the town of Crackleberry. Through Pike's sharp eyes, Hall could see all of the small town.

The buildings of Crackleberry were built into the sides of the many small hills surrounded by higher, some a couple stories buried underground. There were some wooden walls and roofs exposed. The fronts were decorated in bright wooden slat patterns, colorful planters, and vines. Stone walks led to each from the hard-packed dirt roads that meandered through the village. There was no order to the roads as they followed the low points between hills.

He saw a couple dejected Bodin moving about the town. A couple of the homes had been destroyed, gaping maws into the hills with broken and burnt timbers exposed. Hills had been trampled, road stones pulled up. Crackleberry looked like a rampaging horde had charged through and left it behind. There was some reconstruction happening, but it was slow.

Hall wondered where all the Bodin were. He didn't see enough for a village that size. He did see the half dozen Storv- gardians that roamed the streets. Dressed in leathers and furs, carrying double-handed axes and hammers. The few Bodin that were out made sure to avoid them.

Just seeing them made Hall angry.

Then another person stepped into view. Tall, almost as tall as the Storvgardes, but thin. Not weak-looking thin, but wiry. Pale, almost white skin, a light blue robe, and long silver hair that hung down her back. A Norn. She stopped and talked to the Storvgardians, who listened as if she was in command. They continued on their patrol and she went deeper into the village, disappearing around a hill.

A Player? Chances were good the Norn was a Player. A Beta tester, like Hall. There were Half-Elf and Norn NPCs, a couple Norn villages in the lowest islands. But Norn NPCs were rarely seen outside their home islands. There was no reason for a Norn to be working with, as this one appeared to be, with Storvgardes. But why would a Player?

Hall was tempted to run down to Crackleberry and discover if the Norn was a Player. They had seen so few since leaving Grayhold. What had started as a dozen in the Laughing Horse Inn, he had only run across four. Himself, Roxhard and Sabine. Caryn had never been in the Inn and there had only been that murderous Bodin, Davit. Where had all the others gone? He didn't remember a Norn from the Laughing Horse.

Or was it a possible quest? The way Urit had prompted the conversation from Dreden, it had the feel of the beginning scene to a quest. If so, it would involve the Norn and Crackle-berry, making the Norn not a Player. Hall could envision a long quest chain using Norn interference to explain why the Storv-gardians had raided the Bodin village.

Raided and occupied.

Which was not normal behavior for the tribesmen.

Hall remembered a quest chain out of Colds Ridge that had involved convincing a tribe that had broken away from the Jarl's rule to come back into the fold. They were at war with another tribe and the quest involved the Player picking a side in the conflict. Different rewards depending on which tribe the Player sided with and convinced to follow the Jarl's rule.

Conversations with the Dwarves had not launched a quest prompt, so he was sure there had to be more before it would activate. He also wasn't sure he wanted to get started on a quest chain that could involve the Jarl of Storvgarde and travel to Dragonsky Hall. Hall wanted to get back to Skara Brae, and Leigh, as soon as possible and taking on a quest like that would be a distraction.

He had Pike fly away from the village, wanting to leave Crackleberry behind. He was angry at the Storvgarde raiders and wanted to avenge the Bodin, but wanted to avoid starting another quest chain. As Pike circled away from the village within the hills, the sharp eyes spotted more destruction in the land around Crackleberry. Hall almost had Pike fly away but curiosity won.

The fields and orchards had been trampled. Hall could see a wide swath of grass that was no more, a path leading into a nearby forest. On the other side of the trees, at the bottom of another valley, Hall saw the remains of an invading army's camp. The remains of fire pits, churned up muddy ground from many booted feet, animal bones, and other refuse.

Why had a tribe of Storvgarde needed to have a camp? They had their own villages nearby.

Severing his connection with Pike, Hall tried to force the thoughts away from Crackleberry. Not his concern. Not yet and hopefully not ever.

Hall felt for the Bodin, but what could he do? He had enough on his plate. Turning away from the railing, Hall felt a pang of guilt. He should do something. He was the good guy after all. The hero. Or he thought of himself that way.

Most of the time.

Neither Urit or Dreden looked at him or said anything. Neither appeared to be waiting on him to say something either. A clear indication there was no quest attached.

But he still felt the guilt.

One thing at a time, he told himself, forcing his mind to focus on the here and now. Trying to convince himself it was the right call.

Maybe after helping Roxhard, they could help the Bodin of Crackleberry.

He chuckled at the thought of what Sabine would say and how much the Witch would complain. Actually, the more he thought about it, Hall really didn't want to hear more complaining from Sabine.

CHAPTER EIGHTEEN

IT WAS A RESTFUL NIGHT AND IT WASN'T.

The bunks were made for Dwarves so all, but Roxhard and Caryn had to curl up, pulling their legs tight. Jackoby barely fit even when he did that. That meant barely any room or ability to roll over. But they were all so tired it didn't matter.

Then there was the noise.

Greystone Watch was an active post. There were always Dwarves on duty. The garrison was only nine Dwarves, including Dreden Blueboulder. Three to a watch shift, three watches a day. So there was always activity. For the most part, the Dwarves were quiet, but their boots could be heard on the stone ceiling above, the floor of the open level. It was cold in the bunks as wind blew the chill air down from above, the trap door open all night. Torchlight also filtered down from above and below. Not enough to make the bunk level bright, but just enough to provide flickering shadows of movement that teased the eyes.

The mountains themselves made noise throughout the night. Wolves howled, their cries echoing across the tundra. In the middle of the night, a huge roar woke them all. Just the one call and nothing after that. There was no excitement from the Dwarves, so Hall assumed it wasn't anything out of the ordinary. As he fell back to sleep, he wondered what could have made such a loud sound.

Even with all the restlessness and relatively uncomfortable beds, the time still counted as good sleep and they all awoke with full Vitality.

They had been given dinner the night before and a full breakfast. Dreden was asleep, along with the rest of his watch, the second shift eating what was essentially their dinner before taking their rest. Try as hard as they could, they still made noise as they ate. Hall felt awful as he was afraid of waking the sleeping Dwarves but realized that this was their normal and they were used to it.

Urit led them out of the watchpost and into the cold mountain morning. Sabine pulled a fur-lined cloak from her inventory, pulling it around her body as her breath clouded the air.

"It'll warm up," Urit promised as he led them to the path that led deeper into the mountains.

They passed by the cave Hall had noticed the day before. The mouth was thin, barred by a wooden fence and gate. Moos and braying came from the dark interior, the Rams and Yaks waking up and looking for their morning meal.

The trail thinned out as it rose steeply up from the plateau. It cut between the mountains, climbing over a ridge and turning back around so they seemed to be heading back the way they had come, just much higher up.

Hall had no idea how high they had climbed. Axestorm Hall, the lake, and the shipyards started at a high elevation compared to the rest of Huntley, and they had been climbing most of yesterday and all of the morning.

Finally, the trail leveled out at another wide plateau. An almost half-moon shaped area. They had been heading south, and the path continued to the west heading to another mountain. A ridge, the trail and only that wide, spanned between the two peaks, the sides sharply sloping down to a deep chasm on both sides.

On the near side were two short stone columns with statues on top. Each depicted a Dwarf in full armor. One had a shield and ax, the other a shield and hammer. Across the ridge, Hall could see two more statues. Similar but those bore double-handed weapons, an ax and hammer, with no shields.

"That looks fun," Sabine said, pulling the cloak tighter as the wind whipped through the pass.

Urit had been right. It had gotten warmer. Only a handful of degrees but it was warmer. The wind was stronger though, threatening to push them off the mountain.

They settled down to rest before venturing across the ridge. Dropping travel packs, they pulled out waterskins and dried jerky. Matron Lydi had allowed them to empty their packs of extra items, giving them more space for essentials they'd need in the mountains. As well as more inventory space for anything they might find.

With his back against the mountain, Hall looked up into the sky. Pike was circling above, a distant and black dot. The dragonhawk screeched, and Hall connected his senses with that of Pike.

He could see himself and the others sitting on the plateau. Roxhard was talking quietly with Urit near the statues. Caryn and Sabine were huddled against the mountain wall, and Jackoby was staring down the way they had come. But it wasn't his companions that captured Pike and now his attention. It was the dozen forms scurrying down the steep mountainside.

Gray against the gray stone, only Pike's sharp eyes able to see their slow movements.

"Incoming," Hall shouted, jumping up and severing his connection to Pike.

He stepped away from the wall, turning and pointing up with his spear.

"Cragglers," Urit barked.

Now that Hall knew they were there, he could make out the details. The creatures' skin was the color of rock. Grays in various shades. They were short, only two feet tall, with half that height being legs. Their arms were just as long. Spindly but strong-looking, they had very long fingers and toes, both multi-jointed. Their heads were squat and wide with thin noses, small eyes, and large wide-set eyes. Completely hairless and wearing rough gray hides over their bodies.

The Cragglers worked their way quickly down the mountain now that they were spotted. Each faced down, their long fingers and toes grabbing onto the mountain, fitting into tiny cracks and ridges.

Skill Gain!

Identify Rank Two +.4

Darknotch Craggler Scrapper (white)
Darknotch Craggler Scrapper white)
Darknotch Craggler Scrapper (white)
Darknotch Craggler War Leader (white)

Hall and his friends spread out, bracing themselves. The Cragglers made odd chittering sounds. As they got closer, the chittering became warbling howls. The creatures paused, their yellow eyes staring down with hate.

He couldn't see, but he knew that Pike was coming. The dragonhawk screeched, the sound echoing through the mountains. He was a blur, a green and orange streak, dive-bombing the mountain. Pike pulled up, just over Hall's head. Wings flapping in the air, he let out a crackling blue-white bolt of lightning. It slammed into the back of one of the Cragglers, smoke rising up at the impact. The force pushed the creature against the mountain, bones snapping. It spasmed, losing its grip and fell. The angle took it to the end of the plateau, falling and slamming onto the edge of the flat area, bones cracking, knocking it away. The creature howled as it fell down into the chasm.

One down, only eleven left.

Facing down, one of the Cragglers pushed off from the mountain. The long legs looked spindly, but they were powerful. The creature flew through the air, quick and with force. Hall got his spear up, the Craggler unable to move. The ironwood tip slammed through the thin creature's body, erupting out its back. Howling madly, the Craggler slid down the spear, leaving a bloody trail. It thrashed its arms and legs, reaching for Hall as its weight and momentum carried it toward him.

Hall twisted, putting the butt end of the spear into the ground. The end held tight, Hall grunted with effort as he changed the angle of the spear and slammed it against the ground away from the mountain. There was a sickening crack as the Craggler hit the ground, smashing against the rock. It still squirmed, arms flailing, but was unable to move.

But it kept Hall from using the spear.

Cursing, he drew his short sword, spinning around in time to block the swiping arm of a Craggler. The long claws scraped against the metal of his sword as Hall kicked out, catching the spindly creature in the stomach. It yelped but didn't move. Pain throbbed from Hall's foot and up his leg. As thin as they were, Cragglers were as hard as the rock they climbed.

Not wanting to physically hit one of the small creatures, he slashed out with his sword. The Craggler was nimble, darting out of the way. The long arms reached in, twisting around Hall's swinging sword, scoring a hit along his side. The leather armor held, the claws skidding along the tough material, but the force of the blow made Hall take a step to the side.

He sidestepped another attack from the Craggler, hearing a noise behind him. Activating *Leap*, Hall jumped straight up, feeling the change in the air as a Craggler dove where he had been. The two Cragglers slammed into each other, falling down in a heap. Hall landed and stabbed down with his sword. Once, twice, and a third time, ending both creatures.

He heard the crack of lightning, another bolt from Pike, followed by the cry of pain from a Craggler. Hall had no idea how many were left. Four accounted for that he knew of, hoping the others had taken care of the remaining Cragglers.

A warbling howl told him there was at least one left.

Hall turned, taking a step back as the Craggler ran at him. It missed, running past. Hall swung his sword, slicing across the creature's tough hide. It yelped in pain but turned quickly, charging at Hall. The Craggler was enraged and Hall easily avoided the attack. He swung again, scoring another hit. The creature tried to turn, but Jackoby's hammer came flying in from the side. The blow slammed into the small Craggler's head. The body stayed, the head tilted, and the neck snapped. The creature dropped to the ground.

Nodding thanks to the large Firbolg, Hall looked around the plateau.

SLAIN: *Darknotch Craggler Scrapper +5 Experience*
SLAIN: *Darknotch Craggler Scrapper +5 Experience*
SLAIN: *Darknotch Craggler Scrapper +5 Experience*
SLAIN: *Darknotch Craggler Scrapper +10 Experience*

Skill Gain!
Polearms Rank Two +.1
Skill Gain!
Small Blades Rank Two +.2

"Everyone good?" Hall asked.

They all nodded. He couldn't see any obvious injuries.

"Things are annoying," Urit muttered bending down and examining one of the two corpses before him. A grayish blood and bits of gore dripped from the head of his hammer. "Scurry all over these mountains like rats."

A hammer was a strong weapon, but it was not pretty as evidenced by the pulverized appearance of the Cragglers Urit and Jackoby had killed. It looked like the Firbolg's giant hammer had blasted the thin creatures apart.

Crouching next to the bodies he had killed, Hall quickly searched them. Nothing. No coins, no items. Nothing to salvage and sell. The thin hide armor they wore wasn't even worth grabbing for scraps. Torn, stained and smelling, Hall didn't even want to touch them.

He stood up, looking at the trail across the thin ridge.

"Let's get going," he said.

Hall didn't want to stay there, not with the bodies. The blood would attract scavengers. Crag Cats most likely, but a Stone Wyvern could be attracted as well. Hall did not want to encounter one of those on the small plateau. He didn't want to run across a Wyvern at all.

Highly poisonous, long and skinny, ferocious and quick. Wyverns were tough opponents. They were as adept at scaling up the mountain as the Cragglers and possessed wings that let them catch the wind currents through the mountains, drifting from peak to peak.

He glanced up into the sky, Pike once again flying high. Studying the sides of the mountain they were on and the one they were going to, Hall couldn't see anything moving. It wasn't a good way to tell if Cragglers were waiting to ambush them. The cursed things blended in so well against the stone.

———

They started across the ridge, past the stone statues of the Dwarves with shields. Carved from the gray stone of the mountain, the statues somehow had not lost any detail to erosion. With the constant wind and the harsh weather of the mountains, Hall had expected to see the features of the Dwarves worn away. He had thought there would be cracks in the stone, pieces missing. But there was nothing. The two statues were as perfect now as the day they had been carved.

Every hair in the two Dwarves beards was visible, the wrinkles around the eyes. Intricate runes covered the heads of the hammers and axes. Studying the faces of the two statues, Hall was amazed to see that he could tell the hammer wielder had been older than the one with the ax. He could even detect some family resemblance.

"Who are they?" Hall asked Urit.

The Dwarf looked up at the statues almost reverently. The pedestals they stood on where the height of Urit, putting the head of the statues almost even with Jackoby's eyes.

"That there be Bradlet Axestorm himself," Urit said, pointing at the statue with the hammer. "His son, Dornlet," he finished, pointing at the one with the ax.

That was who Hall had suspected the statues to be. Now he understood there was some magic involved that kept the statues from eroding.

The ridge wasn't as thin as Hall had first thought. Wide enough for two to walk abreast. But it was slippery, a thin layer of ice covering it in spots with the fierce wind funneled between the two mountains. Hall avoided looking to the side as he carefully stepped across. He knew there was a long drop and didn't need to be reminded. The distance wasn't great, and it only took a couple of minutes to cross.

Hall looked at the other two statues in passing, seeing the same level of detail and lack of erosion. The ridge ended at another plateau, this one not as large, the trail continuing to the north around the peak.

It wrapped around the mountain, the group walking in single file. The wind blasted them, no longer protected by the peak, they were exposed to the full blast. Cloaks fluttered and snapped, no matter how hard they tried to hold them tight. Hall could feel the chill blast against his exposed cheeks, glad he was able to cover up his arms and wondering when he would find some armor with sleeves. The wind wasn't constant. When it stopped, Hall found the temperature to be pleasant. The sun was warm. Hall could feel it against his skin, the chill leaving his cheeks. But it would immediately come back with the wind.

They were only exposed to the wind for almost an hour before the trail curled around the peak, putting the wind to their backs. Jackoby was in the rear, the large Firbolg making an excellent break.

Hall realized the trail was starting to slope gradually down. He was still surprised how well maintained the trail was. It didn't show heavy usage, but there was a lack of loose stones that should have gathered, falling from the slopes above. No leaves or sticks or other debris was evident. Aside from the Craggler ambush, Hall would have thought the entire trek was within the confines of Axestorm and not the wilds of the mountains.

———

"Wow," Sabine said.

Hall agreed with her.

They stood at the top of a valley high in the mountains. The peaks surrounded them, keeping the wind out and letting the sun shine bright. A waterfall crashed down at the far end, forming a small pond and brook that flowed through the valley to disappear into the side. The steep sides were exposed stone, no trees or bushes. Slopes of loose shale. A handful of small groves of trees filled the floor of the valley, with wide-open spaces between.

What had amazed Sabine and the others, were the things in the open spaces. Varied in design and size, numerous mausoleums littered the floor. Random in location, no set patterns, with a lot of space around and between. No two were alike. Some only a single story, others three or more. Flat blocks with no ornamentation and those that were almost garish in the decorations. Gray stone or other materials added. A couple caught the sun, showing the glint of gold or jewels. Stone bridges, as varied as the buildings, passed over the brook.

Even more amazing was the number of caves that dotted the sides of the valley. Dozens of dark openings at random elevations, switchbacking paths leading to each. Some were close, others with dozens of feet between. Some high up the slope, some just barely above the floor. The openings were as varied as the buildings. Some ornate, others plain.

"Welcome to the Valley of the Ancients," Urit exclaimed. "Impressive, is it not?"

Hall nodded. It seemed Sky Realms Online was still surprising him. The Dwarf graveyard was new. He had wondered what they would encounter when they got to the end of the trail. He had never imagined something like what he was looking at. He had lost count between the caves on the sides and all the buildings below.

The name was plain, Hall thought. Nothing fancy or special, but it worked. It described the valley perfectly.

"It's best not to venture down there in the dark," Urit added, looking up at the sky and the location of the sun. "I know it's still early enough but…"

The Dwarf left it hanging. Hall agreed with the thought. He had no wish to wander those paths in the dark. Even if there were no undead, graveyards were not places to spend time at night.

"We can camp there," Urit said.

Hall tore his gaze away from the valley, looking to where Urit pointed. He hadn't noticed that the trail didn't just run down the slope to the floor, it also continued along the top of the ridge. At the end was a small tower. Three stories, very few windows, and a domed roof. A single door led inside, another cave stable just to the side.

They followed the Stonefire Dwarf into the tower. Pike lifted off Hall's shoulder, spiraling into the air. Hall was the last one into the tower, taking a last look up into the sky, watching Pike disappear into the mountains. He walked inside, closing the wooden door behind them. The round tower was only about twenty feet in diameter, a railing less stair curving up the side. Mostly empty, the first floor looked like it was used for supplies. Stacks of cut wood were piled to a side, pieces of bark across the floor like a trail to the stairs. Axes, shovels, and cloaks hung on racks along the walls. A stone hearth lay directly across from the entrance. The group walked up the Dwarf sized steps. Hall was thankful that the rooms were still sized for humans and others, the Dwarfs liking high ceilings in their architecture.

The stair stopped at a small landing before continuing to the third floor. Three tables filled most of the second floor, cabinets against the wall and another stone hearth filled with mostly burned logs.

"Do a lot of travelers come up here?" Hall asked.

He couldn't imagine regular travelers. The distance was just too great.

"Pilgrims and priests mostly," Urit answered. "Sometimes the spirits are restless," he explained, leaving it at that.

Hall and Sabine exchanged glances, the Witch obviously wanting to learn more. Hall just shrugged. They were at a massive graveyard, hundreds if not thousands of dead Dwarves. Of course, there would be frequent Undead problems.

"Beds upstairs," Urit said, pointing to the ceiling. "Just frames, no mattresses."

"Better than sleeping on the ground," Hall said. "Let's get a fire going and some food. Probably be a long day tomorrow."

———

Hall leaned back in his chair. He could feel the heat coming from the fire in the hearth. They had stocked it high with fresh logs. They had only trail rations for dinner, not like the meal they had gotten at Greystone Watch, but combined with the fire, it made for a pleasant enough meal.

There had not been much conversation, but they were not a vocal group. Jackoby sat at the end of the table, with them but not. Sabine and Caryn sat across from each other and not talking much outside themselves. Most of the conversation had come from Urit and Roxhard, Hall listening in.

The young Stonefire, already calling Roxhard 'cousin,' had asked what it was like growing up in human lands with human foster parents. Roxhard answered as best he could, most lacking in real depth. Dismissive, barely answering the questions. But Urit accepted them all.

Just need some ale, Hall thought. *And Leigh*.

"I need some air," Roxhard said, abruptly standing up as Urit kept up with the questions.

"Ah, I understand cousin," Urit said cheerfully, not understanding Roxhard's sudden need for space. "Not every day one meets their ancestors."

Hall watched Roxhard move slowly downstairs, lost in thought. He waited a moment for Urit to become distracted, the Dwarf trying to talk Jackoby into a game of dice. Hall stood up, waving aside Caryn's questioning look. He followed Roxhard downstairs, seeing the wooden door shut.

Opening it quietly, Hall stepped out into the cold night. He stepped away from the tower, letting his eyes adjust and his racial *Limited Night Vision* to activate. He saw the shadowed shape of Roxhard standing near the edge, where the land sloped sharply down to the valley floor.

"How's it going?" he asked, walking to stand next to the Dwarf. He crouched down, putting his head just below Roxhard's shoulder.

The Dwarf was silent for a while, standing like a stone.

"I don't know," he admitted finally speaking. "It should be overwhelming, but it's not."

Hall glanced at him, a reflex action at the strange statement, knowing Roxhard couldn't see it. That had not been the answer he had expected. Only fourteen, Roxhard had barely been hanging on, for the most part. He had gotten better, but Hall suspected the Dwarf had been walking a razor's edge. Constant activity and action hadn't given him time to stop and think or reflect.

"It's like I said back in Axestorm," Roxhard continued. "It's kind of like coming home."

He paused again and looked up at the moon. Most of it was visible, a bright circle missing small pieces as islands and clouds passed in front of it.

"I miss my home," he said. "My real home. Not here," Roxhard waved his hand, indicating the world around them. "I do. Everyday. But I had started to accept that this was my new home forever, and then we came here and it feels right."

Hall looked out across the valley. He couldn't hear anything or see anything. Nothing moved. The night was silent.

"Where did that stuff about the Dwarven parents come from," he asked, glancing behind him to make sure Urit had not come out.

Roxhard chuckled.

"That was crazy huh," he said. "It came from my Character Sheet. I started to panic when Matron Lydi asked me their names. We had never talked about them and even if we had, any names we had made up would get us caught. She asked and something told me to check my Sheet. So I did." He looked down at Hall and even though he couldn't see the Dwarf's features, Hall knew he was smiling and excited. "The names were there. All in the backstory."

Hall was shocked. There was never anything in the backstory beyond the standard race and location information. Nothing personnel. There had been hardcore role players that had made up their own, crafting generations of lineage and inventing towns or villages they came from. Hall had never done anything like that, had never seen the need. He hadn't even looked at that section of his Sheet since the first days trapped in the game.

He opened it now, cycling through the tabs to the right screen.

It started out with the standard script he was used to seeing.

Half-Elves are a mix of Human and Elven parents. They can live in either culture but are never truly at home anywhere. Most Half-Elves tend to wander, never staying in one place, but can be incredibly loyal to anyplace they end up calling home. Half-Elves have the Starting Skills of Herbology, Skinning, and Survival. Each gains at an accelerated rate and can be used without formal training. Half-Elves also receive a starting Attribute bonus of +2 to Agility and +1 to Wellness. Half-Elves also receive a bonus of +5 to Health, +2 to Energy and +2 to Vitality at each level.

But there was more. Much more. All new. He swore it had not been there before.

You were born in the small village of Hillspan on the island of Scorrow, a medium-sized unclaimed realm between Essec and the wilder lands of the Elves. Scorrow had a mixed population of Gael and Wood Elves, sometimes at war with each other and sometimes not. Your father was a Wood Elf Hunter that died when you were just a young boy, when defending the area against raiding Ursotan. He had been named Torrin, a member of the WildOak tribe. Your mother, named Dorothea who had lived her life in Hillspan, raised you until you left to find your fate at the age of eighteen.

"What the…" Hall said as he read it again. "That is insane," he added after the third time.

"Right?" Roxhard said, chuckling. There was a strange note to his laugh. Disbelief tinged with a little panic. "When did this happen? How did it happen?"

Hall shook his head. "I don't know," he said, realizing Roxhard couldn't see the movement.

He was dumbfounded. He knew from Roxhard's encounter with the Stonefires that his backstory extended far behind his own character sheet. It was real, it was true, and all the NPCs knew of it. Did that extend to Hall's own backstory? His new backstory?

He had never heard of any of the places mentioned. No Scorrow, no Hillspan, and no WildOak tribe. Where had those names come from? His parents? Thinking on the names, saying them aloud, conjured no memories. He couldn't picture them because they did not exist.

Not yet.

He thought about what Roxhard had said about Axestorm feeling like home. What would happen if he set foot in this Hillspan? Would it feel like coming home? Would he suddenly remember these parents?

It was too much. Hall felt himself on the verge of losing it.

How had Roxhard been able to handle this new discovery?

Hall sighed, taking a deep breath.

He forced himself to calm down, to think it through. The Devs, Electronic Storm, in the mail he had received the first day had said that they would be adding to the content to keep Sky Realms Online engaging for those trapped in it. Was that what was happening?

They also said it had been two years since the Glitch had happened. Two years of possible development before Hall and the others had been relaunched. Was all the backstory, connections, and new areas created during those two years? If so, why hadn't it appeared right away?

Or had the tech developed so Electronic Storm could do live patching? Update the world without having to do any uploading or downloading? No downtime at all? Instant patching? Able to add content on the fly? The implications of that were staggering. And a bit scary. Were the Devs watching everything they did? Adding content based on their actions? They saw that Roxhard would need in-game parentage and quickly added it in? That didn't seem possible. Not for humans to code, test, and patch in.

Some kind of AI?

"Wild," he said.

CHAPTER NINETEEN

THEY ATE QUICKLY JUST AS THE SUN CRESTED THE PEAKS TO the east. The morning was chilly, the fires gone out during the night. No one bothered to light a new one, knowing they would be leaving first thing in the morning.

Standing at the top of the long and switchbacking trail that led down, Urit pointed out the largest of the mausoleums. It stood near the waterfall, just to the side, the edge of the building also the edge of the pond. Smooth gray stone with a slight taper toward the top. The base was wide, three or four stories tall, with a sloped roof leading to a point. A statue-lined walk led to the large double doors.

"That there is the Axestorm Crypt," Urit said.

Hall nodded, studying the large building. It wasn't ornate, more functional than built for form. But there was a stark beauty noticeable even from this distance. The valley was long and wide. Now that he was looking, Hall saw that there was a stone-lined path that led from where they were all the way to the Axestorm Crypt. The trail wasn't straight, there were gentle curves and turns to it. This path passed over the river and back, meandering around other crypts, rolling over small hills. Hall could see it pass through some of the trees, trying to create a feeling of traveling through a park. A peaceful field. If Urit hadn't warned them of the possibility of Undead, Hall would have thought it a nice enough place for a stroll. He could imagine the ceremonies the Dwarves would have when they buried their honored dead.

Urit's leather-gloved finger moved off the Axestorm Crypt and settled on a cave halfway up the back wall, on the opposite side of the small pond. Before it jutted out a small shelf, the steep trail cutting into the side of the valley as it switchbacked down to the floor. It was too far away to make out any details.

"And that is the entrance to the Stonefire Crypt," Urit said with a note of pride.

Hall studied the crypt openings along the valley walls. There were no others on the back wall, no buildings near the Axestorm Crypt. The proximity of the Stonefires cave seemed to indicate a position of high rank. The long sides of the valley were covered in openings, which would make the crypts beyond not that big. There wasn't that much space to spread out. But at the end of the valley? The lone crypt on the wall? It could be sizeable.

And, of course, it would be a long walk.

"We better get going," Hall said.

———

The sun was high, just hitting noon, and they were just over three-quarters of the way through the valley. It had seemed long from high above, but this was far longer than Hall had estimated. Taking the path was slow, the worn stones not going in a straight line. None of them wanted to step off the path though. This valley was a graveyard, and stepping on potential graves seemed offensive.

Instead, they resigned themselves to the long walk. It was

chilly in the valley. The sun did provide some warmth but not enough came down to the depths of the valley. Or maybe it was just the atmosphere? Hall couldn't tell. He had always gotten a chill when walking through graveyards. The hairs on the back of his neck and arms standing up, goosebumps across his flesh. Even in real life, he had felt like he was being watched.

It was even worse in a world, game, where ghosts and other Undead existed.

Pike flew above, and Hall would use his *Shared Vision* ability to connect with the dragonhawk's eyes. With the increased detail he could see most of the valley, the group appearing small but trackable. He did this every half hour to hour, using Pike's vision to reassure himself that there was nothing following them. That it was just his imagination.

Urit pointed out some of the crypts as they walked, naming clans and sharing some of their history with an emphasis on the connections to the Stonefires. Hall knew it was for Roxhard's benefit, educating the lost Stonefire Dwarf on his heritage, but most of it Hall just ignored. For his part, Roxhard was paying attention and seemed to be absorbing it. Hall wondered if the information was somehow being imported into Roxhard's Character Sheet.

Ever since his thoughts on the world's potential Live Patching, Hall was looking at everything differently. He had almost forgotten that it was a game world, but this was just hammering it home that he was trapped in a game. Which meant that Leigh was truly nothing but lines of code.

But so was he. So was Sabine and Caryn and Roxhard.

Nothing but lines of code that the Devs could alter whenever they choose. They controlled this world, as evidenced by how completely Roxhard's Stonefire history had been adapted into the lore of the Axestorm Dwarves.

He sighed. Angry at the reminder that they were not in full control of their lives.

Was everything they encountered and went through all at the whims of the Devs? Was Electronic Storm guiding their lives? If so, why? There had to be a reason. Hall just couldn't think of one.

But was this really guided content? There was no way. Yes, they were only on Huntley and at Axestorm because of the plans Hall had found in Cornet's lockbox in the forest outside Silverpeak Keep. They had only gone to Silverpeak Keep because they needed supplies to start rebuilding Skara Brae. The village had only been found because Hall had encountered Leigh in the Green Flow Forest on Cumberland.

There were some connections, but it had still been his choices to take the quests, to do that content. He had not been guided to where he had met Leigh. Or Roxhard or even Sabine. And they were still in an MMORPG environment. Still subject to the game mechanics. That was the purpose of quest chains, to lead from one event to the next and one area to the next.

So how much freedom did they really have in this new version of Sky Realms Online?

It had been their decision to go to Green Ember where they met Jackoby. He could see how events in Silverpeak Keep would have been different if they hadn't detoured to the Firbolg village. There was plenty of evidence that they were following their own paths.

He was feeling less angry, more in control of his life.

Adding in-game parents for Roxhard could have been the Devs way of easing his transition into this new life.

Hall pushed those thoughts away, locking them in the back of his mind. He had accepted this as his reality, and there was no point in dissecting it. Life was what it was now.

The stone slabs of the path were worn with age but well

set. There was very little difference in the heights, no random corners sticking up to trip them as they walked. Two-foot square, an inch or so between, grays and blacks. Some lighter colored stones. Statues stood at intervals, near the small stone-lined paths that led to the different crypts. Each depicted something different. Dwarves, weapons, mountains and other objects. Identification for what clan each crypt held. Other trails set with the stone slabs led to other areas of the large graveyard. Urit led them down the main path, the widest trail.

"How often do you come here?" Hall asked their guide.

"Not since me own communion with the ancients," Urit answered from where he walked ahead. "That was near twenty years ago."

———

They stopped at the edge of the pond, the path continuing to their left and heading straight up to where Axestorm Crypt towered over everything. The mausoleum dominated, larger than Hall had first thought. The plain starkness of the design lent it more weight. Even the sound of the waterfall crashing into the pond lent weight to the massive Crypt.

The main trail continued along the shore of the pond, but a smaller side trail led the other way, following the pond and then turning to start the climb up the side of the valley.

Hall could see the opening to the Stonefire Crypt. A dark shadow against the gray-white stone of the valley. It was higher than the steep roof of Axestorm, having its own presence. The sun shone down into the valley but seemed to stop at the cave as if it were afraid. Something felt off about the Crypt.

It was a Crypt, and Hall knew what that meant. In all the games he had ever played, Crypts and Graveyards meant undead. He fully expected to see Undead within the Stonefire Crypt. But something still felt off about it. It was warm now

272 • TROY OSGOOD

that the sun had burned off the morning's chill, but Hall could feel the cold coming from the cave.

Even Urit felt something was off.

He eyed the opening warily as he led them down the side path. Statues lined it at intervals, ancient Stonefire heroes Urit explained, pointing them out and naming them for Roxhard. Hall shook his head, seeing resemblance to Roxhard in all the carved stone faces. It was weird how deep the game had taken it. How much processing power had been, and still was, involved? The Devs could have just made the statues eroded, not putting similar features to Roxhard on every Dwarf and changing each one just a little to make them all unique.

Would they all disappear or change when we leave, Hall thought, wondering if all this was just temporary. Was all this some kind of instanced area?

Did it matter?

Hall kept his eyes off the Crypt opening, watching the waves caused by the waterfall as they rippled across the pond. He could see fish swimming around beneath the waters. Clear water with few weeds. Then he saw a darker shadow moving along the bottom. Thick and long, it flowed from side to side like a snake, disappearing in the turbulent waters under the falls.

"What was that?" he asked, pointing into the water.

They all watched the water, looking for the shape Hall had described, but none saw it again. Hall kept one eye on the pond as they continued walking.

The side of the valley was steep, the path cutting back and forth. Wide enough for two to walk side by side, it was smooth and free of loose rocks. Hall felt a sense of familiarity. It was like climbing the trail up Breakridge and coming to the top to look down into the meadow and Skara Brae. This trail went up to a wide landing and turned back, continuing up, doing this multiple times.

The shadow of the shelf jutting out from the cliffside kept them in darkness for most of the trip. The temperature dropped, the stone around them radiating chill.

"Something is wrong here," Hall said.

None of the others answered, but all agreed.

They came out of the shadow and back into the sun, feeling warmth against their bodies once again. The path crested, and they walked out onto the shelf.

Two more statues stood at attention to either side of the opening. Each was carved from solid black stone. Both in full plate armor with visors lowered. Each carrying a shield held in front of their bodies, a hammer held over the shield. Guardians of the Crypt. The opening was large, stone blocks framing it with the now-familiar symbol of the Stonefires carved into the keystone.

All of them stepped out onto the shelf, arraying themselves in front of the opening.

They could feel the cold and the darkness coming from inside. Each gripped their weapons tighter.

"Something is very wrong," Urit said.

"You think?" Sabine muttered.

Hall stepped forward, stopping at the edge of the opening. He could barely see inside, the darkness was so deep. It was a room, an antechamber of some kind with a large sculpture in the middle. Darker openings led off in all three directions. Nothing moved.

At least nothing he could see.

But he felt eyes on him. Something watching him.

"Let's just go," Sabine said.

"Ye can't," Urit said, and all eyes turned to him. "Roxhard needs this to be confirmed as a true Stonefire. Without speaking with the Ancestors, he'll be clanless forever." The way Urit spoke, it sounded like that was the most horrible thing that could happen to a Dwarf. He gave a brief shudder

274 • TROY OSGOOD

at the thought. "And I need yer help in finding out what is wrong."

Urit Stonefire has led you to the Stonefire Crypt. You do not know why but all feel like something is wrong. The Crypt is cold and dark. Urit has requested your aid in finding out what has happened.

CRYPT FINDINGS I
Find out what has happened to the Stonefire Crypt 0/1
Reward: +300 Stonefire Clan Reputation, +50 Experience

ACCEPT QUEST?

Hall glanced at the others. Roxhard was staring into the Crypt, eager to get started. He had already accepted the quest. Caryn nodded. Jackoby, like always, appeared indifferent. Sabine glared at him, clearly not happy. She finally rolled her eyes, giving him a wave of her hand. Whatever she was saying.

He turned back to Urit.

"Okay."

CHAPTER TWENTY

Jackoby went first, Caryn right behind.

Sabine and Urit entered, leaving Hall and Roxhard outside. The Dwarf looked up at the statues and into the Crypt. Nervous.

"You got this," Hall said and shot his fist out to Roxhard.

Smiling, Roxhard knocked his fist into Halls. Together they walked into the Crypt.

It was becoming their standard formation. Hall a couple steps behind Jackoby in the lead and Caryn behind the Warden. It made tactical sense, Hall knew even though he wanted to be in front. He hated putting people—his people and his friends—in harm's way first. Caryn had the *Increased Perception* Skill and her *Trap* Skills. That meant she could spot and disarm any traps before Jackoby could spring them. The Firbolg was in front to take the brunt of any ambushes. Hall was the next as he could use *Leap* to clear the other two if need be, to take a second wave of attackers or attack from behind. Spellcasters, just Sabine now, were next with Urit Stonefire and Roxhard bringing up the rear. Protecting the rear.

Jackoby was the Warden tank, where Roxhard was now

their DPS. When the Firbolg had joined the group and took over as the primary tank, Hall had thought Roxhard bothered by it. Jealous or feeling inadequate. Which the Dwarf had been for a short time, but he had gotten over it. He enjoyed just dealing damage and not having to worry about all the duties of the tank.

If Jackoby had an issue with it, Hall didn't care. The Firbolg had the right equipment, was stronger and better suited for it. In the back of his mind, a very small section in the far back, Hall secretly hoped that by serving as the meat shield Jackoby would eventually think his Life Debt honored. It wasn't that Hall disliked Jackoby, he didn't, but he also didn't like the Warden. The Firbolg doing nothing to allow himself to be liked.

They had gone maybe ten feet in when Caryn tapped Jackoby on the back. The Firbolg stopped, glancing down at the small woman. She crept forward, staring down at the ground. Crouching down, she ran her fingers along the surface of the stone.

The room was smaller than Hall had thought from outside. Only twenty feet square. Three arched openings, each on a wall, led off into darkness. In the middle of the room was the statue. It reached almost to the top of the room, at least the large two-handed hammer the statue held uprised in one hand did. A Dwarf. The same as the statues outside. Hall assumed it to be of Brignir Stonefire, the patriarch of the Clan. The great Dwarf who had founded the Stonefires, carved stone likeness the same as the tapestry in Matron Lydi's audience chamber.

There was just enough light to see the details of the statue, which was taller and broader than Jackoby, sitting raised on a pedestal.

Caryn raised her hand, motioning that it was okay to proceed. The duo, Firbolg and Gael, did a quick sweep of the room, spending time at each of the openings. Hall moving parallel across the room but not into, ready to jump to their assistance if need be. They found nothing. Safe to enter the antechamber.

Urit handed out torches he had taken from the supplies at the tower they had stayed the night in. Lighting them, they set the flaming brands in brackets attached at intervals along the wall. Light filled the room, casting flickering shadows.

Roxhard and Urit walked forward to stand before the statue. They both looked up at it, Urit reverently and Roxhard somewhat in awe. Hall studied the sculpture. It wasn't made of the same black stone as the others outside. This one was carved from a shining gray stone that started to catch the light from the torches being lit. The craftsmanship was near perfect. The details were smooth, no chisel marks anywhere. Polished, the stone shined.

Hall could see writing in the pedestal, which was a dark gray and different type of stone. Flowing lines of script in the Dwarf language, alternating with runes. More runework framed the writing. Hall could read none of it. He knew Urit could, possibly Roxhard, but didn't bother asking. He assumed it spoke of Brignir's life and accomplishments, as well as the history of the Stonefire Clan. The runes probably provided the magic that kept the statue from eroding and cracking.

"Which way?" Sabine asked.

The Witch stood just in front of the statue, looking from opening to opening. Coming to stand next to her, Hall could feel the cold in the room. Not just physical cold and damp, but mental as well. The Crypt felt worse inside then it had outside. Darkness practically flowed from the openings, especially the one in front. It seemed that one was the largest concentration of the dark feeling.

"Straight," Urit answered.

Sabine groaned.

"Of course," Hall muttered.

———

The arch opened into a dark tunnel, with a slight slope, about fifteen feet wide and that high, the walls curving up to match the arch. Thicker beams and columns were built into the walls every twenty feet. Small stone blocks made up the wall and ceilings, larger blocks the floor. Each was tightly fit together, none loose. Brackets were set into the wider columns, and they lit the first couple.

The light showed a long tunnel, darkness at the far end.

"It goes fer about a hundred feet," Urit explained, "before the first side corridors. The main heads straight fer another hundred feet before emptying into the first crypt."

"That's where Brignir is?" Hall asked.

"Aye."

Hall took a couple steps forward, looking down the tunnel. He wished he had brought Pike into the Crypt, instead of leaving the dragonhawk outside. The feeling of eyes watching him had returned as he had stepped into the tunnel. He had felt it outside on the cliff but not in the antechamber. Why was it back now? Because they were heading for the main crypt where Brignir was laid to rest?

Or possibly unrest.

"We have three goals," Hall said, not turning around, but keeping his voice low. "First is to get to this Brignir's coffin so Roxhard can commune with him or whatever he's supposed to do." Hall glanced at Urit for confirmation that was where they needed to go for that quest. The young Stonefire Dwarf nodded. "Second is to lay his father to rest." Again, Hall looked to Urit.

"Down the first right-side corridor," Urit replied.

"And third," Hall continued, "is to find out what is wrong with this place."

"Where do we start?" Caryn asked quickly, and Hall

wondered if she was jumping in before Sabine could utter a snarky comment.

"Brignir," Hall replied. He had a hunch that the source of the Crypt's odd feeling would be found in the same place.

No one said anything so he took it as agreement.

They moved relatively quickly. Caryn still checked for traps, which slowed progress, but Hall kept them walking steadily forward. Pausing at the first intersection, they did take some time to move down the side corridors a couple dozen feet to be safe. They found nothing, just long corridors, built the same as the first. The torches provided enough light. Hall had thought it would be dark in the corridors, but some material of the gray stone reflected the light, adding to it and sending it further then it would have naturally. He had paused to examine the stone the first time he had noticed the effect.

There was nothing special that he could see. It just worked.

It wasn't long before they entered the crypt of Brignir Stonefire.

A curved room with a high vaulted ceiling. Gray and black stones with small tiles along the floor that were set flush with the larger stone blocks of the corridor floor. Between each of the vaults was a carved niche, the details lost in shadow as was the top of the domed ceiling. In the center of the circular room was a simple stone sarcophagus. It sat on the floor, not on a raised dais, just low on the ground. A solid block of dark stone, a thin joint where the lid sat. No runes or writing that any of them could see. Even the walls were plain.

Hall was a little underwhelmed.

This was the founder of a large and powerful clan.

He had expected more.

More grandeur, more decorations.

There were no tapestries. No statues.

He looked into one of the niches, his eyes adjusting to the darkness which activated his *Limited Night Vision*. It was empty.

A quick check of a second one showed that to be empty too. Turning back to the middle of the room he saw the others looking into the alcoves.

"Nothing," Sabine muttered, her voice strangely loud in the space.

It didn't quite echo as much as it reverberated. Not repeating, but shuddering and skipping.

All eyes darted around the chamber, hands gripping weapons tighter. They all expected something to happen. Sabine at least looked apologetic as her eyes scanned the dark shadows of the ceiling.

After a moment they grew less tense, not truly relaxing and still on guard, but releasing coiled up energy. Hall could still feel the darkness flowing through the crypt, an oppressive weight pushing down on him. He shivered, staring at the sarcophagus, where it all seemed to be coming from.

Urit walked slowly forward. The young Dwarf stopped in front of the black stone coffin, eyes going wide.

"By the ancestors," he exclaimed. "It's gone."

He spoke quietly, his voice not causing the strange echo effect.

"What's gone?" Hall asked as they all crowded in close.

"The ax," Urit replied, visibly shaken, his voice having a slight tremble. "The Stonefires' sacred weapon. The Ax *of Obsidian Flames*."

As Urit spoke a breeze came rushing down the corridor, a howling sound with it. Blowing into the chamber, it curved around them, cloaks fluttering. It swirled around the sarcophagus, driving them all back. Tighter and tighter the wind seemed to swirl, a cloud of smoke appearing in the middle of the small cyclone.

The chill in the room grew but not the feeling of darkness.

Faster and faster the wind swirled, harder and harder. The smoke began to take shape, becoming a wispy figure of a

1

Dwarf. One that Hall instantly recognized. Only the top half of the Dwarf was revealed, the edges loose, bits of smoke floating into the air, the bottom half a swirling mass of cloud.

It was Brignir Stonefire.

"Who disturbs my rest," the Dwarf said, his voice deep but somehow insubstantial. Hall could hear it, understand it, but it was barely heard as if carried away by the wind. "Who has stolen from me?"

———

Skill Gain!
Identify Rank Two +.1

Animated Spirit of Brignir Stonefire (Purple)

Anger radiated from the translucent ghost. Anger and power. The feeling of cold and darkness grew, causing Hall to shiver. He involuntarily looked behind him at the shadows thick in the room, expecting things to burst forth. The wind continued to swirl through the room. Hall noticed a smell, something new coming with the wind. Death. The scent of death.

"Return that which ye have taken," the spirit of Brignir Stonefire growled. Hall could feel it cutting through his head, slicing into his mind.

You have been struck with Ghostly Thought. Each word spoken by the Spirit deals 5 damage.

"Grandfather," Urit croaked, trying to force the words out. "We did not take yer weapon."

The spirit howled, Hall clutching at his head.

"Ye are here. It is gone," Brignir spoke slowly each word a

flare of pain. "My place of rest has been defiled. Return it or face the wrath of the ancients."

Then it stopped. The spirit disappeared, the wind gone instantly.

"What was that?" Sabine said in shock, turning around and looking all over the room.

They all were, turning fast circles, clutching weapons tight. Eyes searched the shadows.

"What is the wrath of the ancients?" Roxhard asked nervously.

"I do not know," Urit replied, staring at the sarcophagus and the indent on the top that was empty.

Hall noticed the feeling of cold and darkness remained, greater than before. The air was heavy, thick with expectation. Something was waiting. Many somethings. Hungry and angry.

QUEST COMPLETE!

You have discovered what has caused the darkness to enter the Stonefire Crypt. The clan's ancient and sacred weapon has been stolen. This has awakened and angered the spirit of Brignir Stonefire.

CRYPT FINDINGS I

Find out what has happened to the Stonefire Crypt 1/1
Reward: +300 Stonefire Clan Reputation; +50 Experience

"Can you feel that?" Caryn asked, eyes darting around, her twin swords drawn. "It's like something is watching us and waiting."

"Whatever it is," Sabine said slowly," it doesn't like us."

On her shoulder Salem was crouched, fur along his back raised. The Minx Cat's large yellow eyes looked everywhere, a low growl coming from its throat.

"We need to find the Ax," Urit said, not moving from where he still stared at the sarcophagus.

"Not our concern," Sabine said. "Let's get out of here."

"I won't be able to complete my quest if the Ax isn't returned?" Roxhard asked Urit. The other Dwarf nodded.

Roxhard looked to Hall, eyes desperate. He really wanted to be accepted as a Stonefire. How could Hall deny him that?

"We'll find the ax," he answered, earning a dirty look from Sabine that he ignored.

The Ax of Obsidian Flames, the Stonefire Clan's ancient artifact, was stolen. You have agreed to find and return the Ax to the crypt of Brignir Stonefire.

CRYPT FINDINGS II
Find the Ax of Obsidian Flames 0/1
Return the Ax to the crypt of Brignir Stonefire 0/1
Reward: +300 Stonefire Clan Reputation; +100 Experience

ACCEPT QUEST?

Hall quickly accepted the quest, glancing at the others who nodded. Even Sabine, who did so reluctantly.

"Okay," Sabine muttered. "If we're really going to do this, where do we start?"

That was a good question. Hall had no idea. He had half expected the quest to provide some hint or direction. Something. Anything.

He walked over to the sarcophagus, where Urit still stood. It only came up to his knee, sized for a Dwarf. Crouching down for a closer look, he examined the top, studying the indentation where the Ax had rested. It ran the length of the top, taking up most of the width with the head. The ax was massive. The head was double-bladed, each curling high and low in toward the shaft. Two smaller indentations were in the center of each head, perfect hexagonal shapes. Gems mounted to the ax heads?

"How was it mounted to the top?" Hall asked. "Traps?"

Hall saw no evidence that the Ax had been pried out, or any traps activated. It was just missing. He reached out and ran his hand over where the weapon should have been. He wondered if it has just been rendered invisible. His fingers touched nothing, running along the smooth indentation. The spirit of Brignir would have known if it was just invisible. But Hall had to eliminate the possibility.

"The stone was magically formed around the Ax," Urit said. "The weapon was half contained within the block. No need fer traps as there was no way to remove it."

There had been a way because it was gone.

"How long has it been missing?"

"Less than a week I would think," Urit replied. "Maybe only a day or two."

Hall had hoped for a more solid timeline.

No solid timeline, no hint at how it had been removed. Nothing that would help Hall solve the mystery or provide a clue.

Cursing he stepped away from the sarcophagus. There was no evidence there. There had to be some kind of time limit to this quest. But how long did they have before Brignir unleashed the ancients? Whatever those were.

"Over here," Caryn said, drawing their attention.

She was crouched at the rear of the room, inside one of the shadowed alcoves, torch in hand. The niche was different from the others. Deeper, with runes and writing carved along the curved back wall. Hall couldn't read any of it. He beckoned Urit over.

"That is the history of Brignir," Urit explained. "Every crypt has one fer the occupant. It tells their greatest deeds. Not all are as long as Brignirs."

The writing covered the entire surface of the wall, from top to bottom. A height of ten feet and down to the ground. Every inch in the flowing runic script of the Dwarves. Hall could imagine what deeds the clan founder had accomplished.

But it wasn't the writing that Caryn was pointing at. It was the marks along the stone floor. Thin lines scraped into the hard stone coming out from the wall a couple of inches.

Skill Gain!
Increased Perception Rank Two +.1

Hall knew what the marks meant.
There was a door in the back wall.

CHAPTER TWENTY-ONE

"All the crypts have back doors like this," Urit explained as Jackoby pulled the carved stone door open. "One of the first things we build after making the main chamber. In case of a cave in."

Hall had heard of that practice with mines and underground chambers in the real world. It made sense. But he would have assumed that once the crypt was done, the back door was sealed. He said as much to Urit.

"Aye," the Dwarf replied, frowning into the dark corridor beyond. "It was."

They all looked into the opening. The tunnel beyond was only as wide as the door, just as high. Made for Dwarves to quickly exit. It would be a tight fit for all of them. Jackoby would have to crouch to make it through. *No way is he leading*, Hall thought. He glanced at the javelin over his shoulder and spear in hand. Hall stepped back out of the way.

"Rox," he said, motioning toward the tunnel. "You're on point."

Nodding, adjusting his grip on his two-handed ax, Roxhard stepped into the tunnel.

He paused, letting his eyes adjust and his racial dark vision to activate. Hall didn't think there would be traps. No reason the Dwarves would have installed any and the thief, or thieves, wouldn't have left any behind. Even though he was sure the tunnel was trap free, he made sure to space the group out, keeping at least ten feet between them.

The floor was smooth enough, but the walls and ceiling were not. Quickly and roughly cut, sharp edges stuck out, catching them in the dark. The torch that Sabine carried provided some light but served to increase the depth of the shadows at the edges. The tunnel ran straight, sloping up, for over a hundred feet before it curved sharply to the right or what Hall took to be east.

Roxhard smartly paused at the bend, listening and waiting. A perfect ambush point. The Dwarf glanced back at Hall who nodded. Taking a deep breath, Roxhard turned the corner, weapon ready. He saw nothing, felt nothing. No trap, no attack. Stepping back, he signaled to the others and continued down the tunnel.

It curved once more before, back to the left and the original direction. Or so Hall thought. It was hard to tell in the darkness of the tunnel, hand running along the wall. He had lost track of time. Had it been an hour? Less?

Finally, he thought he saw a thin strip of light ahead. Bright against the dark.

As they got closer, the light took on the shape of a door. One that was open, a wider strip to the side. They could feel a draft, cold, blowing down the tunnel.

Pausing at the door, Roxhard shifted to be more in the shadows and out of sight from anyone outside. He listened, watching. Shrugging, he pushed at the stone slab. It slid open.

Loudly.

Stone grating against stone.

Grimacing, Roxhard stepped back. He looked sheepishly

down the tunnel. Hall could hear Sabine muttering behind him as the light from the torch was blown out by the wind. The open door provided enough light to see, and Hall quickly made his way to stand next to Roxhard.

The view wasn't much, but he saw mountains, the green of treetops, dark gray stone all around. And a cliff not that far from the door. From where he stood, it looked as if a trail followed the mountainside to the east. He could just see the sun, enough to orientate himself for directions.

Hall sent his thoughts out, searching for Pike. The dragonhawk was distant, miles away. Too far to be used as a scout. Hall still asked Pike to fly their way. He missed the comforting weight of Pike on his shoulder or the feel in his mind of the dragonhawk circling nearby. Even when he didn't consciously activate their bond, to see through Pike's eyes, Hall always felt Pike. He knew where the dragonhawk generally was and what Pike was doing.

Thankfully the impressions were just basic. He knew when Pike was eating and didn't have to experience it.

Hall stepped out into the light, immediately feeling the cold wind slam against him. He stood on a small shelf, barely deeper than the stone door, a trail leading off to the right. The trail, what he could see before it curved around the mountain, didn't widen out. Wind slammed against him, pushing him back and swirling around the mountain face.

Mountains loomed around him, great peaks with steep sides, directly across a deep ravine. The shelf outside the door dropped off into the ravine, tops of trees barely visible. He could hear the sound of water below, rushing across rocks and down a fall a short distance away. The sun was bright, Hall had to raise a hand to shield his eyes.

Taking a step closer to the edge, he looked down. It wasn't that deep, trees growing tall with the wide river cutting a path through them, the tips sticking up just above the shelf. Evergreens, the wind carrying the piney scent to Hall. He breathed it in. The clean mountain air, the pines, it reminded him of the mountains near where he had grown up. Except better. So much more pure and untouched.

He turned around and looked at the door. It was a solid stone slab, not worked or smoothed. It looked as if the Dwarves had cut into the mountain to form the door, just adding hidden hinges for it to open. He saw chisel marks in the stone wall and more on the door, deep gouges along the shelf. Indications that someone had broken through whatever had kept the door locked.

The thieves had obviously come and gone by the trail, but where had they gone after?

Thinking of his map, it appeared in front of him. Translucent, able to see the side of the mountain across and the top of the trees through it. The blinking dot that indicated his location was in the middle of the mountains, the area around him revealed but surrounded by bands of gray haze. Areas he had not been. He could see Axestorm Hall and the Valley of Ancients, a band of gray and then his present location. They had traveled further than he had thought.

Hall stepped down the trail, making room for the others, as he closed his map. There wasn't enough space for them to gather, only able to stand single file.

"Where does this go?" Hall asked, having to raise his voice for Urit to hear over the roar of the wind.

The young Stonefire was in the middle of the group.

"I donnae know," Urit replied. "Somewhere on the backside of the mountains around the Valley of Ancients."

Hall thought about asking where the trail would lead but knew he'd get the same answer. The thief, or thieves, had probably been the first Dwarves, or humans or anything, to use the trail in centuries.

They started down the trail. It was slow going, parts of it

eroded and gone. Thin, just as wide as a Dwarf, it cut across the face of the steep mountain. The wind pushed at them, threatening to push them off. Each leaned close to the cold stone, grabbing what handholds they could find, which were few and far between.

Loose stones fell beneath Hall's feet, clattering down the mountain and disappearing below. Whole sections of the trail had fallen away. They were able to step over all of them, but it made for extremely slow-going. The wind was loud, drowning out all sounds. Hall thought he heard the yowling of Salem at one point. Distant, even though the Minx Cat was not that far behind him. Haunting as it drifted across the mountains.

The trail continued around the mountain, curving as it slightly sloped down. The ravine, river, and trees followed them. The pines started to block his vision of the mountains as they descended further down the trunks until the far mountain was lost. Blocked by thick branches of pine needles. The wind died down, turning to a light breeze that rustled the needles. Hall heard the sound of the forest. Small animals darting through the branches and the undergrowth. The roar of the river and the falls that were still out of sight.

He stepped from stone and onto the leaves of the ground. Hall smiled as he stepped away from the mountain. Glad to be on flat ground and something besides stone and mountain. He felt the tension melt, his shoulders loosening as he let out a deep breath. The walk down the trail had been nerve-wracking, and he was glad it was over.

They all were, even Urit.

"Let's rest a bit," Hall suggested as his eyes roamed the trees around them.

Even before he had finished speaking, he heard his companions sink to the ground, sighing and groaning in relief. Food and drink were brought out of pouches, each too tired to talk. Hall didn't relax.

Opening up his map he saw that they were facing back toward Axestorm. The area between the forest, the parts that had been revealed, and the home of the Dwarves were still fogged out. No idea if the walk back would be over mountains or through more forest. He didn't remember any woods around the Hall or the Valley, but it could have been hidden by ridges. There was nothing visible on the map that might indicate where the thieves might have gone.

He walked around the small area at the base of the mountain trail, looking for signs of passage. It had been days, maybe a week, so he wasn't expecting to find anything. He didn't even know what to look for.

Opening his Character Sheet, Hall tabbed through the options until he found the quest log. He hadn't spent much time looking through it. There had been no need. Ever since first appearing in Grayhold, he had very little need to review the quest logs. The urge hadn't been there, not like it used to be. There just weren't as many quests. Pre-Glitch, he had always checked the log, reviewing what he needed to do and where he needed to go. His log had always been near to full with quests, even at endgame. But now he only had a handful. Hall tried to think of the last time he had even opened it Post-Glitch, having a hard time remembering. Quests just seemed to happen.

Finding the one he wanted, Hall reread the text. What little there was.

The Ax of Obsidian Flames, the Stonefire Clan's ancient artifact, was stolen. You have agreed to find and return the Ax to the crypt of Brignir Stonefire.

CRYPT FINDINGS II
Find the Ax of Obsidian Flames 0/1
Return the Ax to the crypt of Brignir Stonefire 0/1

He looked around the forest again, trying to find some indication of where to go next. Which direction would the thieves have gone? Not back toward Axestorm? The culprit had to be a Dwarf. They would be the only ones to even know about the possible back door entrance and what the crypt contained. But no Dwarf would possess the magic required to remove the hammer from the sarcophagus lid. And no Dwarf would violate a clan's crypt either. That left Hall back at the same place. No idea.

"Any thoughts on where the thief would go?" Hall asked Urit.

The Dwarf stood up, walking around the trees, pushing at the low bushes. He paused and stared off into nothing. Checking his map, Hall assumed. Urit's eyes flickered, moving back and forth quickly as he scrolled around his mental map. His eyes came back into focus, and he looked back at Hall.

"I think there's a Storvgarde longhouse a couple miles to the north," he said, pointing in that direction.

"Think?" Sabine asked, not kindly.

Urit shrugged.

"I've never been to this part of the Hardedges," he explained, ignoring her tone. "But I know others who have and what they have told me. The plains are filled with Storvgarde clans. They do not live in the mountains but some have hunting lodges in the peaks and valleys. Beyond Axestorm Hall, those would be the only places to stay in the mountains."

It wasn't much, but it was all they had. Hall sighed and looked in the direction of the Dwarf fortress city. It would be easier to just head back that way, see if there was another way for Roxhard to get recognized as a Stonefire. He sighed again. No. They had the quest and couldn't abandon it. Back in the old game, he would have without a thought about the consequences. But now?

Much like in Silverpeak Keep, when they had followed the quest chain through to the end and fighting Cronet and the Silver Blades, he had felt there would be negative reactions to not finishing the quest. In that case, it would have been a closing of doors he would need to make Skara Brae flourish.

Here? The consequences might not be something that would affect him or Skara Brae, but they would affect Roxhard.

And he could not let that happen.

Hall cursed.

"Where is it?" he asked Urit.

The Dwarf shrugged.

"Along the river, past the falls but before it gets out of the mountains."

Hall nodded and reached into his pouch, pulling out the physical copy of the map. He spread it out, motioning for Urit to show him. Most of the area beyond the river was still grayed out, but Urit was able to estimate the location based on what was shown.

Hall ran some quick calculations in his head, using the scale he had already established. Not quite a day's travel.

Skill Gain!

Cartography Rank Two +.1

They would need to find a place to camp for the night, he knew.

"Rest up," Hall told the others, finally allowing himself to sit down with one of the trees to his back. "We leave in ten."

———

They trekked through the forest, staying on this side of the river and trying to find a place to cross. All pines, the trees were thick, and they had to stay on a well-used game trail to make any progress. With so much of the sky open, they could track the sun when it was visible through the mountain peaks on either side of the ravine. At one point, Hall could see the trail they had come down as it curved around the mountain, the now-closed door to the crypt invisible from the distance and angle.

The river was wider than he had thought from above. At least twenty feet of raging white water that crashed over rocks, a couple feet below the level of the banks. The trees ran right to the edge. The crash and roar were loud, forcing them to head back into the treeline a dozen feet or so. Enough to keep the river's edge in their sight as they turned to the east and followed it toward the foothills.

Pike had made it over the mountains and was circling above, his sharp eyes looking ahead for the Storvgarde long-house, a place to cross or any potential dangers.

Hall was getting tired. It was hard pushing through the thick branches of pine needles, barely any space between them. The needles were sharp, biting at any exposed skin. Even though they weren't as high in the mountains, it was still cold.

They pushed on, the roar of the river to the side, needles digging into skin.

Hall sent his thoughts to Pike, having the dragonhawk fly closer. It was time to start looking for a place to camp for the night. Looking up, Hall saw the shadowed form of Pike flying just above the trees. With a screech that echoed through the ravine, Pike swooped off to the south.

Stopping, Hall mentally connected with Pike, seeing through the dragonhawk's eyes. A side of rock rose to the southeast, part of the mountain extending out into the forest.

Before it was a small clearing, the trees set back a dozen feet or so.

Not the best but it would do. The sheer face of the rock would give them some protection, and the trees could provide a break from the wind. It would still be a cold night. Hall had Pike fly around the mountain, looking for signs of Cragglers. Finding none, the dragonhawk settled down on a ledge just above the small clearing to wait.

Hall altered their direction, stepping off the game trail that paralleled the river. They had to push through the trees, but it wasn't as hard as he had expected. There wasn't a trail, but something big had come this way. He reconnected with Pike, having the dragonhawk scan the small clearing, flying up to look at the cliff. There were no signs of anything there currently, but scruff marks and what appeared to be an old track marked the passage of something. Hall started examining the ground more closely and almost immediately spotted an impression in the soft ground.

Skill Gain!
Tracking Rank One +.1

Crouching down, he ran his fingers over it. Deep and large, with four toes. Thick claws cut into the ground. Hall recognized it. Bear. But bigger than any he had heard of. Deeper the other bear tracks he had seen. Whatever bear had made the print was large and heavy.

"Mountain Bruin," Urit said, standing over Hall's shoulder.

Hall looked up at the Dwarf, who didn't look happy.

"Nasty beasties," Urit muttered.

"Should we be worried?" Roxhard asked.

"This looks old," Urit replied. "It must have been passing through."

There were more marks of the Bruins passage. Other

tracks, broken branches and the marks in the small clearing. Hall and Urit walked the perimeter, which didn't take long, finding the tracks Hall had hoped for. A clear set walking out of the clearing.

It didn't take long to set up their small camp, and Caryn got a fire going quickly. The smoke rose into the air, the logs and sticks crackling merrily. Night fell and they spread out with their backs to the mountain, keeping the fire between them and the trees. Hall took the first and last watches, as was his habit.

Except he didn't get woken up for the last watch.

His inner alarm clock woke him. Eyes opened to see some stars up above, not that many, as well as large areas of blackness. Other islands. The night was quiet, all the nocturnal animals having found their dens and nests for the coming morning. He sat up, letting the thick wool blanket fall. The fire was still going, light flickering across the small clearing. Roxhard gently snored, Jackoby turning in his sleep. Urit's snoring was a new sound, something Hall wasn't used to hearing, but while it was thick and deep, it wasn't loud. Caryn made no sound or movement. Pike was nowhere to be seen, off hunting somewhere.

Looking around, he saw the shadowed form of Sabine, who should have come and woken him for his turn. Getting up quietly, he made his way to her, fully expecting to find her asleep. But she wasn't. She stared off into the dark forest, not bothering to look up at him as he sat down beside her.

"I should have woken you," she whispered. "Sorry, but I was enjoying the night."

She fell silent again, shifting slightly as she rearranged the blanket that covered her legs. The robe she wore was tight, form-fitting, with long slits up the side. It was made of a thick material, not as thin as the one she customarily wore, but it still had to be cold.

"And the peace," she said almost a minute later, so quiet that Hall barely heard.

"Are you okay?" he asked, thinking it was a question he should have been asking earlier.

The Witch had been moody lately. Moodier, he amended. Never an ideal traveling companion, she had only gotten worse the last few weeks. It had really started months ago when he had claimed the lordship of Skara Brae. He had hoped that the addition of Caryn to their group, and her new relationship with Sabine, would have helped fix the Witch's mood.

She was silent for a time, and Hall thought she wasn't going to respond. Sabine shifted again and sighed.

"Not really," she replied. "I'm sorry if I've been a total..." She paused, and Hall waved the comment away. He could see her give a small smile in thanks. "I don't mean or want to be but..." She leaned back, turning to look up at the stars. "You make it seem so easy," she said and glanced at him. "This whole situation and you're as calm and collected as can be. You treat everyone the same. You take things as they come and nothing seems to bother you. And that manages to hold us all together. We should all be freaking out with this new existence but not you, not Hall. Nope. You just go marching on like nothing bothers you."

Hall gave a quiet chuckle.

"That's not true," he said but wondered if it was.

He thought of himself as a practical person, only worried only about things he could control. He couldn't control the game world so he had decided early to just go with it. Do what he had always done in Sky Realms Online and play the game. Did any of it really bother him? He hadn't thought about home or earth or real life in days, maybe weeks. Since he had accepted his relationship with Leigh?

Hall looked up at the stars, trying to imagine where the island of Edin was in the skies above. What was Leigh doing right now? How was she doing? Did she miss him like he missed her?

"Of course you don't see it," Sabine muttered, not angrily, but Hall thought he heard a very faint tone of bitterness. "Sometimes it can be too much for the rest of us. We can't all be like you," she said and pushed herself up.

He looked up at her, wondering if she was going to say anything else. She stared up at the stars, looked back out into the forest. Sabine started to speak but stopped, just shaking her head before turning and moving back toward the fire.

Hall watched her go, saw her settle down on a bedroll close to the dwindling fire. She pulled the blanket up tight, her back to him. After a moment he looked out into the forest, wondering what that had been about.

Something about the conversation nagged at him, afraid he had missed something important.

CHAPTER TWENTY-TWO

THE DAY DAWNED COLD, THE SAME AS THE OTHERS THEY HAD experienced in the deep mountains. More of the same.

Only Urit seemed to enjoy it.

Hall stoked the fire to give them some morning warmth, watching his breath cloud up in the air. The Stonefire Dwarf stood at his full height, stretching and breathing the crisp and chilly air deep into his body.

"Us Dwarves love the inside of the mountains don't ye be doubting," he said with a smile. "But we love the outside of the mountains just as much."

None of the others seemed to care, which didn't bother Urit.

The small fire gave off some warmth, letting them work the chill from their bones. They ate a quick meal of jerky, water, and made some tea. Bedrolls and blankets were stuffed into inventory pouches, armor was adjusted, and they were back on the trail.

Hall led them the way they had come, working to find the game trail. Once they got there, the roar of the river rising as they got closer, he turned to the east again and led them down the trail. He paid more attention to the ground and any tracks he found. There was no evidence that the Mountain Bruin was still around, but he didn't want to take chances.

After a couple hours, he felt Pike touching his mind. The dragonhawk was flying above, scouting out the way. From high above the trees, Pike had seen the green of the treetops change.

Because of that Hall knew what to expect when they saw the light of day between the trees ahead. The green and branches thinned out, showing the blue of the sky and distant peaks. The roar of the river changed. No longer the crash of raging water against stone, becoming the sound of water continuing without end, disappearing as it faded.

The pines ran right to the edge of the cliff. More trees spread out far below them, a wide and deep forest. The river turned into a waterfall, crashing into a small pond very far below, the river continuing through the trees to the east. But it was what was nestled on the shore of the pond where the river exited that drew their attention and caused them to step back into the shadow of the trees.

Smoke curled up from a small chimney in the middle of the sloped roof that was the Storvgarde longhouse. Built to parallel the pond, the land around the longhouse had been cleared for a couple dozen feet in all directions, green grass and flowers growing. The land sloped up from the pond's edge, with part of the longhouse built into the hill. With a steeply pitched roof with deep overhangs, the back half covered in green grass and the front in wooden shingles, there wasn't much-exposed sidewall to the building. Wide and dark wood planks made up the walls, carved beams running past the walls at the eaves and ridge.

They saw no sign of life, but the smoke was a clear indication someone was staying at the longhouse. Hall watched for about ten minutes with no one appearing. No way to know if the thieves they were looking for would be using the longhouse and only one way to find out.

Hall opened his connection to Pike as the dragonhawk soared over the pond. Sharp eyes scanned the sheer cliff, finding a way down to the south.

It took them a couple miles out of the way and showed evidence of recent traffic.

The cliff sloped down, steep but navigable. Trees grew along the side, loose rock, leaves, and branches. They found more of the Mountain Bruin's paw prints along with marks left by booted feet. Not that old. Small collections of leaves and rocks, pushed into piles, showed where travelers had slipped and slid down the slope.

Hall leaned back, one hand behind him to help steady his descent. He worked hard to keep the loose stones and sticks from sliding down, but it was hard. A steady stream flooded and tumbled down the steep hill, joined by more from his companions. Especially the heavier Jackoby. The Firbolg growled as his feet slipped on loose pine needles, reaching out to grab a small sapling that bent, but held, under his weight. The others shifted their positions, not wanting to be directly in line with him.

Once on ground that didn't slope as bad, Hall led them toward the pond and the longhouse. He didn't want to get too close, didn't want the noise to travel, but knew they would have to follow the river further to the east to find a place to cross. Pike could remain above, keeping an eye on the longhouse.

They walked through the forest, oaks, and birches replacing some of the pines. Not as thick, there were more places to walk, the trees spaced out. Good sightlines for a decent distance, Hall thought as they spread out, no longer in a single line. His eyes looked everywhere, to the sides and ahead. They passed a large group of boulders. Gray rocks, broken and cracked, covered in moss. Just one more like the dozens they had paused already. Pieces of the cliff that had fallen millennia ago.

Hall barely paid it any attention, concentrating on the forward course. He checked his map, the translucent screen appearing before his eyes. They were getting close to the pond. He paused, raising a hand to slow the group. Should he adjust the course and bring them closer to the river, further away from the longhouse?

A low growl came from behind. Hall turned to see a dark blur charge out from the boulders. It slammed into Roxhard and Urit, the two Dwarves sent bouncing along the ground. Urit rolled up against a thick tree, not moving. Roxhard came to a stop sitting, breathing heavy and shaking his head, his weapon lost.

The others were yelling, scattering as a deep roar filled the forest. Taking his spear in both hands, Hall turned to face whatever was attacking them. He paused, looking at the largest bear he had ever seen.

It was at least ten feet high, six feet wide. A massive creature. Thick legs, huge head, sharp teeth. Sharp claws dug into the ground as it reared up, almost fifteen feet tall. The huge paws swiped at Jackoby, the strength pushing the large Firbolg back.

Skill Gain!

Identify Rank Two +.1

Gray Mountain Bruin (blue)

Caryn slashed at the bear, her swords sliding across its thick fur. Different shades of mottled gray, the bear had blended in perfectly with the boulders. It growled, roaring, turning to swipe at the Duelist while still attacking Jackoby with the other large paw. Caryn dashed out of the way, the massive claws gouging deep marks through a tree. Purple bolts of energy hit the Bruin, streaking across its body. The bear just shrugged the bolts off, ignoring the following *Shadowbolt*.

Hall pulled the javelin out of the holder on his back, taking aim and let it fly. The weapon streaked through the air and slammed into the Bruin's shoulder. It quivered for a moment, Hall thinking it had lodged into the creature's shoulder, but the Bruin roared and the weapon fell to the ground, a small trickle of blood following.

The Bruin's fur and hide were thick, almost like armor.

Doubting it would do much, Hall threw one of the throwing knives from his bracer. It slammed into the side of the Bruin, erupting in sparks and bolts of energy. The fur blackened, smoke rising, but the Bruin ignored the small amount of damage.

Lowering to all fours, the Bruin continued to swipe at Jackoby, taking a couple small hits from Caryn who had to dart in and out before the massive paws struck. Hall ran, spear held in both hands. He waited until he was close and triggered *Leap*. Keeping the arc low, he jabbed out with the spear as he jumped over the Bruin. The Ironwood spear struck a glancing blow. Hall landed on top of the bear, taking the spear in both hands and stabbed down.

The *Exceptional Breakridge Ironwood Spear* activated its special ability, and a large splinter stuck into the bear. It roared, rearing back, and Hall was thrown off. He managed to hold onto the spear as he crashed to the ground. The impact knocked the breath out of him, body and ribs hurting.

A *Shadowbolt* slammed into the large head. The Mountain Bruin roared in pain, growling and swiping wildly. Caryn's twin blades slashed across its side, distracting the Bruin so Jackoby was able to get a solid hit with his hammer. The weapon smashed into the Bruin. Skin and fur exploded, bright with red blood. The Bruin stumbled, turning and exposing its back to Caryn who stabbed straight out with both swords.

Hall stood up and jabbed his spear into the Bruin's side, just under its front leg. He twisted the weapon as he pulled it out. The Bruin turned, growling in pain as Jackoby slammed his hammer into its back. Another hammer slammed into the Bruin's side, Urit swinging again as blood dripped down his head.

The Bruin turned, trying to fight off all of them at once. It swiped with the great paws, driving one or two back but leaving itself exposed to the others. Blood dripped from its many wounds, great gashes in its fur from the hammer hits.

A streaking form barreled into the Bruin, causing it to rear back from the impact of a Warden's *Battle Rush* ability. Roxhard stood before it, two-handed ax in hand. The Dwarf growled and swung, a great overhand chop. The ax bit deep into the Bruin's exposed chest. It roared once more, falling back to crash into the ground. Trees shook, leaves fell, as the great weight slammed down hard.

Hall leapt up, spear pointing down. He slammed the tip into the anger-filled eye of the large bear. It gave a quiet roar and fell silent, the body falling limp.

SLAIN: *Gray Mountain Bruin +10 experience*

Skill Gain!
Polearms Rank Two +.1
Skill Gain!
Thrown Rank Two +.1

Hall jumped off the bear, eyes scanning the forest. The others picked up on his reaction, turning to face the trees. The fight had been short but loud, the Bruin's roars would have been heard for miles. There was no doubt that whoever was at the longhouse had heard. Hall doubted there was much in the mountains that would have been a match for the great bear. Whoever was in the longhouse had to be wondering who else, not what else, was in the forest with them.

He examined the Bruin's corpse. He knew he could skin it and get a good number of hides from the creature, but anyone that might come exploring would immediately know no animal had killed the Bruin. *They'd know by the wounds*, Hall thought as he set his spear down and pulled out his skinning knife.

Congratulations!
You have received six Large Mountain Bruin hides.

Skill Gain!
Skinning Rank Two +.5

He quickly stuffed the hides into his pouch, staring at the bleeding corpse of the creature, wondering if there was anything else that could be looted. Jackoby stepped up next to him, pulling some items from his own pouch. Ignoring Hall, the Firbolg started cutting off large hunks of the bear meat. As he did so, Jackoby sprinkled salt or something else onto the meat.

"We should not waste any of this magnificent creature," Jackoby growled as he placed the cuts of meat into his pouch.

Hall agreed. He hadn't liked killing the Bruin. They had been the intruders into its domain.

"We need to move," he said, picking up his spear and javelin, replacing both in the harness he wore.

———

Hall's ribs hurt. At least he had regained his Health by drinking one of the few potions they had. Roxhard and Urit had each taken one, the Stonefire Dwarf's additional healing coming from Hall's *Triage* skill which had given Hall two gains. Roxhard was still a little unsteady on his feet. Not even a healing potion could help a concussion.

Or heal Hall's sore ribs.

He changed the angle of their march. Instead of heading straight to the river, he instead took them toward the pond. Anyone coming from the longhouse would cross the river. It would be easier to avoid any scouts if they headed northwest to the pond and then followed the water's edge to the river.

They could see the water through the trees, hear the song of birds and the gentle flow of the river as it exited the pond. Hall kept well back from the edge, not stepping out of the shadows formed by the trees' thick branches. He could see the longhouse on the far shore. They had come out near where the river exited the pond, close to the longhouse.

There was movement, and Hall could see six Dwarves moving about the shore. Two more walked out of the longhouse carrying large bundles wrapped in tarps. Tightly wrapped, Hall couldn't make out what the objects were. The other Dwarves, dressed in chain mail and leathers, took up positions around the two with the bundles. Guarding them. Most carried axes or hammers with shields while two had crossbows. Those two stepped away from the others, giving themselves clear line of sight into the forest. One of the hammer-wielding Dwarves stood a couple steps in front of the others, the leader of the band, the hammer leaning casually over his shoulder, his steel booted foot tapping on the ground.

All were looking toward the river and what looked like a trail coming out of the forest. Waiting.

Hall heard Urit curse angrily. He glanced at the Stonefire Dwarf.

"Unclanned," Urit said quietly but harshly, practically spitting the word out. "Exiles."

Hall studied the Dwarves across the river, not seeing anything different about them. He had no idea why they stood out to Urit. How he was immediately able to identify them, but Hall took him at his word. He didn't need to know more. If they were exiled from Axestorm Hall and stripped of their Clan, then they were criminals of the worst sort. Becoming clanless was the harshest punishment that could be given to a Dwarf. Most would rather die than be exiled from their clan.

What had those eight, possibly more, Dwarves done?

Hall could sense the hate coming from Urit, and he hoped the Stonefire would not do anything rash.

He was about to signal the group to start moving toward the river when other figures stepped out from the forest. They walked out of the trail, coming out of the shadows. Four heavily armed Storvgardes carrying axes and two-handed swords, dressed in leathers and furs. They paused when they spotted the Dwarves, spreading out and stepping out of the way of the trail.

The two groups stared at each other, sizing each other up. Neither moved, neither said anything. Finally, one of the Storvgardes turned to the trail and said something.

Four more of the tribesmen came out, two women. Slightly outnumbering the Dwarves. Three of them stood out from the others. All were armed, but two of the three had staves topped in animal skulls, bones hanging down off leather straps. Each was dressed in leather robes, fur trimming along the hoods and sleeves. Rough runes covered the robes, painted in what looked to be dried blood.

Some kind of spellcasters. *A Shaman and Witch*, Hall thought, judging by their clothing and staves. It was hard to tell with the Storvgarde tribeswomen. They were dressed in wool robes lined with fur, painted runes covering the tan hides. Both could have been Shamans or Witches or even Druids, but Hall thought his first impression was right.

The third was the largest man Hall had ever seen. Equally the size of Jackoby, if not bigger. He wore a fur cloak over his leather vest, arms bare. A large sword was strapped across his back. He walked out of the forest and stopped only a couple feet from the lead Dwarf, looking down.

They stared at each other, the other Dwarves and Storvgarde moving nervously. Hall could feel the tension across the pond. Neither group liked each other.

Finally, the Dwarf barked a laugh and signaled at the two in the middle of the guard. They stepped forward, holding the large bundles out. The lead Storvgarde motioned to one of his people who took one of the bundles while he took the other. They unwrapped the wool tarps, letting them fall to the ground.

Urit growled in anger.

The smaller of the Storvgarde, still almost a foot taller than Hall, held a two-handed mace. The metal glinted in the sun, some kind of dark material. The head was huge, nine inches if not more, and studded with rounded bulbs instead of spikes.

"That's Rockflight," Urit muttered, rage filling his voice. "The sacred artifact of the Forgecrush Clan."

Hall looked beyond the mace to what the larger Storvgarde was holding. The man held it up high for all to see. The weapon, one that Hall recognized from seeing it in a tapestry, seemed to soak up the sun. It gathered the light in the shining dark depths of the obsidian it was made from.

The Ax of Obsidian Flames.

The Stonefire Clan's sacred weapon.

———

Hall reacted quickly, turning to grab at Urit before the enraged Dwarf could charge out of the trees. But Jackoby had been quicker. He grabbed Urit by the Dwarf's cloak and pulled hard, knocking Urit off balance. A glare from Hall prevented the Stonefire from saying anything but rage smoldered in his dark eyes.

"We know," Hall said. "We'll get it back."

He turned his attention back to the gathering across the pond.

Even from this distance Hall could tell the Ax was incredible. The craftsmanship was amazing. All one piece of obsidian, the double head was razor-sharp. He couldn't see all the details, but he remembered it from the tapestry. Runes carved down the shaft that was wrapped in leather. More runes along the edges of the heads. No decoration. Just a single piece of shining black rock.

The Storvgarde gave the weapon a few practice swings.

Once he was done, he looked back at the Dwarf and spoke a few words that didn't carry across the water. The Dwarves all looked at each other and the leader clapped. Everyone relaxed.

Until a Norn walked out of the forest.

Tall, thin, dressed in white that wasn't quite as pale as her skin. The robe was trimmed in gray, simple with no frills or decoration, just belted at the waist. She carried nothing. Her long gray hair hung straight down her back. A coal-black raven was perched on her shoulder.

The Dwarves and Storvgardes all took a step back as she entered the clearing around the longhouse, except for the leaders of both groups. They stood side by side, confronting her.

Words were exchanged, the Dwarf gesturing wildly. The Storvgarde clutching the Ax.

"I think those are the Storvgardes that attacked Crackleberry," Hall said quietly.

He couldn't be sure it was the same Norn, but how many of the White Elves were roaming Huntley and working with Storvgarde tribesmen?

"No," a voice said from behind them.

Hall turned, thinking he recognized it. Vaguely familiar. He had heard it, but just briefly and a long time ago.

Weapons were raised, as each of his companions took a defensive stance, cursing that they had been snuck up on.

"We're the ones that attacked Crackleberry," the voice said casually.

Six people stood ten feet or so away from Hall and the others. Four Storvgardes, their weapons raised and ready to attack. But it was the other two that had Hall's attention.

The speaker was a Wood Elf, and Hall knew him. He had seen the Elf in Grayhold on the first day. A Duelist with long green hair, some pulled up in a top knot, grayish-brown bark colored skin and bright green eyes.

Hall struggled to remember the name. He had only seen the Elf briefly. Speaking up and exiting the Laughing Horse Inn, proclaiming it was just a game and he was going to have some fun before it got fixed.

Cuthard.

That was the name.

He stood there smiling, nonchalant, weapons sheathed.

Hall was surprised that he knew the last person as well. A Half-Elf, female and a Skirmisher like him. She had straight black hair with deep purple streaks. She wore leather armor that covered her from head to toe, a dark blue cloak over her shoulder. Two javelins and a spear were in the harness, a short sword belted at her waist. On her shoulder was a purple and green dragonhawk. Its eyes stared at them all as if sizing them up for a meal.

He knew her. From the very first day he had ever played Sky Realms Online.

Thellia.

PART THREE
IRON'S ARMY

CHAPTER TWENTY-THREE

"LONG TIME," THELLIA SAID.

Hall was confused and surprised all at once. What was Thellia doing here? How was she here? The Elf, Cuthard, how did he get to Huntley? Who were the Storvgarde with them?

And they were responsible for the attack on Crackleberry?

And what did they have to do with the Dwarves, Storvgarde, and Norn across the pond?

He didn't know what to say or do.

"I think we surprised him," Cuthard said with a chuckle.

"Understandable," Thellia replied with a shrug. "This is kind of a strange situation we find ourselves in."

Hall shook his head, trying to get control of the situation.

"Why are you here?" he asked, thinking it was the simplest and most direct question.

"That's a long story," Thellia said, and Cuthard laughed. "I don't think you're referring to how I wound up on Huntley. You and this guy," she said and pointed at Cuthard, "started out in Grayhold and I started out in Darkice. I think the question refers to the here and now."

Hall nodded, wishing she would just get on with it. He had

forgotten how long-winded she could be. They had met the first day of Beta, the first Player Hall had come across. The first in-game friend. It hadn't lasted as she was always more of a power gamer and he was a casual. She also worked for one of the online sites devoted to VRMMORPGs and other games. Thellia had quickly outleveled him, leaving him behind.

Not that he minded. She played the game her way, he played it his.

"Why we're here is well," Thellia paused, glanced at Cuthard and back at Hall. "Let's just say that those folks across the pond are our enemies and leave it at that."

"And the way you lot were spying, think they're enemies of yours," Cuthard said.

Hall instantly disliked the Elf. Cocky, arrogant. Cuthard thought he was more charming than he really was. The Elf's eyes locked on Sabine and never left her. For her part, the Witch ignored him. Hall noticed the four Storvgarde hadn't moved or relaxed. Each had their weapons out, eyeing Hall and his companions warily.

"Who are your friends?" Sabine asked, waving at the Storvgarde.

Cuthard glanced at the four tribesmen, still smiling.

"They are part of the Jorgunmund Clan," he said with a shrug as if it didn't matter. "They're part of our army now."

"Iron's Army," Thellia corrected.

———

"The top guild," Roxhard blurted before Hall could say anything. "Iron's Army was always the highest ranked guild in the game. First to enter and solve all the new areas and all the raids."

The Dwarf, excited, would have gone on and on, but Hall raised a hand to stop him.

He had heard of Iron's Army of course. No one that played Sky Realms Online could avoid them. All the forums were filled with their accomplishments. Somehow the Guild was always the first to solve any of the myriad puzzles in the game. Whenever a new Raid dungeon appeared, there was Iron's Army pushing their way through it. They were efficient and calculating, well planned and organized. The other top-ranked Guilds had been jealous, always trying to figure out a way to beat Iron's Army. Trying and failing.

No one ever beat Iron's Army.

Skill Gain!
Identify Rank Two +.1

Thellia, Skirmisher (orange)
Faction: Iron's Army, Captain

Orange? That meant she was at least three levels higher than he was. That put her around Level Eight or Nine, compared to his Level of Five. How had she gotten so high so quickly? Experience had come so slow for him and the others.

"Hey," the Elf, Cuthard said with a chuckle, drawing Hall from his thoughts. The Duelist was staring at Roxhard in recognition. Hall knew what was coming and couldn't react fast enough to stop it. "I know you. You're that Dwarf that cried the first day in the Laughing Horse. Broke down and just sniffled mommy over and over."

Cuthard was laughing. Roxhard's face turned beat red, embarrassed. Neither Jackoby or Urit seemed to be paying attention. They were staring at the Storvgarde, who stared back, all hands tightening around their weapons.

"You should have seen it," Cuthard said to Thellia. "Balling like a little baby, crying for his mommy."

The Elf laughed but stopped when Thellia glared at him. He shrugged, still smiling and looked at Roxhard with a sneer.

"Why are you after those Storvgarde?" Hall asked, trying to steer the conversation away from Roxhard's behavior months ago. He glared at the Elf who returned a wicked smile.

If Thellia was three or four levels higher, Cuthard was most likely that high as well. Hall would be no match if came to a fight. And Cuthard knew it. He was just backing down because Thellia wanted him to.

"They belong to the Svertleim Clan and have been harassing our supply lines," Thellia explained.

Hall wondered what she meant by that. Supply lines? What was going on?

"Iron wanted them eliminated," she continued. "So here we are." She looked at Hall with a 'your turn' tilt to her head.

Hall explained most of it. He explained about coming down to Huntley and Axestorm Hall and how they had gone to the Valley of Ancients for Roxhard to become fully integrated into the Stonefire Clan.

"Looks like your enemies are upgrading their weapons," he finished and pointed behind his group.

She glanced beyond him at the longhouse just barely visible through the trees. Her gaze returned to him, and he motioned her to join him. Together they walked to the edge of the forest and looked out across the pond. The Storvgardes and Dwarves were still there, talking with the Norn.

"The Norn is new," Thellia said. "We had suspected the Svertleim were getting aid from somewhere but had not suspected Norns. What are they doing in Huntley?"

"Brokering that deal," Hall replied and pointed to the two Storvgarde with the Dwarven artifacts.

Thellia studied the Storvgarde and the weapons. Hall had tried to pull up the stats on the weapons, but they were too far

AXESTORM • 321

away. He could tell by the way her eyes unfocused that Thellia
was doing the same and failing.

"Lovely," she replied and stepped away from the edge of
the trees.

Hall followed.

Nothing much had changed with the others. Cuthard still
sneered at Roxhard and glanced with what he thought was
charm at Sabine, giving Caryn a similar glance that she turned
away from. He ignored Jackoby and Urit completely. Thellia's
Storvgarde allies had relaxed slightly. Only slightly. Tension
was still high between the two groups.

"So what's the plan?" Cuthard asked Thellia.

Before the other Half-Elf Skirmisher could reply, Hall
spoke up.

"I don't know what your goals are, but we're here to
recover those weapons," he said, looking at Thellia, ignoring
the Wood Elf Duelist.

She tilted her head, fingers tapping her leg, the other hand
reaching up and scratching her dragonhawk's neck. Lost in
thought. Finally, she smiled.

"We don't care about the weapons," she said.

"Weapons?" Cuthard said, showing some excitement and
interest. "What weapons? Iron will want…"

Thellia sharply rose her hand, stopping the Duelist.

Anger flashed across his features but passed quickly,
replaced by the sneer he commonly wore.

"The one with the ax is the Svertleim Clan chieftain,"
Thellia continued as if Cuthard hadn't interrupted. "He's our
target. The rest is just collateral. Same for the weapons."

Her eyes unfocused, irises flicking back and forth as she
scrolled through her menus.

Hall was startled as a notification appeared before his eyes.
The standard translucent half unrolled parchment that he was
used to seeing.

Thellia wants to share a quest.

*The Svertleim Clan have been harassing Iron's Armies supply lines
and stealing much-needed resources. You have been tasked with
eliminating the Svertleim Chieftain and recovering any supplies you
can find.*
Faction Quest: Svertleim Thieves II
Eliminate the Svertleim Chieftain 0/1
Recover supplies 0/1
Rewards: +100 Experience

*Attention: You are not a member of the Iron's Army Faction and
cannot receive Faction and Reputation rewards from this quest.*

ACCEPT QUEST?

Hall stared at the wall of text. Shared quest? Faction quest?
And it was the second part of a chain? He glanced at the
others who were all indifferent, except Sabine. She was
nodding, seeming more excited than Hall had seen her before.
He accepted the quest.

"Now that all that is out of the way," Cuthard said with an
exaggerated roll of his eyes. "What's the plan?"

"We need to get across the river first," Hall said. "Need to
find a place to ford."

Cuthard and Thellia exchanged quick glances, the Skirmisher motioning the direction they had first come from.

"I think we know where that is."

———

Hall was amazed that the large group was able to stay relatively
quiet as they walked through the forest. He and his five

companions, Pike still flying above, Thellia, Cuthard, and the four Storvgarde who brought up the rear.

Having the Storvgarde behind them made Jackoby nervous. The Firbolg kept looking over his shoulder, lips curled in a silent snarl. For their part, the four blond warriors ignored him. Cuthard, twin long swords sheathed in scabbards across his back, prowled in front a dozen feet or so. Once they were moving, the Duelist was all business. His arrogant attitude was gone. Hall still didn't like him and definitely didn't trust him.

Thellia was still a question. How far could she be trusted? Cuthard had shown interest when Hall had mentioned the Dwarven weapons. He obviously wanted to claim the weapons and bring them to his leader, this Iron. Thellia had said they had no interest, but would that last? With Thellia and Cuthard being high level, Hall and his friends were outnumbered. He glanced over his shoulder at the Storvgardes.

Skill Gain!

Identify Rank Two +.2

Jorgunmund *Berserker (white)*
Jorgunmund *Berserker (white)*

He wasn't sure what special Abilities being a Berserker had, but white indicated they were equal level or only one higher. Those four shouldn't be an issue by themselves, but with theLevel Eight or Nine Players, it made any potential fight very one-sided.

Hall hoped it wouldn't come to that. But he wasn't sure.

There had been some strange comments. They talked about the Svertleim like soldiers talking about their enemy. Talk of supply lines and even hinting that they had been involved with the attack on and conquest of Crackleberry.

Iron's Army had just been a guild name. Now it sounded like something more.

It was a little unsettling.

"Hey," Thellia said, looking over her shoulder from where she walked just ahead of him.

She was waving her hand to get his attention.

"Sorry," Hall said. "What did you say?"

"Asked about that Lordship title you have," Thellia said with a smile. Her eyes were alight with curiosity.

That was the Thellia he knew. The one that had worked for Wikikazam, more interested in learning about the game than actually playing it. She had been good at the job.

"We were on a quest for a Druid we met," he started to explain. "Leigh." He felt a quick stab in his heart as he thought of her, missing her.

"NPC," Thellia interrupted.

Hall nodded, not sure why it made a difference.

"She needed to find a Druid's Grove on Edin. We joined her and found the Grove and the ruins of a village near it. When I touched this gray pillar in the center of town, I was given the village."

Thellia faced ahead, digesting what he had said. She looked at the ground in front of her, searching it for tripping hazards. Seeing nothing she glanced back at Hall.

"How did you wind up down here in Huntley?"

"That's a bit of a long story," he replied and told her about what had happened in Silverpeak Keep, Cronet, and finding the airship plans.

He was about to ask for her story when Cuthard spoke up. No alarm, just telling them to stop just ahead. Hall heard Caryn gasp in shock. Stepping past two birch trees standing like sentinels, he saw the bodies.

Dwarves.

Three of them. Cut to shreds. Their weapons and armor

had been stripped, leaving nearly naked and bloody corpses. They looked fresh, the blood just barely drying.

"We ran across them before we found you," Thellia said in answer to Hall's unspoken question.

"Probably sent out to investigate that loud roaring," Cuthard remarked with a smirk. "We figured that was you killing some beast."

"A Gray Mountain Bruin," Caryn said absently as she stared down at the corpse closest to her.

The slices across the Dwarves body were in patterns, lots of small cuts and few deep. Hall recognized the moves the same as Caryn obviously did. Made by the twin swords of a Duelist. One that had played with the Dwarf before delivering the killing blow.

"What's that?" Cuthard asked, and shrugged, not caring anymore. "Whatever it was, you all made some noise."

He glanced at Hall, the ever-present smirk plastered on his face. His eyes were filled with malice.

"We took care of them for you."

Hall shot him a quick glare, which only made the smirk deeper.

"You said you knew how to cross?" he asked Thellia.

"Technically I said I think we know where to cross," she said and walked into the trees to the side.

Hall followed and saw evidence of booted feet, steps in the soft ground. He was heading to the river, the footsteps were coming away. Smaller in size. Dwarf feet.

Skill Gain!
Tracking Rank One +.1

Together, the two Skirmishers stepped out of the trees and onto the riverbank. Hall looked to the west and couldn't see the longhouse. Trees and a slight curve to the river hid them from sight. The river was still wide, but the ground before them had been built up. Piles of stones only a foot or so below the surface of the water. A man-made ford.

"We saw the Dwarves right after they had entered the trees," Thellia said. "Could see the river so guessed they had crossed nearby."

He took a step into the water. Hall could feel the river against his boot, hitting it and flowing around. Not that strong but the rocks under his feet were somewhat loose making for treacherous walking. Slow and careful, he made his way across the river.

The other bank showed more evidence of the ford being used. The bank was muddy, the grass torn up. He could see a worn trail leading into the trees. A short walk brought him to a larger trail. The one the Storvgardes and Norn had come down. He looked to the right, wondering where it led. Glancing over his shoulder he saw the others trying their best to walk through the river quietly.

Looking to the left, toward the longhouse, Hall pulled up his map. He adjusted the scale, seeing where the marker indicated his current location and how far they were from the longhouse. Only a couple hundred feet.

Closer than he wanted.

The chances of getting noticed were high, and at some point, the Dwarves at the longhouse would start to worry about the scouts they had sent out. Because of the meeting, the Dwarves and Storvgarde at the longhouse would already be weary. With the roar of the Bruin and the loss of the scouts, they would be even wearier. They would be expecting trouble.

Not ideal, Hall thought, picturing what little he had seen of the longhouse.

He was tempted to have Pike do a flyover. His gaze drifted to the purple and green dragonhawk on Thellia's shoulder.

Would the Storvgarde be on the watch for a dragonhawk? Better to just keep Pike in reserve.

The others all gathered around, eyes looking both ways up the trail. At a motion from Thellia, the four Storvgardes spread out behind them, walking down the trail a dozen feet or so. Hall wasn't comfortable with them at his back but couldn't think of a reason to protest, and he wasn't going to send one of his companions to the rear and take them out of the upcoming fight.

"How many did you say there were?" Cuthard asked in a loud whisper. Hall shot him a glare. The Duelist just gave that arrogant smirk that made Hall want to throw his javelin.

"Six Dwarves, Eight Storvgardes," Hall replied, answering as quiet as he could. "Two of the Storvgardes are spellcasters. Witch and Shaman, I think. And the Norn Witch."

"Corvandr, the Svertleim Chieftain is there," Thellia added. "He's got the large black ax."

"One of the Dwarves, the band's leader, is named Gundar," Urit said.

For some reason, both Thellia and Cuthard gave the Stone-fire Dwarf odd looks. Cuthard's was condescending, as if he didn't want to hear what Urit said. Thellia's wasn't as bad, but there was still something odd about the way she glanced at Urit, almost dismissing him.

Was it because Urit was an NPC? Hall hoped not. But he had seen both of them treating their allied Storvgarde as servants, not as equals.

Cuthard glanced at the entire group, his hand raised and pointing at each in turn. "Fourteen and eight of us. Two a piece," he said with a smile. "Providing you lot can hold your own at your low level."

The last was said with a smile, but Hall picked up on the condescension. He bit back a retort.

"What about them?" he asked instead, motioning to the four Storvgarde behind.

"They'll guard our backs," Thellia replied. "And be reinforcements if needed."

"Which it won't," Cuthard added with a chuckle. "So this is what we'll do," he started to say, but Thellia held up a hand. Again. And again, a quick flash of anger crossed the Duelist's face, but he stopped speaking.

"You know your group," Thellia said, turning to Hall. "You set the battle up."

Hall nodded his thanks, looking down the trail in the direction of the longhouse. Two to one weren't bad odds, but it was the make-up of the enemy forces that was the issue. Two mini-bosses with Gundar the Unclanned and Corvandr the Clanchief. Possibly a third with the Norn Witch. Two spell-casters and a bunch of warriors. They needed to occupy the bosses and the spellcasters otherwise it wouldn't matter how fast they could get through the warriors, spells would be slamming into their backs and they'd be finished.

It took a minute, but he came up with a plan. It was really just for the first attack as after that, it would be all chaos and on-the-fly adjustments.

"I'll take the Norn," Cuthard said before Hall could say anything.

He wanted to say something, order Cuthard to attack one of the other mobs, but the move made sense. Hall nodded. The Wood Elf Duelist had the best chance of taking out the Norn the quickest.

"Jackoby and Roxhard, you two take Corvandr and Gundar. Your main task is to keep them occupied. Thellia," Hall said, turning to her. "You and I will deal with the Storvgarde Shaman and Witch." He turned to the others. "Caryn and Urit, the warriors are yours."

He had wanted more to deal with the warriors, but they would have to do.

"Thellia and I can send Pike and," Hall paused and looked at Thellia.

"Screech," she supplied.

"We'll send the dragonhawks to help you," Hall finished and turned to Sabine.

"*Hexbolt* them all," she said with a sigh, knowing her role.

Hall looked around at them all, locking eyes, looking for doubt and uncertainty. There was none. They were in agreement or if they weren't, they didn't say anything.

"Okay," he said. "Let's do this."

CHAPTER TWENTY-FOUR

HALL ACTIVATED *LEAP*.

Beside him, Thellia did the same.

They were at the front of the group on the trail, just breaking past the edge of the trees.

As he jumped into the air, he heard the pounding feet of Jackoby and Roxhard charging across the clearing at their respective targets.

The group had spent a couple minutes in the shadows of the trees watching the Dwarves and Storvgarde, getting the positioning down, before making their attack. Cuthard had disappeared into the forest, away from them.

"Don't worry," Thellia had said in a soft whisper. "He may be a jerk, but he's good at what he does."

Hall put Cuthard out of his mind. He put all the worries out of his mind.

There were people to kill.

———

His target was the Svertleim Witch.

The Dwarves and Storvgarde had spread out, still keeping their distance, but no longer as wary. The two leaders and Norn were still talking in the middle of the two half circles formed by the others. Hall had been thankful and amazed they had still been there. He had half expected them to have all disappeared. But they had not.

The Witch was to the right, her attention on the dialogue between her chieftain and the others. None of the Storvgarde were paying attention to the forest.

As he soared through the air, Hall heard the Dwarves start to shout. They were facing toward the forest and saw Hall and his companions attacking. But it was too late for the Storvgarde.

The Witch turned as Hall used *Leaping Stab*. The spear tip caught her in the shoulder, scoring a deep gash and turning the woman. As he landed, he turned and thrust out with his Attack of Opportunity. The ironwwood spear sliced a glancing blow across her side.

Critical Hit!

Leaping Stab lands a critical blow dealing 2x damage.

Hall saw the notification flash across his vision as he twisted his spear around his body, bringing the tip to jab out at the Witch. She stepped back, the attack missing, but it stopped her from casting a spell.

Skill Gain!

Identify Rank Two +.1

Svertleim Hex Mistress (white)

He pulled her Health bar, seeing that it was down almost a third. She was clutching at her shoulder, and Hall saw the large splinter lodged there, blood dripping from the wound. Her Health bar lost more red. He hadn't realized his *Breakridge Spear* had activated its Special Ability and lodged a splinter in the wound.

Taking advantage of the damage over time wound that broke the Witch's concentration, Hall stepped forward putting more force behind the jab of the spear. The Witch stepped back, but Hall twisted, grabbing the shaft with both hands and rotating the weapon. Ironwood slammed into the Hex Mistress' side as Hall rotated the spear, using it as a quarterstaff.

He pulled the weapon toward him, sliding his grip and rotated it around his body. Point facing the Witch, he stabbed it forward and into her chest. She folded around the weapon, hands grasping at the shaft to try to pull it out. Hall helped by yanking the spear back before he slammed it forward again.

Watching the Hex Mistress' Health bar, he saw it drop, flash briefly and disappear. She fell backward, landing on the ground and didn't move.

SLAIN: *Svertleim Hex Mistress +25 Experience*

Skill Gain!
Polearms Rank Two +.2

Turning, Hall surveyed the chaotic battle. There was fighting everywhere. The Norn was backing up, forced to move by Cuthard's whirling blades. Blood dripped from a wound on her side, most likely from a sneak attack by the Wood Elf. The raven was cawing, unable to defend its mistress, as Thellia's dragonhawk slammed into it. Hall heard the crackle of Pike's lightning attack followed by the pained yell of a Dwarf.

Jackoby was being hard pressed by the Chieftain. The Firbolg was giving up ground. Ax blows crashed against his shield, which he had to hold with both hands. Purplish-black flames surrounded the head of the Stonefire's artifact weapon. Hall understood where the name came from. Luckily, whatever magic was in Jackoby's wooden *Torklir's Shield* it was resisting burning from the magical flames.

Skill Gain!

Identify Rank Two +.1

Black Corvandr the Dread (orange)

The Unclanned Dwarf leader, Gundar, and Roxhard were on equal footing for now. Hammer and ax clashed, metal against metal, as the two Dwarves exchanged blows.

Hearing a clipped off scream to the side, Hall turned to see the Shaman fall to the ground. Thellia pulled her spear from the body. Without looking she activated *Leap* and jumped into the chaotic melee. She landed in front of a Storvgarde, stabbing out with her spear.

Off to the side, Sabine was casting *Hexbolt* after *Hexbolt*, alternating between the group of Unclanned Dwarves and the Storvgarde. Unable to move or fight, the Witch's spell was helping control the numbers that Urit and Caryn had to deal with while the others finished off the larger threats. A quick glance at Sabine's Energy bar showed it rapidly depleting. In combat, she wouldn't be able to recharge quickly. Hall saw an empty vial at her feet. Sabine had already downed one of the few *Minor Potion of Energy* they had.

One of the Dwarves fell, Caryn's twin blades stabbing straight into it. As the body collapsed to the ground, the Duelist was already turning and blocking an attack from a Storvgarde warrior.

Hall started to activate *Leap* when he saw Cuthard fall to the ground. Something had struck him from behind, but there was no enemy near. The Duelist was up quick, dodging an attack from the Norn Witch. Hall searched the battlefield for a ranged attacker. The Dwarves with crossbows were occupied with Pike and dealing with the effects of Sabine's *Hexbolt*. Cuthard had not been struck by an arrow or bolt. The only spellcaster still active was the Norn and the attack had not come from her.

Cursing, Hall realized his mistake. The Svertleim had been given two ancient Dwarven weapons. The second was a huge mace called Rockflight.

Flight.

Hall found the Storvgarde warrior with the mace. He stood further back from the others, out of the range of Sabine's *Hexbolt*. The warrior had just moved out of the range, Hall realized. He stared at the weapon in the Svertleim's hand. A metal shaft, leather wrapping the bottom half. No mace at the top. Hall remembered the head of the mace. Round, studded and huge. It was gone.

And then it wasn't.

The round head just appeared as if it had never disappeared. Not growing back or forming in a swirl of smoke or light. It was just back.

The warrior smiled, gave the huge mace a swing to make sure the balance was the same, and stepped toward the chaotic melee.

A cooldown, Hall knew. The weapon was somehow able to launch the mace head, which is what had struck Cuthard. But it had a cooldown before it could be used again. Otherwise, the warrior would stand there and just launch large cannonball-like mace heads at them.

Skill Gain!
Identify Rank Two +.1

Herlitgar of the Svertleim (blue)

Hall activated *Leap*. He arced over the melee, over the clash of sword and ax. Using *Leaping Stab*, he thrust the spear forward. Somehow Herlitgar sensed the attack. The large warrior swung the mace, knocking aside the *Leaping Stab* attack. Hall landed and struck a solid blow before he skidded back out of the way of the huge mace.

Rockflight slammed into the ground, bits of dirt and rock flying up.

Can't let that thing hit, Hall thought. One blow from the mace would be brutal.

Blood flowed down Hertligar's side from where Hall's spear had sliced across it. The Svertleim wore hide armor, padded and fur-lined, which were good for keeping the cold out and against blunt weapon attacks. Not so good against slicing weapons.

Hall darted to the side, jabbing out with the spear. A quick attack, just piercing the hide armor and drawing blood, before he had to pull it back out of the way of the swinging mace. He wasn't sure if the ironwood could handle a direct hit from Rockflight, but he didn't plan on finding out. Pulling Hertligar's Health bar, Hall saw that it was down to just over three quarters left.

The Svertleim growled and dashed forward, Rockflight held over his head.

Hall waited until the last second and rolled to the side. The mace slammed into the ground, Hertligar out of position because of his momentum. The spear thrust jabbed into the warrior's side. Growling in pain, Hertligar swung the mace which Hall easily avoided. He thought to call Pike in for an attack, but the dragonhawk was needed to distract the Dwarves. Hall tried to make sense of the battle but couldn't see who was fighting or how they were doing, not from his angle. The only thing he saw was a Storvgarde fall to the ground and not get up. He hoped it meant his side was winning.

He heard the screech and felt a sharp jab of pain in his head. Glancing up, Hall saw Pike struggling to stay aloft. A crossbow bolt had pierced the dragonhawk's right wing. Pike managed to keep it flapping, but it was painful. He tried to rise higher but failed.

Fly away, Hall sent his thoughts out to Pike. The dragonhawk let loose a final lightning bolt, missing the target, and started to fly to the forest. Hall saw the Dwarf crossbowman take aim.

He activated *Leap* and jumped into the air. With Leaping Stab, he slammed the tip of the ironwood spear into the Dwarf's shoulder. The trigger was pulled, the aim pushed, and the bolt missed the fleeing dragonhawk. Hall landed and stabbed out, the spear catching the Dwarf in the neck. The tip pushed through the other side, the Dwarf trying to speak but failing. Hall kicked out, pushing the Dwarf off the spear as he pulled it out with a loud pop. The Dwarf fell to the ground.

Hall turned to *Leap* back to Hertligar but fell to the ground as a great weight slammed into his chest. Ribs cracked, one possibly breaking. Breathing came hard as he impacted roughly against the ground. He glanced at his Health, seeing a good chunk removed. Hall tried to push himself up, having a hard time. He couldn't catch his breath, each attempt painful.

He could see the Svertleim warrior across the battlefield, two-handed mace shaft in hand, smiling cruelly. A second later, the mace's large head reappeared. Hertligar started to run, charging straight at Hall with his mace raised.

Hearing a noise to his left, Hall turned to see a Dwarf's heavy hammer heading toward him.

———

Hall rolled to the side.

Just barely in time.

The hammer slammed into the ground. He could feel the force of the blow against his back, not even an inch away. Vibrations ran through the earth, through Hall's hurt ribs. He hadn't been hit, but it still hurt. Rolling had hurt.

He couldn't see Hertligar, but the Svertleim was his second concern now. The Dwarf was his first.

Hall kept rolling, each movement causing pain to shoot through his body. Holding his spear in tight, he heard the javelin crack as he rolled. He could also hear the footsteps of the Dwarf, booted feet slamming against the ground, not that far away. And a new sound. Water gently splashing against the shore.

He kept rolling, forcing himself to move faster. The pain was excruciating, but he pushed past it. Hall felt like screaming. His chest was on fire. His lungs felt like they would burst. But he pushed, hearing the water coming closer, and then he felt wetness. The stomps were still coming but they were a little further away.

Bracing himself, Hall pushed himself up. Grunting, mouth clamped shut to hold in the scream. Hall slammed the butt of his spear into the soft mud along the pond's edge. Bracing himself, holding the weapon tight against his body, tip pointing at the charging Dwarf.

Who the move caught completely by surprise.

He had not expected Hall to be able to do anything but keep rolling away. The Dwarf was not prepared and could not pull up in time.

The spear tip slammed into his chest, lancing through the chain mail armor, bursting out the other side of the startled Dwarf. But his momentum kept the Dwarf pushing, sliding down the spear's shaft.

Hall yelled now, body trying not to move as the spear seemed to bend but held. He let himself fall backward, lifting the spear over his head with a scream. The heavy Dwarf lifted off the ground, falling down hard on his back in the water with a great splash. Hall lay there, head in the water, trying to breathe. He growled, working to slide his body around to get out of the pond. Each movement hurt, unable to push himself up.

The spear had been pulled from his hand as the Dwarf was flipped over. He looked into the pond and saw the unmoving body, spear sticking straight up into the air. Hall could hear the sounds of fighting behind him. Metal on metal, grunts of pain.

Taking a deep breath, Hall forced himself to a sitting position and from there to standing. Each breath was labored, his chest tight.

He heard a war cry, a great bellow.

Black Corvandr the Dread stood back to back with Hertligar. Stolen ax and mace swinging, blocking. Purple-blackish lightning cascaded around both Svertleim. They fought through the pain. Caryn faced Corvandr, twin swords darting in and striking quick. Thellia stood to the side, spear jabbing in at both Storvgarde when she could. Against Hertligar, Cuthard's brutal and quick slashes were getting through his defenses more often than not. The warrior was enraged, swinging wide, sloppy strikes.

Hall felt a surge of panic, not seeing Jackoby against Corvandr. Was the Firbolg hurt? Dead?

He breathed a sigh of relief as the battle shifted, and he saw Jackoby fighting against a Storvgarde. The Firbolg Warden was obviously hurt but faring better against the Storvgarde than he had against Corvandr. The Chieftain had been two or three levels higher, and Jackoby had held Corvandr at bay as long as he could.

Urit faced off with one of the Unclanned Dwarves, slipping around an ax strike. His hammer swung, connecting with the other Dwarf's shoulder. Near the entrance to the longhouse, Sabine, two shadowy and blurry images of the Witch, shot off a *Shadowbolt*, the black bar slamming into the chest of a Storvgarde warrior. He doubled over, the black energy spreading around his body. Hall saw the small Minx Cat, Sabine's familiar Salem, appear on the Storvgarde's back, sharp little claws digging into the man's back. Hall knew how sharp those claws could be.

All his people were injured, but all were still standing.

What they faced were the remainders of the enemy. Two Storvgarde and a Dwarf. But also Corvandr, Hertligar, and Gundar.

Water splashed as Hall stepped into the pond, clutching his chest. He stomped on the dead Dwarf and yanked the spear out. Using it like a crutch, he surveyed the battle, trying to see where he could do the most good.

———

Spear in hand, Hall activated *Leap*. He soared over the battle, landing behind the Storvgarde facing Sabine. Stabbing out, the spear punched through the back of the warrior, out the front. Pulling the spear out, Hall kicked the warrior who fell to the ground. He moved, trying to push himself up, but an *Arcane Missile* from Sabine ended the warrior's life.

She nodded her thanks.

Hall took a step, staggering a little, clutching his ribs. He turned around, seeing Urit kill the Dwarf he was facing.

"Gundar," Hall shouted to both Sabine and Urit.

He wasn't sure they heard and didn't waste time finding out. He turned and took the few steps needed.

His spear stabbed out, catching Hertligar in the side. The Svertleim warrior collapsed to that side, *Rockflight* dropping from his grasp. Cuthard took advantage of the opening, both long swords slashing across Hertligar. Crying out in pain, the warrior dropped to the ground.

Corvandr roared, swinging the *Ax of Obsidian Flames* in a wide arc, pushing everyone back. He saw the battle, knew it was lost. The last Storvgarde facing Jackoby was wreathed in purple-black lightning. Gundar faced off against both Roxhard and Urit. The Unclanned might be higher Level than the other two, but he could not face two-to-one odds for long.

And now Black Corvandr faced two Skirmishers and two Duelists.

The fight would be over in seconds.

Roaring again, shouting out in rage to the Spirit of his clan, Corvandr activated one of the *Ax of Obsidian Flames* special abilities. The shining black rock head of the weapon flared, all the runes along the edges lighting up in bright purple energy.

Hall felt the impact. A wave of heat and energy and flames shot out from the ax in all directions. Even somehow passing through Corvandr. The flames burned, the energy pushing Hall back. He fell, rolling along the ground. So did the others. Even those not directly fighting Corvandr. The force slammed into him, already hurt ribs cracking more, another breaking. He rolled, kicking up dust and stones, dropping the spear. Grunts and groans sounded across the clearing, wood cracking as someone slammed into the longhouse.

Black Corvandr the Dread unleashes Obsidian's Wrath. You suffer 10 fire damage, 10 force damage, and 10 impact damage.

Hall forced himself up, using both hands, to a kneeling position. He looked out over the field of battle. Corvandr was nowhere to be seen. Bodies lay everywhere. Dead and alive, all pushed and thrown around.

SLAIN: *Herlitgar of the Svertleim +10 Experience*
SLAIN: *Hardedge Unclanned Hammerer +25 Experience*

SLAIN: *Svertleim Bloodrager +10 Experience*

Skill Gain!
Light Armor Rank Two +.1
Skill Gain!
Polearms Rank Two +.3
Skill Gain!
Strategy Rank Two +.2

"What was that," Sabine said, coughing as she stood up.

"I don't know how that Storvgarde was able to activate the Ax's abilities," Urit growled as he kneeled on one knee, breathing hard and leaning on his hammer.

Hall pushed himself up by using his spear, leaning against it. Only his people, Thellia and Cuthard were getting up. He saw the last Storvgarde had died by impacting against the longhouse, breaking the plank wall and himself. He looked for the body of Gundar the Unclanned and saw the Dwarf lying dead on the ground at Roxhard's feet. Urit kneeled next to them, turned and spit on the corpse.

"Where's Corvandr?" Thellia said, looking around the clearing.

"Fled," Cuthard replied with a curse. "You fools, let him go," he said accusingly, pointing the tip of a sword at Caryn.

Growling, frustrated with the Wood Elf Duelist, Hall forced himself to stalk forward. He wanted to just lay on the ground, let the game's accelerated healing start to work, but he had enough of Cuthard.

"Last I saw," Hall said, stopping in front of the taller Elf. He stared up at the angry eyes, not backing down, "you were the last one in his way. If anyone let him go it was you."

Cuthard's hands tightened around his blades. He looked ready to attack and was in better Health than Hall was. But Hall, clutching his ribs, did not back down.

Thellia got between them, Screech on her shoulder, pushing Cuthard back. The Wood Elf went, eyes not leaving Halls.

"You know Iron's rule about Players," she said in a whisper, but Hall caught it, wondering what the statement meant.

Cuthard visibly relaxed but still stared daggers at Hall.

"How bad are we?" Hall asked the group without taking his eyes off the Wood Elf.

The others all spoke up, one after the other. Even Urit after a nudge from Roxhard. Most were in decent shape with himself and Jackoby the worse. He wished Leigh was here with her healing magics. Sighing, he reached into the leather potion case on his belt and removed the two *Potions of Minor Healing*.

He heard a quiet screech and glanced up. A shadow fell across the ground as Pike slowly circled above. Unsteady, the wounded wing not as strong as the other, landing on Hall's shoulder. Talons dug in as Pike tried to settle, holding the wounded wing out. Somehow the dragonhawk had removed the bolt, blood still dribbled slowly down the wound, but it seemed to be healing nicely. Pike would be as good as new in a day or two.

"Jackoby," Hall said, walking over to the Firbolg and handing over one of the potions. "Who else?"

"You," Caryn replied.

Hall started to protest. He could manage. One of them should use the Potion, but one look at the others, even Sabine, told him it wasn't worth it. Nodding his thanks he popped the cork and downed the bitter thick liquid, leaving a small amount in the bottom of the vial. He could feel warmth spreading through his body concentrating on his chest. Breathing became a little easier, the tightness leaving. He grunted as sharp pains came from his ribs. Fractures and breaks fusing back together, new bone material rapidly growing.

It stopped and he could breathe again, just a dull ache

coming from where the pain had been seconds before. A glance at his Health bar showed no movement, the Potion used on his battered body. The Health would regenerate over time, but it was the low Vitality he was worried about.

The wounds added up over time, and only true rest healed them completely. For now, he had lost Vitality. Too much more and it would start to affect his stats.

Hall laid his hand palm up, dumping the last of the healing Potion into it. He held it up to Pike, letting the dragonhawk lap up the last of it. He scratched Pike's chin, feeling the warmth radiate through the dragonhawk's body, feeling it through the bond Hall shared with Pike.

"We need to go after Corvandr," Thellia said, stepping up to Hall.

He nodded. They needed to kill Corvandr to meet one of the quest conditions. But more importantly, the Svertleim chieftain still had the Ax of Obsidian Flames.

"Loot quickly," Hall said, glancing at the longhouse. Should they search it? He wasn't sure if there would be anything of importance and nothing that affected their current quests. They could always return this way he knew. "We leave in five minutes."

CHAPTER TWENTY-FIVE

"No," Jackoby said again, his voice defiant.

Urit stood before the much taller Firbolg, the Forgecrush Clan's artifact weapon in hand. He was holding *Rockflight* out to the Firbolg, again offering it to him to use. Jackoby was the only two-handed blunt weapon user in the group, and Urit felt the Firbolg should use it. But Jackoby kept refusing.

"That is a sacred weapon," the Firbolg said, his deep voice softer, almost revenant. "I could not use it."

Finally, Urit nodded, stepping back, understanding.

He could see in Jackoby's eyes that the Firbolg did want to use the mighty weapon but honor forbade it. Urit opened the pouch at his side, holding the large mace over it. Hall watched as the weapon distorted, shrinking and twisting as it was sucked into the magical bag.

They had gotten a fair amount of loot from the Unclanned Dwarves and Svertleim clansmen. A lot of silver, copper, and even a large bag of gold coins. The payment for the Dwarf weapons. Divided between all of them, at Hall's insistence and Cuthard's grumbling, the Wood Elf thinking it should have been weighted toward damage and the most kills, it didn't come to much, but Hall was happy for the additional gold.

Axes, hammers, and assorted pieces of armor made up most of the loot. They picked through the pile quickly, looking for the best examples and leaving the rest. From the Norn, Shaman, and Witch, they took a total of four rings and two necklaces. None of them could identify them. Cuthard grumbled, loudly, when Thellia insisted that Hall's group take them.

There was something else that was looted from the Norn. A small leather cylinder, similar to the map cases Hall had found. Only three inches long and not even an inch in diameter. Brown leather with gold-colored rune work. It was a language that Hall recognized but was unable to read and unsure who it belonged to. Not one of the more common rune languages. Opening the cylinder, it was not trapped, a rolled-up parchment fell into his hand. Thin, only two inches long, he slowly unrolled the scroll. It was a note or letter of some kind, the words written vertically down the long parchment.

"I think that's Norn," Thellia remarked, looking at the scroll.

You have discovered a letter in an unknown script. It could possibly be Norn. Find someone to decipher the script. The letter could possibly explain why the Norns are aiding the Svertleim.

The Long Scroll I
Find someone to read the scroll 0/1
Reward: deciphered scroll, +100 experience

Hall rolled the scroll back up, slipping it into the case which he dropped into his inventory.

"Let's get this stuff packed up," he told the others.

———

It took closer to ten minutes, but they set off down the trail after Corvandr.

Hall had entertained a brief hope that the four Jorgunmund clan Storvgarde they had left down the trail would stop the Svertleim chief. They had heard nothing, and when they got to where the Storvgarde had been, there were just bodies.

Victims of a quick attack. Strong and fierce. Corvandr had caught the four by surprise, completely. Overwhelming them in seconds. One had managed to land a blow. A fresh wound with dripping blood left marks on the hard-packed dirt. An easy trail to follow.

"Should we bury them?" Caryn asked.

Cuthard almost laughed, Thellia shaking her head.

"No time," the Skirmisher said.

Cuthard once again took the lead, ranging a dozen feet or so ahead. They stayed to the trail, watching the markers for where Corvandr could have darted into the forest on either side. It didn't appear as if the Svertleim was trying to evade them. He was just running, taking the easiest route available.

But he had a decent lead on them. Though he was wounded, it wouldn't make a difference as they were all hurting as well.

The sun was high and still they had not caught up. Desperation drove Corvandr, pushing him beyond when he should have collapsed.

"We're not going to catch him," Hall said. "Not before dark."

He said it loud enough for Cuthard to hear from further ahead. The Wood Elf Duelist didn't stop though he obviously heard. He had paused but ignored the comment. Thellia did stop, glancing at Hall, up at the sun and ahead to Cuthard. She cursed and sighed.

"Cuthard," she called out.

This time the Duelist did stop. He glanced back at them,

clearly annoyed. Thellia waved and reluctantly he came back to the group.

"We need to move," he said. "The Storvgarde can't be that far ahead of us."

"Hall is right," Thellia told him. "We need to stop. We're all hurt and need rest."

The Duelist was about to say something else, but a glare from Thellia stopped him. He grumbled something under his breath but immediately put on the sneering smile.

"Sure, whatever Hall says," Cuthard muttered behind the fake smile.

He ignored the second glare Thellia sent him.

"Where are we to camp, fearless leader?" Cuthard asked, spreading his arms wide.

Hall sighed and glanced at Pike. The dragonhawk stood up, flexing his wings. He flapped the wounded one a couple of times and let out a squawk. With a leap, Pike lifted rapidly into the air, rising above the trees. He circled in ever-widening spirals before disappearing out of view.

Eyes going out of focus, Hall connected with the slowly flying Pike. The forest spread out before them. The high cliff behind, the mountains to the sides, trees filling the space between with the river running down the middle. In the far distance to the west Hall could see the plains spreading out.

He had Pike concentrate on the area near, looking for a defensible place to camp for the night. The forest was full of tall trees, grown thick together. The trail disappeared beneath their branches, appearing for a time before being hidden again. Hall saw that it turned to the north a half mile further down. Or at least it looked like it did. He couldn't see if it turned back east or even west. Putting the trail out of mind, he continued to look for a campsite.

And found one.

———

"You call this a campsite," Cuthard exclaimed with a mocking laugh.

The river flowed past a bowl-shaped clearing ringed by trees. The land was flat, grass for most of it, turning to sand at the shore. A couple small rocks lined the river's edge, a larger boulder near the tree line. There was nothing wrong with the site, Hall knew. Cuthard just wanted to complain.

And do so loudly.

"It'll do," Thellia said.

Bedrolls were spread out around a fire in the middle of the clearing. Watches were assigned, Hall putting Cuthard at the worst watch in the middle of the night. It was petty, Hall knew, but he didn't care. The sooner they could be rid of the Duelist, the better.

They ate a cold meal of travel rations, not wanting to hunt in the forest. They had not seen or heard anything during their trek, and even though no one said it they were worried that Corvandr could have doubled back, just waiting to ambush them in the depths of the woods.

The sun set, darkness setting in. Hall stood on the shore of the unnamed river looking up at the stars and dark spots that were higher islands. A peaceful night, the fire burning behind him casting flickering shadows. He wondered which of the dark spots was Edin. Was it even visible from Huntley?

"I was surprised how quickly I got used to that view," Thellia said from behind.

He turned as she walked up. She had been sharing his first watch, looking into the forest.

"The stars and the islands," she said, looking up into the night. "Before getting trapped here, I never bothered. I used to look at the stars all the time back home. I loved the stars. But in-game? There was no need."

Hall knew what she meant. There were a lot of aspects to the world of Hankarth that he had either ignored or took for granted. Now that it was his life, and he could never log out, he took the time.

"Now I try and look at them every night," Thellia continued. "It gives me peace."

She paused, looking back at the fire and the bedrolls. No one seemed to be stirring.

"I don't know how to explain it."

Hall looked up at the stars as she fell silent. Clouds floated by, obscuring and revealing stars and islands. Bits of the moon showed, hidden by a large island.

"I know what you mean," he said finally. "It's so different from home but just," Hall paused, trying to find his thoughts.

"Feels right," Thellia supplied.

"Yeah," Hall replied. "It does."

And she was right. This new life was starting to feel natural, like it was the true life. The changes to their backstory, where they had real history in the world, was helping with that. They fell silent, staring up at the stars.

———

"I know that look," Thellia said a half-hour later. She had walked the perimeter, taking another look into the dark depths of the forest. She found Hall in the same position, looking up at the stars. "That's the look of someone missing something."

She stood next to him, looking up.

"Or someone."

Hall smiled, not sure if she could see it.

"Someone," he said. "Leigh. She's that Druid we met and recently become the Custodian of the Grove on Edin."

"When you became Lord of Skara Brae?"

"Yeah," Hall answered and told her about how he and Roxhard had met Leigh, then Sabine and about the fight with the corrupted Custodian. He didn't go further, didn't talk about his relationship or feelings about Leigh, but Thellia got the idea.

"That's interesting that a Player can become Custodian of a Grove," she said after Hall had finished telling his story.

"I don't know if they can," Hall told her. "She's not a Player. Leigh was born on Hankarth."

"An NPC," Thellia exclaimed, struggling to keep her voice a whisper. "You're missing an NPC?"

"What's the problem?" Hall asked, shocked at Thellia's reaction.

"That's right, you said this Leigh was an NPC," she said, remembering.

"Yes. What difference does that make?"

Thellia looked back at the campfire. Hall followed her gaze. She was focusing on Jackoby and Urit, he knew, wondering what she was thinking. And why being an NPC mattered.

"You care as much about an NPC as," she gestured to herself and Sabine, who was starting to get up, hearing the conversation. It was the Witch's turn for watch soon. "They are just lines of code given form."

"And now so are we," Hall said, anger in his voice.

This was the same argument and views that Sabine used to have, but she had changed. He didn't know why, but he hadn't expected it from Thellia. He really didn't know her well, just a couple days, years ago, playing side by side for a bit and various small conversations through the years. But to think of NPCs as less than equal? She had been living in Sky Realms Online since the Glitch, the same as he had. Hadn't she seen enough to know that NPCs were every bit as real as they were now?

352 • TROY OSGOOD

Thellia was silent, looking down at the gently flowing river as it lapped against the shore.

"Watch is over," she said stiffly, turning and walking away.

Hall turned, wondering what had happened. The conversation had taken an odd turn. It seemed like Thellia was mad at him. That made no sense.

The Skirmisher ignored Sabine, who was standing up and stretching. Thellia laid down, pulling a blanket over her, turning to face the fire and away from Hall. The Witch glanced down, stepping over the sleeping bodies. She stopped next to Hall.

"She seemed mad," Sabine said, looking up at the stars. "What did you say?"

"I have no idea," Hall said with a shrug.

"It might be a good idea not to piss her off," Sabine said with a grin. "She is higher level than us."

Hall shook his head. Nodding goodnight to Sabine he headed for the fire. He crouched down next to the sleeping form of Jackoby, reaching out and lightly touching the Firbolg's shoulders. Eyes instantly opened, awake and alert.

"Your turn," Hall whispered.

Jackoby grunted, pushing off his blanket.

Hall moved out of the way, grabbing some more of the logs and branches they had quickly collected before settling in. He lay them across the fire, watching the flames start to hungrily eat the wood, sending out heat.

Skill Gain!

Survival Rank Two +.1

He was shocked to see a *Survival* Skill gain. It had been awhile. Which made some sense. The game mechanics had been designed to reward repeated actions, but only if the difficulty of the action increased. Smithing iron daggers a million times would max out the skill, but it would take years. The skill would only get so high off iron daggers and then it would take a long time between skill gains. To begin, there would be a gain for each dagger, then a gain for every five, a gain for every ten and so on until it reached the time where it was a single skill point for every thousand daggers. He had assumed the *Survival* skill was like that. He was good at making fires now so the gains would come few and far between. He wondered what he would need to start doing to get steady gains in *Survival*.

Satisfied the fire was high enough, giving off enough heat, Hall laid down on his bedroll. He pushed at his rolled-up cloak that served as a pillow, getting it as soft as possible. Shifting, rolling over onto his side, he pulled the blanket up and tried to get some sleep.

———

The sun rose, blocked by the trees. Just enough light to know it was dawn, but none of the warmth that came with the morning's rays. It was a cold morning.

Hall sat on the lone boulder in the clearing, cloak pulled tight. His breath fogged as he looked out into the shadowed depths of the forest. First and last watch. Just like always

Wood in the fire cracked and sparked. They had kept it going all night, the bedrolls all huddled close. Roxhard stood near the river's edge, idly tossing small stones into the water and watching the ripples.

He had managed to get some sleep and even regained a couple points in Vitality. While his body felt stiff from the hard ground and the cold, he knew his ribs had healed more. They no longer throbbed when he breathed.

Hearing screeching above, he looked into the blue sky and saw two circling forms. Pike and Screech, back from their morning hunt. The two dragonhawks had been wary of each other at first but finally accepted each other. Dragonhawks were not solitary creatures, bred to work with their Skirmishers which usually meant alone, but they would work with other dragonhawks if need be. Pike and Screech had accepted each other as troop mates.

Hall jumped down from the boulder, wincing slightly at the pressure on his ribs.

"Time to get up," he said to the group of sleepers.

They grumbled and moaned but got up quickly. Except Cuthard. Unsurprisingly, the Wood Elf Duelist was slow to wake. Pulling the blanket tight, he cursed. Thellia poked him with her spear, and he finally sat up.

"What's for breakfast?" he asked as the others were already packing away their few camping supplies.

"We eat on the road," Hall said, using a long stick to break apart the ashes and remaining logs of the fire.

Cuthard grumbled some more, loudly.

It didn't take long to make their way back to the trail, eating jerky as they walked.

All knew that Corvandr had a bigger lead on them now. The Svertleim Chieftain had most likely run through the night, or part of it, increasing the distance between them. Hall wasn't concerned. They would track him down and reclaim the Ax. He knew that the supplies Thellia and Cuthard required to complete their quest would not be found along the trail. They needed to track Corvandr back to his camp. Hall reasoned that Corvandr had a camp, maybe at another of the deep woods longhouses, where the raiding party had brought the supplies and a place close to the meeting with the Dwarves.

Thellia had given him a brief history lesson on the tribes that inhabited the Whitegrass Tundra and Greystone Foothills. Besides the Jormungdr and Svertleim, there were at least another dozen scattered throughout. Each numbered only a hundred to two hundred people, a large number of fighters and casters. Hall remembered the few tribes on Huntley before, four at the most, and how there had been no non-fighters in the quest related villages, or clanholds as they were called. Things had changed.

Again.

Some of the tribes were more closely aligned to the Jarl but most were not. Always at war with each other.

Iron had taken over the Jorgunmund, turned the tribesmen into his own personal army. Hall wasn't sure how he felt about that. He knew he didn't like the idea, but maybe there was more going on than he thought. It was best to reserve judgment for now.

Once that had happened, the Svertleim started to raid the supply lines that went from Crackleberry to the Jorgunmund clanhold of Great Deer, further east near Colds Ridge. *Probably feared that Iron was going to attack them next*, Hall thought, knowing he was right.

But again, maybe there was a reason. Maybe Iron was following his own quest chain.

Hall wasn't sure what the sacking of Crackleberry might have to do with it, but he would find out.

The Svertleim clanhold of Grey Rock was just over a days journey north of Crackleberry, nestled in the lower Greystone Foothills.

Thellia had marked locations on Hall's map showing Great Deer and Colds Ridge in relation to Crackleberry as well as the general area where the Jorgunmund had told Iron the location of Grey Rock was.

As they walked Hall pulled up his map, adjusting the scale. Grey Rock was a good distance from them. They wouldn't make it in a day, especially through the forest and the foothills further on. Hall knew that once they were in the hills, their pace would slow.

An hour into the trek the trail forked. The main trail

continued directly east while the new side trail, much thinner and more overgrown, headed north.

"Which way?" Cuthard asked, looking at Hall with a smirk.

Ignoring him, Hall walked down the side trail, eyes examining every inch of the ground and the bushes along the path, looking for some sign of Corvandr's passing. He couldn't find anything. He had gone about ten feet or more down the trail, seeing nothing.

Turning back to check the other trail he stopped, looking to the bushes and branches to his left.

Skill Gain!
Increased Perception Rank Two +.1
Skill Gain!
Tracking Rank One +.1

He saw the marks now. Corvandr had walked past the trees and doubled back, entering and breaking the branches from this side. Hall had expected to see signs of passage from the other direction, the one they had come from.

Pushing them aside, Hall could now see footsteps in the soft ground and what looked to be a pine branch snapped off, laying on the ground. Used to sweep away footsteps in the trail.

"This way," Hall said.

———

Following Corvandr through the forest slowed them down. Tracks were hard to find, especially at Hall's low skill level. None of them were high in tracking. Turned out that Thellia was the highest and had only just barely gotten to Rank Two in the Skill.

Hall managed to gain another four times as they followed the passage of Corvandr. The chieftain didn't go out of his way to leave a trail, but he didn't try to hide it either, thinking they would have lost him at the fork. He seemed to be moving quicker, which told Hall that his destination was near. It couldn't be Grey Rock, the clanhold was still too far away and Corvandr wouldn't push himself to cover that distance.

A longhouse. The chieftain was making for another hunting lodge.

Corvandr's trail headed west before turning north and then east again, finally south to meet up with the original small trail.

They found the longhouse three hours later.

The trail had angled toward the encircling mountains, the longhouse built tight against the cliff. Walls made of stone, a single sloping roof with the ridge against the stone. Not as large as the other, with the gray stone walls it almost blended in with the towering cliff. The trees had been cleared for a good distance around the longhouse creating a clearing of grass.

An open area that was filled with Svertleim.

Hall had heard the noise before they had entered the clearing. Voices talking in the Storvgarde language. They had slowed, spreading out and using Stealth. Hall had gained a couple points creeping up to the edge of the trees. He knew he was lucky the shadows where thick and the Svertleim occupied or he would have been noticed. Cuthard had disappeared almost completely. If Hall hadn't known Cuthard was there, he wouldn't have seen the Duelist.

Corvandr was near the longhouse, a woman in front of him. Blue energy spiraled up her bare tattoo-covered arms. It flowed out her palms that lay against Corvandr's chest.

A Druid.

She was healing the chieftain.

Hall counted another half dozen warriors and what looked to be another Shaman. But he also saw stacks of small crates and pouches against the wall of the longhouse.

Iron's stolen supplies.

CHAPTER TWENTY-SIX

THEY DIDN'T PLAN. THERE WAS NO NEED.

They just attacked.

Pike and Screech, summoned by the two Skirmishers, flew out of the sky. The dragonhawks attacked two Storvgarde warriors, unleashing lightning bolts before spiraling back into the sky. Smoke curled up from the two warriors' chests, each doubled over in pain as sparks shot across their hide-covered chests.

Their attack was followed by streaks of purple energy. Bolts slammed into five of the Storvgarde warriors, including the two the dragonhawks had attacked. Sabine's *Hexbolt* sent bolts of energy around their bodies, preventing them from moving, shocks erupting as they tried.

Falling to the ground, they cleared a path for the two Wardens.

Roxhard charged into the last Storvgarde warrior, his *Battle Rush* ability increasing his running momentum. The warrior was pushed back, grunting in pain that turned into a scream as Roxhard's ax slammed into his side.

Corvandr turned, trying to get the Ax of Obsidian Flames

up in time to block but moved too slow. Jackoby slammed into the Svertleim. The Firbolg led with his shield, pushing Corvandr off balance, knocking the chieftain off his feet. Before Corvandr could react, Jackoby struck with his hammer.

The two Duelists rushed out of the forest. Caryn and Cuthard split, each taking a side and going to work on the Storvgarde warriors.

That left just the casters.

Hall arced through the air, jumping over the *Hexbolt* afflicted Storvgarde and running Duelists. He struck out with *Leaping Stab*, catching the surprised Druid in the shoulder. The woman staggered, crying out in pain. Hall landed, immediately stabbing forward with the spear. He caught the Druid in her side. She clutched at the wound, trying to back away from him.

He didn't give her the chance. Stepping forward, he whipped the spear around, slamming the shaft into her back. She staggered, falling to her knees.

Hall hesitated. She was down, wounded. A quick glance at her Health showed it near critical. She wasn't his enemy, just in the way. It didn't feel right. Not like this.

He took a step back, pulling the spear back from where it had been only inches from the Druid's back.

The wind slammed into him, knocking him off his feet. He was able to stop himself from rolling or sliding as the air buffeted him. Small twigs and rocks crashed against him, knocking a small amount of Health off. Hall cursed, pushing against the howling wind buffeting him by the *Gust of Wind* spell.

He also cursed himself. His hesitation had caused this.

If he had just killed her, treated her like any monster, he would be able to help Jackoby or the Duelists. They'd be out of this fight quicker and with fewer injuries.

Hall activated *Leap*, jumping above the wind attack, using the momentum giving him by the Special Ability to fight past the gusts. He stabbed down with the spear, striking the now risen Druid. Catching her in the shoulder, she dropped hard and didn't get up. Looking at her Health bar, the red disappeared as it dropped to zero.

He turned, rotating the spear around his body. The shaft caught Corvandr in the back of the knee, staggering the tall Storvgarde. The Svertleim chieftain stumbled and Jackoby took advantage, delivering a powerful swing from his hammer. Hall heard bone breaking, but Corvandr did not shout out.

Dropping the spear, Hall pulled one of the magical throwing knives from his *Quickdraw Bracer of Sharp Teeth*. He launched the small blade across the clearing. It struck one of the Storvgarde warriors facing Caryn in the shoulder. Lighting crackled as the weapon's special ability activated scoring a Critical Hit. Smoke rose from the burned hides, the warrior grunting as the energy spread around his body.

Quickdraw Bracer of Sharp Teeth

Protection +4

Attack Power +2

Agility +4

Durability: 20/20

Weight: 1 lb.

Contains two Throwing Knives (1d4 +2 DMG, +6 Lightning DMG, 25% chance of Critical Strike bonus of +10 DMG). Once thrown a knife will reappear in the Bracer after ten minutes. Cooldown of twenty seconds between throwing knives.

Mentally Hall counted down from twenty, wishing he could see the Bracer's cooldown. Once he reached zero, he pulled out the second throwing knife and let it fly. It slammed into the kidney of another Storvgarde, not scoring a critical hit, with small sparks erupting on impact. The warrior shifted, lowering his hammer, and Cuthard's longsword snaked past the Svertleim's defenses. The blade sliced into the warrior's stomach. Cuthard twisted it as he pulled the blade out, blood trailing through the air. The warrior fell, dropping his weapon as he clutched at his stomach trying to stem the flow of blood. Cuthard didn't acknowledge Hall's aid as he concentrated on the next foe.

Hall picked up the spear, giving the battlefield a quick glance. Roxhard's first target was down and out, the Dwarf moving on to one of the two Caryn was facing. She squared up with the one that Hall had stabbed in the back shoulder with a throwing knife. Cuthard had one of his foes left, quickly moving past the warrior's defenses. He saw Thellia roll by, avoiding a flame burst from the Shaman.

He turned to Corvandr and Jackoby, smoke rising from the Firbolgs arm, a smell of scorched fur filling the air. The chieftain had managed to take back the initiative, which angered the proud Firbolg. Jackoby had learned from the duo's first fight, had an idea of how Corvandr fought, and was doing a much better job at holding back the stronger and higher level chieftain. If they had been equal Level, Jackoby would have won the fight.

Hall was impressed.

It didn't stop him from jumping into the fight to help Jackoby.

Activating *Leap*, he covered the short distance to Corvandr. Coming down on the arc, he stabbed out and caught the chieftain in the shoulder. The spear slammed into the Storvgarde, the sharp point plunging in deep. Sticking in Corvandr, Hall twisted the spear down as he landed, pulling the tall man with him. Corvandr yelled now, feeling his muscles tear as the spear was forcibly ripped out of his body. Bent awkwardly, he could not defend himself from Jackoby's attack.

The hammer slammed down onto Corvandr's chest. Bone

shattered, rib cavity collapsing. The large man fell to the ground, struggling to get up, breathing hard. He coughed up blood, hands reaching up and grasping for something only he could see. Hall walked over to the side of Corvandr, Jackoby on the other. The two looked down at the dying man.

Holding his spear point down, Hall stabbed it through the Svertleim chieftain's hide armor and into his heart. The body spasmed, fingers reaching. Corvandr's arm dropped. He gave one last cough, the breathing stopping.

Hall looked around the clearing. The warriors were down, all eyes drawn to the last battle. The Shaman staggered as a *Shadowbolt* from Sabine slammed into her stomach. A following thrust from Thellia and the last enemy was down.

SLAIN: Black Corvandr The Dread +20 Experience
SLAIN: Svertleim Bloodrager +10 Experience
SLAIN: Svertleim Bloodrager +10 Experience
SLAIN: Svertleim Earthraiser +30 Experience

Skill Gain!
Polearms Rank Two +.2
Skill Gain!
Thrown Rank Two +.2
Skill Gain!
Strategy Rank Two +.1

Faction Quest: Svertleim Thieves II
Eliminate the Svertleim Chieftain 1/1
Recover supplies 0/1

Hall dismissed the notifications, studying his companions for wounds. It looked like only Jackoby had sustained any wounds.

His fur was blackened along his right arm, his weapon side. The Firbolg held it up, grimacing as he sniffed at the singed fur. There was nothing that a healing potion could do for that wound. It would just need to heal naturally, the hair growing back over time.

"You," Cuthard growled walking over to Hall.

His swords were still out, blood dripping down their lengths and onto the ground. The Duelist was angry. He stopped right in front of Hall, looking down the couple inches.

"Don't be stealing my XP," Cuthard said, eyes hard, fingers gripping the hilts of his swords tight.

Hall stared up at him, not intimidated, calm.

"You're welcome."

That caused Cuthard to pause, stop what he was going to say. He looked confused, not relaxing but taking a step back.

"What?"

"You're welcome for the assist," Hall said calmly.

He turned away from the Duelist, putting his back to Cuthard. Hall walked away, ignoring Cuthard who just stood there looking unsure what to do.

Approaching the pile of small crates and packs stacked outside the longhouse, Hall let out the breath he had been holding. He had half expected Cuthard to attack him, stab him in the back.

Thellia was already at the pile of loot, sorting through it, while the others took weapons, armor, and coins from the dead Svertleim.

"Is this what you're looking for?" Hall asked her.

She was opening one of the crates, and Hall looked in. Mostly foodstuffs, some potions in another. The packs held linen, wool, flint, tinder, and other small items. No weapons or armor, but just basic living items for an army on the move.

"Yeah," she said, standing up.

. . .

You have assisted the members of Iron's Army in defeating Dread Corvandr the Black, the chieftain of the Svertleim clan as well as recovering the stolen supplies.

> *Faction Quest: Svertleim Thieves II*
> *Eliminate the Svertleim Chieftain 1/1*
> *Recover supplies 1/1*
> *Rewards: +100 Experience*

Cuthard gave Hall one last scathing glance before he started picking up some of the supplies, starting to stuff them into his inventory pouch. He got one pack in there before he stopped, holding another in his arms.

"This isn't going to work," he muttered. "We were counting on the four Jorgunmund to help us lug this stuff back."

Hall had a feeling that it wasn't the supplies that Iron cared about. There really wasn't that much here and most of it was easily replaceable. This was about image, Hall realized. Iron did not want word getting out that his supply lines could be raided.

He realized that Thellia was looking at him.

Thellia wants to share a quest.

Iron's Army supplies have been recovered, but Thellia and Cuthard require assistance in returning the supplies to their Faction.

> *Faction Quest: Svertleim Thieves III*
> *Return the supplies to Iron's Army 0/1*
> *Rewards: +100 Experience*

. . .

Attention: You are not a member of the Iron's Army Faction and cannot receive Faction and Reputation rewards from this quest.

ACCEPT QUEST?

Hall looked at his companions. Sabine and Caryn were off to the side, sorting through the collected loot from the Svertleim. Weapons and hide armor mostly. There were some rings, necklaces, and trinkets. All made from bone and covered in runes. Most likely magical but no way to know at the time. Hall figured that the ring, necklace, and trinket that Corvandr had been wearing would end up having good stats. The two Dwarves were standing next to the body of Corvandr, looking down at the obsidian ax that lay on the ground. Urit motioned to Roxhard, pointing at the ax. Roxhard opened his pouch, sliding his own two-handed ax into the magical pouch. Bending down, he lifted up the *Ax of Obsidian Flames*, staring at it in awe.

You have recovered the Ax of Obsidian Flames from Black Corvandr The Dread.
> *CRYPT FINDINGS II*
> *Find the Ax of Obsidian Flames 1/1*
> *Return the Ax to the crypt of Brignir Stonefire 0/1*

"Give us a minute," Hall told Thellia, walking away.

Hall motioned to the others, gathering them together at the forest's edge as far from Thellia and Cuthard as they could get.

"We came here to get the Ax," he started, motioning to the

weapon in Roxhard's hand. "I wasn't expecting to find them," he continued, waving toward the Skirmisher and Duelist.

"I'm curious about this Iron," Sabine said.

"So am I," Hall told them. "From what Thellia has said, it seems like he's looking to take over Huntley."

"May I speak?" Urit asked. The Stonefire Dwarf had lagged behind when they had gathered, unsure if he was to be included. Hall nodded and Urit continued. "I think I need to learn more about this Iron and his Army. If they are indeed working to take all the land in Huntley, this would affect us in Axestorm Hall."

Hall looked to Jackoby and Caryn. She shrugged, indicating she'd do whatever they all decided. The Firbolg just grunted, not caring. Hall's gaze turned to Roxhard who was still staring at the ax in his hands. The Dwarf ran his gloved fingers over the runes carved into the two heads.

"Rox?"

No answer. He was lost in the depths of the stone weapon. There was a shine to the obsidian, polished, the edges catching the light.

"Roxhard," Hall said louder, more forceful.

"Huh," Roxhard said. "Sorry," he muttered as he saw all eyes on him. "What?"

"We came here for you and the Ax," Hall said, trying to keep his voice level, not wanting to make Roxhard feel pressured. "We got the Ax. It's up to you if we follow them to Iron or we return to the Valley of the Ancients."

Roxhard looked at his companions and back to the Ax. He looked over at Thellia and Cuthard, finally settling on Hall.

"If you think it's important to meet Iron, then returning the Ax can wait."

Hall nodded, turning back to Thellia.

"Share the quest again," he said.

CHAPTER TWENTY-SEVEN

Caryn signed, watching Sabine walking ahead of her. The Witch, her girlfriend, was chatting with the other Skirmisher, Thellia. Talking like old friends. Laughing.

Maybe flirting.

The two had been talking non-stop since they had left the longhouse. Cuthard, the arrogant Wood Elf Duelist, a total jerk, was ahead of them. Scouting. Something she would have been doing, but he was higher Level.

Instead, she was walking a couple steps ahead of Hall. The two Dwarves were pulling the litter, their turn. The sled, which had quickly been constructed, held the supplies they had found, making it easier to transport them. It dragged across the rough trail, getting snagged often. The travel was slow, which suited Caryn as it gave her time to think.

She knew she wasn't really happy with Sabine. Not truly.

A relationship of convenience?

On Sabine's part anyway. Caryn knew she was naive but wasn't that naive. Sabine was only with her because there was no one else. Caryn knew she was with Sabine because the Witch showed interest in her.

When learning she had been trapped in Sky Realms Online, without her real-life girlfriend, Caryn had hoped it would mean a fresh start for her. But here she was, falling into the same old patterns. Why had she been so quick to get into a relationship with Sabine?

Why did she do the same thing over and over?

No matter where she was.

She wondered what Sabine and Thellia were talking about and why it couldn't involve her. She thought about walking up there, forcing her way into the conversation, almost increasing her pace to cover the small distance. But she stopped.

Why should she? She was her own person. She didn't need to be involved in Sabine's life every minute of it. Caryn knew she didn't want to be.

Her hope had been that being stuck in Sky Realms Online could break her out of the spiral her life had become. She had only started playing the game because Cassandra, her girlfriend, was a player and Caryn thought it was the only way to spend time together. Or she had hoped. Didn't seem like it was going to turn out like that. Cassie had been a high-level endgame player and didn't have time to play alongside the noob that was Caryn.

Then the Glitch had happened and Caryn was here. Cassie was? One of those dead? Trapped like her? Safe? Caryn had no idea, and it had surprised her how quickly she ended up not caring. She realized she had never really loved Cassie, hadn't really been comfortable in the relationship. She had just been going through the motions.

She had freedom now in the game. Until she met Sabine and in a matter of weeks, she found herself back in the same routine.

When she was fighting, everything else disappeared. She had confidence, grace, strength. Everything she lacked normally.

She had only been playing for a couple of hours before the Glitch, but she had found a freedom in the game she didn't have in real life. She had found that confidence and strength. Through battle, of all things. Part of her understood why Cassie chose to play the game over spending time with her, but that part was quickly pushed aside in favor of the fun that she was having.

The Glitch had scared her, but it had been a short panic. What had the real world offered her? Dead-end job. No family. Few friends. Cassie.

Which hadn't been good.

Why not reinvent herself as Caryn the Duelist?

And it had worked until Sabine showed an interest early on during those few weeks in Skara Brae after the adventure in Silverpeak Keep. She had fallen quickly back into being the same old Karen.

Except when she was fighting. Caryn the Duelist appeared. Calm, confident, strong.

Why couldn't she be that way all the time?

"You okay?" came Hall's voice, drawing her from her thoughts.

Which she was thankful for.

It had been a long time since she had let herself spiral like that.

"Yeah," Caryn replied, feigning a smile. "Just thinking."

"Of?"

"Life," she said, looking at Sabine ahead of them.

She glanced up, seeing Hall look that way. He studied the two women ahead of him. Sabine in her dress, slit up the sides, belt, and jewelry, hoop earring visible around her short blonde hair. Salem, the Minx cat familiar, was curled around her shoulders. Thellia wore tight leathers, arms covered, Screech sitting on her shoulder, javelins and spear in her harness, pointed ears sticking out of her hair. They were the same height, same build, looking like friends just out for a walk.

"When we first became trapped in the game," Hall said quietly, thoughtfully, "I made the decision to just go with it. If this was to be my life, then I'd enjoy it. Never expected it to lead where it did." He paused, looking up into the sky as the shadow of Pike flew by. "Or who it led to. I have my moments where it's a game, but more and more, it's becoming just my life. I am Hall. I'm not who I was."

He stopped and just gave a shrug.

Caryn thought about it. It was true. This was her life now. She was Caryn the Duelist.

But what did that really mean? Who was that person?

———

They made quick time. Not having to follow a trail or move quietly, they were able to keep their pace. Cuthard kept checking his map, keeping them on course. Knowing where to go helped. They kept their eyes open, watching for Svertleim Raiders and other potential menaces in the woods. The sound of animals followed them. Bears and wolves. But none attacked.

Night came, and they weren't even halfway to their destination. Hall had expected the Svertleim raiders to be closer to where Iron was camped. He had thought they started raiding Iron's supply lines because their clanhold was the next target on whatever list the Army had. But from what Thellia had said, to Sabine since she was effectively ignoring Hall, Iron was moving away from the Svertleim village.

"Securing the southern border," she had said. "Before moving north."

The target was another clan, the Hagnar.

Hall didn't understand any of it. Which is why he wanted

to meet Iron, find out the plans. Urit had been right. Whatever Iron was doing would affect the Axestorm Dwarves. Once he had conquered all the Storvgarde clans on the Whitegrass Tundra would he turn his attention to the Dwarves?

They spent the night in a shallow cave carved out of the side of a grass-covered hill. The trees were thinning out, the land sloping down in a series of hills, the mostly flat tundra spread out before them as they crested the small hills.

As Hall stood at the cave's mouth, on his last watch of the night, he thought about plans and armies, clanholds and battles. He was no tactician, he knew. Large scale battles were not something he had engaged in. The large raids, which Iron's Army had excelled at, were not something he had led. He grudgingly admitted that these smaller battles they had been in, those were things where he was a good leader. Somehow he knew how to fight those.

The movements of an Army? A battle of dozens versus dozens, or worse hundreds versus hundreds, that was beyond him. But As he watched the night sky through the trees, the movements of the Storvgarde started to make sense. Or at least he thought it did. There were pieces he didn't have, but he started to think his assumption was right.

It was the Norn that had led him down this path. Not as much of a wild card as first thought. What if the Norns were organizing the Storvgarde against the threat that Iron posed? He wasn't sure why the Norns were concerned about Iron, but that one was there brokering the deal between Corvandr and the Unclanned Dwarves, it meant they were concerned. The various clans had only united once before. The first time the Jarl had come to claim Huntley as part of his kingdom. That fight had ended with the clans swearing loose allegiance to the Jarl but not under direct control. Since then they had gone back to their tribal ways, warring with each other.

Was the threat apparently posed by Iron large enough for

them to unite once again? With some prodding by the Norns, it seemed like it was.

If the Svertleim raided the supply lines, it would force Iron to send part of his army after them. That would weaken them for the fight against the Hagnar. Would the Svertleim then advance on Iron's back, catching his forces between them?

Skill Gain!
   Strategy Rank Two +.1

Interesting, Hall thought as he dismissed the notification. Apparently, he was on the right track.

But why was this all happening? Why was Iron trying to take over Huntley?

Was that even his plan?

Hall had thought there had to be a quest chain that Iron was following. But what was the goal?

After Silverpeak Keep, Hall had started to wonder if he was being led to some bigger goal. Since claiming lordship of Skara Brae, it had seemed any quests he found were ultimately helping fortify, rebuild or increase the population of Skara Brae. Even the chain they were on currently. They had come to Axestorm Hall to get an airship for the village.

Was he ultimately going to be sent on a similar path as Iron?

That idea bothered him.

The sun rose, and Hall was still in the same spot, thinking about the future.

———

Up and down the hills, following paths along the low gulleys between and up along the ridges. The sun rose above them, clear with barely a cloud in the sky, just the distant islands overhead. Pike and Screech soared above them, spiraling lazily through the air, riding the wind currents.

The wind blew across the tundra, across the hills and into them as they crested the tops. Cloaks were pulled tight. No one talked as they trudged along, heading in a relatively southeast direction.

It was midday when the first of the smoke appeared. The mountains rose up to the west, peaks towering above a long cliff wall. Hall thought he could make out Greystone Watch along the cliff. Dozens of pillars of smoke rose up beyond the hills. A large collection to the south and another to the east.

Consulting his map, Hall knew the smoke to the south belonged to the Bodin village of Crackleberry. The one to the east had to be Iron's Army. Why hadn't he seen the smoke days before when they had been at Greystone Watch? There had been a clear view of Crackleberry. The smoke from the Army should have been visible, but they had only seen Crackleberry. Where had the Army been?

Cuthard turned them east, cutting across the hills toward the smoke that was Iron's Army. From a distance, there had only been a half dozen or so pillars of smoke, but as they got closer, it became more. Dozens of cookfires, the smoke rising lazily into the air.

How big was this Army? Hall thought, a little worried.

The group continued across the hills for two or three more hours. The sun rose high overhead, starting its descent, and they still hadn't gotten out of the foothills. The smoke got thicker, closer, so they were making progress even if the landscape didn't reflect it.

Hall didn't like the timing. Part of him wondered if Cuthard had done it on purpose. They were too close to stop for the night, and when they arrived, it would be time to camp.

Hall and his friends would be stuck at the Army's camp unless they wanted to venture into unfamiliar and hostile territory at night. Which probably wouldn't be the smartest move.

He was probably overthinking it. There was no reason to be worried. Cuthard may be an arrogant jerk, but he wasn't threatening. Thellia was fine, even if she was a little frosty now. Better safe than sorry he thought. He had no idea what to expect. Not one to really pay attention to the forums and inter-guild drama, Hall didn't know much about Iron or the Guild he had run back in the Pre-Glitch game. And how much had the man changed? Hall knew he had changed. Not just from being stuck in Sky Realms Online, but being thrust into a leadership role had started to change him as well.

The same had to have happened to Iron. But it seemed to have made him a conqueror.

Hall still hoped it was some kind of quest chain with a grand purpose behind it. He didn't want to think that it was just Iron wanting to take over Huntley.

But what if it was?

He thought back to Davit, the Bodin Player they had met back in Auld when first arrived on Edin. Davit had murdered some citizens, NPCs. The Bodin hadn't thought it a big deal. They were just NPCs. It was a callous attitude, one that instantly made Hall dislike him and dismiss him. Both Cuthard and Thellia seemed to share at least some of that attitude toward NPCs. Sabine had early on as well.

Was he the odd one?

Did the feeling that Players were superior to NPCs exist with all Players? If so, conquering Huntley made more sense. But Hall couldn't believe it. People were bad, but just being around the NPCs would change people's attitudes. It had to. They were as real as the Players, both nothing but digital code. NPCs were as alive as Players. There was no difference between them.

Hall had to believe that there was another motivation for what Iron was doing. Something beyond misplaced feelings of Player superiority.

He would find out soon.

They started up yet another hill, Cuthard standing at the top. The Wood Elf was staring out over the tundra, waiting for the others. Hall was the first up the top. The last stretch was up almost a dozen feet of steeply sloping exposed rock. Hall watched his feet and hands as he climbed, pulling himself up onto the ridge.

Standing he looked out where Cuthard pointed.

The hill rose high above the tundra, a steep slope down to the grassland. Smoke rose high into the air, caught in the wind as it was pushed across the land. Dozens of campfires dotted the grassland at the base of the hill. Tents of various shapes and sizes, all arrayed in neat and orderly lines, campfires set up between groups of them. People moved about the camp, patrols visible on the outer edges. A single large fire in the middle of the camp with three of the largest tents positioned around it.

"Let's go see the boss," Cuthard said with a chuckle.

CHAPTER TWENTY-EIGHT

CUTHARD LED THEM THROUGH THE CAMP, PASSING THE sentries with ease. They recognized him and Thellia, who brought up the rear, no words exchanged though the sentries eyed Hall and the others warily.

Hall had gotten a good look at the camp as they descended the steep hill, the tents and fires in view the whole way down, as they worked their way down with the sled of supplies. All he saw were Storvgardes. The majority were men from the plains, the Jorgunmund clan. The rest had to be from Colds Ridge. Their armor was leather, some with pieces of metal armor. They carried swords and shields instead of axes and hammers and kept themselves apart from the Jorgunmund. A quick count had around three dozen Colds Ridge men and women, three or four times that for the clansmen from the tundra.

But it was the group to the south that had caught Hall's attention for most of the trip down from the Greystone Foothills to the Whitegrass Tundra. Only about two dozen. Shorter than the typical Storvgarde, covered in furred hides. They had their tents outside the main group, a circle of them around a central fire. Between each set of tents were lines attached to thick posts set into the hard ground. Tied to the lines were creatures twice the size of horses but looking like mammoths. Wide and relatively short, they stood on four thick legs, long tusks with even longer trunks. Large ears flapped in the night as the creatures grunted and shifted.

Tunoths.

Tundra Mammoths.

That meant the two dozen Storvgardes were from the Mamonog Clan.

The only known clansmen in the Storvgarde islands that rode animals. They raised their special mounts, training them from birth, breeding the qualities they wanted.

That explained where the Army had been days before. Finding or conquering their new allies.

"Told you he didn't need us," Hall had heard Thellia say to Cuthard when she had caught sight of the Mamonogs.

A quick glance had revealed an angry Cuthard.

Hall wondered how many Players Iron had with him. It couldn't be many. From all he had seen, Hall didn't think there had been many Players restarted in Sky Realms Online. He had only encountered four and only maybe a dozen or so the first day in Grayhold. If the numbers held for those that had appeared in the Storvgarde Islands, at Darkice, then there couldn't be more than a dozen Players if all that had restarted joined up with Iron.

The Wood Elf led them through the tents, not that straight a path. The tents were laid out in a pattern, one that Hall had seen from above. Set groups and lines but staggered so that there wasn't a straight walk from the outer edge to the center where Iron was located. Cuthard led them left, then right, always moving ahead.

Until finally they passed the last line of tents and approached the largest campfire. Flames roared to the height of a man, logs that were more trees laid in a pyramid shape burning and crackling.

There were about a half dozen people seated around the fire, some on the ground and some on logs. All faced toward the blaze, talking quietly. Only one turned at their approach, standing up.

"I saw the quest completion notification," the figure said, lost in the shadows cast by the fire.

He was large, a Storvgarde but big even for that race. He stepped away from the flames, stepping out of the shadows where details could start to be seen. Over six and a half feet tall, a couple hundred pounds of solid muscle. A Warden, no weapons visible, but evident in the way he carried himself. Sleeveless brigidine leather armor with metal plates covered a wide chest, blue and black tattoos running up his thick arms. Leather armor and bracers, studded leather gloves, armored boots, and leather pants with metal plates. Clean-shaven except for a patch on his chin that grew long down his chest and tied in a thick braid. The sides of his head were shaved and tattooed, the hair on top tied in a long braid that hung down his back. A thick fur cloak hung over his shoulders.

His eyes roamed the group, studying them. Gray, they stopped on each member for seconds, measuring and focusing as he used the *Identify* Skill, before finally locking on Thellia.

"I take it you were successful?"

Something in the man's tone told Hall that if Thellia and Cuthard were not successful, then they shouldn't have bothered to come back.

"We were," Thellia replied and motioned to the sled that was now being towed by a couple of Storvgardes she had co-opted for the labor.

QUEST COMPLETE!

. . .

You have returned the stolen supplies to Iron's Army.
  Faction Quest: Svertleim Thieves III
  Return the supplies to Iron's Army 1/1
  Rewards: +100 Experience

"We have news as well," Thellia continued.

The large Stovegarde held up his hand to stop her. Hall had already guessed his identity.

"Who are these visitors?" he asked.

Thellia gave introductions, starting with Sabine and glossing over Urit and Jackoby. The others around the fire had turned to look, to see the newcomers, and Hall could feel the eyes of others in the camp on them. "And this is Hall," Thellia finished motioned to him.

Hall thought he heard a sharp intake of breath followed by a curse come from the side of them. He turned to look but saw nothing but motionless Storvgarde staring at him. Not friendly but not kindly either. The large Storvgarde had also apparently heard the noise as well and was looking curiously in that direction. Seeing nothing he turned his attention back to Hall.

"Welcome to our camp," he said. "I am Iron."

———

Skill Gain!
  Identify Rank Two +.1

Iron, Warden (orange)
  Lord of Colds Ridge
  Chieftain of the Jormungund Clan
  Chieftain of the Mamonog Clan
  Faction: Iron's Army, Commander

· · ·

"Thank you for your assistance," Iron said once Thellia had given the Warden a detailed debriefing.

Iron hadn't said a word, waiting until she was done, and then asked questions. He asked of both Thellia and Cuthard, looking for discrepancies. Cuthard's answers were obviously colored by his bias, and it seemed Iron understood that. He even asked questions of Hall and Sabine.

The five had left the fire and entered one of the large tents, the inside serving as Iron's bed and study. A large table was in the middle, a bed pushed against the back wall. Covering the table were maps and notes, wooden figurines carved to reflect troops. Hall didn't get much of a chance to study it before Iron started the questioning.

The others were enjoying food and drink by the fire along with the members of Iron's Army that had been there before. All Players. A half dozen of them. They had been introduced as "Players like us", as Iron put it. Urit and Jackoby were there but had not been given the same attention as Caryn and Roxhard. Hall suspected that Iron did not want to alienate him yet, but he was realizing his assumptions of the Army's Player feelings of superiority were on point.

"No problem," Hall said in response to Iron's question. "Just worked out that our goals aligned."

Iron was standing at the head of the table, the others down the sides. His fingers tapped on the wood as he thought.

"The appearance of the Norn is interesting," Iron said, fingers still tapping. "Brokering a deal with the Unclanned for weapons to undoubtedly use on us."

"I can see why the Svertleim would worry about us," Thellia said. "But why the Norn? There aren't any Norns on Huntley?"

"There was at least one," Iron said with a laugh. "Most likely there are more."

Hall wondered who Iron really was, or had been before the Glitch. Most Players that chose Storvgarde did it because they liked the large size of the race, the physical aspect. Iron came across as cultured, smart. Not the typical Player that went Storvgarde. Hall still wanted to know why Iron was on this apparent path of conquest. He was about to ask when Iron spoke again.

"It is late," the Storvgarde said. "We can talk more in the morning. Eat and drink your fill. Thellia will get tents prepared for you and your people."

It was a clear dismissal. Hall glanced at Thellia as Iron turned away from the table. The Skirmisher motioned them to follow her.

Outside the tent, she led them to the fire and the others, who stood up at their approach.

"Hall," Roxhard said excitedly. "There's another Player from one of the top guilds, the Gold Dragons."

He nodded, not really sharing Roxhard's enthusiasm.

"I used to watch their Streams," Roxhard continued, acting fully like the fourteen-year-old kid he was.

With a laugh, Thellia led them around the fire to a table covered in food and drink. An elderly Storvgarde woman was dishing out stew and pouring tankards of mead. Hall took one, following Roxhard back to the fire. He took a seat on a vacant log. Next to him was a Norn, a female Shaman named Corinth.

"Welcome," she said as Hall sat. "Roxhard has been telling me all about your adventures."

Hall silently cursed. He hadn't wanted to reveal much to them. He wasn't sure why, but he didn't feel comfortable around these people. Not yet at least.

"Looks like you've been up to more than we have," Hall

said, motioning to the camp of Storvgarde around them. Maybe he could get some more information out of them.

Corinth laughed. This was a hint of coldness to it, like she saw through Hall's feeble attempt at fishing for information.

"This is all Iron," she said finally, looking at him out of the corner of her eyes, smirking. "We're just along for the ride."

"And what is the ride?" Hall asked.

Again, Corinth gave the laugh.

"I'll let Iron fill you in," she said.

Hall gave up and started eating the food. It was good, probably tasting better because it had been days since he had anything that hadn't been burnt over a fire. Corinth was looking at him with that sly smirk, like she knew more than he did. It made him uncomfortable. He studied her, the first Norn Player he had seen in a while. Like the race he had chosen, Half-Elf, the Norn race was a special reward for Beta Players, those first ones allowed into the game to test it out. Corinth had been a first day Player just like him. He knew he'd never come across her before and wondered if she had been part of the Iron's Army Guild back pre-Glitch. He cursed quietly, berating himself for being an idiot.

Setting the plate and mug down on the ground, he pulled the small leather cylinder out of his inventory. Opening it, he pulled out the parchment. Corinth was watching his actions, curious and interested. Holding it by the ends he showed her the text. Her eyes lit up.

"Can you read this?"

She nodded, hands reaching forward to take it.

"May I?"

QUEST COMPLETE!

Corinth of Iron's Army has agreed to read the scroll and decipher its contents for you.

The Long Scroll I
Find someone to read the scroll 1/1
Reward: deciphered scroll, +100 experience

Holding the two-inch-wide scroll by the ends, Corinth's eyes roamed the paper. She read it from the top to the bottom, following the vertical lines of text. Then she read it again. And a third time.

She shook her head, handing it back to Hall.

"It doesn't say much," Corinth told him. "I'm not sure what it even means."

She leaned back, looking up at the stars and shadowed islands in the sky overhead.

"The Champions must be defeated," she started to say, reciting the translated letter. "Do what you must."

Corinth looked at Hall and shrugged.

"That's it. No idea what any of it means," she told him. "Not sure what a Champion is. I'm going to tell Iron what it says."

Hall nodded, going over her translation.

"There has to be some connection," he mused. "Why they are aiding the Svertleim and what this Norn was ordered to do."

Corinth nodded.

The scroll has been translated, but you are no closer to discovering what it means. The best way to figure it out would be to capture a Norn and ask them. If you can.

The Long Scroll II
Capture a Norn 0/1
Discover more information on the Norn's mission 0/1
Reward: +100 experience

. . .

The Norn's eyes perked up.

"Weird," she said. "I just got that quest."

A quick look around and he saw all the Players react, as well as the two NPCs, Urit and Jackoby. Apparently, they had all gotten the quest. He had expected his companions to get it as they always did. But the Iron's Army Faction members? Thellia had to actively share the other quests for him to receive them. He hadn't done that. What was different about this one.

He studied the other Players around the fire, apparently Iron's inner council. Besides Corinth, there was another Shaman. A Wood Elf. His name had been given as Torit. Two Wardens sat on the other side from Hall, barely visible through the flames. A Gael and Arashi. Nero and Tig. Next to Tig was a Wood Elf Druid named Tashy. The last was a Gael Skald, Tabitha.

Caryn and Sabine were deep in talk with Torit, Roxhard talking with Tabitha who must have been from the Guild he had mentioned. Urit and Jackoby stood by themselves off to the side, near the fire but not. They each held a mug of ale, eyes constantly moving around. None of Iron's people seemed interested in talking with them.

"Excuse me," Hall said to Corinth.

He got up, returning his plate to the table, got a refill on the mug and walked over to the two NPCs. He could feel the eyes of the Players following him. A glance showed Corinth watching him intently, not trying to hide her interest, a small amused smile on her face. He felt more than just those around the fire. Turning he saw Iron standing just inside his tent. The large man was watching him. Iron nodded, as if confirming something, and disappeared back inside. Hall continued his survey of the nearby camp. None of the Storvgarde NPCs that made up Iron's Army were paying any attention to him, but Hall could feel another set of eyes following him.

It made the hairs on the back of his neck stand up.

Skill Gain!
Increased Perception +.1

He couldn't find the interested party, the person lost among the tents and Storvgarde.

"Are ye okay?" Urit asked when Hall stopped in front of him. "Ye act like ye seen a ghost."

"Just feels like I'm being watched," Hall said, taking a sip from the mug as he did another survey of the camp.

"Besides that lot," Urit muttered, motioning with his head toward the Players gathered around the fire.

Hall nodded.

"I do not like these people," Jackoby growled.

I don't think they like you, Hall thought to himself looking back to the fire. All of Iron's people were back to what they had been doing, except for Corinth who still watched him.

"We're not here to make friends," Hall said. "Just get some information."

He looked around for Thellia, seeing the other Skirmisher walking toward the fire. He raised a hand, signaling her.

"Let's find our tents and get some sleep," he told them.

CHAPTER TWENTY-NINE

"You do not have a Faction yet?"

Hall heard the voice and turned, looking up at the tall Storvgarde. Iron stood behind him, looking down, dressed in his armor with a shield over his shoulder and a large warhammer in hand.

Iron took a seat on a log next to Hall.

They sat in front of the fire. The ashes had been set ablaze, new logs added, warding off the morning's chill. A cold wind blew in off the tundra, sending sparks swirling into the air. Hall had been up for an hour, the sun just starting to rise in the east. A red glow across the horizon. There was not much activity in the camp, people just starting to get up. None of his companions were up yet. Pike was off across the grasslands hunting for breakfast. Hall could feel the dragonhawk as a presence in the back of his head, always there but in the background.

Hall wasn't sure why he had gotten up. His sleep had been good. Not the most restful but he had managed it. Most likely his body was just used to being up before the sun. He almost always took the last watch so it was natural for him to be awake.

He glanced at Iron. The man held himself in a stiff but relaxed posture. The way he talked, his body language, Hall suspected that Iron was older in real life. The Storvgarde Warden looked to be in his late twenties, much like Hall, but mentally most likely in late forties or early fifties. There was just something formal and mature in the way he talked. There was also something charismatic about the man. He didn't come across as friendly. Somewhat aloof, but still people willingly followed him. And it wasn't just for strength alone.

"What do you mean?" Hall asked.

Iron grabbed a long stick lying on the ground. He poked it into the fire, pushing burning logs around. Flames leaped up sending a fresh wave of warmth.

"You are Lord of a town," Iron stated, not a question. "Hall, Level Five, Lord of Skara Brae."

Hall winced a bit. Level Five, where Iron was at least three or four Levels higher. He wondered what the man's *Identify* Skill was at if he could see Hall's exact level. He also wasn't happy that he didn't know how to answer the question without coming across as ignorant.

"Not sure what you mean," he said finally.

Iron nodded, as if the answer confirmed something.

"As the Lord of a Settlement, you can create a Faction based out of that Settlement."

Hall stared into the flames, mentally pulling up his Settlement Interface. He hadn't bothered looking at it since leaving Skara Brae. There had been no need.

Skara Brae
  Lord: Hall
  Status: Ruins 25%
  Morale: Productive

. . .

Government:
    Appointed Officials: Timmin, Administrator
    Brient, Sheriff

Population: 13
    Production: Carpentry Rank One - 25%
    Farming Rank One - 15%

Faction:
    Allies:Gnomes of Valedale
    Brownpaw of Fallen Green
    Trade Partners:
    Enemies:

The statuses were all the same, as it should be expected. Hall figured he was too far away from the village for the statuses to update. He looked at the Faction listing, one he really had not spent any time exploring. Leigh had said that Guilds had to be registered so he had put it out of mind at the time. Roxhard kept wanting to come up with a name for their group, which Hall supposed was a Guild, but it was just low on the priority list.

Concentrating on the heading a new notification popped up, filling his vision.

Factions are autonomous groups associated with a particular Settlement. They usually work with that Settlement's goals in mind but can sometimes work counter to the Settlement or for goals of their own. The Settlement serves as the Founding location for the Faction as well as its base of operations. They are allies of the Settlement. A Faction can only be founded in a Settlement if accepted by the Lord of that Settlement. If Founded by the Lord of the Settlement, or chosen Representative, the Faction is more closely tied to the Settlement and the Faction goals more closely align with the Settlement.

Settlement Requirements: Minimum population of 20, Settlement Status of Village

There was more to the notification, another page at least, but Hall didn't read any more. He dismissed the screens.

"There are many benefits to forming a Faction," Iron said, noticing Hall's eyes regained focus.

"Skara Brae is still classified as ruins," Hall said, wishing he had read the Faction note earlier. "And we don't have the population yet."

Iron nodded in understanding.

"I did luck out in gaining Colds Ridge," he admitted. "It saved me a lot of the early development time."

"How did you get Colds Ridge?" Hall asked.

"The old-fashioned way," Iron said with a laugh. "I took it."

Hall was shocked by the answer. Straight forward. No lying. He hadn't expected Iron to just admit it like that.

Iron laughed again.

"Shocked?" Iron asked, poking the stick into the fire again. He shifted some ashes around, stirring up flames. A Storvgarde warrior on the other side tossed a couple logs into the blaze. "Thought there was a good reason to do so beyond just I wanted to?"

"Yes," Hall replied, not quite sure where to steer the conversation.

Iron leaned forward, reaching his hands out to the fire, palms out. He left them there a moment, feeling the warmth.

"Like you, I have played Sky Realms Online since the Beta," Iron said, his eyes roaming the campsite as more and more people awoke. He nodded to Torit as the Shaman sat down on a log next to Hall. "I had played all the others, always one of the best if not the best player in the game. That was a goal of mine. To always be the best. There are reasons for it, I assure you, but they are irrelevant now that we are trapped in the game." He paused, leaning back, rubbing his hands together. He stared at them, opening and closing into fists. "Even trapped the need to be the best is still there, but as I soon learned, and I'm sure you learned, the game was different."

Hall nodded. It had not taken long. He was as opposite a Player from Iron as there could be. While not casual, Hall had never been as driven as Iron. He liked the endgame content, but it was the journey to get there that he Played for. Iron, it seemed, just played for the endgame.

"Long story short," Iron said with a chuckle, leaning forward as more people joined them around the fire. "I received a quest with an end goal of taking control of Colds Ridge. It wasn't a hard decision to make."

Iron finished the story, nodding and waving to the others.

Hall wondered if there was more. He had a feeling there was.

"But what about them?" Hall asked, motioning to the Jorgunmund around them. "And Crackleberry?"

Iron didn't say anything, didn't move, just stared into the flames. Hall was about to ask again when the large Storvgarde quickly stood up. He was looking across the fire at Cuthard. The Wood Elf Duelist had disappeared soon after returning to camp. He was dirty and tired, breathing heavy.

"They're on the move," he said. "And have Norns with them. Lots of Norns."

———

They assembled in Iron's tent at his war table. Hall was surprised to be invited, but he was along with Cuthard, Thellia, Corinth and the Skald, Tabitha.

Some of the carved icons had been rearranged, the ones representing the Svertleim Hall had been informed. He saw markers carved as axes that had to represent Iron's Army, assembled in a valley just past Crackleberry. On the town was a carved hammer. Hall assumed it meant the town was under Iron's control.

He still didn't have an answer on why Iron had attacked the Bodin town but was starting to form some conclusions. Iron had not said much, but Hall had read between the lines. Iron had already conquered all the endgame that Sky Realms Online had offered. He was the best. Now starting over at Level one, why do the same content? Why not try a new approach to being the best? Why not take over the lands?

"Where did the Norns come from?" Tabitha asked.

A female Storvgarde, she was tall and muscled. Long blond hair was tied in a thick braid that fell down her back. Pale skin with bright blue eyes, she had multiple piercings in her ears. Dressed in leather with a fur cloak, her lute hanging across her back, Tabitha was standing next to Hall. Her question brought his attention back to the map.

Rough and crudely drawn, he knew even at his *Cartography* Level he could have done better. It showed the southern half of Huntley and had enough detail in what was supposed to be the mountains and lakes, that Hall could follow where they were even without labels.

Further to the southeast, near the edge of the island, was

another hammer marker. That would be Colds Ridge, Hall knew. Two other hammer markers indicated the Jorgunmund and Mamonog clanholds. Sword markers to the north of Iron's Army were presumably the Svertleim. Others to the south would be the clanhold of the Hagnar.

Cuthard had moved the Svertleim markers closer to the Army's location, pulling out some new ones from a bag off to the side. He added a couple carved in the shape of stars. The Norns.

"They're maybe half a day out," Cuthard said, glancing at Hall. If he wondered why Hall was there, he didn't ask. "No idea where the Norns came from."

Iron looked down at the table, large fingers tapping against the wood.

"I did not expect the Svertleim to react this quickly after the death of Corvandr," Iron said finally. "I'm surprised they even know of his passing." He glanced at Thellia.

"None escaped," she said, Cuthard nodding in agreement.

Fingers tapped against the wood table again.

"Interesting," he said. "I would like to know how, but it is no matter."

Leaning forward, Iron began moving pieces of his Army across the map. Hall noticed that a couple of the ones moved were carved like the Tunoths he had seen just outside the camp.

"We have two fronts," Iron explained. "The Svertleim to the north and the Hagnar to the south. The Hagnar are stationary and from what the scouts say, do not know we are coming. The Svertleim are a different story. They have been harassing us since Crackleberry. The smart move would be to move against the Svertleim. Deal with them first."

He paused, fingers tapping against the table still. Hall glanced around at the others, they were all smiling, anticipating what Iron was going to say. Hall wondered if there had been more villages that he didn't know about. He looked back at Iron. The man was calm, didn't seem rash. Hall expected Iron's Army to break camp and attack the Svertleim.

Iron surprised him.

"That is what they expect us to do," Iron said with a smile. "I suspect the Hagnar are not as complacent as they appear. I suspect they also have Norn allies. If we move against the Svertleim, the Hagnar will attack from the rear."

He finished moving the pieces. Half his army was near the Hagnar clanhold, the other half near the Svertleim.

"We will attack both fronts."

Cuthard and Tabitha exchanged fistbumps. Thellia just nodded, in complete agreement.

Hall looked down at the map, wondering if the markers indicated the true numbers in each of the three forces. If they did, Iron's Army was outnumbered. He looked up, feeling all the eyes on him.

"And what will you do?" Iron asked.

———

"What do you think?" Hall asked the others.

He had gathered his companions just outside the camp, past the last of the sentry lines. They were in the middle of the tundra, nowhere for anyone to hide, in a close circle and facing each other. No way for anyone to listen in.

The others were silent. He had explained Iron's plan and the request for their aid. Hall didn't think Iron really expected them to make a difference. He suspected it was a way of trying to get Hall and his friends to join up with Iron's Army.

He had been tempted to just say no. Take his people and walk away. But they had come here for a reason, part of it to gauge any potential threat to the Dwarves of Axestorm. It seemed the Norns were brokering a deal between the

Unclanned Dwarves and the Svertleim, possibly the Hagnar too. They had seen two weapons traded, but were there more?

If so, they needed to recover those weapons.

"Iron has said we can take any recovered ancient Dwarven artifacts back to the Valley," Hall told them.

"That's good since they be not his," Urit grumbled.

Hall nodded, agreeing.

"Look," he said with a sigh. "I'm not liking this. Iron is the aggressor, without a doubt."

"But what?" Sabine asked when Hall paused.

"There's the quest we got last night," he said. "The Norns are with the Svertleim. Iron would like us to assist in that attack. It seems the only way to complete the quest."

"But do we even need to?" Caryn asked. "How does it concern us?"

Like Hall, and most of the others, she was having reservations about attacking the Svertleim. Iron was the invader in Huntley, the other clans were just defending themselves.

"It seems these Norns be allying with the Unclanned as well," Urit interrupted. "That be of interest to me and Axestorm Hall."

"It would help us get in good with Iron," Sabine added.

"That we do not need," Jackoby growled.

Sabine glared up at the Firbolg.

"The guy has an actual army," Sabine said, her tone incredulous. "They outnumber us by a lot. They could slaughter us. It seems being on his good side would be a smart move."

"But he's down here in Huntley," Roxhard spoke up. "Edin is a long way from here."

"Yes," Sabine said, rolling her eyes. "But your family, the Stonefires, are not."

Hall caught the mocking tone when Sabine had said family.

She didn't think Roxhard or Urit did. In response to her point, which was accurate, Roxhard looked to Urit who shrugged.

"I doubt this Iron could ever take Axestorm Hall but having an enemy right outside our stone would nae be good," Urit admitted. "I think the King would be agreeing with me."

Jackoby appeared like he was going to say something, Sabine glared at him, almost daring him to. Hall sighed.

"Enough," he said sharply, drawing their attention. "Sabine has a point. The whole reason we went to the Valley of Ancients was to help Roxhard with the Stonefires. This seems an extension of that. Like Urit said, it seems the Norns are working with the Unclanned. It all looks connected and the next step would appear to be confronting the Norns that are with the Svertleim."

"The Storvgarde clans of the tundra left us Dwarves alone. They had no interest in Axestorm Hall. Now, this Iron is building himself an empire in the Tundra," Urit growled. "Fer the first time in centuries, there's unrest and he's the cause." The young Stonefire paused, sighing and shaking his head, not happy. "But the King would want peace with our new neighbor."

They were all silent, working it all out in their heads. Hall let them think for a couple minutes before speaking again.

"I don't think any of us really like this," he started and glanced at Sabine, mentally excluding her. The Witch seemed almost eager to align with Iron. "But it seems our goals align with Iron's as far as the Svertleim and Norns are concerned."

They all nodded slowly, reluctantly accepting the reasoning.

"There's also this," Hall said and shared the quest.

Iron's Army is being attacked on two fronts. The commander of the Army, Iron, has requested your aid. He has asked that you assist part of his forces in facing the approaching combined Svertleim and Norn attackers.

The Two-Front War

Attack the Svertleim and Norn 0/1

Rewards: +100 Experience

Special Condition: For the duration of the fight you will be granted temporary Iron's Army Faction Enemy Combatant rights. This will double your experience gain per kill.

ACCEPT QUEST?

CHAPTER THIRTY

THERE WAS ONE OTHER THING THAT IRON WAS OFFERING.

Hall and his companions were led to a tent just outside the ring belonging to the Players of Iron's Army. This meant it belonged to one of the more important NPCs in the Faction. Thellia opened the flap and ushered them all inside.

A circular tent with a high ceiling, there were piles of furs against one wall that served as a bed. Chests lined the other walls and a collapsible table in the middle. Walking around the tent, pausing to look up as they entered was an elderly Storvgarde woman. Her long gray hair was tied in a single thick braid, dressed in a long hide robe decorated in stitched runes. Black eyes regarded them coldly.

Skill Gain!
  Merta, Witch of the Jormungund (blue)

Shutting the chest, the Witch stood up, studying each of them before her eyes settled on Thellia.

"Yes," she said, her voice aged but strong.

"Iron needs some Scryings done," Thellia replied, a bit sharply, a little annoyed.

It wasn't at them, Hall knew. Thellia had been happy to help them get their magical items Identified and revealed. He realized her annoyance was toward the Witch, an NPC, and one that was probably not too happy to be part of Iron's Army.

"Of course," the Witch muttered and walked to the table. She took a seat on the single stool. She glanced up at them and then motioned impatiently. "Come on."

Looking apologetic, Hall reached into his magical pouch and pulled out the collection of magical items. He set them down on the table. A sword of medium length, the baldric to carry it, leather pauldrons, two leather belts and a handful of rings, necklaces, and trinkets.

Merta the Witch glanced at him angrily, saw his look of apology and sighed.

"That is a lot young man," she told him.

"Sorry," Hall replied. "We can pay you," he offered.

The Witch glanced behind him at Thellia. Hall looked over his shoulder to see the Half-Elf Skirmisher shake her head. No.

Merta grumbled something under her breath but smiled at Hall.

"There's more," he told her.

The Witch grumbled even more, this time loudly.

———

It took over an hour and many potions before Merta was finished. Hall and his companions had been collecting gear since they had crashed on the island further up the sky. Most had not been magical, and those pieces had been sold in Axestorm Hall or traded to the Jormungund in the camp for coins, but they had still amassed a large collection of magical items.

And it was a varied lot.

Hall had only three magical items up to that point. His short sword, spear, and bracer. With the new gear, he replaced the short sword and gained leather pauldrons, a belt, two rings, a necklace, and a trinket. They had spread the items out among all of them, including Jackoby and a couple to Urit.

He pulled up his Character Screen to look at the gear and how it affected his stats.

Exceptional Breakridge Ironwood Spear
  Attack Power +2
  Damage 1d6 +2
  Agility +1
  Durability 12/12
  Weight 3 lbs.

On successful hit, has a 50% chance of causing Splinter. A shard of wood lodges within the wound causing 1 DMG every 3 Seconds for 15 Seconds.

LEATHER CHEST
  Protection +1
  Durability 6/6
  Weight 5 lbs.

Exceptional Dusky Wyvern Hide Pauldrons of Fast Strike
  Protection +1
  Agility +1

Durability 20/20
Weight 1 lb.

Quality Green Kiot Hide Baldric
  Strength +1
  Durability 15/15
  Weight 1 lb.

Quality Crag Cat Hide Belt
  Protection +1
  Wellness +1
  Durability 15/15
  Weight 1 lb.

LEATHER LEGGINGS
  Protection +1
  Durability 6/6
  Weight 5 lbs.

Quickdraw Bracer of Sharp Teeth
  Protection +4
  Attack Power +2
  Agility +4
  Durability: 20/20
  Weight: 1 lb.

Contains two Throwing Knives (1d4 +2 DMG, +6 Lightning DMG, 25% chance of Critical Strike bonus of +10 DMG). Once thrown a knife will reappear in the Bracer after ten minutes. Cooldown of twenty seconds between throwing knives.

LEATHER GLOVES
Protection +1
Durability 6/6
Weight 5 lbs.

LEATHER BOOTS
Protection +1
Durability 6/6
Weight 5 lbs.

Yeti Bone Ring of Strength
Strength +1

Tundra Fox Bone Ring of Quickness
Agility +1

Obsidian Pendant of Icy Chill
On successful hit, all Water/Cold based attacks deal an additional +2 DMG

Quality Carved Bone Idol of Yeti's Howl
On successful hit has a 25% chance of causing Yeti's Howl, granting carrier +3 unprotected DMG to attack's total damage

. . .

JAVELIN
>Attack Power +1
>Damage 1d6
>Range 30 Yards
>Durability 6/6
>Weight 1 lb.

DAGGER
>Damage 1d4
>Durability 4/4
>Weight 1 lb.

Exceptional Sword of Cold's Edge
>*Damage 2d4 (+5)*
>*Agility +3*
>*Strength +2*
>*Fire Resistance +25%*
>*Durability 20/20*
>*Weight: 5 lbs.*

On successful hit, has a 50% chance of causing Ice Shock. Extreme cold spreads out from the area of impact causing 2 DMG (Water/Cold based) every 3 seconds. Damage increased to 4 DMG every 3 seconds for creatures with weakness to Water and Cold based attacks. Ice Shock does no damage to creatures with resistance to Water and Cold based attacks.

He was down to just one bracer. The *Quickdraw Bracer of Sharp Teeth* was just a single one, covering only his left wrist. He had been wearing one of the *Hunter's Bracers of Quick*

Strike, the first magical bracers he had found, but had been receiving no benefit from just the one beyond a single +1 to Protection.

Hunter's Bracers of Quick Strike
  Protection +2
  Parry +2
  Agility +2

The pair had originally been meant for a Duelist, with the +2 to the Parry Skill. Caryn had been given the two. Hall knew he could find a spare leather bracer in the camp somewhere.

He had lucked out with the swords. They had all the same stats, the new one just having more. The weapon's special ability was a nice bonus. Hall still found it odd that each of the weapons, plus Caryn's, had seemingly been made by the same swordsmith.

Each of the rings was made of bleached white bones, small runes carved into the surface. They were rough shaped, not smooth, and formed thin, fitting tightly with no discomfort. Not attractive, but they worked, and they slid easily into his leather gloves.

Hall dismissed his Character Screen, happy with what he saw. He still needed to upgrade his basic armor, but that would come. Thellia had said the clan's leatherworkers would be able to fully repair it for him before they set out.

That thought jarred Hall from his contemplations. He hadn't forgotten what they had agreed to do, but the excitement in the new gear and upgrades had pushed it from his mind. From all their minds. Now it was back.

With a vengeance.

He sighed, again pushing his concerns and worries away.

They had agreed to assist Iron's Army with the Svertleim. There was no going back now.

"By the Spirits let that be it," Merta groaned.

She had just finished the last of the rings, which was going to Sabine. The Witch was old and looked it. Her eyes drooped, shoulders sagged. The Scryings had taken a lot out of her.

"Yes," Hall told her gently. "Thank you."

He knew how much it had taken out of her. He was grateful because they had all received at least an upgrade or two in their gear, which would help out in the coming battles. But Hall felt bad they had piled it on the Witch.

With a quick glance at Thellia, he stopped himself from saying and doing more. He felt bad, like they had taken advantage of Merta.

They left the old woman to her sleep; she had already started for the pile of furs before they were all out of the tent. Thellia pointed deeper into the camp, leading them that way.

"Leatherworkers and smiths are this way."

"I feel bad for Merta," Hall said, walking alongside the other Skirmisher. "That was a lot to dump on her."

"Don't worry about it," Thellia replied. "She's an NPC, it's what she's here for."

Hall glanced at her, biting back an angry remark.

———

Midday, Hall found himself again in Iron's tent at the war table. Before he had felt out of place. Now he felt for sure he didn't belong. Throughout the morning, the idea that all of the Players in Iron's Army felt superior to the NPCs was on display.

Even Torit and Tabitha, who seemed to be two of the nicest people, treated all the NPCs differently. They treated them like NPCs, how Hall had treated them before the Glitch.

They were there to serve the Players. Cannon fodder, part of the story, not free-thinking and independent beings.

He couldn't understand how they felt that way. It hadn't taken him long to realize the Post-Glitch NPCs were different. More alive. More like the Players.

And now the Players themselves were just bits of code in the Sky Realms Online servers. There was nothing that made them different from the computer-generated characters that populated the world.

But he kept quiet. Didn't try to rock the boat in the camp.

And it made him ashamed.

What would Leigh think if she were here?

The Storvgardes and other NPCs still got that strange blank look like their attention was elsewhere whenever the Players talked about outside game items. The way the Players in the Army carried on, the NPCs seemed to always have that look.

There was a rudeness to it, an arrogance.

Beyond the feelings toward the NPCs, Hall overall liked most of the people he had met. Cuthard was an obnoxious jerk. Corinth was cold and haughty. Iron was rarely out of his tent. But besides those three, Hall liked all the others. From the few conversations and interactions he had.

Iron started talking, and Hall forced himself to focus.

"With Cuthard's recon to the north and the Svertliem and Dav..." Iron paused. "Our scouts report from the south and the Hagnar, we know the numbers of our enemy. It appears the Norns are only with the Svertliem." He looked and focused on Hall. "Since the Norns are your concern, you and yours will go north."

Hall couldn't tell if it was a question or an order.

He nodded.

"Thellia, Cuthard, Tig, and Torit will lead half our Army north," Iron continued almost immediately after Hall's nod, like he would have said it regardless of what Hall did. "I will take the rest of it south. You will get half the Tunoths."

It was a quick meeting. There was not much to go over. They were heading out to engage the opposing clans in the field. No set or known battleground. The majority of the strategy would be decided on the point of attack. Hall was just glad he didn't need to lead the Army's forces and deploy them.

They filed out of Iron's tent, separating to gather their forces. Hall walked to where his companions were gathered. They stood in a rough circle, talking. He was surprised to see Salem, Sabine's Minx Cat familiar, laying across Caryn's shoulders.

"We good to go, boss?" Roxhard asked, trying to put some energy and excitement in his voice.

He failed. None of them looked happy.

"We head out in an hour," Hall confirmed.

Hearing a screech, he looked up to see Pike descending, spiraling slowly. The dragonhawk came down, feet outstretched and wings flapping. Hall felt the weight of Pike against his shoulders, the talons digging in. With a quick flap of wings to steal his momentum, Pike settled and squawked. Hall reached up, petting the dragonhawk under the chin.

"Are we sure about this?" Caryn asked, petting Salem.

Sabine shot her a glare.

"No," Hall replied. "But we're too far into it now."

———

Jormungand scouts ranged ahead, spread out and looking for Svertleim scouts and movements. They cut overland, following the lower edges of the Greystone Foothills. A long line spread out behind Hall. He and his companions were near the front. Thellia and Tig led with a small group of the Jormungand. Two of the Mamanog on Tunoths led the whole force.

Arrayed in organized lines behind them were the Jormungand warriors and casters, a mix of Witches and Shamans. More Tunoths followed.

Hall had counted around fifty Jormungand and twelve of the Mamanog. Not a large army but still a sizable force. He had no idea how many Svertleim they would come up against. Iron had not supplied that information, most likely deeming it irrelevant.

For such large animals, the Tunoths moved silently. Their thick, tree-trunk-like legs, kicked up a small shower of twigs and leaves with each step, but little noise. Hall could imagine the noise a charging Tunoth would make, let alone a dozen of them. He wondered how Iron had managed to take the Mamanog clan if they had such beasts.

The Tunoths should have trampled Iron's forces.

Could it have been willingly? Could the Mamanog have chosen to join Iron? It was possible.

Did the Jormungand do that as well? Hall thought Thellia had said that Iron had defeated the Jormungand's clan chief in single combat. Little to no bloodshed. The clans respected strength, and Iron had plenty of that.

That made Hall rethink some things. Could Iron really be following a quest chain? If so, he was following it in a hard and cold way. Methodical, efficient. Just how he had dealt with the raids and endgame content before. Iron just saw NPCs as pieces on the board, pawns to be used to further his goals.

Which is how they had always been treated in RPGs since the first one was created.

Hall pushed the thoughts back down. It was more of the same since they had encountered Thellia and Cuthard. It got him nowhere. Even if Iron was on a quest chain, Hall didn't approve of the man's methods or how he treated the people in the game world.

He just wanted to return to Skara Brae.

And Leigh.

He had thought that rebuilding the village was overwhelming, too much, and it was. But now he missed it, looked forward to having to deal with it all again. There, on Edin, it was just him and his people. Their troubles and how they chose to deal with them.

Hall had once wondered why he didn't run across more Players, where they had been hiding. Now he wished to go back to where there were no others beyond the few in his immediate group.

They continued walking through the day, camping in a large clearing at the bottom of the hills. The Jormungand spread out around them, the Mamanog again keeping themselves and their mounts separated. Tents were staked but no fires were lit. They were too close to the Svertleim. The scouts had returned, saying the enemy forces were only miles away. It would be early morning when the two would meet.

Sentries and watch were set. Hall was tempted to set his own with his people, but they were surrounded by supposed allies. There shouldn't be a need for a watch in the middle of the camp. He tried to relax but was having a hard time.

He sat outside of the tent he shared with Jackoby, using his cloak as a blanket. Pike perched on the tent pole above, sleeping. Hall could hear the snores of the large Firbolg inside. Roxhard and Urit shared another tent to the side, Sabine and Caryn on the other. The only ones moving about the camp were the sentries. Everyone else seemed to be asleep.

Looking up at the stars, the shadowed undersides of the islands, he tried to clear his thoughts. To focus on anything else but the upcoming battle. He wasn't sure why this was affecting him like it was. There had been quests before that fell on either side of the morality line. The Essecian Brothers, where one was the rightful ruler but had disappeared allowing the younger to become King. A decent enough King. Then the elder had returned with an army to try and take his rightful kingdom back. The younger had prevailed, but there were valid reasons for each to be King. The Players could have picked either side.

Hall had even been part of an army during that quest, similar to what he was doing now.

So why was he bothered by what Iron was doing? Was it because Iron was the focus of the quest, the one spearheading it and not just acting on the sides like Hall and others had been in the Pre-Glitch quests? Before they had been working to push NPCs along the path, not the ones directly on the path.

But what about Crackleberry? How was that justified?

And was there another reason, something more personal?

Was he jealous?

Iron had an army that seemed like it would grow bigger. Was the ultimate goal to take over all of Huntley? Forge his own kingdom? He had Colds Ridge, a fully functioning town. He had two Storvgarde villages. Hall just had a ruined village.

The quest chain they had followed in Silverpeak Keep could have led to Hall becoming a Councilor in that city, replacing Cronet. It could have led to Hall getting power over the Silver Blades or even the Door Knockers, the two thieves guilds that had gone to war for control of the city. There were lots of ways that Hall's own power could have risen as a result of the quests.

Instead, he had gotten a couple citizens and not much else.

He really didn't think he was jealous.

He hoped not. But had to admit that part of him was. Skara Brae would never be more than a mid-sized village. It was locked in by the mountains and Breakridge. The nearest neighbors were weeks of travel away.

With a sigh, a last look up into the sky where he thought Edin would be, Hall crawled into the tent to try to get some sleep.

It felt like he had just barely closed his eyes when shouts ran through the camp.

Yelling, screaming, the clang of metal on metal. People running. Pike screeching as the dragonhawk flew into the air.

But one word rose above the sounds.

"Attack."

CHAPTER THIRTY-ONE

HALL RUSHED OUT OF THE TENT, PULLING HIS SPEAR BEHIND him, new sword and baldric in hand. He let them drop to the ground in a clatter, working to strap on the new leather pauldrons. Glad he slept in the majority of his armor, no matter how uncomfortable it was, Hall scanned the chaotic camp looking for the attack.

He could hear men yelling and screaming, see the glow of flames in the dark night down at the southern end of the encampment. Metal on metal. He could see the Jormungand running that way, toward the sound of fighting. Around him the others came out of their tents, working to pull on armor, holding weapons at the ready.

"What's going on," Sabine asked.

"No idea," Hall replied.

Roxhard and Urit started to follow the Storvgarde rushing to the south, but Hall held out a hand, stopping them. They needed to figure out what was happening first.

"Come on idiots," a voice said, rushing by. "Make yourselves useful."

Cuthard rushed by them, both swords out. The Duelist

glared at Hall as he passed, barking out something that was lost in the noise.

Hall was glad they hadn't rushed off when a new voice broke out.

Clear and smooth, accented. Arashi.

Tig, the Warden leading the Army.

Hall couldn't see him but could hear the voice, loud, speaking out over the noise of the fighting to the south and the commotion of the camp.

"To the north! Rally! Form lines!"

Hall still didn't move. He wanted a clear idea of what was happening.

More voices started shouting from the north.

"You're here," Thellia said, coming to a stop next to Hall. She was breathing hard, just coming up from the south end of the camp. "Good."

"What's going on?" Sabine asked as they all gathered in close to Thellia.

"Raid," she replied, pointing to the south. "A small group of Svertleim flanked us and came up from the south. They started harassing us. Burning tents, attacking the sentries."

"A distraction," Hall said, pointing to the north.

"Yeah," Thellia agreed. "It sounds like the main force of Svertleim kept marching."

She paused, listening as Tig's voice rang out again.

"Rally! Form Lines! To me!"

Hall looked that way, seeing the flow of Storvgarde now moving to the north where Tig seemed to be assembling the Jormungand. They couldn't hear any other noises from that end of the camp, just their people. No idea how far away the Svertleim were. He looked back to the south where the sounds of fighting were getting louder, closer.

"Leave them," Thellia said with an angry shake of her head. "Torit and Cuthard are there. They should be able to stop the raiding party. They better," she spat with a growl. "Come on," she ordered.

The others all looked to Hall, who nodded.

They followed the other Skirmisher through the camp, dodging around tents and fires, pushing aside the Jormungand who were not moving. When she came across those, Thellia would yell and order them to the front. Most responded quickly, others more reluctant.

As they got closer to the edge of the camp the sounds became less chaotic. Torches were lit, driven into the cold and hard ground. Shadows danced, flickering in the flames. Hide clad warriors, all of them large, stood side by side. A long line of them running to the sides. Hall could make out shapes of others in front. Ranks, three men deep.

Which was something the Jormungand were not used to, that was obvious. They shifted from foot to foot, pushed the man next to them, trying to get more space. Hall wasn't a tactician, but he could recognize that aligning the Storvgarde this way wasn't the best use of the warriors. There was a mix of two-handed weapons, axes and swords, shields. Archers were spaced randomly down the back line, bows held ready.

He was going to say something to Thellia but stopped. This wasn't his Army. It wasn't going to be his part of the battle.

Following Thellia, they ran behind the line to the right, to the east. Shadows covered the ground, the torches throwing a little light. Hall was able to see, his racial *Limited Night Vision*, activating and showing shadows on shadows, different shades of grays. Behind him he could hear Sabine and Caryn stumbling, the two Humans didn't have access to night vision of any kind. The ground was covered in blackness, shadows that the flames didn't penetrate.

Ahead were large areas of black, odd shapes without definition. More details revealed as they got closer and Hall realized he was looking at a group of Tunoths huddled together. The animals shifted from foot to foot, trunks raising and lowering as they quietly made noises. Deep and rumbling. Mamanog held reins, others working to tie saddles.

Before them stood Tig. The Arashi Player stood out among the Jormungand. He was shorter and much thinner. But he still commanded their attention. Dressed in overlapping plates of light steel, leather pants, and steel pauldrons, the Warden held an oval-shaped shield. Long and thin, designs covered the metal, but the shadows prevented Hall from studying them. A long and thin sword was belted at his waist.

Tig glanced at Thellia, motioning her over. Not sure what else to do, Hall and the others followed.

"They're only a couple hundred feet out," Tig told them, pointing to the north.

Hall saw the plain spreading out in front of the Jormungand. Dark shapes were on the other side, not in lines but small groups gathered together. Too far away to make out details, they just looked like oddly shaped shadows, but Hall knew what they were. Massed as they were the Svertleim were able to hide their numbers.

"That collection of shadows are the Svertleim?" Sabine asked. "Why are they just standing there?"

"Waiting to see what we will do," Tig answered. "They had been rushing across the tundra when they realized we had responded quicker than they thought we would. The hope was that the southern raid would take all our attention."

Hall knew the Svertleim should have kept going, charging across the tundra still. The Jormungand wouldn't have been able to fully prepare and while the attack wouldn't have the full impact, it still would have hurt the camp. He thought to point that out but like before, didn't bother.

"Why didn't it?" he asked instead. He was curious about Tig's quick reaction time.

"As soon as the attack in the south happened, I realized it

was a feint," Tig replied. "Classic maneuver. The raid was meant to distract from the main attack."

"Tig was in the Marines," Thellia said.

Hall looked back out across the tundra at the mass of Svertleim, wondering what they were waiting for. Why weren't they attacking?

"Why are they waiting?" he asked Tig.

"I don't know," the Arashi replied. "But we will wait until they start to move then," he stopped and motioned to the Tunoths.

Hall knew what that meant.

―――――

"That's what they were waiting for," Tig growled.

The sun was just rising in the east, a red tinge to the sky, the dark of night welcoming the light of the day. It was that in-between time, when the shadows are gray but the light hasn't come yet. That time when night vision wasn't useful.

They came charging across the tundra, a chorus of war cries. No one was the same, the individual calls lost in the common roar. So many Svertleim. No order, no discipline, some outpacing the mass.

And they were not alone.

Six large creatures ran ahead of the warriors. Each almost fifteen feet tall, six feet wide. Each lumbering stride slamming into the tundra, causing the ground to shake. How they moved was a mystery. Thick legs that lacked knees, wide bodies and long arms, squat heads with no necks and no eyes or mouths. Masses of hardened mud, some still dripping down to the ground.

Elementals.

Skill Gain!

Identify Rank Two +.1

Shaped Mud Elemental (blue)

Hall stood at the edge of the Jormungand line, Tig next to him. They watched the elementals separating themselves from the charging Svertleim. The warriors still roared, but the Jormungand line did not answer. Hall looked down the length of it, seeing men shift nervously, clutching weapons tighter.

The elementals had burst out of the ground in front of the Svertleim. Rock and stones erupting up in fountains of mud. Long arms reached out, followed by the squat bodies and the legs, the ground sealing and closing behind them. The gashes healing.

Down the Jormungand line, three figures stepped forward. Two women, one man. They were dressed in hides and furred line robes, staves carved from bone in hand. Shamans.

Each of the three raised their staff high into the air, pointing a hand out across the tundra at the charging Elementals. Flames shot out, great gusts from the ends of the staves. They soared across the tundra, the ground smoking in their wake. Fire splashed around three of the elementals, wrapping around the creatures, engulfing them.

Still, the Mud Elementals ran. They pushed against the geysers of flame, slowing. Steam rose off their bodies, more mud falling to the ground. Cracks formed in the bodies, larger pieces breaking off.

One Elemental collapsed in a heap, breaking apart into steaming chunks. The others kept coming, pushing against the flames that died out. One by one, the shaman's spells ended and they stepped back.

"Hold," Tig shouted, the call echoed down the line of Jormungand.

To their credit, faced with the charging elementals, the Jormungand held.

Now they shouted. A cry of defiance. A roar that grew louder and louder. Hall could see numbers and the Jormungand were outnumbered. But they shouted louder, roaring their rage.

The elementals reached the front ranks which stepped aside, flowing around the large creatures. Some of the Jormungand turned to face the Elementals, others staring down at the charging Svertleim.

Tig looked behind him, raising his hand above his head. Hall heard a horn blow, looked back and up to one of the Mamanog mounted on a Tunoth. He held a curved ivory horn, blowing long notes through it. The call was echoed by the mounts themselves, trunks raised as they trumpeted out their war cries.

They watched Tig's raised hand. It lowered, and the eight massive Tunoth took off running. The sound was deafening. Heavy legs slamming into the ground, the creatures large but fast. They thundered across the tundra.

Not aiming for the elementals or the lead Svertleim but charging for the middle of the opposing warriors. Spread out as they were, no disciplined lines, they weren't prepared for the massive Tunoths. Some saw the creatures but were unable to avoid them trapped as they were between their own allies.

The beasts burst into the rushing warriors. Bodies flew, the ground shook. The trumpeting of Tunoths echoed through the morning. The mass of Svertleim broke apart, bodies left trampled under the massive feet of the Tunoths.

Hall heard a crack, turned, and saw another of the Elementals falling apart. Only three of the creatures remained, the Jormungand Shamans turning their attention to the Svertleim. Fire shot out across the tundra, flooding over the warriors. Men screamed, flesh burned, smoke curling into the air.

"Why are you still here," Tig barked, not turning.

Hall looked at the Arashi Warden, confused, but then saw Thellia motioning them to follow. She was running, not to the battle, but around the edge. Hall chased after, his companions following.

They took a wide arc, crouching low, trying to avoid attention. There was no time to talk, Thellia keeping them at a fast pace. She kept glancing toward the battle, gauging the movements of the various forces. The Tunoths had turned, charging across the field once more, but this time the Svertleim were ready. They stepped aside, leaving wide paths for the charging beasts, attacking the flanks. Men still died, trampled, as the riders turned their mounts. One Tunoth didn't turn fast enough, swords and axes cutting into its flanks. The giant creature cried out in pain as it collapsed to the ground, crushing men beneath its bulk. Svertleim cheered only to be cut down by streaking arrows coming from the Jormungand lines.

Thellia kept them moving.

———

She held up a hand, telling them to stop. Crouching lower, she shifted to hide behind the tall grass and bushes. Hall crept up alongside her.

Skill Gain!
Camouflage Rank One +.1
Skill Gain!
Stealth Rank One +.1

They were a little behind and to the side of the Svertleim army. Sentries were posted, looking out across the tundra, but their attention kept drifting to the fighting they were missing. Mostly young warriors, eager but not allowed to go to battle.

Past the watch, Hall could see the leaders of the Svertleim. At least those in charge now that Corvandr was dead. Three of the Storvgarde with two Norns. Just ahead of the small group, more sentries stood along with two more Norns, arms raised in the act of spellcasting.

The ground shook, Hall having to brace himself. He watched an explosion as a geyser of mud and rock burst from the ground. Another Elemental being born.

Roaring in rage, the lumbering creature took off at a run.

"Those are our targets," Thellia told Hall in a whisper.

The two sentries were closest, the only ones facing their direction. The others all looked toward the battle.

Skill Gain!

Identify Rank Two +.1

Svertleim Unblooded Warrior (white)
Svertleim Unblooded Warrior (white)

A large Svertleim, that reminded Hall of Corvandr, seemed to be directing the battle. Next to him were two other warriors and the two Norns, both female and both dressed in pure white robes trimmed in green.

Skill Gain!

Identify Rank Two +.3

Novtan of the Svertleim (blue)
Svertleim Shield Warrior (blue)
Svertleim Shield Warrior (blue)
Testria of the Cerulean Regency (blue)
Cerulean Icemage (blue)

Beyond them were the last of the Norns and four more Svertleim. The tundra stretched for almost fifty feet between the commanders and the rest of their army. Enough distance that Hall didn't think reinforcements could arrive from the army, if the Svertleim would even discover their commanders were being attacked.

Skill Gain!
Identify Rank Two +.3

Svertleim Bloodrager (white)
Svertleim Bloodrager (white)
Svertleim Bloodrager (white)
Svertleim Bloodrager (white)
Cerulean Earthmage (blue)
Cerulean Earthmage (blue)

Thirteen enemies, including four spellcasters. Hall wasn't a big fan of the odds. The highest Level was only blue, only one or two levels higher than Hall himself. Not that bad. There were six of them plus the two dragonhawks. The trick would be to take out the two sentries first without being seen or heard.

Thellia had the same idea.

They pulled back, further away and huddled in a circle, laying out the plan.

CHAPTER THIRTY-TWO

HALL LIFTED HIS HEAD UP, BARELY CLEARING THE TALL GRASS. The Svertleim sentry was turned, once again looking longingly toward the battle that still raged. Men screamed, metal hit metal, and the young warrior wanted to be in the midst of it. Hall could just barely see Thellia crouching a couple dozen feet away from the second sentry, that one also looking toward the battle.

She held up an arm, two fingers aloft. One finger and then zero.

Turning back to his sentry, Hall activated *Leap*.

He covered the distance between them, the sentry turning back in looking on in shock at the jumping Skirmisher. Hall stabbed out with his spear, the tip catching the Svertleim in the shoulder. The man turned, a large Splinter lodged in the wound. Landing, Hall pivoted and slammed his spear through the hide armor and the young man's chest.

SLAIN: *Svertleim Unblooded Warrior +10 Experience (+10 Faction Bonus Experience)*

QUEST COMPLETE!

You have engaged the Svertleim and Norn attackers.

The Two-Front War

Attack the Svertleim and Norn 1/1

Rewards: +100 Experience

Special Condition: For the duration of the fight you will be granted temporary Iron's Army Faction Enemy Combatant rights. This will double your experience gain per kill.

Hall brushed the notifications aside as he saw two rushing forms charge past. One tall, the other short. He kicked out, pushing the dead Svertleim off his spear. The body landed on the ground with a thud as the rest of Hall's companions ran past.

Sabine's hands were raised, crackling purple-black lightning shooting out. The bolts slammed into the four Svertleim Bloodragers. The warriors spasmed as the bolts of energy crackled around their bodies. Putting on a burst of speed, Caryn covered the last of the distance, twin swords slashing out at the two Norn Earthmages.

Screeching, diving out of the sky, one on either side, the two dragonhawks flew over the four warriors and the Earthmages. Bolts of lightning shot out from open beaks, slamming into warriors. Smoke curled up from the wounds. Pike and Screech flew past each other, darting back up into the sky for another pass.

Activating *Leap* again, Hall soared across the tundra. He arced up into the air, coming down toward the two Norn Icemages. He didn't know which was the named, the leader, and which wasn't. They had shifted and looked too much alike. It didn't matter. They both had to fall and fall quickly.

The Norns were in the act of casting, trying to get spells off against Roxhard and Jackoby who were engaged with the

Svertleim, Jackoby somehow taking on the two while Roxhard engaged the leader. Stopping her casting, the Norn saw Hall's shadow across the ground.

She shifted, avoiding the *Leaping Stab* attack. Landing, Hall pivoted and stabbed out again. The spear caught the edge of the Norn's robe, ripping through the fabric and scoring a slash across her chest. Hall saw the red of her blood, seeming brighter against her pale white skin. Cursing the Norn took a step back, her bright blue eyes filled with rage.

Barking a quick word, the Norn flicked her fingers at Hall launching small snowballs at him. They impacted, exploding against his leather armor. He braced himself for the cold damage. He knew the spell, and it didn't do much damage, but there was nothing. The Norn looked surprised, almost as much as he was until he remembered his new sword and its cold resistance.

Smiling, he darted forward, leading with the spear. The ironwood tip slammed into the stomach of the Norn. She cried out in pain, hands reaching to clutch the shaft, trying to pull it away. Hall pushed forward, stepping and driving the point harder. He was stronger than the Norn, the spear pushing deeper into her body.

She fell to the ground, hands grasping at her stomach as the point tore a larger gash. Hall stepped forward, looking down at her sadly. He drove the spear down.

Pulling the weapon up, blood spraying into the air, Hall turned to survey the battle.

Sabine was casting *Hexbolt*, refreshing it on the four Svertleim Bloodragers. There were two of her, the purple-black bolts streaking out from four hands. She alternated with a *Shadowbolt* followed by the *Arcane Missiles*, little blue streaks of light slamming into one of the warriors. The attack canceled out the *Hexbolt* effect on him. Growling a war cry, the warrior charged her. He swung his two-handed ax, the weapon passing harmlessly through one of the images of the Witch that wavered for a brief moment. He looked confused and then cried out as Salem disappeared from Sabine's shoulder and onto the warriors, small claws digging into exposed flesh.

Hall knew from experience how sharp those claws were as well as the effects of Salem's *Minx Maul* attack. Though small, the Minx Cat's claws contained a toxin that caused bleeding damage as well as weakened the target to Shadow damage.

Like that from Sabine's *Shadowbolt*.

She cast it quickly, the black bar at point-blank range. It slammed into the Bloodrager's face, inky black liquid surrounding him. He fell back, Salem disappearing and reappearing on Sabine's shoulders. The Minx Cat hissed at the Bloodrager as Sabine cast an *Arcane Missile* that ended the man's life.

Hall pulled one of the throwing knives from his magical bracer. He launched it, the weapon streaking and slamming into the shoulder of one of the Norn Earthmages facing Caryn. Sparks erupted on impact, the Norn's spell fading. Caryn pivoted and her sword sliced across the Norn's throat. She danced, stepping back, bringing both blades forward and around, driving the second Earthmage back.

Using *Leap*, Hall jumped across the battlefield. His spear jabbed out, taking a Bloodrager in the shoulder. The Storvgarde twisted, stepping back and Hall landed where he had been. Twisting the spear around his body, Hall slammed the point into the Bloodrager's chest. He pulled it out, one of the warrior's hands going to cover the wound while the other swung a heavy hammer. Hall easily evaded the attack, rotating the spear around and stabbing the point into the Bloodrager's now exposed side. Growling in pain, the man fell, weakly trying to stand up.

Turning, stabbing down and ending the Bloodrager's life, Hall slid the shaft of the spear through his hands. The butt end slammed into the back of the Norn facing Caryn. The Earth-mage could not get off a spell, working hard to avoid the Duelist attacks. Stumbling as the spear caught him in the knee, he could not fend off a rapid strike from Caryn.

The last of the Earthmages fell to the ground. Caryn lifted a blade in salute as Hall pivoted and activated *Leap*. From above, Pike and Screech launched another attack on the remaining Bloodragers.

As Hall arced over the tundra, he saw one of the Svertleim Shieldwarriors fall. Roxhard had the *Ax of Obsidian Flames* swinging to block the second Shieldwarriors attack. The Dwarf Warden was moving fast, like a Duelist. The head of the shining black stone double-headed ax was glowing with purple flames, a line of sparks trailing as it split the air.

The Norn leader, Testia, made a motion with her hands. Thellia was thrown backward, sent tumbling. Shamans cast spells connected to the four elements of the world. Air, earth, fire, and water. They all had access to the four but could specialize in one element to get different spells and make their other spells associated with the element stronger. It made fighting a Shaman difficult. No matter how high the resistances, there was an elemental spell at the Shaman's fingertips that cold nullify that resistance.

Testria staggered, blood soaking through her white robe.

Hall used *Leaping Stab*, the attack missing as Testria somehow sensed him behind her. She twisted out of the way as Hall landed, swinging the spear toward her. The tip sliced along her side, drawing more blood. Growling the Norn took a couple steps back. Hall took one toward her. With a flicking motion of her hand, the ground around her surged up forming a barrier.

Cursing, Hall activated *Leap* again, jumping over the wall. He could hear Thellia behind him, also leaping around the barrier.

Testria had used the time well, moving further back and giving herself space. Her hands moved in a complex series of motions, a large gem hanging around her neck glowing. The movements were odd, not like the normally smooth motions a Shaman made. These were jerking, stuttering, as if her arms and hands were not used to moving that way. It looked unnatural.

As did what surged out of the ground.

The explosion of mud and rocks slammed into the Skirmishers as they were still in the air. The force sent them flying. Hall slammed into Testria's earthen barrier. He grunted in pain, feeling like he hit a concrete wall at high speeds. Sliding to the ground he watched as something huge pulled itself out of the newly formed hole.

Mud flowed from the gash in the ground, black and brown, moving like water as it spread like blood coming from a wound. And it did look like a wound in the earth. Jagged, ripped, and torn.

The creature was large. Fifteen feet tall, half that wide. It was shaped like a giant ape. Short legs, long arms, thick body with broad shoulders and a squat head. Large horns grew from the forehead, curling up and back, flaming red eyes filled with rage. Canines jutted from the upper lip, each tooth the size of knives. Long claws grew from the thick fingers that dug into the ground as the creature roared its rage.

Hall recognized it.

A demon.

Instead of fur, scales, or a hide as thick as armor, it was covered in thick plates of stone and ice. Or what looked like ice. The segments along the demon's lower arms, shoulders, and legs were semi-translucent and green, a strange glow seeming to come from beneath.

Skill Gain!

Identify Rank Two +.1

Minor Cormlig Demon (orange)

"What in the…" Thellia growled from the side. "Since when can Shamans summon demons?"

She was right. Summoning had been a Skill that only Witches could learn. How had a Shaman been able to do it? Hall couldn't see Testria past the large Cormlig, but he remembered the glowing gem around her neck. Some kind of magical item? But what item could summon a demon like a Cormlig?

The demon roared, stretching and raising its long arms to the sky. The hands came down, curled into fists, slamming into the tundra causing it to shake. Hall had just gotten to his feet and now stumbled, falling back down.

It took a step forward, covering half the distance to Hall in one move. One arm dug into the ground, pulling up a large chunk of earth. With an almost contemptuous throw, the Cormlig launched the earthen ball at Hall. He ducked to the side, the missile exploding against the Norn's earth barrier which shattered on impact. Small pieces struck Hall, bruising and drawing a line of blood across his cheek.

Activating *Leap*, Hall pushed off from the ground. He didn't get a chance to attack while in the air. The Cormlig swung one long arm, slamming into Hall. He landed hard, losing his spear, and skidding across the ground.

Pushing himself up, Hall saw Thellia land two blows against the Cormlig. One in the air and one as she landed. She had to dart out of the way quickly as the long arm slammed into where she had been. Hall saw that the Cormlig's Health bar had barely moved.

"Where did this thing come from," Caryn shouted as she darted in, a black bar of energy shooting past her.

Sabine's *Shadowbolt* slammed into the waist of the tall

demon. Black swarmed around the impact, spreading across the demon's body. It stumbled back a half step, growling as Caryn's twin swords sliced across its tree trunk thick leg. The blades scraped across the stone plates, drawing sparks and making more noise than damage. The dancing Duelist curled around the leg, swords striking the Cormlig's back as she darted around to the front again.

The kick caught Caryn off guard, launching her into the air. She curled into a ball, rolling across the ground to come up standing. Shakily. Blades in hand, she wavered, trying to clear her head.

Drawing his sword, Hall *Leapt* into the air. The Cormlig had turned to Sabine, who was firing *Arcane Missile* after *Arcane Missile* at the beast. The small darts of energy seemed to be doing the most damage, knocking off a tiny fraction of Health with each impact. Hall came down, his new sword slicing across the Cormlig's shoulder and down the back as he landed. The sharp blade drew a thin line of blood.

Feet touching the ground, Hall kept running away from the demon. He could feel the air moving as the giant Cormlig turned to attack. Skidding to a stop, turning with his sword held across his body, Hall waiting for the Cormlig's charge.

Which didn't come.

The large demon stared down at Hall, growling. Hall tightened his grip on the sword, waving at the demon to come and get him.

It still didn't move.

"Come on, you dumb beast," Hall barked, but the words were lost as the growl became a shout of pain.

Shards of ice slammed into his side, cutting across the exposed flesh on his arms, finding gaps in his leather armor. He managed to twist his head in time, shards slamming into the back of his head and not across his face. He felt the impact of each, knowing blood was leaking down his back from gashes across his skull.

He staggered to the side, limping, glad the new sword gave him cold resistance. It didn't help protect him from the physical damage, but at least he didn't get the cold damage over time. The attack had taken a good chunk of his Health.

The Cormlig barked, harsh and guttural. A deep laugh.

Hall looked over his shoulder, behind him, seeing the Norn Shaman. She was smiling, a wicked and cruel smile, hands moving in spellcasting, her robe stained a deeper red from blood loss.

Testria the Norn Icemage never saw Thellia landing behind her. The Norn's cruel face changed to shock, eyes wide as the tip of a spear burst from her chest in an explosion of gore and guts. The eyes looked down at the weapon, shocked. She uttered a single word in the language of the Norns before her body collapsed in a heap. The dead Testria fell forward, sliding off the spear. Thellia pulled it up, giving the weapon a shake, throwing off blood. She stared defiantly at the Cormlig.

Red eyes looked from Hall to Thellia, growling. Hall braced himself, watching the demon. Neither Skirmisher was prepared for how fast the Cormlig was.

It took one step leaning down, the right arm reaching down and digging into the ground. Another step and the arm whipped across its body, the hard chunk of ground flying toward Thellia. Another step and the other arm shot forward, directly at Hall.

Stepping to the side, he avoided most of the blow, but even the glance was enough to knock him off his feet. Hall fell, barely holding onto his sword. It felt like his shoulder was broken. More Health dropped from his bar. The ground was hard as he hit, immediately moving into a roll. The Cormlig's foot slammed down, the ground shaking. He kept rolling, narrowly avoiding the other foot.

Hall rolled again, expecting another stomping foot, but it never came. He stopped and pushed himself up, looking at the demon that was roaring in pain.

A dark black object, shining in the morning sun, wreathed in purple-black flames pulled out of the Cormlig's lower back. The double-headed ax slammed down again. Roxhard stood behind the Cormlig, strong arms driving the *Ax of Obsidian Flames* deep into the Cormlig's armored back. The Dwarf adjusted his swing, slicing the ax across the back of the Cormlig's legs.

With a cry, the demon fell to the ground.

Roxhard shifted his arms, ready to swing the ax down into the demon's chest. The Cormlig reacted quickly, a swing of the long arm catching Roxhard and knocking him off balance. He slid back a couple of feet before falling to his back.

The Cormlig jumped to its feet, pushed up by the strength of its long arms. Growling it turned to Roxhard. It took a step, roaring in pain as Thellia stabbed it in the shoulder as she descended. Landing on the ground, she turned and stabbed out with her spear, catching the Cormlig in the back of the leg. It staggered but did not fall, turning to try to hit Thellia with a grasping arm. She used *Leap* and jumped out of the way.

Growling in rage, the Cormlig returned its attention to Roxhard, but before it could swing the arm forward again, Hall L*eaped*. With just his sword, he couldn't use the *Leaping Stab* ability, but it didn't matter as he landed right behind the Cormligs moving arm, behind the Cormlig where it couldn't see him.

He swung the sword, cutting across the Cormlig's arm, slicing into an earthen plate. Cracks formed as the blade bit deep, black blood oozing out. He growled against the pain through his shoulder as the blade struck hard armor. Hall jumped backward as the enraged Cormlig turned quickly, exposing itself to Roxhard.

The Dwarf was up from the ground, ancestor's ax swinging. It slammed into the Cormligs side. Large chunks of the armor plating cracked and broke off, pieces falling to the ground. Underneath was night-black hide, thick and leathery.

An arm slammed into Roxhard, sending the Dwarf flying.

Hall darted in, slicing across the Cormlig's back as it turned and stalked toward Roxhard. The demon ignored Hall's attack even though it drew a long line of black blood across the cracked plates along its back. It ran forward, ignoring the two attacks from Thellia as she leapt in.

It covered the distance to Roxhard in three long strides, both arms raised. One closed in a fist, the other open with the long claws ready to slash.

Roxhard lifted the *Ax of Obsidian Flames* before him. The Dwarf locked eyes with the Cormlig, defiant. The flames around the head flared, and Hall felt the rush of heated air as far away as he was. The Cormlig took the full brunt of the force waves sent by the Ax. It was pushed back, thick legs digging furrows in the ground. Steam rose from the icy parts covering the demon's body, water dripping to the ground.

Hall watched the Cormlig's Health drop to below twenty-five percent.

He pulled a throwing knife from his bracer, launching the small weapon. He aimed for the exposed flesh on the Cormlig's side. The small blade landed true, cutting deep into the hide of the demon, its special ability activating. Lightning sparked up on impact, bolts of energy wrapping around the creature. A javelin stabbed deep into the Cormlig. The demon roared, twisting as it tried to find the attackers, trying to decide which to deal with first.

Twin bolts of lightning slammed into the Cormlig. Two streaking forms dived out of the sky, passing each other over the demon. Pike screeched as he twisted higher into the sky, passing Screech as both dragonhawks prepared for another attack.

Thellia landed a blow from the spear in the Cormlig's shoulder and another in the creature's back as she twisted on landing. Roxhard's ax slammed into the side of the Cormlig, more pieces of plating flying away from the impact.

Hall replaced Thellia as she *Leapt* out of the way. He aimed for the exposed hide, lightning still sparking from the throwing knife. Driving the sword at the Cormlig, Hall pushed the tip into the side of the creature, feeling it in his throbbing shoulder but pushing past the pain. Not made for piercing, Hall forced the blade in deeper, twisting and sliding.

The Cormlig roared in madness, the sound echoing across the tundra.

Thellia struck from the side, Roxhard from the front. All three kept up the attack, the two dragonhawks adding their lightning bolts.

Already at twenty-five percent, the Cormlig's Health dropped quickly. Flashing brightly and then disappearing.

With a final weakened roar, the Cormlig dropped to the ground.

They all stood around it, breathing hard, leaning on weapons.

Skill Gain!
Light Armor Rank Two +.3
Skill Gain!
Polearm Rank Two +.4
Skill Gain!
Small Blades Rank Two +.3
Skill Gain!
Thrown Rank Two +.2

SLAIN: Cerulean Icemage +30 Experience (+30 Faction Bonus
Experience)

SLAIN: Svertleim Bloodrager +25 Experience (+25 Faction Bonus
Experience)

SLAIN: Svertleim Bloodrager +10 Experience (+10 Faction Bonus
Experience)

SLAIN: Cerulean Earthmage +10 Experience (+10 Faction Bonus
Experience)

SLAIN: Cerulean Earthmage +10 Experience (+10 Faction Bonus
Experience)

SLAIN: Testria of the Cerulean Regency +20 Experience (+20 Faction
Bonus Experience)

SLAIN: Minor Cormlig Demon +20 Experience (+20 Faction Bonus
Experience)

Hall stared at the notifications that flashed across his vision. That was a lot of experience. The Faction bonus was amazing. *We really need to form our own when we get back to Skara Brae,* Hall thought or tried to as he started yelling in pain.

With the adrenaline from the battle fading, the full pain in his shoulder flared up.

Hall dropped to the ground, clutching at his wounded arm.

The others ran to him. Roxhard pointed down at his pouch.

"He's got healing potions in there," the Dwarf said, indicating the potion pouch Hall wore on his belt.

Hall tried to move out of the way to give Thellia access to the pouch, but the pain was too much. She pulled a small vial out, popping the cork and holding it up to Hall's lips. Grunting in pain, he tipped his head back, and she dumped the full contents down his throat. He could feel the warming energy spreading through his body, healing his other wounds but not the shoulder. The magical liquid tried. He could feel the bones pushing and rubbing against each other as they tried to fit back into their natural alignment. The torn muscles reached out, grabbing for the other ends but unable to connect.

Thellia leaned back, looking at Hall as he still clutched the shoulder, unable to speak past the pain.

"It's dislocated," she said finally. "We have to knock it back into place or it won't heal."

Roxhard fell back, holding his hands up.

"Nope," the Dwarf said. "No way."

Thellia shot Roxhard a hard look, shaking her head.

"You, Firbolg," she yelled as Jackoby jogged over to them. "Hold onto Hall."

Without a word, taking the scene in and understanding, Jackoby dropped his hammer and shield. He leaned down, grabbing Hall around the body, an arm across the shoulders.

Looking up at Jackoby, waiting for the nod, Thellia grabbed Hall's arm and shoulder. With a quick movement, she slammed the arm back into place.

Hall screamed and fell silent, panting as his arm lay limp.

"Thanks," he managed to spit out, as Jackoby released him.

Thellia just shrugged.

"Could you?" he asked and pointed to the potion pouch with his good arm.

———

Hall looked down at the barely breathing Norn Earthmage. Caryn had managed to leave one alive. He was breathing hard, blood bubbling up from his lips. He didn't have long to live. The Earthmage spoke slowly in his own language, coughing.

Pulling out the small scroll they had recovered at the hunting lodge, Hall held it up for the Norn to see.

"What is this?" Hall asked. "Why are you here and who are the Champions?"

The Norn growled, eyes filled with hatred. He spoke in his language. Hall looked at the others, waiting for a translation.

"Basically, he told you to go to hell," Thellia said. She shrugged at Hall's look of surprise. "I learned the language from Corinth."

Kneeling down closer to the Norn, Thellia started talking to the Earthmage in his language. Like Highborn Elven language, it was musical. The words and cadence sounded like poetry, an unheard song surrounding it. But where the Highborn was soft and light, the Norn's was harsh and cold. Just like the race.

The Earthmage still refused to answer questions.

With a quick glance at Hall and the others, Thellia turned her attention back to the Norn and punched him in the side where he had been stabbed. The Norn yelled in pain, the scream turning to a whimper. More blood gushed out of the wound.

"What the..." Hall exclaimed taking a step forward and reaching a hand to Thellia.

"Don't," she growled, her tone of voice threatening harm to Hall if he touched her.

He hesitated, debating, but finally fell back as the Norn started speaking. Rapidly, spitting out the words. Each was painful, an effort to say, but he did. Thellia asked a couple more questions, received her answers, and stood up.

The Norn looked up at her with sad and pleading eyes. Nodding, she pulled her spear off the harness on her back, flipped it around so the point was down and slammed it into the Norn's throat. He convulsed, giving a quick spasm, and then lay still.

"What was that?" Hall demanded.

"A quick death," Thellia said in response, wiping the blood off the spear tip with the dead Norn's robe. "In exchange for telling us what he knew. No one wants to die in pain."

Hall was about to speak, but she held up a hand.

"They are part of the Cerulean Regency, one of the Nine Norn ruling families," Thellia explained. "Apparently, there's some internal strife in the Norn kingdom and the Ceruleans want to take over and become the new Overking of the Nornic Cliffs. To accomplish this, they've allied with some others," she paused and glanced down at the Norn. "He's just a low-level mage in the Regency hierarchy. Just a soldier following orders. He doesn't know who they are aligned with. These allies are the ones that want the Champions dead."

She stepped away from the fallen Norn.

"And no, he doesn't know who these Champions are."

QUEST COMPLETE!

The Long Scroll II
Capture a Norn 1/1
Discover more information on the Norn's mission 1/1
Reward: +100 experience

None of it explained anything. Why were the Norns allied with the Svertleim? Who were the Champions and these allies of the Cerulean Regency? And why couldn't the allies kill these Champions themselves?

You have learned that the Norns allied with the Svertleim are part of the Cerulean Regency, one of the nine Nornic ruling families that want to make a bid for power. They have allied with some mystery others to kill some entities called the Champions. Find out more about the Cerulean Regency and the Champions.

The Long Scroll III
Learn more about the Champions 0/1

Learn more about the Cerulean Regency's allies 0/1
Reward +100 experience.

ACCEPT QUEST?

Hall quickly accepted it, pushing the walls of text out of his vision. He looked over his shoulder at Thellia who was walking away, heading for the Norn's leader and the demon.

"You didn't have to torture him," Hall said.

"What's it matter?" Thellia called back, not bothering to look at him. "He was just an NPC."

CHAPTER THIRTY-THREE

Urit knelt next to the body of Novtan. Grumbling, cursing, he grabbed at a one-handed hammer, forcing open the fingers of the dead Svertleim. Standing up, Urit held the hammer up to the light, examining it. A long handle, the head was small and rectangular, covered in angular script. The weapon was a dull gray color, no reflection and all one shade.

"I think this be the hammer of the Understones," he said, shaking his head angrily. "How many of our dead did those cursed Unclanned loot?" Growling he kicked the body, turning away and placing the hammer in his pouch. "We need to tell Matron Lydi," he said to Hall. "The Hall must be told that our ancestors have been desecrated."

Urit Stonefire has discovered that a third Dwarven clan's artifact weapon has been stolen from the Clan's crypt by the Unclanned. The Dwarves of Axestorm Hall must be informed so they can find out if there are more artifact weapons missing and seek to reclaim them.

THE UNCLANNED THEFTS
Inform Matron Lydi of the Stonefires about the thefts 0/1

Reward: Stonefire Clan reputation +100, +50 experience

ACCEPT QUEST?

They looted the other corpses quickly, leaving anything that was non-magical or didn't feel as if it contained magic. There was still a decent-sized pile of items, coins and jewels when they were done. Hall had hoped to try and skin some of the earthen armor plates off the Cormlig but could not figure out how to do so without ruining them, so he quickly gave up.

The sounds of battle were still coming across the tundra. Not as loud, less steel on steel. But the Svertleim and Jormungand were still fighting. Wearily, they all made their way toward the sounds.

Blood and bodies covered the grassy tundra. Storvgarde and Tunoth. Hall lost count of the beasts, thinking most of them were dead. He could see a couple further back where the Jormungand lands had been. Tig bringing them out of the fighting to keep them alive.

There were no more lines, just one large chaotic mass of fighting. Storvgarde versus Storvgarde.

"Guess they don't know their leaders are dead," Sabine said in disgust.

"Or they just don't care," Thellia replied.

Hall didn't care. He just wanted the fighting to end. He shifted, Pike adjusting his weight. The dragonhawk was on the opposite shoulder from where he normally perched. The potions had healed Hall's wounds, even the shoulder, but it was still sore.

"Come on," he growled, angry. "Let's end this."

———

And they did. Not quickly. There were still too many Svertleim for that. Hall hoped they would surrender, but they never did. They just kept fighting.

And dying.

A lot of Jormungand joined them. The pile of bodies grew higher, thicker, vultures circling above and the yips and yaps of Tundra Jackals coming closer, just waiting for the fighting to end so they could feast.

Hall was disgusted.

Even as he drove his spear through yet another *Svertleim Bloodrager*. This was senseless, he thought, spinning and blocking the attack of yet another *Bloodrager*. The Svertleim's ax went wide, and Hall got his spear past the man's defenses, the point slamming into his chest. He fell backward and Hall let him fall, not following up for a killing blow.

He just didn't have it in him anymore.

Skill Gain!
Light Armor Rank Two +.1
Polearms Rank Two +.2

SLAIN: *Svertleim Battlerager +25 Experience (+25 Faction Bonus Experience)*
SLAIN: *Svertleim Battlerager +25 Experience (+25 Faction Bonus Experience)*

Looking around he didn't see any Svertleim. At least none rushing to try and kill him. Leaning against his spear, Hall took a deep breath, trying to get his heart and nerves under control. It felt like he had been fighting for hours. Probably had.

"Just give up," he growled at the Svertleim that were still fighting.

Without the magic of the Norns, the Svertleim were no match for the Jormungand and their Player allies. Hall watched the other Players, his group and Iron's. They ran about the battlefield, leaving carnage in their wake. Most of the deaths came from them. There was a difference in how a Player fought and how an NPC fought. The Players were stronger, quicker, more powerful. He hadn't noticed before but couldn't deny it now. Not watching the fighting going on around him.

"They won't," a smooth voice said from beside him.

Hall, cursing that he had been caught by surprise, it could have been a charging Svertleim, turned and saw Tig walking toward him. Blood covered the Arashi Warden's sword and shield, dripping down to the ground. He had wounds of his own, blood dripping down his shoulder.

"They should," Hall said, turning back to the battle.

The last of the Svertleim were falling, pulling together into a defensive position. Just delaying the inevitable.

"Have you ever known mobs to give up and run?" Tig asked.

He was right. In all the games that Hall had played, unless there was a story-driven reason for the mob to retreat, they never did. Just fought until the end.

"But they're being slaughtered," Hall said. "Don't they want to live?"

"They are just NPCs," Tig said with a shrug. "They can only follow their programming."

Hall shook his head. There had to be more. They weren't just NPCs, they were people, the same as he was. Lines of code but still people.

Maybe they weren't fighting because they were programmed to. Maybe they were fighting because they had nothing else to fight for. It was either die in battle or become part of Iron's Army. For the proud warriors, dying in battle was the preferred choice.

He still hated that the Svertleim were not surrendering.

"They won't respawn so we won't have to fight them again," Tig said, calmly, eyes roving the battlefield. He winced as two of the Jormungand were cut down. "Sadly, ours will not either."

Hall glanced at the Arashi. He had said it so calmly, dispassionately. Uncaring. Just numbers to be pushed around as he saw fit.

"You're losing your army," Hall pointed out.

"Price of doing business," Tig replied. "I was a Marine before getting trapped here. Lost soldiers all the time. Never gets easier. I wish soldiers didn't have to die but…"

He trailed off, watching the battle.

"Here at least they are just," he started to say, but Hall cut him off.

"Don't say it," he barked and walked away.

———

What was the point? Hall thought. All this death for what? So Iron could expand his territory? So the Svertleim could protect theirs?

He stood at the edge of the field of carnage. All the Svertleim were dead or dying. The Jormungand were licking their wounds, getting healed. His friends were resting, finding some food or just relaxing. Pike perched on his shoulder, Hall scratching under the dragonhawk's chin as he watched some of the Jormungand looting the corpses of friend and foe. Nothing was going to waste. Mamanog skinners were taking pieces of hide off the dead Tunoths, cutting slabs of meat to cure later. A huge pile of weapons and armor was being collected. Sleds were being rigged together from branches to carry the loot back to Iron's camp.

It was all being done quickly and efficiently, like they had done it all before. Which they had.

Had he accomplished what they had set out to do? He didn't feel like they had. No closer on solving the mystery of the Norns involvement and even more questions had been raised. The market for the Unclanned Dwarves weapons was dried up. Without the Svertleim or the Hagnar there was no one to buy the weapons from the Dwarves. No reason for them to plunder the crypts. At least for now. The future could change. The Unclanned would need to be dealt with at some point.

Was their part in it done?

"You okay?"

Hall didn't turn as Caryn walked up next to him. He didn't answer, just continued to look out at the bodies. Flies were buzzing in increasing numbers, the vultures flying down at the edges away from the people, starting their feasting.

"Was the game always that graphic," she asked and pointed at the vultures.

Hall had forgotten that Caryn was a truly new player. She had only been playing for a couple hours before the Glitch. There was a lot that she had never encountered.

"No," Hall replied. "That's new."

At least the part where the vultures pulled the corpses apart. There had been vultures and they were around the aftermath of battles but not to eat. Just for effect, to add to the overall battlefield immersion.

Hall missed Leigh. He had been missing her since they had left, but at that moment, he wanted nothing more than to hold her. He wanted to be home with her. He didn't care if she was "just an NPC." She was real to him.

With that thought, it all clicked. Iron, Thellia, and the others, they were clinging to the idea that they were different from the characters created in the game. That there was some hope, no matter how small, of escaping the game. They kept the separation between Player and NPC because they needed to feel different. They needed to feel like they were still Players in the game and not truly living the game. They were afraid.

Afraid of losing themselves.

But he wasn't. He was fully embracing this new life. It was his life. The NPCs were as real and as equal as anyone in real life. The old life.

He wasn't better than the NPCs, he was their equal.

And that made him better than Iron and his people

Hall smiled, at peace since meeting Thellia outside the hunting lodge.

It didn't matter what Iron or anyone thought. He knew what was right.

"Come on," he said to Caryn, "let's get out of here."

CHAPTER THIRTY-FOUR

TIG AND THELLIA LED THE TRIUMPHANT IRON ARMY'S BACK TO the camp. There were fewer of the Jormungund, but more than Hall had thought had survived. Only two of the Tunoths were killed, a couple wounded, all of the large creatures in the rear, the survivors pulling the sleds of weapons and armor.

Shouts rang out as they were spotted, those that had remained behind rushing to greet them. To see who had survived. Among them was the old Witch, Merta. She stood at the edge of the tents, watching the army enter the encampment. Her eyes were hard, and she shook her head, angrily and a bit sadly. She stared daggers at Tig and Thellia, turning and walking away, disappearing into the crowd.

Not all Jormungand were happy with Iron and his war.

It didn't look like Iron was there.

The procession broke apart as they entered deeper into the tent encampment, warriors leaving to find their tents and the ability to finally and fully relax. Hall and the others found the tents they were borrowing, still set up around the central campfire, which was going. Large logs laid in a pyramid pattern, flames hungrily eating away at the wood. It was late afternoon, and Hall could smell the meat roasting on the cooking fires. It smelled good, and he wondered if it was Tunoth.

He crawled into the tent he shared with Jackoby, quickly searching through the packs to make sure everything was there. It was. He laid his spear on the ground, tempted to lay out the bedroll and go to sleep. He was tempted to just take his people and leave.

There was nothing left for them here.

No, he thought, crawling out of the tent. There was one more thing. He had to make sure Iron would not invade Axestorm Hall.

He had no idea how he would accomplish that.

———

Iron returned a couple hours later, just as the sun was setting.

He came back at the head of a much larger army.

Instead of fighting to the end, like the Svertleim, the Hagnar had surrendered and joined Iron's Army. He was now the chieftain of the Hagnar, almost doubling the size of his forces. It didn't even look like there had been a fight. The Colds Ridge warriors, that had gone with Iron, shouted loud, the triumphant returning. There were cheers from the Jormungand, loud as Iron walked into the camp. Some of it seemed forced in Hall's opinion.

It didn't take long for the celebrations to start.

The central fire was stoked, more logs added, the flames growing higher and higher. Other fires were started, larger than just the cooking fires from before. From somewhere, drink was produced and the noises got louder and louder.

Hall was surprised to see Jormungand and Hagnar celebrating together as if they hadn't been enemies only hours before. It was surreal. The Hagnar acted as if they were fully part of Iron's Army. Not as conquerors but as volunteers. They acted like they wanted to be there. Had been there from the start.

Men and women from both clans mingled together. Drinking, eating, and other acts.

Hall wandered through the camp, watching it all, taking it all in. He was offered drinks from the Jormungand that had fought the Svertleim, asked to join their fires. He politely declined. From what it looked like there were no sentries that he could see. Which made some sense as there were no enemies anywhere nearby. Tonight was a time to party before the next step.

He wondered what that step was going to be. Where was Iron going to go next? What clan was going to be the next one to become part of the Army? To give up their independence? Or the next to be destroyed?

There was no pattern to his wandering through the camp. Hall just picked a direction and went in it. Once he reached the edge of the camp, he'd change direction and keep walking.

If it hadn't gotten dark, he would have left. Now, they were there until morning. He didn't want to be celebrating. He had found peace with Players and NPCs being equal but was not at peace with what Iron was doing.

He found himself back at the central fire again. He'd walked the perimeter and almost everywhere inside the ring. Still the celebrating raged on. Even louder than before as more and more of the Storvgarde got drunk off the drink. Fights broke out, most good-natured tests of strength, a few not. Those were quickly ended, the other Storvgarde around the combatants pulling them apart and shoving more drink at them.

His friends were gathered around the central fire with Iron's Players. None of them were drunk, though Roxhard looked like he was getting close. Hall saw Urit shove a mug into Roxhard's hands, nearby Storvgarde urging him to drink. He almost said something. Roxhard was only fourteen after all, but to Urit the Dwarf was the same age as he was. Hall just smiled. Let Roxhard have his fun.

Caryn stared morosely into the fire. Next to her Sabine was chatting with Corinth, the two with their heads bent together. Sabine seemed to be ignoring Caryn. Jackoby was near the far edge, engaged in a contest of wrestling with a Storvgarde of equal size. Neither seemed to be winning.

Iron was nowhere to be seen. Light could be seen coming from within his tent, leaking out the cracks in the canvas. Thellia and Tig were missing as well, most likely inside with the leader of the Army.

Hall sat down on the log next to Caryn. She looked up and smiled.

"Where's Pike?"

"Out there somewhere hunting with Screech," Hall replied. He leaned forward, looking past her at Sabine and Corinth. He nodded at the pair, a questioning look.

Caryn looked that way, shook her head and turned back to Hall with a shrug. A female Storvgarde, dressed in a wool dress with an apron, handed Hall a mug of ale and some food.

"Thank you," he said, smiling at her.

She smiled back and winced as Cuthard yelled sharply for her. Grabbing a fresh mug, she walked around the fire. Once there the Elf Duelist smacked her on the behind, laughing. The girl gave a weak smile and quickly left.

"He's been hitting on me non-stop," Caryn said with a disgusted look at Cuthard. "Hitting on Sabine as well."

She shook her head, dark hair framing her dark skin, flickering shadows from the flames playing across her face.

"I don't see it with Iron's people. Probably gave up on them," she chuckled.

Hall laughed, taking a deep pull from the mug. The ale was good and rich, a nice light brown color. Setting the mug down, he picked up a piece of the meat. Taking a bite, it was tough and greasy but had good flavor.

"Tunoth," Caryn said, pointing at the meat.

Hall tried to think of a comparison to something he had before but couldn't. It was unique.

"It's good," he said, reaching up to wipe a bit of grease off his beard.

The fire was warm, the food was good. Hall felt himself relax, thoughts pushing to the back of his mind as he let himself enjoy the night.

———

He woke to the sound of commotion outside by the fire.

Pushing off the blanket, Hall crawled out of the tent. Standing up, shielding his eyes from the rising sun, stretching and stifling a yawn, he looked around the camp. There was a lot of activity. Storvgarde were breaking down tents, kicking fires apart. Hall was amazed at how efficient they were. The celebrating had continued long after he had gone to bed, and the Storvgarde had drunk much more than he had. They should have all been fighting hangovers.

Instead, they were breaking down the camp. And doing so quickly.

This was not a normal breakdown of an army on the move back home, this was the breakdown of an army with a purpose. A quick target and location to move to. Hall looked to the north and saw some elements of the army already on the move. Led by half the remaining Tunoths, it was a mixed group of Colds Ridge, Jormungand, Mamanog, and Hagnar.

When was the last time that many of the wild tribes of Storvgarde had banded together for a common purpose?

It looked like some of Iron's inner circle were going with the initial wave of the Army. Hall saw Tig leading them, along with Cuthard, Tabitha, Torit, and Tashy. He found his friends around the central fire. It had lowered, started to go out during the night and some of the Storvgarde were in the process of breaking the remaining logs apart. Working to put the fire out. The elderly that had prepared and served the food were now cleaning pots, disposing of the remains of last night's celebratory feast. There was no sign of Iron. Only Thellia stood by the fire talking with Sabine while Caryn stood off to the side with Urit. Jackoby was grumbling behind Hall, just emerging from the tent. Next to them, Hall could see Roxhard pulling himself out of the tent he shared with Urit. The Dwarf was holding his head, moaning quietly, clearly hungover.

Hall glanced around, feeling eyes on him once again.

Skill Gain!

Increased Perception Rank Two +.1

He thought he saw a fleeting movement, a shadow darting between tents, but it was gone. *Weird*, he thought, not the first time he had felt angry eyes on him in the camp. It had to be some of the Storvgarde.

"What's going on?" Hall asked, coming over to where Thellia and Sabine were talking.

They fell quiet with his approach.

"Getting ready to move out," Thellia answered. "First elements are to set up a forward camp a couple miles from the target while the larger force follows."

Hall fought the urge to roll his eyes. That part of it was obvious.

"Who is the target?"

It was too soon to move on another clan, he thought, and they wouldn't move the Army in pieces but move the total force at full strength. Overwhelm the next clan with the size of the Army and try for a bloodless takeover like Iron had accomplished with the Hagnar. That seemed the most logical, but it appeared that Iron didn't follow the most logical path. There was no logical reason for the attack on Crackleberry. Hall started to have a suspicion where the Army was going.

Thellia didn't say anything, glancing at him quickly before looking away. Clearly, she didn't want to tell him. Which made his guess much more likely.

"Where's Iron?"

"Here," the man's voice said from behind.

Hall turned to see the large Storvgarde walking out of his command tent. Nero and Corinth were with him. The Gael Warden was smiling wickedly. Almost hungrily. Hall hadn't spent any time with Nero, had no idea what the man was like. He had kept apart from all the others in Hall's group. Just the way Nero carried himself, it reminded Hall of Cuthard. Which made him instantly dislike Nero. Tall, thin but athletically built, with flaming long red hair done in two braids that hung down his back. No beard, but blue tattoos around his eyes gave Nero a fierce look. He wore chainmail armor, leather pants and iron boots, a two-handed claymore strapped to his back.

Iron stopped in front of Hall. Nero continued walking to stand next to Thellia. The two briefly whispered. Corinth stayed with Iron a moment before moving off to the side.

"Where is the Army going?" Hall asked.

Iron had no expression as he studied Hall, the gray eyes piercing. The large Storvgarde smiled. There was no warmth to it.

"Why does it matter to you?" he asked. "The reason you came here is done and you are not part of the Army."

He paused, the smile growing deeper.

"But you could be," Iron said. "Or an ally," he added with a soft chuckle.

Hall thought he detected a small note of arrogance in Iron's voice and the chuckle. Like he didn't think Hall worthy of being an ally. Hall knew what Iron really meant. It meant being used by Iron, controlled by Iron.

"You would be on your own," Iron said as if reading Hall's thoughts. "Your village," he said with the condescention and chuckle, "would serve as a good launching point for operations on Edin. We could fly some of the Storvgarde and some of my people," he nodded toward Nero and Thellia, "with you to assist in whatever direction you want to go."

There it was. An ally but with the illusion of free will reinforced by Iron's people to push Iron's agenda. Iron's much higher level people and more numerous soldiers that would follow Iron's orders.

It was obvious that Iron had thought this through, planned multiple steps ahead. Had probably started thinking through his plans the moment Hall and the others appeared. Hall knew how it would go. It would start with gentle pushing to move on to the cities and towns on Edin, starting slow, gently prodding. They would move from one village to the next, slowly Nero and Thellia pushing Hall aside. Until finally all of it, including Skara Brae, was Iron's to control.

Hall wasn't a conqueror. He had no desire to expand the territory of Skara Brae. Just the small village was all he could handle. He didn't want more. But if he allied with Iron, that is what would happen and it would not be his choice.

Iron was a bully. A sophisticated one. Power-hungry. But still a bully.

"No," Hall said, looking up at the much taller and bigger Iron.

The smile disappeared. Anger flashed in Iron's eyes, bright and hard, but then they were back to the typical calm gray.

"No what?" Iron asked, his voice cold. "No to the offer of our aid? No to being our ally?"

He looked down at Hall, waiting.

"Where is the Army heading?" Hall asked instead of answering.

Iron smiled, giving a small shake of his head.

"Gray Rock," he answered.

The Svertleim clanhome. Just what Hall had guessed.

"Why? They're defeated. There won't be anyone but women, children, the old and sick."

Iron was quiet for a minute. He stared at Hall, looked past at Neo and Thellia, glanced around at the watching Storvgarde, Jormungand and Hagnar both. Hall watched a flurry of emotions cross Iron's face. Pride. Anger. Remorse? The Storvgarde Warden's face settled on the calm and composed expression that was Iron's standard.

"A message," he finally said. "To the other clans that live on the Whitegrass Tundra."

"A message?Hall growled, angry. "What kind of message does slaughtering the weak send?"

"To not stand in our way," Iron said, his voice growing angry. He leaned down, the full weight of his stone glare on Hall. "That to rise up against us means death for all that you hold dear." He calmed down, sighing, letting his anger leave. "The Hagnar joined because they did not want to be destroyed like the Svertleim will be. They saw the future, and they wanted to be part of it. They want to live."

It was Hall's turn to fall silent. He pushed down his growing rage. This was wrong. So wrong. The tactics of a bully, using strength and fear.

"They fear you," he said, spitting the words out.

"Good," Iron replied with a hard smile. "As they should. These people respect strength," he said, pointing at the watching Storvgarde. "They respect my strength because they fear that strength."

"Fear is not respect," Hall said sadly, a small shake of his head.

Iron leaned back, laughing loudly. Behind him, Hall could hear Nero chuckle. At least he thought it was Nero. He also wondered when the Gael had moved behind him.

"If that is what you think," Iron said, stopping laughing and looking down at Hall. It was a serious expression that said Iron was done with this conversation. And done with Hall's apparent foolishness. "Then you are a fool."

Hall took a deep breath, forcing himself to calm down and bite back his retort. This was getting them nowhere. He just had to stop talking, grab his people, and leave. There was nothing he could do for the people of Gray Rock. Nothing he could do for the other clans in the tundra. He took a step back, eyes locked with Iron.

"And what was Crackleberry," Hall asked quietly, not sure why he did. "Did they not show you the proper respect?"

Iron's eyes hardened, growing flinty. It was clear he had enough.

"That was also a message," Iron said, each word harsh and sharp, clipped. Frustrated, aggravated, annoyed.

"To who," Hall barked, no longer able to keep it in. "They were Bodin. Women. Children. No match for the Storvgarde. They had been left alone because they had nothing of value. But then you came and killed them. For what? A message? What was the message? To show off how strong you are?"

Iron didn't reply, not right away. His eyes glanced around the fire. At Hall's companions. At his own people. Lingering on the Jormungand, Mamanog, and Hagnar that watched. Hall saw Merta near the edge, watching the exchange intently. Hers was the only seemingly dissenting expression among the Storvgarde. Hall didn't look behind him to see what Nero and Thellia were doing, but he could imagine. They believed in Iron. They followed Iron.

"Yes," Iron finally said. "To show my strength. To let the watchers know me and to grow to fear me."

With that one word, watchers, Hall understood. Nothing about the attack on Crackleberry had made sense. The Hagnar and Svertleim wouldn't have cared what Iron did with the village of Bodin. They would have wanted him to waste resources, men and equipment, on destroying and conquering the village. Wasting more men and equipment on keeping control of the village.

But there was one other group in the area. One with a vested interest in having non-aggressive neighbors. Hall glanced at Urit. Iron followed his gaze.

"Now you understand," Iron said with a nod, seeing the knowledge in Hall's eyes. "The message was for them," he continued, pointing at Urit and Roxhard. "It was for the Dwarves of Axestorm Hall."

"Ye won't be getting to the Hall," Urit barked, stepping forward.

Jackoby reached down and grasped the angry young Stone-fire on the shoulder holding him back.

"He doesn't plan to," Hall said, knowing he was right. As he spoke, Iron smiled, pleased that his grand plan, his intelligence, was revealed for all to see. Not just physical strength, but tactical. "He knows he wouldn't make it through the mountains and never get into the Hall itself." Hall paused, angry at himself that he understood what the conquest of Crackleberry meant and that for Iron's plans it made sense. "But he also knows that the Dwarves won't leave the mountains. As long as he keeps a force in Crackleberry, he's drawn a line around the mountains. The Dwarves on one side, him on the other, and neither will make a move."

Skill Gain!
Strategy Rank Two +.1

Urit looked like he was going to argue, most likely say

something about Dwarven bravery and how no one would lock them into the mountains. But he didn't, knowing that Hall was right. That Iron respected, and possibly feared, the might of the Dwarves in the mountains but also knew they would not venture out. They never had before and they wouldn't now. Not when there was an army camped on their borders just waiting for that to happen.

"Fear," Iron said, the word echoing through the camp.

He stepped back from Hall, arms raised to encircle the whole camp. He turned as he spoke, smiling and proud.

"Strength and fear are the driving forces in the world," Iron said, his voice loud so all could hear. "We are the strong," he said, punching his chest, and Hall knew he meant the Players and not the NPCs like his Storvgarde army. "And we should rule."

Hall shook his head.

"You're the fool," Hall said. "We have a chance at something new and you treat it the same as back in the real world. It didn't work there. It won't work here." He looked around at the Storvgarde, seeing a lot of blank stares, the way NPCs got when they talked about the real world. About Earth. Staring at nothing. He looked back at Iron who was staring down at him, grinning but with a hard edge in his steel-gray eyes. "You don't get to decide who rules."

Iron laughed.

"Oh, but I do," he replied. "But I grow tired of this. It's obvious you will not fall in line." Iron lost the smile, face hard.

Hall tensed. He looked at the circle around them, the dying fire to his left. Behind Iron, his companions stood in a line, Storvgarde surrounding them. Behind him were more Storvgarde along with Nero and Thellia. Corinth was off to the right withmore Storvgarde. He had made a mistake. He had gone too far. They should have left earlier.

"I had wanted to work with you," Iron said with a small

shake of his head. "But you refuse to see the truth. I am sorry," he said, and Hall knew it was sincere. Misplaced but sincere.

"Take them," Iron commanded, not harshly, just a statement.

Hall dropped into a fighting crouch, not yet drawing his sword but hand on the hilt. Behind Iron, who had not turned, the Storvgarde surrounding his friends, closing in on them with weapons drawn. The Storvgarde did not attack. His friends eyed the weapons angrily, hands ready to draw their own. They looked to Hall, ready to fight.

"I will not kill them," Iron said, and all knew who he meant. "They will be spared but you," he growled, pointing at Hall. "You will be a message."

CHAPTER THIRTY-FIVE

HALL DREW HIS SWORD, THE SOUND LOUD IN THE HEAVY silence. Iron made no move to pull his large hammer from the harness across his back.

"Do you think you will respawn?" Iron asked, mocking. "Is that what makes you brave? You think you will live forever? Reborn?" He took a step forward, still not drawing his weapon. Hall held his ground. "Truthfully, we do not know what will happen. None of us have died. Shall we use you to answer the question?"

Hall slid back a step. He reached out to Pike, the dragonhawk screeching far above. Followed quickly by another screech. Panic came through the bond. Surprise and betrayal. Hall wanted to look back at Thellia. She had sent Screech to attack Pike. A surprise attack. But he could not take his eyes off Iron.

"Let us find out," Iron said and reached for his hammer.

Hall tensed, ready to activate *Leap*.

Most of the Storvgarde had continued on to the north, leaving a small number behind. If Hall could jump over Iron, land a single blow, and then run to his friends. Could they clear away the few Storvgarde surrounding them? Then run through what was left of the camp? Would Iron bother chasing them?

It was the only chance they had.

Skill Gain!
Strategy Rank Two +.1

The plan flashed through Hall's mind in seconds. In the time it took Iron to lift his hand, fingers closing around the hilt of his hammer. He waited for Iron to hold the hammer, to charge, then he would *Leap*.

But it didn't happen.

Instead, Iron smiled.

"I know you have been wanting to do this for a while," he said, confusing Hall, eyes locked on Hall. "Now."

Skill Gain!
Increased Perception Rank Two +.1

Hall saw the shadow appear on the ground. The sun behind him, he saw his shadow change shape, distort, as something joined it. All the warning he got.

He twisted to the side, crying out as a sharp knife tore a bloody gash across his side. He felt his leather armor rip, his side tear, blood dripping down. Landing hard on his side, he rolled, keeping hold of his sword and bringing it up in defense as he looked at the small form staring hatefully down at him, holding two short swords, one with an edge dripping blood.

A Bodin.

One he knew.

———

Davit.

The murderer. The Bodin they had encountered when landing on Auld. The one that had been fleeing the guards.

Skill Gain!
Identify Rank Two +.1

Davit, Duelist (blue)

The higher level murderer.

Hall tried to move, but the cut in his side was deep. Almost a quarter of his Health was gone. Only catching the shadows change had saved him from a Critical Blow.

It was Davit he had been feeling around the camp, the angry eyes. Davit stealthed. Davit that Iron had kept hidden.

"You abandoned me on Auld," Davit said, the hate in his voice odd in the high-pitched tones of a Bodin. "I was hunted. Hounded."

With each word, the small Bodin swung a sword. Hall blocked the strikes, but each blow sent pain ripping through his side. Davit altered one of the swings, the sword slashing down the length of Hall's leg. He cried out in pain, more Health disappearing from his bar. The wound felt hot. A burning pain as if his flesh was melting.

A small icon flashed beneath his Health bar.

You have been afflicted with Burning Rot. The edges of the wound are on fire, melting away at the skin and burning the muscles beneath. 2 DMG every 1 second for 10 seconds.

Hall tried to slide across the ground. To put some distance between himself the murderous Bodin.

"Kill him," Iron commanded.

"NO!"

The voice was deep. Loud. Strong.

The hard tundra exploded as running feet slammed down, the ground shaking. Hall watched as a blurry form slammed into Davit, sending the Bodin flying. The Duelist managed to get into a roll, coming up standing and facing his attacker.

Roxhard stood in front of Hall, the *Ax of Obsidian Flames* in his hands, the head burning with purple-blackish flames.

Behind Iron, the sounds of fighting erupted. Hall looked quickly, seeing his friends pushing aside the Storvgarde, using their now drawn weapons to form a perimeter. Back to back, they stood, swiping at the Storvgarde, keeping them at bay.

"Kill the Dwarf," Iron commanded.

Hall turned just in time to see the large Storvgarde Warden lunge toward him, hammer swinging. Pushing against the pain in his side and legs, Hall rolled out of the way, the hammer's head slamming into the tundra, sending up chunks of hard ground. He activated *Leap*, jumping high over the Warden. He didn't try to attack, just wanting distance.

Landing behind Iron, Hall sheathed his sword and pulled his spear from the harness on his back. He turned to face the Warden, who shrugged his shield off his shoulder. Iron thumped the head of his hammer against the metal of the shield. Once, twice. Three times.

"I said they could live," Iron said to the Storvgarde. "As long as they do not interfere," he added, eyes locked on Hall.

"Don't attack," Hall said to his friends, hoping they would listen.

He couldn't look to see if they had. Iron rushed at him, heavy hammer swinging through the air. Hall jumped back, avoiding the sweep, and stabbed straight out with his spear. Somehow, Iron got the heavy hammer back and swinging upward, knocking the spear aside. Behind the large Warden, where he could not see, Hall heard the sound of metal on metal.

Roxhard against Davit.

He knew he had to somehow end the fight with Iron quickly or Roxhard would lose.

Stabbing with the spear, he darted to Iron's side. The tip hit Iron's armor and glanced aside, not penetrating. He took a couple quick steps, pulling the spear back, and stabbing out again, trying to score a hit on Iron's unprotected back.

The shield blocked it, metal against wood, almost knocking the weapon from Hall's hand.

He felt the vibrations through the wooden spear, down his arms, and through his body. His side screamed out in pain, his wounded leg shaking as it barely supported his weight. The damage over time effect of the *Burning Rot* had faded, but the wound had not closed. His Health was at seventy-five percent.

Activating *Leap*, Hall shot straight up as Iron's hammer barely missed his feet. With *Leaping Stab,* he scored a glancing blow against Iron's upper arm, drawing first blood. Landing behind Iron, he jabbed out with the spear and got the bonus from the Attack of Opportunity, scoring a solid blow in Iron's side. The Warden grunted in pain, stepping away from Hall.

"Excellent," Iron said, smiling. "I do not like easy fights."

He turned to Hall but stopped as they heard a loud scream.

Hall looked past Iron, seeing Roxhard fall to the ground.

Davit stood over the Dwarf, both swords bloody.

Roxhard lay on the ground, pushing himself up with one arm, the *Ax of Obsidian Flames* held defensively in front of him. He bore wounds across his legs and chest, blood dripping down from a cut above his left eye. Davit twirled his twin swords, turning them to point blade down.

A wicked grin on his face, he took a step toward the wounded Roxhard.

"NO!" Hall yelled trying to race to save his friend.

His brother.

He grunted in pain as a heavy blow slammed across his back. He felt ribs breaking, losing the spear as he slammed chest down onto the tundra. Breathing was hard, his chest heavy. Then the booted foot pressed against his back, driving him harder against the ground.

Hall could barely breathe. Barely cough, spitting up blood.

"Watch," Iron said. "This is where your weakness brings you."

Davit took one more step, not hesitating. In one motion, he stepped and stabbed down.

Hall couldn't even cry out as he watched the swords stabbing down to finish off Roxhard. From his position, the Dwarf might have been able to fend off one sword, but not both. It was over. Down the swords stabbed.

A bright light flashed. A blinding purple that caused all to look away.

Blinking, tears in his eyes, Hall thought to see Roxhard dead or dying, but instead the Dwarf was alive.

Before him stood another Dwarf. Taller, broader. A shining purple translucent Dwarf in full armor. Every line in the Dwarf's craggly face was visible, every surface of the armor, every hair in his beard. Blurry in the purple glow, Hall could see through the ghostly Dwarf. No helm, but bearing a two-handed ax identical to the one in Roxhard's hands.

Brignir Stonefire stood protectively over his descendant. Hate and anger shone in the ghostly being's eyes. Dark black in the purple glow.

Davit's blades, both short swords, were held up by Brignir's spirit Ax. Shock was frozen on the Bodin's face. Shock and some fear. He shifted, trying to bring one weapon to attack, but the ghost Dwarf was too quick. Turning slightly, Brignir brought his Ax of Obsidian Flames down and around, catching the attack from Davit.

The blade was knocked from the Duelist's hand, clattering across the ground.

Davit stepped back.

"Get up, young Stonefire," Brignir's ghostly voice said, a hollow but deep voice. "There are enemies near."

Amazingly Roxhard stood. Purple flames spread across his body, flaring brightly. The wounds healed. Blood stopped flowing, skin stitching together.

"No," Davit squeaked as Roxhard stalked forward.

With a roar, the Stonefire Dwarf charged.

Iron stepped off Hall in surprise. Pushing himself up, fighting against his own pain, Hall watched Roxhard swing his weapon. The Ax slammed into Davit's hasty block. Metal snapped, the cracking loud, as the Stonefire's ancestral weapon broke Davit's last short sword.

Davit didn't have time to run.

A quick swing of the Ax sliced through the leather armor on Davit's chest, a bright red gash as blood sprayed into the air, almost cutting him in half, and the Bodin fell to his knees. He clutched at the massive wound in his stomach. Eyes looking down in surprise.

"How," he croaked and fell to the ground.

He did not get up.

———

Silence fell across the tundra. Everyone watched, staring at the body of Davit the Bodin.

They waited, watching.

Nothing happened. Blood flowed from the wound, pooling on the ground. Davit did not disappear. He did not get up.

He was dead.

And did not respawn.

CHAPTER THIRTY-SIX

"Now we know," Iron said, moving a couple steps away from Hall who struggled to push himself up.

On his knees, Hall reached out and grabbed his spear. He used the weapon as a crutch, pushing himself up to stand.

Roxhard stared down at the body of Davit, shock and horror across his rough face.

The spirit of Brignir Stonefire faded away, taking the strange purple glow with him. Flames still encircled the head of the magical ax, but they were weaker, not as bright.

Two angry screeches came from the sky, drawing all eyes. Hall watched as two darting forms chased each other over the camp. They spiraled, diving at each other before breaking apart and flying down. Screech landed on the ground near Thellia's feet, stumbling. He bore scratches down his chest, a couple feathers missing.

Pike looked worse. Blood dripped from the many scratches across his body, burned feathers smoking, but he landed on Hall's shoulder steadily. Squawking angrily at Screech. Roxhard did not move, just stared at the corpse. Hall turned to face Iron, spear held tightly as he somehow managed to stay standing.

Corinth stepped out from the line of Storvgarde, laying her hand lightly on Iron's arm. He bent down, and she whispered something to him. Iron nodded, and she stepped back. Raising her hands, Corinth signaled to the Storvgarde.

All of them that remained—Colds Ridge, Jormungand, Mamanog, and Hagnar—all stepped away from the clearing. The circle broke apart, each turning to walk away to the north. Including the ones surrounding Hall's companions.

They took up defensive positions around Hall and Roxhard.

Soon all that remained of Iron's Army was the commander and his three Player followers. Now outnumbered, they did not care.

"I told you that they could live," Iron said. "I shall allow you and the Dwarf to live."

He pointed the head of his hammer at Hall.

"For now. You can leave Huntley, but if you return, then I will kill you and everyone you hold dear."

It was not an idle threat, Hall knew, but the truth. He didn't relax his grip on the spear, eyes never leaving Irons. Each breath was painful. At any second his leg would give out. The wound down the length burned, screaming with each tiny movement and shake.

"You, Dwarf," Iron said and pointed at Urit. "Take a message to your King. We will be talking soon. He can have the mountains, but the rest is mine."

Urit growled something that Hall could not hear.

Iron looked at each of Hall's companions, except Jackoby, gaze lingering on each.

"I invite any of you to join me," he said. "You have seen my strength. We are the true rulers of this world, and we will take what is ours. What we deserve."

Hall growled, fighting through the pain. He took a step forward, Pike rearing up and screeching angrily. The dragonhawk spiraled up into the air, circling overhead.

"You deserve nothing."

He crouched, ready to activate *Leap* when Iron smiled.

Hall screamed in pain, his body on fire, muscles spasming. Purple-black bolts of energy crackled around him. He fell to the ground, on his knees, struggling to get up but shock stopping him. A purple robe walked past, smooth skin visible through the slit. He turned against the pain, looking up at Sabine.

She looked down at him sadly. Hall growled, trying to stand, but the bolts flared, his muscles locked, and he fell back.

"Fool," she said. "Stay down. I just saved your life."

She walked past, stopping in front of Iron. On her shoulders, Salem the Minx Cat looked back at them. The familiar's eyes were sad, reluctant, unhappy. Pike swooped down, landing near Hall, stepping close but darting back as lightning shot out from Hall's pained body.

"Excellent choice," Iron said with a warm smile looking down at the much shorter Witch.

"I want to rule," she said. "Caryn?" Sabine asked, looking over her shoulder.

Hall turned, lingering sparks of energy flying across his body, to watch the small Duelist. Caryn looked betrayed, devastated. She took a step forward, tears starting to fall.

But then she stopped.

The anguish disappeared, replaced by anger.

"No," she said resolutely. "This is wrong. They are wrong. Don't do this Sabine."

Surprise flashed in Sabine's eyes. Annoyance.

"Caryn, don't be silly," she said. "Come here."

"No."

Sabine shrugged and turned away. She walked past Iron to

where Corinth and Thellia waited, the two women giving Sabine welcoming hugs. Together, all smiling, the three walked away, following the Storvgarde. Only Iron and Nero remained.

Caryn watched Sabine disappear, tears flowing down her cheeks. Cursing to herself, Hall thought he heard a muttered "weak", she wiped away the tears. Turning from Iron and Sabine's lost form, Caryn walked over to Roxhard laying a hand on his shoulder. The Dwarf still stared down at the body of Davit.

Hall pulled his spear to him, holding it tightly. He pushed himself up, growling against the spasms that shot through his body as the last of Sabine's *Hexbolt* faded. Breathing was hard, his leg shook beneath him, muscles twitched, but he stared across the tundra at Iron.

"One of these days I will come for your tiny little ruin," Iron told him. Calmly, a simple statement.

"I'll be waiting," Hall growled, forcing the words out.

Iron nodded.

"Good."

He turned and walked away. Nero waiting until Iron had walked past, chuckled and waved, before turning and following.

Hall watched them go until their shadowed forms disappeared.

Then he fell, leg no longer able to support him. Jackoby caught him before he hit the ground. The Firbolg helped Hall stand, holding him up.

"Let's go home," Hall said, tired.

PART FOUR
RETREAT

CHAPTER THIRTY-SEVEN

It was a silent and hurting group that made the long trek back to the Valley of the Ancients. Between Urit's limited knowledge of the area and Hall's *Cartography* Skill, they were able to go through the foothills and not up into the mountains the way they had come from. Hall hoped the time would be the same, if not less. Urit wasn't sure if they would be able to enter the Stonefire crypt through the back door, which would have meant days of walking only to turn around and start back.

None of them wanted that.

"How are they higher level?" Caryn asked the first night. She didn't need to specify who they were.

It was a question that had been bothering Hall. The Faction Bonus helped but didn't account for the difference.

"Dungeons," Roxhard replied.

The Dwarf had been quiet most of the trip, lost in his thoughts. Killing Davit had hit him hard.

"The Druid, Tashy, said they had found an active dungeon south of Colds Ridge."

"Aye, that would do it," Urit said, throwing another log on

the fire. "Ye get double experience when in a dungeon. That's why people became Adventurers. The experience and the loot found in dungeons."

They had camped in a shallow cave, lighting a fire. A miserable, quiet camp. Even when Caryn had started the conversation, it didn't change the mood.

"We were told that all the dungeons were empty," Hall said.

He sat at the edge of the cave. Pike nestled in the branches of the trees around them. He had been looking out into the thick woods, not seeing, just staring. Most of his wounds were healed. It had taken pretty much all the Healing potions they had and he was still incredibly sore, but at least he could stand and walk.

"They are," Urit said. "Or were. Sounds like some might be active again."

Silence came again, as each returned to their private thoughts. Hall felt that he should say something. Anything. He was the leader. Wasn't it his job to motivate his people? But what could he say? Iron had beaten them. Sabine had betrayed them. They had participated in the slaughter of an entire clan of Storvgarde. And for what?

Nothing.

Surprisingly it was Jackoby who spoke. The Firbolg who had always acted aloof, as if he truly didn't want to be there. Had never tried to be one of them.

His voice was deep but gentle.

"There is no shame in losing to a stronger opponent," he began.

Hall turned, looking into the cave. Jackoby stared down at the flames, shadows dancing across his face, the orange glow highlighting his brown fur.

"Is there shame in doing what we did, no matter the reason?" Jackoby continued but paused. The others all looked at him, waiting. "Yes, there is," he said finally, a slight growl in his voice. "But there is greater shame in not standing back up, accepting what you did, and not doing better. The greatest shame comes in letting the failure drag you down." Jackoby lifted his head, turning and looking straight at Hall. The others did as well.

Hall felt them all looking at him. Not measuring, not judging. Caring. Loyal.

He nodded.

"The shame is in not learning from the mistakes we have made and in not striving to do better," Jackoby finished.

Hall stood up, walking the short distance back to the fire. He sat down, reaching over to clap Jackoby on the shoulder, locking eyes with each of them. He didn't need to say anything. No need to apologize or ask forgiveness. They were all hurting and shocked. It would take time, but they would recover.

He looked across the fire at Caryn. She smiled. It didn't get to her eyes, which were still sad, but it was a start.

———

They found a game trail that led up the mountain. Steep but an easy walk up the forested slopes. By midday on the third day, they crested the ridge and looked down into the Valley of the Ancients. It looked much the same as before. Nothing had changed. On the south side of the valley, the tower to their left and the cave entrance to the Stonefire crypt on the far-right wall.

It took most of the rest of the day to find a way down and make their trek across the valley and up to the cave.

Hall thought about camping for the night, entering the crypt in the morning. He could still feel the cold and wrongness emanating from the dark interior. The idea of being near that crypt during the night was not appealing, even if they back-tracked and went higher up the ridge.

They knew why the crypt was wrong. There was no reason to delay in returning the *Ax of Obsidian Flames* to where it right-fully belonged.

Roxhard and Urit led them into the dark interior of the crypt. As soon as the two Dwarves crossed the threshold, the feeling of cold and wrong dimmed. Hall looked around as a low moaning came down the corridors, but it didn't make him afraid. It was welcoming.

Pulling the ax off his back, Roxhard held it out in both hands. The purple-black flames spread around the double-bladed head, casting an odd glow over the room as they walked. The flames seemed to drive the cold away.

As they passed the intersection, the moaning stayed behind, filling the space. Caryn glanced back nervously, but nothing followed. A barrier of spirits, the ancients, and dead of the Stonefire Clan.

No one spoke as they entered the final chamber that contained the sarcophagus of Brignir Stonefire. Nothing had been disturbed, a faint line of light at the far end where the secret door to the tunnel stood open. In the middle was the sarcophagus and the indentation where the *Ax of Obsidian Flames* was supposed to rest.

Roxhard stepped closer and the flames around the ax heard flared brightly. Flickering fire flowed around the sharp edges, now growing out thick beyond the metal. Roxhard stepped back, shocked, almost dropping the weapon.

"They're not hot," he said in awe, staring at the flaming axehead.

The moaning grew louder, now coming from the middle of the room. They all watched as a purple glow appeared over the stone coffin. It swirled, growing and brightening until the ghostly form of Brignir Stonefire appeared before them. The spirit hovered over the crypt, eyes hard and staring at Roxhard.

"Welcome son of the Stonefire," Brignir said, his voice echoed through the hall, but unlike the first time they had been there, it did not cause pain.

"Thank you, grandfather," Roxhard said, bowing his head.

Hall motioned the others to step back, leaving Urit and Roxhard alone by the sarcophagus and the spirit of their ancestor.

Urit was kneeling while Roxhard held the ax before him. He walked forward, slowly, eyes staring up at the floating spirit. Stepping to the side Roxhard stopped in the middle of the sarcophagus. He laid the ax down horizontally, holding the shaft with both hands. The spirit of Brignir looked down on him, smiling, and nodded. Roxhard laid the Ax of Obsidian Flames down onto the stone. The flames around the head flared, no longer flames but a bright purple light. It flowed out from the ax head, following the shape of the weapon, filling the thin space between the stone of the crypt and stone of the ax. Outlined in bright purple, the stone of the weapon gleamed in the odd light.

Flaring once more, so bright they had to turn away, the light disappeared and the Ax was where it belonged once more.

"Excellent, my grandson," Brignir intoned.

You have returned the Ax of Obsidian Flames to the resting place of Brignir Stonefire.

CRYPT FINDINGS II
Find the Ax of Obsidian Flames 1/1
Return the Ax to the crypt of Brignir Stonefire 1/1
Reward: +300 Stonefire Clan Reputation; +100 Experience

Roxhard moved his iron gloved hand over the ax, smiling.

"You have shown yourself to be a true Stonefire," Brignir said, his voice deep and sounding real, not echoing anymore. All eyes looked toward the ancestral patriarch of the clan. "We are honored to call you one of us."

With a nod to Roxhard, the spirit of Brignir disappeared. Not fading away. It was just gone. With it went the purple glow, the room returning to dark except for the torch held by Caryn. The distant moaning faded, silence coming to the crypt.

Brignir Stonefire has accepted Roxhard as a member of the Stonefire Clan.

A CLAN'S HISTORY I
Assist Roxhard in communing with the Stonefire ancestors 1/1
Reward: +200 Stonefire Clan Reputation; +25 Experience

"The cold and that odd feeling are gone," Caryn said. "It feels like a crypt should." She chuckled. "That's just odd to say."

Hall agreed with both statements. That strange wrongness was gone, a calmness replacing it. He could feel the weight of the stone around them, the weight of the history and lives entombed around them. But there was no feeling of cold, or undeath or anything else associated with a desecrated place of burial. It was musty with a natural chill from being deep within the mountain. But that was all.

Just like a crypt should feel.

Return to Matron Lydi of the Stonefire. She will be eager to learn of Roxhard's acceptance into the Clan by the Clan's Ancestor.

A CLAN'S HISTORY II
Inform Matron Lydi of Brignir's decision 0/1

Reward: +200 Stonefire Clan Reputation; +25 Experience

Waiting on Roxhard to Accept or Refuse Quest.

*Roxhard has Accepted **A CLAN'S HISTORY II***

ACCEPT QUEST?

Roxhard had not moved. His hand rested on the ax. Urit had gotten up, standing on the other side of the sarcophagus, his own leather-gloved hand resting on the ax. Both Dwarves had their heads bowed, silent.

Hall stepped around them, walking to the other end of the room. He leaned in close to where the secret door was open, looking up the tunnel. Even his Limited Night Vision had a hard time with the deep blackness. Stepping back, he put his shoulder against the stone door and pushed.

It scraped across the stone floor, loud and echoing. The heavy stone moved slowly then it slid faster as Jackoby leaned against it next to him. It slammed shut with a crash.

"Are ye ready to lay yer Da to rest?" Urit asked.

"Yes," Roxhard answered.

———

Urit led them back to the intersection, turning left. The new corridor wasn't as large as the main. Only ten feet wide. Through the light from Caryn's torch, Hall could see pilasters evenly spaced as they walked. Small niches were cut into the smooth walls.

Hall stopped to look into one. Not that deep, it was taller than wide. Where the walls were carved from the mountain, smoothed by hand, the niche was made of small blocks. Only one small object was contained within the larger space. A stone statue.

Standing about four inches tall, it depicted a Dwarf. Female with long hair done in two thick braids that hung over her shoulders. She was dressed in full plate armor, a sword and shield in hand. A helm sat at her feet.

Stepping back, he glanced at the other niches. The entire wall, all the walls, were filled with them. Each contained a statue. Different poses, different weapons, male and female. Different Dwarves.

The others had continued down the long corridor, stepping through an opening into a dark room. He joined them, walking into a square room. Much smaller than the crypt that housed the tomb of Brignir Stonefire, this new space was not plain. Pilasters lined the walls, in the corners and midpoints. A single wide column, made of smoothed stone, rose up from the center of the room. It looked as if it had been carved directly from the stone, one solid piece with the floor and ceiling. Through the flickering flames of Caryn's torch, Hall could see scenes of battle carved into the walls between pilasters. There was no sarcophagus. Instead, a statue of a Dwarf stood in front of the column.

Hall stared at the statue in amazement. It was Roxhard. Just older, the face slightly different. Chainmail shirt, iron legs and boots, no helm. Long hair hung down his back and shoulders, longer beard hanging past the iron belt. The stone Dwarf had his arms crossed over the top of his ax, the shaft of the weapon against the ground.

"Ye never saw her father, did ye?" Urit asked gently as he and Roxhard stopped in front of the statute. "That be Dern Stonefire."

———

"Looks just like Roxhard," Caryn said in awe, looking from the statue to Roxhard.

Hall glanced at Urit, expecting the Dwarf to say something, but he was talking quietly with Roxhard and didn't hear. Most likely would have just ignored it, Hall thought. Caryn knew about their histories being tied into the lore of Hankarth, but it was still hard to accept.

"It's how I would expect his father to look," she said, looking at Hall. "Does that make sense?"

He nodded.

Hearing Roxhard and Urit step closer, Hall and Caryn moved back to stand next to Jackoby at the arched entry to the room. It was not a crypt or tomb. There was no body to entomb. Hall didn't know what to call the space.

Roxhard stood in front of the statue, eye to eye with the carved image of his father. Or what the game had created to be Roxhard's father. Or had taken an existing NPC and altered to fit Roxhard's image. Hall stopped pursuing those thoughts. Too much unknown.

All that mattered was that in Sky Realms Online, Dern Stonefire was Roxhard's father.

Reaching out, Roxhard removed one of his gauntlets. He lay his hand on the stone ones of the statue, flesh on stone.

Bowing his head, Roxhard spoke quietly. Too softly for Hall to hear.

Whatever was said was private anyway.

Raising his head to look into the statue's eyes, Roxhard stepped back. Hall thought he saw a flicker of movement in the eyes of the statue, a quick blink, but it had to be a trick of the flickering torchlight.

Without a body, the Stonefire Dwarves built a statue to honor Dern

Stonefire. By visiting, Roxhard has done what is needed to lay the spirit of his father to rest. Dern is at peace with his ancestors.

THE FINAL REST

Accompany Roxhard to the Stonefire Crypts and lay the spirit of his father to rest 1/1

Accompany Roxhard to the Amberbar Crypts and lay the spirit of his mother to rest 0/1

Rewards: +200 Stonefire Clan Reputation; +25 Experience

————

They stopped on the cliff outside the Stonefire Crypt, looking down into the Valley of the Ancients. The sun had set, the moon high, casting its light down into the massive graveyard. So deep, the valley floor was mostly covered in shadow, the light hitting the taller hills and mausoleums.

"We know of at least two weapons that were stolen," Urit stated, patting his magical pouch. "Ye can be sure there are more."

Hall stepped to the edge, eyes following the paths, searching the darkest shadows under the groves of trees. He thought he saw movement, short and staggering motions. Another trick of the eyes and light, or were there Undead down in the Valley?

Combination of both, he thought.

His eyes roamed to the mountain and the ridge. They could make it to the ridge and find a place to camp for the night. In the dark. Or go down into the Valley and try to make it across to the tower on the other side. With the possibility of Undead.

"Will it be safe to stay in the entry chamber?" Hall asked Urit, motioning to the Crypt behind them.

"Aye," Urit answered, already turning to walk back in.

"Now that the Ax is back. He's supposed to spend the night anyway," he said and pointed at Roxhard. "Even if Brignir accepted him without it." He chuckled, clapping Roxhard on the shoulder, pulling the other Dwarf into the dark entry chamber.

Hall was the last to enter. He paused before stepping over the threshold, looking up into the night sky. A small form flew across the face of the moon, a lone screech through the night. Hall smiled. Pike had healed up nicely from the fight with the higher level Dragonhawk. Most of the burned feathers had grown back. He had picked up a scar along the orange scales on his chest. The impression Hall got through their bond was that Pike was proud of it. A mark of his fight against a stronger enemy, a fight that he had not won but not lost either.

Inside the entry hall of the crypt, the others had spread out their bedrolls. No fire but they didn't seem to mind. Caryn had relit her torch, placing it in one of the brackets mounted to the walls.

"I'm jealous that you all can see in the dark," she said, chuckling, as she lit another torch and set it in a nearby bracket on the other side of them, framing them in light.

"Where is the Amberbar Crypt?" Hall asked Urit as he took his own bedroll out of his pack.

It had been a surprise to find all their gear remaining in Iron's camp. Nothing had been stolen. Even when the Army had left, not a single item had been disturbed.

"Off the main path," Urit answered, ripping a piece of jerky apart. "We'll pass the trail on the way back. Not out of the way at all." He paused, glancing quickly at Roxhard. "It's not much of a Crypt. Not really," he said with a shrug. "Not like this. The Amberbar's werenae no Stonefires if ye catch my meaning."

Hall nodded. Even Dwarf Halls had different levels of society.

"It was a bit of a scandal when Dern Stonefire wed Carli Amberbar," Urit continued. "They had never been a large Clan. Good crafters and miners but never rose high in the ranks."

"Had to be love," Caryn said cheerfully. They all looked at her. "That's usually the reason someone goes below their social class. True love."

Urit laughed.

"Probably," he replied. "There were some that accused her of bewitching ol' Dern. Making him love her so she could become a Stonefire." He shook his head. "Weren't true, of course. Ma always said that just had to see them together and knew it werenae true."

Hall glanced at Roxhard, seeing his Dwarven friend smile. He didn't talk about his mother much, just that she had loved him deeply, and Roxhard never talked about his father. His real father. Hall wondered why that was and knew it would not be a good story.

None of them stayed up that much later past eating.

For once Hall didn't bother posting any sentries or watch. He still woke up, used to doing it multiple times a night, but there was a sense of peace in the Crypt now. He knew nothing would harm them.

He was still surprised by the notification he received when waking up.

You have received a full night's rest. All Vitality has been restored. The spirits of the Stonefire Ancestors have watched over you through the night. Thankful for the return of the ancestral weapon, they have granted you a boon. +5 HEALTH for Five Hours. +5 VITALITY for Five Hours.

CHAPTER THIRTY-EIGHT

THEY HAD EASILY PASSED BY THE PATH THE FIRST TIME WALKING through the Valley of the Ancients. Small, overgrown on the sides, not that well maintained. It had been easy to miss. Hall would have walked right past it if Urit hadn't known where they were going.

Pointing out the path, he looked a little embarrassed. It wasn't the embarrassment of showing something below their station, but the embarrassment that it existed in such condition. Someone should have maintained better care of the path that led to the Amberbar Crypt.

The Clan was no more, which explained some of the problem. But there were still honored dead buried at the end of the path. Axestorm Hall should have done more to maintain it.

It was a short path, only about a hundred feet. Tall trees and overgrown hedges lined the sides. The Crypt itself was small. A small pyramid, a square entry built off the front with a single door. The blocks of the building were a dull brown, rectangular, with no carvings. Two statues stood to either side of the door, carved from the same material as the pyramid. Hall knew the stone was not amber but just colored to resemble the material that had given the clan their name. Carved into the door was a large metal bar with a sun rising behind it, the symbol of the Amberbars.

As he got closer Hall could see chunks of amber embedded in each statue's eyes. Dwarves dressed in plate armor, holding a shield and a one-handed hammer. Nearly identical. There was a different style to the statues. Not as detailed as others Hall had seen. The work was still excellent, the features of the Dwarves and the lines of the armor, but they just looked different. Hall thought he liked these better.

Urit motioned Roxhard to the door. Looking from Hall to the others, somewhat nervously, Roxhard walked forward. He grasped the round handle to the door, carved from amber, and pulled. There was some resistance, the door hadn't been opened in decades. Setting his feet, grabbing the ring with both hands, Roxhard pulled. With a grinding noise, stone against stone, the door pulled out an inch. Then two and finally a couple of feet. Enough for Roxhard to enter.

Without looking back, he stepped into the dark opening.

"Are you coming?" he asked, looking over his shoulder at them.

"This be for ye alone," Urit replied.

Roxhard nodded, looking deeper into the Crypt. He took another step and stopped.

"Hall?" he asked, not looking back. "Would you please come with me."

Pike stretched his wings, flapping and pushing off from Hall's shoulder. He flew the short distance, landing on top of the square section of the crypt, settling down. Reaching up over his shoulder, pulling his spear from the harness. He handed it to Jackoby and followed Roxhard into the Amberbar Crypt.

There was no entry chamber, just a wide set of stairs that led down. Roxhard was waiting just inside, still looking nervous. Hall would have thought meeting the spirit of Brignir Stonefire would have made Roxhard nervous. It hadn't. But this was.

Neither spoke as they walked down the stairs.

Hall pulled a torch from his pouch, quickly lighting it.

The walls of the stairwell were smooth, made of the same blocks at the exterior. He ran his leather-gloved hand along the surface. The joints were still tight, no block shifted out of place, or heavily cracked. Hall was surprised he didn't have to duck, the ceiling a foot or so above his head. He reached up and touched it, running his fingers along the tightly packed stones.

They didn't descend long, the stairs ending in a large open room. It was bigger than the pyramid above, but not by much. Open with no columns or supports. Numerous niches were cut into the walls, the resting places of the majority of the Amberbars. A series of sarcophagi were lined up in the middle of the room. Hall could see the shape of a weapon on top of the middle one, a one-handed weapon.

But what drew the eye was the statue in front of the middle sarcophagus.

A Dwarven female. Not dressed in armor but in pants and a work apron, sleeves of her woolen shirt pulled up, wearing leather gloves. Her long hair was done up in a bun, two braids hanging over her shoulders. She was smiling, one arm raised and holding a small carving in the palm of her hand.

Carli Amberbar.

Hall wondered who had carved it. Like the Stonefires had done for Dern, with nobody to intern, they had built a statue of the lost Carli. It was not a style similar to the ones above. This was more detailed, reminding Hall of the statue of Dern. Had the Stonefires carved it?

Roxhard took a hesitant step off the stairs and onto the floor of the crypt. His foot touched stone, and a blue mist rose, swirling around the statue. Hall couldn't see where the mist came from, it appeared to just seep out of the stone of Carli's statue.

As they watched, the mist started to take shape. It spiraled before the statue, widening. First, an arm appeared, then legs, the other arm, chest, and finally the head. Hall gasped as he saw the ghostly form of Carli Amberbar.

She was smiling, looking at Roxhard.

The Dwarf had stopped, unable to move.

"Hall, it's my mom," he said in a choked voice, hand reaching out. "It's really my mom," he cried and ran forward.

Roxhard fell to his knees in front of the ghost, crying loudly.

He held out his hands, and the spirit reached out. Her fingers wrapped around his, not solid, somewhat merging into his hands. Her smile was soft, proud, and Hall thought he saw tears falling down her cheeks as well.

"My son," she said, her voice gentle, loving. "How I have missed you."

"Mom," Roxhard cried. "I'm sorry. I didn't want to leave you but…"

"Hush," Carli Amberbar said. "You did nothing wrong. I am proud of you. Always remember that."

"I miss you."

"And I you. Always. But you are here for a reason."

"A reason," Roxhard asked, looking up at the spirit. She smiled down at him.

"Yes. You have much to do, my son, my champion."

The ghost of Carli leaned down, kissing Roxhard on his forehead. Somehow the kiss was solid. She looked up at Hall, her eyes not as soft.

"You have much to do, and it is all important to the future of this world," she said. "I wish I could tell you more, but I cannot. All I can ask is that you look after my son."

"I will," Hall said.

Carli nodded.

Her hands were removed from Roxhard's. He looked up at her, reaching for her as she started to fade.

"I love you, my son," her voice said, floating across the room as the last of the blue glow faded. "No matter where you are. Always."

Roxhard remained kneeling, looking at where the spirit had been.

QUEST COMPLETE!

Roxhard has visited the Amberbar Crypts to lay the spirit of his mother to rest but it appears her spirit has helped him.

THE FINAL REST

Accompany Roxhard to the Stonefire Crypts and lay the spirit of his father to rest 1/1

Accompany Roxhard to the Amberbar Crypts and lay the spirit of his mother to rest 1/1

Rewards: +200 Stonefire Clan Reputation; +25 Experience

You are now KNOWN and FRIENDLY to the Stonefire Clan

"It's was her," he said. "I'm not crazy. It was my mom. As a Dwarf. Not some coded NPC." His voice was happy. Even as he still cried, Roxhard was happy. "It was her eyes."

Did he really mean what it sounded like? Hall thought. If the game had somehow managed to recreate Roxhard's real mother in game form, that was unnecessarily cruel. But was it? Hall looked at the still crying Roxhard. He was happy. For the first time since Hall had known him, it seemed the heavy weight of being trapped in the game had lifted from Roxhard's shoulders. Since day one, he had missed his mother, had been nearly overwhelmed by being fourteen in a world of adults.

Now it seemed he had found closure of some kind.

But how had the game copied Roxhard's mother? If what he said was true, and Hall had no reason to doubt it. He would have known his own mother anywhere. It seemed that the developers, Electronic Storm, had copied Roxhard's mother when it created Carli Amberbar. Had turned her into a Dwarf like they had Roxhard. Was such a thing possible? Apparently, it was.

And what did she mean by his being important to the future of this world?

Him?

That made no sense. He was no one special. And how was he important? What future?

Hall thought about the Cerulean Regency and the notes he had found. The Norns were on Huntley looking for these Champions, whatever they were. Was that tied into what Carli Amberbar was hinting at?

Was he a Champion? And if so, what did that even mean?

She had called Roxhard 'her champion'. Was that related or just a mothers love?

Hall didn't want to think of the implications. He didn't want to be important. He just wanted to be himself. It was bad enough that he had the responsibility of Skara Brae and the people that now, and would, call it home. He had chosen that and would do his best to be worthy of it. But important to all of Hankarth and Sky Realms Online?

That was not something he wanted.

But if it was true?

There was nothing he could do about it now. Not without more information. And that would have to come when it came. For now, he had Skara Brae to worry about, not Hankarth.

"You good?" he said to Roxhard, wanting to push the thoughts of a larger role in the world away.

"Yeah," Roxhard said, pushing himself up from the ground. He turned around, smiling. The Dwarf looked better. More mature. Like a weight had been lifted. "I'm good."

He walked toward the steps, one last glance over his shoulder at the statue of his mother.

———

"I don't know where the Forgecrush and Understone Clan crypts are," Urit told Hall as they stood on the ridge looking down into the Valley of the Ancients.

The others had already gone into the tower that stood vigil over the Valley at the end of the road from Axestorm Hall. It was only the afternoon, but they all felt better staying in the tower and getting a full day's walk in back to Greystone Watch. None wanted to camp out on the mountainside.

"Even if I did, they be anything like what had happened to the Stonefire Crypt, I don't think we'd want to enter."

"Agreed," Hall said.

The Valley looked peaceful. Beautiful in its way. Their first trip to the Stonefire Crypt could have gone wrong right from the start, but they had gotten lucky. Hall suspected that having a member of the Stonefires, two members now, with them had been the only thing that saved them from the wrath of vengeful spirits. He had no desire to test that theory by venturing into other Clan's crypts.

The Dwarves could do that.

He hoped there weren't more weapons stolen but had a feeling there were. It was a smart plan by the Norns, who he knew had to be the ones to contact the Unclanned with the idea. Arm the Storvgarde with magical weapons to aid them in their war with Iron's Army. Make the Storvgarde stronger and indebted to the Norns.

Part of him hoped that the other Storvgarde tribes could, or would, unite against Iron and defeat the powerful faction

leader. How long could this go on before attracting the attention of the Jarl? Iron was fighting a small handful of clans right
now but how would he fare against the forces of the Jarl?

Hall didn't want it to come to that. So many lives would be
needlessly lost. It would though, he knew. It was inevitable.
Iron would not give up.

He sighed.

This new version of the game was getting complicated.

Much like life.

CHAPTER THIRTY-NINE

THE RECEPTION THEY GOT WHEN RETURNING TO STONEFIRE Hall was much different than the first time. There was no coldness. They were welcomed with what Hall thought of as eagerness. The reception hall was filled, almost every inch. Somehow word of their return had reached the Stonefires long before they had even entered Axestorm Hall.

Matron Lydi sat on her throne, watching them approach down the aisle left by the Dwarves watching. There had to be at least a hundred, maybe more.

Urit was smiling broadly. Roxhard was not smiling, but he wasn't nervous either. He walked with his head high, proudly. They came to a stop at the bottom of the steps. Hall glanced at the male and female Dwarves again standing off to the side. Urit's elder brother and sister. She, Hall had never learned her name, now looked somewhat accepting. He, the heir to the Clan, didn't look happy.

"Ye have returned," Matron Lydi said. "Long after we had thought ye would."

"Yer pardons, Ma," Urit said, still beaming. "We got waylaid along the way."

Matron Lydi's eyebrow rose in a question.

"Something for less," Urit started and glanced around the crowded room.

His mother nodded, still curious, but understanding his meaning.

"And what of our young friend Roxhard?" she asked, looking toward him. "Are ye a Stonefire?"

Before Roxhard could answer, Urit spoke up, unable to contain himself.

"He summoned the spirit of Brignir Stonefire while in battle," Urit said, his voice filled with awe.

The entire room seemed to gasp in surprise. Voices started talking, whispering, the noise level rising. Lydi leaned forward, looking from Roxhard to Urit and back. Settling back in her chair once more, the elderly Dwarf looked around the room.

"Enough," she said, her voice not loud buy carrying over the noise. Almost instantly the entire reception room, all hundred Dwarves, stopped talking. "It seems there is much to discuss but first..."

Matron Lydi stood up. She touched the head of the large hammer that leaned against the chair, glanced at her two children and descended the short set of stairs. She was shorter than Hall would have thought, a full head below Roxhard. Stopping in front of him, she took his hands in hers and looked up into his eyes. She smiled as Roxhard leaned his head down. Matron Lydi stood up on her tiptoes and lightly kissed him on the forehead.

"Welcome home, nephew."

The entire room erupted in cheers.

———

QUEST COMPLETE!

Roxhard has been accepted into the Stonefire Clan as determined by
their ancestor and Clan patriarch, Brignir Stonefire.

A CLAN'S HISTORY II
Inform Matrol Lydi of Brignir's decision 1/1
Reward: +200 Stonefire Clan Reputation; +25 Experience

QUEST COMPLETE!
Roxhard has proven himself to be a true Dwarf of the Stonefire Clan.
He is now a fully accepted member of the Clan with all rights and
obligations that brings.
A DWARF IS A DWARF NO MATTER WHAT II
Assist Roxhard in proving himself to Matron Lydi and the Stonefires
1/1
Reward: +200 Stonefire Clan reputation; +25 Experience

Hall finally looked at the notifications. They had come right after Matron Lydi's acknowledgment of Roxhard being a Stonefire, but he had been so caught up in the moment that he hadn't bothered to read it when it flashed across his vision.

He had lost sight of Roxhard, his Dwarf friend being swallowed up by the sea of well-wishers. The entire room had surged toward Roxhard, pushing Hall and the rest of his friends out of the way. They had retreated back to the far end of the room, the balcony overlooking the lake, the roar of the waterfall loud. The celebration had gone on for a long time before a guard had found them, directing them to another room just off the main corridor. A smaller reception room.

There they had been given food and drink while they waited for their hosts.

"I apologize," Matron Lydi said thirty minutes later when she entered the room with Urit and Roxhard. "It is not every day that a lost member of the Clan returns to us," she added, looking at Roxhard fondly.

"Understandable," Hall said, setting down the plate of food he had been eating.

"My son tells me there is much to discuss," Matron Lydi stated as she sat down at the end of the long stone table that dominated the windowless room.

Tapestries hung along the wall, statues in the corner. Hall and the others all took seats.

"Where to begin," Hall said, looking around at the others.

"Tell me all," Matron Lydi told him.

So Hall did.

He left out the parts about Iron being a Player. He wasn't sure how to explain it to her and was afraid she would get the typical NPC blank stare when the subject came up. It was enough that she knew Iron was a threat.

Her eyes grew hard when they got to the stolen ancestral weapon. Hall saw her hands grip the stone table, fearful it would crack. Lydi kept silent. Hall could tell she wanted to speak, to ask questions, and to curse, but knew it best to wait until the end.

The others, especially Roxhard and Urit, spoke up now and then. Adding to Hall's story, filling in spots he had missed. Inside the room, Hall had no concept of the passage of time. No windows to look out into the world and watch the sun as it journeyed through the sky. It felt like hours when he finally stopped talking.

Matron Lydi was silent for a while, staring across the room at one of the tapestries, lost in thought and absorbing all that they had said.

"The Unclanned have gone too far," she said at last, her voice angry. "Ye are sure of the other thefts?" she asked Urit.

He nodded.

"We have recovered two other weapons. The mace of the Forgecrush and the hammer of the Understone."

QUEST COMPLETE!

Together with Urit, you have told Matron Lydi of the Stonefires about the stolen artifact weapons. She will take that knowledge to the king and the other clans.

THE UNCLANNED THEFTS

Inform Matron Lydi of the Stonefires about the thefts 1/1
Reward: +100 Stonefire Clan reputation, +50 experience

"The Unclanned are a blight," Matron Lydi cursed. "We should have dealt with them more firmly. Instead, we let them band together. They are Dwarves. Used to be of Axestorm Hall and we let that blind us." She shook her head sadly. "But it is no more concern of ye and yers," she said, looking down the table at Hall. "We thank ye fer the recovery of the three artifacts, but from here on, it is a Dwarven matter."

Hall nodded. He had expected as much. In the Pre-Glitch game, a new quest chain would have activated, sending Hall in search of the Unclanned. It would have ended in a Dungeon with him having to recover the stolen weapons. But not in this new Post-Glitch world. His part in that was done.

For now, at least.

"Understood," Hall told her.

Matron Lydi nodded her head. She looked at Roxhard, still smiling but not as deep. Hall thought he saw some worry in her sharp eyes.

"Now there is the matter of the line of succession," Lydi said.

Everyone around the table caught what she said but Roxhard. His eyes looked at the tapestries and statues, studying them, trying to understand what they depicted. The history of his Clan. His history. He realized no one was talking, all eyes were on him.

"What?" he said, shocked, finally registering what Matron Lydi had said. "What do you mean?"

"Yer father, Dern Stonefire, was my brother," Lydi said calmly. She glanced at Urit. "This ye know. But what ye don't realize is that he was my older brother."

Roxhard's eyes widened. He looked down the table at Hall, almost in a panic.

"I…" he started to say but stopped, not sure what there was to say.

Lydi held up a calming hand. She chuckled.

"It doesn't mean quite what ye think," she told Roxhard. "Yer father would have become the leader of the Clan if he had lived, and ye would have been his successor. But I am now the leader and will remain so. The question becomes who will follow me."

Roxhard glanced over at Urit, who was smiling.

"Never was going to be me," the other Dwarf said. "No worries there. I'm the youngest, remember?"

"I would become…" Roxhard started and stopped.

"Could," Matron Lydi replied. "If ye chose to make yer claim." She leaned forward, hands clasped before her, studying Roxhard. "It would be complicated and maybe not end in yer favor. The Clan could be split. Anger between those that should be clan brothers. In other Clans, this has even led to warfare within the Clan."

Roxhard looked at Hall, who just nodded. He would support any decision. Turning back to Matron Lydi, Roxhard sat straighter.

"I don't want that," Roxhard said. "I don't want to rule anything." Lydi nodded, satisfied and happy with his answer. Hall suspected it was the answer Lydi had thought Roxhard would give. "I'm a Stonefire, but I'm not," Roxhard admitted as he continued, eyes once again on the tapestries. "Not yet, maybe not ever. Just having the name doesn't make it true. I want it to be," he said, looking up at Lydi. She nodded. "But I don't think my place is here." He glanced at Hall. A reminder of the conversation with the spirit of Carli Amberbar. "Not yet."

"I thought as much," Lydi said with a smile. "I am glad. Not that ye will not be here with us," she added. "But that ye are a true Stonefire and think of yer clan, as new as we are."

"Thank you," Roxhard said.

"That is the pressing business dealt with," Matron Lydi said, leaning back. "And I have been in contact with the Battleforge Shipbuilders. There are a couple more days needed on yer ship," she continued looking down the table at Hall. "Please stay as our guests until it is done."

"Of course," Hall said. He wanted to get home to Skara Brae and Leigh as quickly as possible, but they all needed true rest and the airship. "Thank you."

Lydi stood up, clapping her hands.

"Good," she said, smiling, looking younger. "I believe there is a celebration still going on."

———

"Welcome," Corben Battleforge said loudly.

He stood outside the closed doors to his workshop, the shipyard around him busy. No one looked their way as Hall and the others, along with Urit, walked toward the old shipbuilder. Gerdi stood next to him, smiling, wearing workers' clothes and aprons. Various tools fit in straps and loops in her belt.

Corben looked different from when Hall had first met him days ago. The Battleforge patriarch had looked old, tired, worn out. Now he looked full of life. He was doing what he loved. Building ships.

"Are ye a Stonefire?" Gerdi asked Roxhard.

"Yes," he said and got a clap on the shoulder from Urit.

Matron Lydi's youngest son studied Gerdi, saw her eyes locked on Roxhard, and smiled. He gave his new cousin a harder slap on the same shoulder.

"But yer not staying?" Corben asked.

There was an odd tone to the question. Hall noticed it. A kind of hope.

Roxhard shook his head. "Not now," he answered. "My place is elsewhere."

"Good, good," Corben said, clapping his hands together. "Are ye ready to see what ye bought?"

Hall nodded eagerly. He was excited and worried. The ship that Corben, his sons and his daughter, had built was not what Hall had originally wanted. He wasn't sure what the final product was going to be. Would he be disappointed? Would the ship serve his purposes?

Corben made a shooing motion with his hands, pushing them away from the doors. Gerdi walked back to the large iron doors, taking a hammer off her belt. She slammed the small hammer against the metal, the sound loud and ringing, quickly stepping back to join her father and the others. Hall noticed that she squeezed her way into standing next to Roxhard.

The great doors slowly swung open, soundlessly moving on greased rails set into the ground of the shipyard. The shop was dark inside, shadowed, as more and more of it was revealed. There were no lights on within the space, making it dark. A bit of showmanship to add to the moment of reveal. Hall could see a darker shape against the shadows. Two Yaks stepped out into the light, thick ropes tied to the harnesses the creatures wore. One of Corben's sons, Hall wasn't sure which one it was, held the reins of the two creatures, pulling them out into the open yard.

Hall looked past the animals and at the ship they towed. The design was similar to the plans that Hall had found, that had first led him to the Battleforges, just on a smaller scale.

Built of a dark wood and iron plates, the bow was sharply angled, the tip of a ballista visible. Not long, only thirty feet or so, the ship widened out in the middle before tapering back to a square aft. Two rotatable engines were mounted port and starboard of the single-story deck mounted above the main. Two stairs led up to the pilot's house. A single mast stood in the middle of the open main deck. By the low overall height of the ship, Hall estimated it to have only one level, maybe two, below the main deck. Portholes lined the sides, rectangular with plates covering the openings.

It wasn't the prettiest ship that Hall had ever seen, but it looked sleek. There was a stark beauty to it, a unique charm.

"What do ye think?" Corben asked, pride in his voice.

"I love it," Hall replied.

CHAPTER FORTY

QUEST COMPLETE!

Battleforge Shipbuilders have completed your airship, and it is ready for you to take possession.

A SHIP OF OUR OWN II

Claim ownership of an airship 1/1
Rewards: Airship, +100 Experience

"WHAT ARE YE GOING TO NAME HER?" CORBEN ASKED AS HE led Hall around the ship, giving a tour. The shipbuilder pointed out features that Hall, no expert on ships and their operation, quickly forgot about. Even with his limited knowledge, Hall knew there was something special about the ship. It was more streamlined, in design and controls. Corben said the ship required less crew.

"Sometimes it takes a bit before the name comes to ye," Corben added. "Got to get to know her."

Hall just smiled. He already had the name.

The *Ridgerunner*, the name Hall had given the ship, sailed through the blue. The engines, rotated at an angle, propelling the small ship upwards. The single sail billowed in the wind that pushed it forward. Debris islands floated by, larger ones in the distance as the ship's new pilot kept a steady course. The pilot was smiling broadly, hands on the controls, enjoying the feel of the ship.

Gerdi Battleforge whooped, her long hair blowing in the wind. The *Ridgerunner's* pilot was a wild one.

Hall smiled, enjoying watching her excitement. She was a good pilot. So far. A little quick, excitable, but solid. He had been surprised at the level of experience the young Dwarf possessed. She knew what she was doing, had flown ships before, but never served on crews. He had been just as surprised at the expertise of Corben's three sons. The triplets —Borden, Norden, and Korden—served as the ship's crew and engineers, and they knew their tasks well. In addition to the Battleforges, there were two other Dwarves, old friends of Corbens that had served on ships with him in the past. They were the true veteran experience on board the *Ridgerunner*. Gorid Stoneglare was the Captain of the ship, a grizzled Dwarf with graying hair and beard. An old sailor had captained his own merchant vessel for years. Herj Onyxshard was the other. Another aging Dwarf of gray hair and beard. Another veteran sailor.

Hall wondered what had happened to both Dwarves to put them in a position where the *Ridgerunner* was their only option. It had to be something, Hall knew. Corben had told him about the experience both had and with that much, they could have served on any ship they wanted. So why the *Ridgerunner*? Hall wasn't sure he wanted crew with mysterious backgrounds, possible future problems, but he didn't have much choice.

Corben Battleforge had asked it of him.

"What are ye going to do for a crew?" Corben asked as the tour of the ship continued.

Hall ran his ungloved hand across the smooth wooden railing. How had the Battleforges managed to build the entire ship in just over a week? How much help had Corben called in?

"I'm not sure," Hall admitted. "There has to be some for hire."

"There are," Corben said, stopping and turning to face Hall. He looked up at the taller Half-Elf. "And there be some good ones for hire, but might I make a suggestion?"

Hall nodded.

The old Dwarf looked around, seeing no one near. He sighed.

"Ye have to know that ye are getting a huge discount on the ship," he started. "Even with the jewels, gold and the donation from the Stonefires."

Again, Hall nodded. He hadn't been sure but had assumed. He had also assumed it was all part of his quest chain. The game seemed to be leading him toward getting an airship. Corben seemed to be leading toward a new quest.

"Ye know a little about our recent troubles," Corben continued. He sounded a little dejected, still proud, but embarrassed. "The main reason I took on yer contract. We needed the coin, even if it did not pay for the ship."

Corben paused, eyes looking toward the rear of the ship where his three sons were showing the engines to Jackoby and Caryn. They were explaining the finer points of the engineering in their odd triple way of talking. Their audience of two was not understanding. Jackoby frustratingly so. Caryn just smiled, humoring the Dwarves.

"I can pay," Hall said. "Over time. I do not want to cheat you of what you deserve."

Turning back, Corben shook his head.

"Ye misunderstand, boyo," he said. "There's something else I be wanting from ye."

Hall could tell that whatever he wanted to ask, it was hard on the proud old Dwarf.

"Ye be needing a crew and I be needing to get me family out of Axestorm," Corben said, forcing it all out quickly. Now that his request was out, the Dwarf found it easier to talk. "Honor is everything to a Dwarf and once lost, it benext to impossible to get it back. Us Battleforges will be forever tainted by my foolishness. Me boys and daughter, they need a fresh start."

Hall didn't reply, just watched Corben, letting the old Dwarf talk.

"They be a qualified crew and the best engineers in all of Axestorm," Corben said proudly. "I know a couple old veteran sailors to round out the crew." He stopped, locking eyes with Hall. Waiting. Not pushing.

It didn't take Hall long to find the answer.

"If you vouch for them," he said, smiling as the old Dwarf's eyes lit up, a weight lifted.

"Thank ye," Corben said, reaching out and clasping Hall's hand as a fellow warrior. "Who knows, maybe I just might move the business up to that village of yers. Skara Brae, ye said it was? On Edin?"

———

It was hard to tell how happy Roxhard was with Gerdi being part of the *Ridgerunner's* crew. That meant she would be with them a lot. Would be living in Skara Brae. After a week of travel, the young female Dwarf spending every free moment she could find near Roxhard, even he was realizing the extent of her interest in him.

Hall found it funny. Roxhard didn't know what to do or how to act. The more nervous he was, the more it spurred Gerdi on. She treated it like a game.

"Ye just aren't used to a real woman," Hall heard her say once. "Been around them humans. No Dwarf women."

Hall just hoped that she would go easy on him.

He was also glad for an uneventful voyage up from Huntley to Edin.

Gerdi brought them in from the west side, taking them around Cumberland, far enough out to avoid the traffic around Silverpeak Keep. The mountains became familiar just north of the city. He could see the Silverpeak itself, the mountain shining in the sun. A bright spot against the gray of the Thunder Growls. He had walked down from Skara Brae to the city on the land side and flown up along the sky side, watching the mountains. He knew the peaks, and he knew when they were close to Breakridge Meadow.

The gap, the break between the Thunder Growls and Frost Tips, was visible just ahead. A dark line where the continuous mountains ended. No details, just shadows marking the location. As they got closer, Hall could see the Thunder Growls curling in toward the meadow, the grass of the meadow itself and the steps in the first mountain of the Frost Tips.

Gerdi took a firm grip on the controls of the *Ridgerunner*. She had been warned to expect fierce winds, but it still caught her by surprise. The small ship bucked and shifted, buffeted by the winds. The engines groaned as they rotated, the exhaust ends pointing up to push the ship lower to the ground.

Hall stood in the bow, the medium-sized ballista next to him, no bolt loaded, hands on the rail. More of the island was revealed as the Thunder Growls twisted away. The long grass of the meadow blowing in the wind. The grass-covered mounds that were the roofs of the sunken village.

He could see activity in the meadow. Small figures moving

about the roofs of the village. Two large animals, guided by two ranchers,pulling a metal plow as they worked one of the large fields.

Hall shook his head, not fully sure what he was seeing.

The *Ridgerunner* turned into the meadow, heading away from the sky. It crossed over the land, the shadow falling across the grass. They were low enough that Hall could see the ranchers and the animals looking up at the ship as it passed overhead. The two Firbolgs went back to their work, pulling the reins of the Alcest. Grunting, the beasts dug their large hooved feet into the soft dirt and stepped forward, the metal plow digging into the earth.

"Good," Jackoby's voice said from behind, the Firbolg walking up to the rail. "They arrived."

Hall looked up at him in surprise. Jackoby smiled, one of the few that Hall had ever seen from the Warden.

"What? How?"

Jackoby just laughed and walked away.

To their right, the peaks of the Thunder Growls sloped down to the meadow. Still tall, but not as towering, forming a wall that contained the woods known as Greenheight Vale and the protected dock.

The completed airship dock.

Wooden platforms sat on a system of beams, columns, and cross braces. Thick wooden logs, wooden planking. Space for three medium-sized airships to dock at once. There were no ships there now, but Gerdi adjusted the *Ridgerunner's* course to bring the ship in toward one of the spaces. As the ship turned, the bow pointing toward the docks and the now visible trees of Greenheight, Hall took one last look out over the meadow.

And the three figures walking out of the village with the giant Craobh behind them.

———

Before the Ridgerunner had settled in its berth, Pike had lifted off Hall's shoulder and disappeared into the sky, his screech saying he was happy to be home. Before the lines were thrown over the side and the ship tied off, Hall had jumped out, leaving most of his gear still on board. The three figures and the Craobh were making their way across the meadow toward the dock, moving quickly. Two were robed, the brown hoods pulled over their heads. The third, the one in the middle, wore a cloak with the hood up, a small and shaggy cow walking beside.

Hall knew who the center person was.

He ran down the steep plank ramp, booted feet hitting the grass. He slowed to a fast walk, watching the figures as they all closed the distance. The Craobh, a walking oak, towered over them all. Its steps shook the ground, the loud thuds echoing across the meadow, carried by the wind.

The center figure increased the pace, closing with Hall quickly. He recognized the leathers. A skirt, the bottom end angled, the sides stitched, a halter top, light blue tattoos along her arms visible through the cloak that billowed in the wind. Tight red curls were visible through the dark green hood.

Hall smiled as Leigh walked closer. Then she stopped, twenty feet away. His steps faltered, wondering why she wasn't moving.

She didn't say anything, just reached up and grabbed the ends of the hood. Slowly she pulled it back. Hall saw the beautiful face, the green eyes, the red hair.

And the antlers.

CHAPTER FORTY-ONE

"Do they hurt?" Hall asked.

He pushed himself up from the bed, leaning on his side, looking down at Leigh who lay next to him. She reached up and touched one of the antlers now growing out of her forehead. They were small, only a couple inches long and splitting into three points.

"No," she answered. "I know they're there, but they don't seem to affect my balance or anything like that." Leigh pulled herself up, leaning against the headboard. "It does make it a bit awkward as I'm not used to them yet, and they're still growing."

Hall chuckled, trying not to reach up and rub the spots on his head from where the bone antlers had hit him during the night. They would take some getting used to.

"Do they have something to do with being the Custodian?"

He remembered that the corrupted Custodian of the Grove, that Leigh had replaced, Vertoyi, had antlers. One of which had been broken off. But Hall had always assumed them to be unique to Vertoyi. He hadn't thought Leigh would grow antlers.

Neither had she.

"Yeah," she replied. "I hadn't thought about it when accepted." She turned to look at him, shy. "I wasn't sure what you would think. If you would still…"

Hall leaned over, twisting his head to avoid the antlers, and kissed her.

————

Together they walked out of the nearly finished Inn. Hall was amazed at how much work had progressed in the time he had been gone. There was still a long way to go, but most of the buildings had the exterior walls repaired or replaced. Valedale gnomes were hard at work and the high-pitched voice of Duncant could be heard on the other side of the village yelling something.

"Seo and Bealee arrived about a week ago," Leigh said as they walked hand in hand. "Sent by the Druids Council to assist me."

Hall had met the two briefly last night when the *Ridgerunner* had landed. A Gael and a Wood Elf. Both young. Hall suspected that Seo was a Player but hadn't spent enough time to be sure.

"Grayknot was sent along as protection," Leigh continued, referring to the large Craobh.

The two young Druids, male and female, had been sent back to the Grove, but the walking tree had refused. He sat just outside of town, waiting on Leigh. Pike had taken an instant liking to Grayknot, perching in his upper branches. Originally happy to have the dragonhawk back, Angus the cow was a little jealous that Pike had found a new place to rest. But he did enjoy laying down around Grayknot's thick bark legs as the Craobh sat on the ground, waiting patiently and unmoving, head bowed with long branching limbs moving slowly through the tall grass of the meadow.

Along with the Druids and Craobh, there were Jackoby's clanmates from the Brownpaw Firbolgs. Aside from the Valedale Gnomes, the Green Ember Firbolgs were Skara Brae's only allies. So far.

He hadn't expected Ranchers though. Jackoby had sent a message off to his mother in Green Ember. It had gone from the post office in Axestorm Hall to the Season's Goose Inn and from there to Green Ember when the latest carts of supplies made the journey to the Firbolg village. The message had been simple and Yarbole, his mother and clanchief of the Brownpaw, had sent the two Ranchers and some beasts of burden. Harklin and Georwin. An older Firbolg and younger apprentice.

Two Druids, two Ranchers, and six Dwarven members of an Airship Crew. Ten new citizens for Skara Brae.

He hadn't done it last night, but now it was time to make it official.

"Let's get everyone together."

———

Hall didn't need to be at the Settlement Stone, which was outside the building that was serving as the Town Hall. He could have gathered them inside that building. The first floor had enough space, but Grayknot would not have been able to come in, and Hall felt it important to include the Craobh. So he had them all join him up on the meadow, just to the side of the road that came down from the ridge and sloped below ground into the ring road of the village.

He stood with his back to one of the grass-covered roofs, Leigh next to him, Pike on his shoulder and Angus next to her. They all stood near, facing him. Roxhard with Gerdi close. The other Dwarves around them. Duncant next to the Dwarves, the Bodin's eyes looking past to where the Valedale Gnomes were still working. Caryn and Jackoby, the two Firbolg Ranchers behind. Hitchly the farmer and her mother, Dinah. Who seemed to stand awfully close to Brient, the former Silverpeak Guard and current Sheriff of Skara Brae. Timmin, the town's Administrator, stood slightly away from the others. Looking impatient and bored. The two Druids were also slightly apart, but on the other side, near the Dwarves. Behind them all towered Grayknot, casting a shadow over the gathering.

Braniff and Garrick, the two high-level Adventurers, that Hall had somehow convinced to come to the village, were off in the mountains. They had stayed near the village like Hall had asked, setting back out to continue exploring just that morning.

The ever-present wind blew in off the sky, crushed between the towering mountains and blown back into the meadow by the Breakridge, the strip of raised land between the peaks that gave the area its name. Tall grass blew, cloaks fluttered. It was warm enough in the sun.

Without a world, Hall mentally opened the Settlement Menu.

Skara Brae Town Stats
Lord: Hall
Status: Ruins 75%
Morale: Productive

Government: N/A
Appointed Officials: Timmin, Administrator
Brient, Sheriff

Population: 14 (Alert: You Have pending citizens required approval)

Production: Carpentry Rank Two - 15%
Farming Rank One - 75%
Ranching Rank One - 50%

Faction: N/A
Allies:Gnomes of Valedale
Brownpaw of Fallen Green
Stonefire Clan of Axestorm Hall
Trade Partners: Stonefire Clan of Axestorm Hall
Battleforge Clan of Axestorm Hall
Enemies: N/A

He noticed that some of the main screen items had changed. Somehow Duncant had gotten to Rank Two in Carpentry and with the Firbolgs, even though they weren't official citizens, their Ranching Rank appeared. The village was closer to no longer being classified as Ruins.

The citizens pending approval notice had been expected and that was where he went. The number of citizens had gone down by one. It had accounted for Sabine betraying them. Hall started to get angry. Her betrayal still hurt, but he pushed those thoughts away. She no longer mattered. The people in front of him were the ones that mattered.

Mentally clicking on the Population tab, it pulled up a new menu.

Across the top was a progress bar labeled *Population: 14/75*. It was only about a quarter full, almost to a third. Below it was a series of tabs. *Settlement Officials, Settlement Crafters, Settlement Militia, Settlement Merchants, Others, Pending Citizens*. He chose the last one, pulling up a list.

Gerdi Battleforge, Level 4 Navigator
ACCEPT CITIZEN?
Norden Battleforge, Level 6 Airship Engineer

ACCEPT CITIZEN?

Borden Battleforge, Level 6 Airship Engineer

ACCEPT CITIZEN?

Korden Battleforge, Level 6 Airship Engineer

ACCEPT CITIZEN?

Gorid Stoneglare, Level 8 Airship Captain

ACCEPT CITIZEN?

Herj Onyxshard, Level 7 Airship Sailor

ACCEPT CITIZEN?

Seo, Level 5 Druid

ACCEPT CITIZEN?

Bealee, Level 5 Druid

ACCEPT CITIZEN?

Herklin of the Brownpaw, Level 6 Rancher

ACCEPT CITIZEN?

Georwin of the Brownpaw, Level 5 Rancher

ACCEPT CITIZEN?

Hall mentally accepted them all. There was no noise, no bright flash of light. The bar along the top of the menu slid a little bit further toward full, and the number changed to 24/75. A new notification flashed across his vision.

Alert! Your Settlement's population has increased past 20. You must designate a form of Government!

He dismissed the warning and mentally tabbed back to the main page. Mentally choosing the Government tab, he brought up the three kinds he could choose from.

Mayoral: The Lord of the Settlement, or chosen representative, is the sole voice of rulership. There can be a council that assists, but they would be advisers only. The Mayor is responsible for all final decisions.

Lord's Council: The Lord and chosen representatives, chosen by election or appointment, make the decisions together. The council has a say in the decisions, but the final decision is up to the Lord. The Lord can follow the council's advice or chose another direction.

Town Council: A council of chosen representatives, chosen by election or appointment, which can but does not need to include the Lord, make all decisions by vote. The majority vote wins and decides the final decision. The Lord can override if they so choose but would most likely not as they appoint the council to run the day to day operations of the town.

Hall already knew which form he wanted. That decision had been made a long time ago, soon after activating the Settlement. He had just been waiting for the right time, and the right population to need it. He mentally clicked on the one he wanted.

You have selected Town Council as the form of government for Skara Brae.

ACCEPT?

With a quick mental choice, a new notification flashed across his vision. A new menu that he assumed would be accessible from the *Government* tab on the main screen. Along the top was written Town Council 2 / 5. Interesting that the maximum number was set. He liked that it was an odd number, meaning there could be no tie votes and figured the maximum number was based off the maximum population. The rest of the page was taken up with roles and where to assign the councilors. Two of the spots were already taken.

Lord of the Settlement: Hall

Settlement Administrator: Timmin
Councilor 3 (set title): N/A
Councilor 4 (set title): N/A
Councilor 5 (set title): N/A

He shifted his gaze, staring past the translucent menus floating before him, looking at the citizens of his village. Who to pick for the other Councilors? Like picking the style of government, filling out the rest of the Council was easy.

Lord of the Settlement: Hall
Settlement Administrator: Timmin
Settlement Sheriff: Brient
Councilor 4 (set title): Dinah
Councilor 5 (set title): Duncant

Hall smiled as he saw both Dinah and Duncant's eyes widen in surprise. They had received the notifications of their new positions. Duncant especially looked unsure. Hall was a little as well. The Carpenter had proven reliable, but there was a reason he had been unGuilded back in Silverpeak Keep. Hall was putting a lot of trust in faith in the Bodin. He hoped he wouldn't be disappointed.

"Welcome to Skara Brae," he said to the assembled group. "Officially."

They didn't cheer or clap. There were some smiles and nods. They had been living in the village already. This had just been a formality.

"There's one more thing," Hall said, looking at Roxhard. "We wanted to wait until we had a name, and we do now."

Going back to the main screen, Hall mentally clicked on the *Faction* tab. A notification popped up.

There is no Faction associated with this Settlement. Do you wish to align an existing Faction with Skara Brae or form a new allied Faction?

Hall smiled as he chose to create a new Faction.

Choose a name for the new Faction _____

He nodded to Roxhard. The Dwarf had been trying to come up with a Guild name for months. Even before they had gotten to Skara Brae. His desire had only increased after activating the Settlement. It wasn't until they were flying back to Skara Brae from Axestorm Hall that the perfect name had come to him.

Roxhard smiled at Hall as he said the name.

"Breakridge Irregulars."

Epilogue

THE SHIP SAILED CLOSE TO THE MOUNTAIN. ROCK ROSE UP, straight and proud, jagged and hard. But the pilot did not care. This close to the edge of the island, the wind that blew across the sky slammed into the mountain, forced back out and buffeted the airship. Growling, the helmsman fought to hold the wheel, keeping the side of the ship a mere dozen feet from the mountain.

A strong gust could slam the ship into the rocks, destroying it. But they kept the small distance, jerky movements of the ship countered by swift turning of the ship's wheel.

Lines flew out from the railing, heavy anchors and grapples attached. They caught purchase against the jagged sides of the mountains and in the flat shelf under the ship. A thin path carved deep into the mountain, leading away and out to the plains. To one end of the shelf was a cave.

Once relatively secure, a rope ladder was hung over the side of the ship. Long and narrow, built of a dark wood inter-spaced with metal plates. Cannons lined the rails, a ballista in the bow and one in the aft on the upper rear deck. Two sails were furled, the spars tilted and tied to the masts. Three engines, two to the sides and one underneath groaned as they fought against the wind.

A lone figure climbed over the rail and onto the swaying ladder. The wind took it, the weight ends not enough to hold it still. Even with the sailors' added weight, it still bucked and swung. The sailor, short and compact with long arms, hung on tight. He didn't look up or the side, just down where he wanted to go. The swaying of the ladder didn't seem to bother him as he climbed down, making sure each foot and grip was secure before making the next movement.

It seemed a long time, but finally his heavy boots touched down on the stone. He stepped away from the ladder which hung dangerously over the edge of the island.

Four feet tall, not bulky but still with mass. Arms that were a little too long, legs a little too short, feet a little too big. Lanky gray hair hung down his craggy face, with an overly large nose, overly large ears poking out from the hair. He had a scraggly beard, the end long and tucked into the leather belt to keep it from blowing in the fierce winds. Dark eyes stared out from beneath a heavy brow and thick eyebrows. He wore leather armor and carried a one-handed hammer in a loop on his belt. A bright red skullcap fit tightly on his large head. It seemed to glow in the afternoon sun.

Corht, Captain of the Duntinic ship the *Roc Reaver*, stood on the edge of the shelf. He looked down, far down, no other islands directly visible beneath him. The height and the view of nothingness below, didn't bother the Duntin, commonly known as Redcaps. His people were pirates. They lived in the sky around the many islands of Hankarth. Feared and respected. The best shipbuilders and sailors in the entire world.

Ruthless, vicious, and fearless.

He turned away from the edge, walking to the cave.

Something was off. He knew it instantly. It had been many months since Corht had last been here. The visits were infrequent, no a set pattern. He only brought the *Roc Reaver* here when there was something to leave behind. His ship had a singular mission, given by the Duntin King himself. Corht didn't understand it, not completely, but it wasn't his place to question the King.

Not when he was able to do what he would be doing anyway. And get rich at the same time.

The *Roc Reaver's* mission was simple.

Raid the small villages on the many islands. But not enough to draw the attention of any of the major kingdoms' armies. Harass. Hit and run.

Scavenge the many wrecks that dotted the many islands. Take what treasure they could find.

Take from any of the airships flying the sky that they could.

They were looking for magic weapons and items. Gems and other high-value items that could be sold anywhere in the world.

What they found they were to leave in this cave. In a special chest that was locked by a Key Map. A map that was given to someone that Corht did not know.

An ally of the Duntin's new allies. A friend of friends.

An allegiance that would lead to more power for the Duntin and an end to their hated cousins, the Dwarves.

The details were no concern of Corht. He got to kill, raid, and pillage. His favorite things to do.

A loud call came from the rail of his ship. He looked up, motioning at the sailor to wait. He didn't want the bag of the latest treasure dropped just yet.

Something was wrong.

The body of the Duntin, one of his sailors killed during a raid, was moved. The skull was off to the side, somehow having rolled off the pile of bones. That body had been carefully laid out, meant to distract and possibly drive away anyone curious enough to find the cave. Instead, it had been disturbed. A clear sign that someone had been there.

It didn't look recent. Over a couple months old, maybe more.

Slowly he walked into the cave, drawing his hammer. The sun disappeared the deeper he moved into the passage, but Corht didn't care. He could see just fine. The ore and other materials in the stone glowed, giving off varying shades of light. Enough for him to see.

As he got to the end of the passage he stopped, listening. There was nothing, no sounds. But there was a smell.

Something rotting.

Growling, Corht stepped into the wide cavern. He could see the crack in the wall at the far end. He knew it belonged to Caobolds. But there was an arrangement. They left the contents of the chest alone, and the Duntin and their allies left the Caobolds alone.

But it seemed that something had happened.

The smell came from the bodies of Caobolds that lay about the floor of the cavern. Some had been torn apart, cave scavengers going after fresh meat, but there was enough left to identify them and for rot to set in. No scavenger was going to eat them now. Dried blood covered the stone floor.

A fight.

There had been a fight.

Corht ran for the chest. The heavy stone lid was on top of the chest, a single piece of stone growing out of the floor, carved when the chamber had been made. But the lid wasn't on tight, it was angled. Someone had taken it off and replaced it.

Fearful, angry, Corht grabbed the edge of the lid and pushed. He growled and grunted, straining to move the heavy stone. But he did. His long arms shook, but he pushed the lid off. It landed with a loud crash, echoing through the small chamber. Corht glanced at the crack in the wall, where the Caobolds had come from. The noise of the lid against the floor would attract attention.

Turning back to the chest, Corht looked in and yelled.

His scream of primal rage was loud. His men about the *Roc Reaver* heard it above the sound of the engines and the wind. They looked at each other nervously, fearfully. They feared the rage and hate that came with that scream.

It was gone. All of it. Months of hard work and raiding, the deaths of many crewmembers.

Gone.

Not just the weapons and armor but the gems. A lot of gems.

And the redcap.

That was what angered Corht most of all.

It had belonged to Michk, the body in the cave.

Grabbing his hammer, Corht swung at the chest. The metal head hit stone, cracks forming. He swung again, all his strength which was considerable despite his small frame. More cracks, jagged pieces falling to the ground.

He would find whoever had stolen from the Duntin. He would find them and kill them.

Character Name: Hall
Race: Half-Elf
Class: Skirmisher

Level: 5
Experience
Total: 2,290
Next Level: 2,400

Unassigned Stat Points: 0

Health
Base: 64
Adjusted: 0
Total: 64

Energy
Base: 81
Adjusted: 0
Total: 81

Vitality
Base: 22
Adjusted: 0
Total: 22

Attributes
Strength
Base: 11
Adjusted: 4
Total: 15
Agility
Base: 17

Adjusted: 7
Total: 24
Wellness
Base: 13
Adjusted: 1
Total: 14
Intelligence
Base: 12
Adjusted: 0
Total: 12
Willpower
Base: 10
Adjusted: 0
Total: 10
Charisma
Base: 12
Adjusted: 0
Total: 12

Attack Power
Base: 1
Adjusted: 4
Total: 5
Attack Speed
Base: -4 seconds
Adjusted: -2 seconds
Total: -6 seconds
Spell Power
Base: 1
Adjusted: 0
Total: 1
Spell Resistance
Base: 0
Adjusted: 0

Total: 0
Protection
Base: 5
Adjusted: 11
Total: 16
Carrying Capacity
Base: 30
Adjusted: 10
Total: 40

Elemental Resistances
Air: 0%
Earth: 0%
Fire: 25%
Water: 0%

Racial Ability
Limited Night Vision

Class Abilities
Evade (Rank One)
Leap (Rank Two)
Leaping Stab (Rank One)
Shared Vision

Skills
Combat
Light Armor (Rank Two): 13.8
Polearms (Rank Two): 18.8
Small Blades (Rank Two): 15.0
Thrown (Rank Two): 12.7

Activity
Identify (Rank Two): 12.8

Strategy (Rank Two): 10.9
Triage (Rank Two): 10.7

Environment
Camouflage (Rank One): 1.4
Increased Perception (Rank Two): 11.0
Stealth (Rank One): 2.2
Survival (Rank Two): 13.7
Tracking (Rank One): 3.4

Professions
Cartography (Rank Two): 17.5
Herbology (Rank Two): 15.8
Skinning (Rank Two): 14.5

Reputation (Faction)
Druids of the Grove: 1500, Known and Friendly
Kingdom of Essec: 1600, Known and Friendly
Valedale Gnomes: 1000, Known and Friendly
Brownpaw of Fallen Green: 1000, Known and Friendly
Peakguard: 750, Known
Door Knockers: 625, Known
Stonefire Clan: 1550, Known and Friendly

Reputation (Alliance)
Guard Captain Henry: 1300, Friendly
Watchman Kelly: 800, Known
Merchant Dyson: 700, Known
Druid Leigh: 6000, Loved
Smol, Gardener of Greenheight Vale: 1200, Friendly
Jackoby of the Brownpaw: 350, Known
Sergeant Brient of the Peakguard: 1200, Friendly
Captain Hart: 1000, Friendly

Character Name: Hall

Inventory:

Exceptional Breakridge Ironwood Spear

Attack Power +2

Damage 1d6 +2

Agility +1

Durability 12/12

Weight 3 lbs.

On successful hit, has a 50% chance of causing Splinter. A shard of wood lodges within the wound causing 1 DMG every 3 Seconds for 15 Seconds.

Leather Chest

Protection +1

Durability 6/6

Weight 5 lbs.

Exceptional Dusky Wyvern Hide Pauldrons of Fast Strike

Protection +1

Agility +1

Durability 20/20

Weight 1 lb.

Quality Green Kiot Hide Baldric

Strength +1

Durability 15/15

Weight 1 lb.

Quality Crag Cat Hide Belt

Protection +1

Wellness +1

Durability 15/15
Weight 1 lb.

Leather Leggings
Protection +1
Durability 6/6
Weight 5 lbs.

Quickdraw Bracer of Sharp Teeth
Protection +4
Attack Power +2
Agility +4
Durability: 20/20
Weight: 1 lb.

Contains two Throwing Knives (1d4 +2 DMG, +6 Lightning DMG, 25% chance of Critical Strike bonus of +10 DMG). Once thrown a knife will reappear in the Bracer after ten minutes. Cooldown of twenty seconds between throwing knives.

Leather Gloves
Protection +1
Durability 6/6
Weight 5 lbs.

Leather Boots
Protection +1
Durability 6/6
Weight 5 lbs.

Yeti Bone Ring of Strength
Strength +1

Tundra Fox Bone Ring of Quickness
Agility +1

Obsidian Pendant of Icy Chill

On successful hit, all Water/Cold based attacks deal an additional +2 DMG

Quality Carved Bone Idol of Yeti's Howl
On successful hit has a 25% chance of causing Yeti's Howl, granting carrier +3 unprotected DMG to attack's total damage

Javelin
Attack Power +1
Damage 1d6
Range 30 Yards
Durability 6/6
Weight 1 lb.

Dagger
Damage 1d4
Durability 4/4
Weight 1 lb.

Exceptional Sword of Cold's Edge
Damage 2d4 (+5)
Agility +3
Strength +2
Fire Resistance +25%
Durability 20/20
Weight: 5 lbs.

On successful hit, has a 50% chance of causing Ice Shock. Extreme cold spreads out from the area of impact causing 2 DMG (Water/Cold based) every 3 seconds. Damage increased to 4 DMG every 3 seconds for creatures with weakness to Water and Cold based attacks. Ice Shock does no damage to creatures with resistance to Water and Cold based attacks.

Character Name: Hall
Current Quest Log:

TO THE FINDER GOES THE REWARD
Rewards: +500 Experience

You cannot Accept this quest at this time. Earn Minimum Skill of 40 in Cartography and Minimum Level of 20 to become eligible for this quest.

DYSON'S OFFER I
Merchant Dyson has made you an offer for future work. Impressed and thankful for how you helped out his operation, he has a job that he would like you to do when you are ready.
Requirement: Level Six
Rewards: +20 Experience

THE PAINTED SKYBREEZE I
You have found a painting within the treasure of the SkyBreeze. It appears to be of great age and possible value, the true treasure of the map. There is a maker's mark on the canvas. Discover more about the painting and who painted it.
Learn more about the painting 0/1
Rewards: +100 experience

CLAIMING YOUR LAND
You have laid claim to a previously uncharted island. The claim must be secured and notarized with The Guild of Exploration.
Register the uncharted island with the Guild of Exploration 0/1
Reward: +100 Experience; a new island

THE LONG SCROLL III
You have learned that the Norns allied with the Svertleim are part of

the Cerulean Regency, one of the nine Nornic ruling families that want to make a bid for power. They have allied with some mystery others to kill some entities called the Champions. Find out more about the Cerulean Regency and the Champions.
Learn more about the Champions 0/1
Learn more about the Cerulean Regency's allies 0/1
Reward +100 experience.

About Troy Osgood

LitRPG: the genre I always wanted to be writing in but didn't know it until recently.

Things got a little rough for Hall and company and it doesn't look like it'll be slowing down. Things might get worse before they get better. Hall has more questions and precious few answers. Who or what are the Champions? How much of a threat will Iron and his Army be? With the growth of Skara Brae, will Hall be overwhelmed as Lord? The game world seems to be evolving, what does that mean for the future of Hall and the other Breakridge Irregulars?

Axestorm ends the first part of the epic Sky Realms Online saga. Book 4 will be published later this year. Keep an eye out for it.

You can join other fans of Sky Realms Online, and my

other works, in the Ossy's Worlds facebook group. (https://www.facebook.com/groups/200913971032382/)

Visit my blog: www.ossywrites.com
   Join my newsletter: www.ossynews.com

Check out my Patreon where I'll be posting work-in-progress chapters and original works (paid tiers) along with behind the scenes (free) glimpses of where the inspiration for Sky Realms Online came from: www.patreon.com/troynos

Please leave a review on Amazon. Every one helps us authors out.
   Thanks for reading. See you in the next book,
   Troy

Don't forget to join LitRPG Addicts and come hang out with me!
   I'm also very active and thankful for LitRPG Books and GameLit Society

To learn more about LitRPG, talk to authors including myself, and just have an awesome time, please join the LitRPG Group

To learn more about LitRPG, talk to authors including myself, and just have an awesome time, please join the LitRPG Group

SPECIAL THANKS TO:

ADAWIA E. ASAD	EDDIE HALLAHAN	KYLE OATHOUT
JENNY AVERY	JOSH HAYES	LILY OMIDI
BARDE PRESS	PAT HAYES	TROY OSGOOD
CALUM BEAULIEU	BILL HENDERSON	GEOFF PARKER
BEN	JEFF HOFFMAN	NICHOLAS (BUZ) PENNEY
BECKY BEWERSDORF	GODFREY HUEN	JASON PENNOCK
BHAM	JOAN QUERALTÓ IBÁÑEZ	THOMAS PETSCHAUER
TANNER BLOTTER	JONATHAN JOHNSON	JENNIFER PRIESTER
ALFRED JOSEPH BOHNE IV	MARCEL DE JONG	RHEL
CHAD BOWDEN	KABRINA	JODY ROBERTS
ERREL BRAUDE	PETRI KANERVA	JOHN BEAR ROSS
DAMIEN BROUSSARD	ROBERT KARALASH	DONNA SANDERS
CATHERINE BULLINER	VIKTOR KASPERSSON	FABIAN SARAVIA
JUSTIN BURGESS	TESLAN KIERINHAWK	TERRY SCHOTT
MATT BURNS	ALEXANDER KIMBALL	SCOTT
BERNIE CINKOSKE	JIM KOSMICKI	ALLEN SIMMONS
MARTIN COOK	FRANKLIN KUZENSKI	KEVIN MICHAEL STEPHENS
ALISTAIR DILWORTH	MEENAZ LODHI	MICHAEL J. SULLIVAN
JAN DRAKE	DAVID MACFARLANE	PAUL SUMMERHAYES
BRET DULEY	JAMIE MCFARLANE	JOHN TREADWELL
RAY DUNN	HENRY MARIN	CHRISTOPHER J. VALIN
ROB EDWARDS	CRAIG MARTELLE	PHILIP VAN ITALLIE
RICHARD EYRES	THOMAS MARTIN	JAAP VAN POELGEEST
MARK FERNANDEZ	ALAN D. MCDONALD	FRANCK VAQUIER
CHARLES T FINCHER	JAMES MCGLINCHEY	VORTEX
SYLVIA FOIL	MICHAEL MCMURRAY	DAVID WALTERS JR
GAZELLE OF CAERBANNOG	CHRISTIAN MEYER	MIKE A. WEBER
DAVID GEARY	SEBASTIAN MÜLLER	PAMELA WICKERT
MICHEAL GREEN	MARK NEWMAN	JON WOODALL
BRIAN GRIFFIN	JULIAN NORTH	BRUCE YOUNG

CPSIA information can be obtained
at www.ICGtesting.com
Printed in the USA
LVHW021617090721
692281LV00001B/15